JOSH HAYES
ECHOES OF
VALOR

AETHON
BOOKS

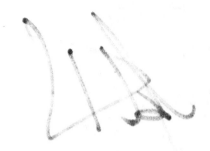

ECHOES OF VALOR

©2019 JOSH HAYES

Print and eBook formatting, and cover design by Steve Beaulieu. Artwork provided by Florent llamas.

Published by Aethon Books LLC. 2019

ALSO IN THE SERIES

ACKNOWLEDGMENTS

I've heard it said that the second book of a series is generally the most difficult to write and for the most part, I disagree. Though, it must be said that the ending of this book was somewhat of a challenge to push through, as many included in the following acknowledgements can attest. We get to explore a lot more of Fischer's world in this book, and where *Edge of Valor* was very limited in its scope, *Echoes* broadens the landscape and I'm excited to see which of the new characters rise to the top.

Edge of Valor took over six years to write. This book took significantly less time, and that can only be attributed to the time and effort of the people listed below.

First, and most: my wife Jamie.

She put up with my 2am sessions , my hibernation in front of the computer for hours and hours trying to get this thing finished and as polished as it could be. She even helped out when I needed ideas—things that I am eternally grateful for. Without her support, this book would not have been written.

If you can't take grief from your editor, who can you take it from? Steve Beaulieu, as always, did a fantastic job editing this book. His careful eye spotted things that weren't readily apparent to me during the writing process. It wasn't until I stepped back, and moved things around, that I realized how much better his red ink made the book. I appreciate his insights and hours spent getting *Echoes* into its final form.

After Walt Robillard's essential input on *Edge of Valor* and *Stryker's War*, I decided to enlist his help during the actual writing process of this book. Not only did he assist with various technical aspects of *Echoes*, he helped orchestrate some of the pivotal scenes and caught several mistakes that helped make the book so much stronger.

Much thanks go to Ralph Kern, Rick Partlow, David Weiner, Meenaz Lodhi, and Thomas Hottle for taking an early look and finding the little mistakes that otherwise might have gone undetected.

And once again, thank you to my fellow writer and friend, Scott Moon, who endured hundreds of phone calls, angry and frustrated text messages, and many breakfast rants. Without his sounding board, I might've lost my sanity in these pages.

And you, my readers. Your messages and reviews have been overwhelming, humbling, and encouraging. I'm eternally grateful for your support and hope you enjoy your continuing journey with Jackson Fischer and his companions.

"Eyes up."

—Josh

CHAPTER 1

ANS *New Washington*
New Tuscany Orbit
21 July 2607

The ship felt like a hollow, steel tomb. Ghosts walked the corridors, reminding him of why he'd spend every waking moment onboard this empty ship. The ghosts of Lieutenant Hastings and his Marines, the Stonemeyer Embassy staff, the countless civilians in Calibri City—they all wandered these corridors, pushing him to find their justice.

And despite all his best efforts, after all the countless hours poring through the *New Washington's* databases, all the interviews, watching hundreds of hours of security footage, Jackson Fischer wasn't sure he'd be able to give it to them.

The link display on Jackson Fischer's left hand activated for the third time, the holographic interface rotating up from underneath his arm to hover over the back of his hand and wrist. He didn't even have to read the words to know who was calling. He swiped a finger through the air, ignoring the request, he wasn't in the mood to talk to his boss. Or anyone for that matter.

Fischer pressed a thumb into the small of his back and winced as he stretched. He stood in the middle of the ANS *New Washington's* Command Information Control center, surrounded by multiple holodisplays, showing everything from the battleship's roster to their communication logs, system access records, even the galley menu. The flagship of the Alliance Navy's Second Fleet was older than most, but she had a significant history, and her crew wouldn't think of transferring the flag to any other ship.

He swiped away the report he'd been reading on their most recent JumpLane transitions and leaned against the console behind him. Three months he'd been scoping through these logs and still hadn't been able to find one single piece of solid evidence to use against the disgraced former Second Fleet Commander, Admiral Marcus Young. It was more than a little infuriating to know he had the right guy, but the evidence only substantiated a fraction of what Fischer knew Young to be responsible for. Misuse of rank, improper contact with subordinates, issuing illegal orders—those were simple charges to prove. It was murder, weapons smuggling, and conspiracy that Fischer wanted, and those were the charges that were going to take more than what he had.

Before the Tribunal Magistrate had issued a gag order on Young during his incarceration, the former admiral had proclaimed his innocence to anyone willing to listen. He'd even managed to do a couple media interviews—arranged by his lawyers—to combat the "unreasonable and ridiculous" charges laid against him. His JAG lawyers had quickly protested the order but were shot down almost before they were able to bring the motion, citing the classified and critical nature of the mission and surrounding political implications.

Fischer's blood boiled at the thought of anyone being able to represent that bastard. Young had shirked everything onto Tobias Delaney, Stonemeyer's ambassador who'd been killed during the failed mission. It was easy to put the blame on the one person who couldn't defend himself.

Delaney, on the other hand, didn't share Young's record, and it was easy for people to believe that he was the driving force behind the operation. Fischer knew better. He knew Marcus Young and knew what the man was capable of. Knew if anyone was going to be able to finally put the bastard away for good, it was going to have to be him.

Sighing, Fischer opened another communication log. The data was incomplete, a victim of Young's habit of deleting everything. Most of the logs he'd gone through already had either been completely emptied or corrupted to such a degree they might as well have been nothing. He keyed in the search parameters and allowed the system to work.

A hatch behind him slid open and he turned to see Aniyah Eliwood enter, carrying two stainless steel mugs, their contents steaming.

Another sigh.

"Please tell me that's not that herbal tea again."

Eliwood grinned, "Coffee, just the way you like it."

Fischer accepted the drink gratefully, inhaling the dark aroma. "Thanks."

"Find anything to nail that bastard to the wall yet?" Eliwood asked, motioning to the open display panel where the trace program was scrolling through fragments of code that looked like power fluctuation logs.

Fischer scratched at his beard. "No."

"I hate to break it to you, Fish," Eliwood said, "but Young might not be your guy. I mean, don't get me wrong, he's a Grade-A asshole, and he deserves to spend the rest of his life locked up, but if that's all the evidence you get…"

"That's not all I can get," Fischer said, biting off the frustration swelling in his chest. "I know he's behind more than just

Stonemeyer. That hellhole was just the tip of the iceberg, I promise you. And there's absolutely no way Delaney set that whole operation up on his own. No fucking way."

"How sure are you about that?"

"Come on, you've seen the files from the DC, same as I have. He was inept and corrupt. That's why they moved him all the way out there in the first place."

The Diplomatic Corps, the Alliance's connection to the rest of the civilized galaxy, liked to think of themselves as a higher class of citizens. For the most part, their members enjoyed unimpeded traffic throughout the galaxy, to both friendly, and not so friendly worlds. Within the Protectorate—the interstellar collection of star nations that gave each of their members a forum for their own worlds in the larger realm of human worlds throughout the galaxy —the ranking members of the DC had unlimited and unrestricted access. Even more than some heads of state.

"Right," Eliwood said. "So he wouldn't cause any trouble. And look what happened."

"Exactly," Fischer said. "Oh, I've already given a couple of their 'investigators' a piece of my mind. Their case," he held up air-quotes at the word, "had so many holes, you could fly a Leviathan class carrier through them. Even then, they had enough to remove him from service or suspend him, at the very least. I just don't understand why they didn't."

"Politics, Fish, you know that just as well as I do."

Fischer shook his head. "There has to be more to it than that. What I don't understand is while their file is so empty. Even with half the charges, I'd have at least double, or even triple the supporting documents."

"Those guys couldn't find vacuum if they fell out an airlock," Eliwood said.

"You're not wrong there," Fischer agreed.

"Carter's looking for you."

"Yeah." Fischer rubbed his eyes. "I'm ignoring him. I'm busy."

"Busy, huh?" She crossed her arms. "What, did you find some new brilliant piece of evidence that's going to pull this all together?"

Fischer glared at his partner, grinding his teeth.

She raised her hands in mock surrender. "What'd I say?"

"Nothing," Fischer growled. "I've found precisely nothing."

"There might not be anything *to* find. Even you said Young was a smart son of a bitch."

"Conniving isn't the same thing as smart," Fischer said. "But sure, he's not stupid. But I'm counting on him making a mistake somewhere. That's how most of the famous ones usually get picked up; they make mistakes."

"I'm sure there's a little bit of police work that goes into it, too," Eliwood suggested.

Fischer grinned, raising a thumb and forefinger just an inch apart. "A little."

"What you looking at now?"

"Communication logs for *New Washington's* secondary array."

"How exciting."

"Not really," Fischer admitted.

A soft chime sounded as the search program paused. A message panel appeared over the original display, several lines of text highlighted. Fischer frowned, leaning forward to examine the alert.

"What is it?"

"Not sure," Fischer said. "It looks like some kind of text string tied into the power core readouts." He tapped several commands on his link, trying to clean up the information. "The systems been finding a lot of jumbled numbers and letters that it thinks are text. Usually, it's nothing."

As the scrubbing routine cleared away some of the random alphanumerics, what looked like words began to appear. Though they were incomplete, it was obviously a message of some kind. The format was unmistakable."

```
S...ER ID: U...OW.
T.: A..N.2.
M..S..E .E..NS:
...L..E W... .O. .. .OL..A..D
...DIN..
M...A.. ..D.
```

Eliwood moved around the display to stand next to Fischer. "What the hell is that?"

Fischer stepped closer to the screen. "I think we might have something here." He tapped a few more commands into his link, and the system attempted to put the fragment back together.

Eliwood's link activated, its orange holographic panel rotating into place over the back of her hand. She glanced down at the display and chuckled. "I guess it is important."

Fischer put a hand up. "Don't—"

Eliwood swiped her finger over her link, accepting the call. "Evening, Boss."

"For shit's sake," Division Chief Dan Carter said, his voice gruff and irritated but loud and clear over the speaker. "Is Fischer with you?"

"Fischer?" Eliwood raised an eyebrow at him. He mouthed "no" and drew a hand across his throat, signally her to hang up. "Yeah, sure, Boss. He's here."

Fischer swore and glared at his partner.

"Fischer?" Carter barked. "Where the fuck have you been, and why haven't you been answering my calls?"

"I've been busy," Fischer said, turning back to the message fragment.

"Bullshit," Carter said. "Listen, I know it doesn't mean much to you, but Division Chief does technically mean I'm your boss, so occasionally, you're going to have to respond when I need you."

"Sorry," Fischer repeated half-heartedly. "I've just been neck-deep in these systems., I didn't really have any time to come up for air."

There was a pause, then Carter said, "Oh? Did you find something?"

"Maybe," Eliwood said before Fischer could answer.

Fischer bared his teeth at his partner, shaking his head. Eliwood was probably the best partner he'd ever had, but that didn't mean she wasn't a pain in his ass. She was slightly shorter than his five-foot-eleven, with dark brown hair, an angular jaw, and moderate cheekbones. Unlike many of the women he'd known over the years, she had no love for makeup, and generally avoided it when she could.

That wasn't to say that Eliwood wasn't attractive. Fischer genuinely thought she was, but to him, she was more like a sister than any kind of romantic attraction. Not to mention that his wife, Carissa, would have his ass if she caught him looking at another woman in any kind of romantic sense.

She wore her hair in her typical fashion, pulled back in a ponytail, and her navy blue suit jacket was open at the front, allowing him to see just a hint of the pistol on her right hip. Just like him, her Alliance Security and Intelligence badge was clipped to her belt.

"What is it?" Carter asked.

"I'm not sure yet," Fischer admitted, mentally willing the computer to work faster. "It looks like a deleted message fragment buried inside *New Washington's* secondary communication relay. The computer's chewing on it now. Could be something, could be nothing."

"Well, I've got something," Carter said. "And you're not going to like it."

"Shit," Fischer said, already not liking it.

"What is it, Boss?" Eliwood asked.

"Young's being transferred back here for his Tribunal," Carter said.

Fischer straightened, instantly alert, forgetting about the message in front of him. "I knew they'd pull something like this. When did it happen?"

"I don't know, we just got the call."

Eliwood frowned. "When he's coming in?"

"Don't know that either," Carter said.

"Don't they have to put the Tribunal on the docket?" Eliwood asked.

"I told you I don't know," Carter repeated, clearly exasperated. "I tried reaching out before calling you, but the closest thing I got to an answer was 'You'll be advised.' Apparently, anything to do with the Tribunal is JAG's business, not ours."

"Bullshit, it's not ours," Fischer said. "It's our fucking case. And I haven't finished it yet. How the hell can they be pushing forward without our full report?"

"As far as I understand it, Chief JAG has decided that what they have is sufficient to move forward. So they are."

Shaking her head, Eliwood said, "But how the hell can they do that?"

"JAG does what they want."

"But I'm not finished investigating this yet," Fischer argued.

"Evidently, they don't need or want anything else from us, Fischer. I'm sorry."

"What the fuck? They don't have anything," Fischer said, his anger rising. "What are they going to charge?"

"Dereliction of duty, conspiracy, insubordination, making false statements, conduct unbecoming, and obstructing justice."

Fischer's stomach twisted in a knot, his fists clenching together as his boss read off the list. "That's nothing!"

"Right now, JAG feels those are the standout charges," Carter said. "He's facing a dishonorable discharge, reduction in rank, forfeiture of pay, probably a max of ten years—"

Eliwood laughed. "Ten fucking years? That bastard caused the deaths of fifteen Marines! Not to mention the Embassy staff and Delaney, that prick. How in the hell do they think all of that rates ten years?"

Fischer couldn't believe what he was hearing. "This isn't justice, Dan. It's a fucking slap on the wrist. Not only that, it's a slap in the face to the memories of everyone that died during that mission. Not to mention their families. It's a slap in the face to everyone who has ever, or ever will, put on this uniform. It's a—"

"Listen, I don't disagree with any particular point," Carter interrupted, his tone noticeably softer. "But the fact is, none of us can control anything about that. JAGs going to do what JAGs going to do. They always have. All we can do is our best and hope they get it right in the courtroom."

"That's such bullshit," Eliwood said. "I think I'm going to be sick."

Fischer bit down hard, trying to keep his rage in check. Carter gave him a fair amount of leeway when it came to his work, but when it came right down to it, he was the Division Chief, and private line or not, Fischer couldn't just start losing his mind on his boss. A part of him knew it wouldn't matter anyway. He had no doubt Carter had already made a similar case to the people above him, and if his words hadn't changed any minds, Fischer's weren't going to either.

"And we have no idea when he's coming in?" Fischer asked again.

"None," Carter said, sounding more than a little frustrated. "All I know is it'll be sometime in the next seventy-two to ninety-six hours."

"That's a hell of a big window," Eliwood said.

"Yeah," Carter agreed.

"So, what about local law enforcement and the Marines? They're going to be the ones tasked with the security for this thing. Aren't they getting some kind of heads up, so they know when to mobilize? It's going to take a few days for them to get spun up."

"They're mobilizing right now," Carter said. "As I understand it, they're going to be on station for the duration of the hearings. The media outlets are all being sent briefings and staging area information, but no one has been giving the dates, times, or location for the Tribunal. That's all been classified Ultra Eyes-Only."

"I mean, I'm all for security, especially for this," Fischer said, "but not informing the investigating agency? By law, aren't they supposed to give us notice?"

"They have," Carter said. "This is it. This is their notice."

"You've got to be kidding."

"Look, this is all happening on levels way above my pay grade. Director Clancy wasn't even invited to sit in on the briefings. The only people that know the exact details of the operation are Fleet Admiral Hunter, JAG Command, Admiral Eriksen and the personnel being detached for escort duty."

"How the hell can we even start to prepare for this thing if we don't have any idea when the son of a bitch is coming?" Fischer asked. "I still have about twenty secure cores to go through, not to mention finishing the complete physical and visual inspections. The team I have right now isn't nearly enough."

"I sympathize, Fish, I really do, but there isn't a damn thing I can do about it," Carter said. "You're lucky I was able to get you that much on extended basis. But Young's case isn't the only one this office is working, in case you forgot, and quite frankly, we've spent too much time on it already. The Director wanted to give *New Washington* back a week ago, and I held him off, but my stall tactics aren't going to work forever. Not with all the new raider activity near the border. Hell, even the Pegasi are standing up their fleets to address the issue on their side."

The thought of losing the *New Washington* made Fischer's stomach turn. He still had months of work to do to completely clear the ship. Just visually inspecting all the compartments was going to take two or three months, and that didn't count all the small mechanical hideaways and cubbies. He could've had a year, and it probably wouldn't have been enough.

"So what do you want me to do?" Fischer asked.

"I want you to put together the best case you can," Carter said. "Collect what you've found so far and we hand it over."

"How much time do I have?"

"Realistically? Thirty-six, maybe forty-eight hours. After that..." Carter trailed off, not finishing his thought.

Fischer understood. Once the Tribunal started, they'd be behind the eight ball. Young's defense would get all the files and see what Fischer had found and—more importantly—what he hadn't found. They'd have the upper hand. That's without the fact that once the hearings started, Young and his team would have access to the media again, and Fischer had no doubts that they would be spending as much time as humanly possible in front of the microphone.

"Fischer?" Carter asked.

"Yeah?"

"I'm sorry."

Fischer shook his head and let out a long breath. "It's not your fault, Boss. I know you did what you could."

"I'll keep you updated," Carter said. "As soon as I hear something, I'll let you know."

"Thanks, Boss," Eliwood said, and the connection terminated.

"Goddammit!" Fischer shouted, kicking the base of the console in front of him. The twang echoed around the empty compartment. "What the hell are we even doing this for? I just don't understand it. Is any of it worth it?"

"Sure it is. It has to be." She let out a long breath, then said, "Hey, look."

Fischer turned, then followed her finger to the display screen. His cheek tightened as he read the now decrypted message.

```
SENDER ID: UNKNOWN
TO: ANON421
MESSAGE BEGINS:
FAILURE WILL NOT BE TOLERATED
CARDINAL
MESSAGE ENDS
```

CHAPTER 2

Civilian Freighter *Bulalo*
Detached Marine Training Center - Absolution Market
Location: Classified
22 July 2607

You sneaky bastards, Corporal Allen Sheridan thought, taking a knee and drawing in a long breath, trying to slow his heart rate. His entire body cried out for relief: muscle aches, lungs burning, legs blown. The initial assault had gone well, but it had involved a lot of up and down running, and in full gear, which weighed just shy of eighty pounds, it was no easy task. But he was a Saber now, not a regular grunt. This was his job, and he'd volunteered for it. There was no quitting now.

Halfway, he told himself, looking down the long corridor ahead. *It's all downhill from here.*

He adjusted his grip on his MOD27, a highly modified version of the standard LR27, which he'd customized further, with a slimmer grip, a carbon alloy stock and two, fully-adjustable and interchangeable optical sights. He'd known Marine Special Operations Command had its special toys, but having all those shiny new pieces of equipment came at a cost—you had to carry it all.

His space-gray-and-black camouflage fatigues were custom-tailored to him, allowing for complete, unrestricted movement and comfort. The body armor he wore over his chest, torso and shoulders doubled as a tactical harness, carrying the majority of his battle gear; extra magazines, fragmentation and stun grenades, tactical knife, comms, and medical kit. He'd been issued the basic MARSOC kit after indoctrination but had been forbidden to modify or add any equipment until he'd passed his final phase of training.

In addition to his basic kit, today he was carrying his extended tour pack as well, complete with extra rations and uniforms, even more ammunition, and everything else a Saber special operator might need on extended detachment from their home ship. The reason for bringing it on this mission was simple: it made things difficult.

Corporal Jonathan Reese came up behind him, tapping Sheridan once on the shoulder. "Six clear."

"Roger," Sheridan said. He nodded toward the "gift" the enemy had left for them. "Bastards set up for an ambush."

"You sure?"

"Portside opening, three hatches down?"

Reese crouched, moving up beside Sheridan. "Yeah? Where?"

"Top corner," Sheridan said, pointing. The opposition forces or Team Two were defending this round, and their team leader, Sergeant Nguyen was notorious for leaving surprises for the attackers to find. Sheridan had been the unwitting victim of more than a few tricks.

Not this time, though, he thought.

A fist-sized cylindrical anti-personal mine had been affixed to the door frame just inside the hatch. In normal conditions, the APM78 would completely destroy anything in its firing area. In this confined space, however, its killing power would be enhanced by an order of magnitude. Not only would the mine's projectiles shred through body armor like a knife through butter, but the blast wave reflecting off the surrounding bulkheads could pulverize internal organs.

"That sneaky bastard," Reese said, verbalizing Sheridan's earlier thought.

Sheridan chuckled. "Yeah. Where are the others?"

"Sarge has Richards and Cole moving to take the shuttle bay. Hanover and Neal are securing main engineering."

Sheridan nodded, still trying to work out how he was going to neutralize Nguyen's boobytrap.

"You know, this is the third time this week we've had comm blackouts," Reese said, "I don't know about you, but I've never encountered anything close to that in a real op."

For this particular exercise, the team's taclink—their primary means of communication—had been deemed compromised, meaning they couldn't use them for fear of being heard by the enemy. It was a rare threat, one that would take someone with exceptional technical knowledge of MARSOC communication encryption and also possess the equipment necessary to penetrate it.

"I have," Sheridan said. "And trust me, it's not fun."

It'd been six months since he'd been extracted from Stonemeyer after a failed mission to rescue the Alliance ambassador assigned there. The mission that had resulted in the deaths of every Marine in his platoon and the exposure of one of the biggest conspiracies in Alliance military history. The single positive thing that had come out of that disaster was Sheridan's assignment to Special Operations Command, a posting that, otherwise, wouldn't have been open to him for at least another three years.

Surprisingly, only a few of the long-time operators had said anything negative about the unusual assignment. The orders had been personally handed down from Fleet Admiral Gary Hunter himself, and no one—not even the saltiest of space dogs—would say anything against that. Not in public, anyway. He'd heard whispers, and received a cold-shoulder or two during indoctrination, but nothing that led him to believe the cadre didn't want him to be there.

And he'd proved himself, hadn't he?

He'd passed every qualification, every physical, every test required, and had done so with excellence. For Sheridan, it hadn't ever been about passing the tests. It'd been about proving himself to the men and women he'd be serving. That was the real test, and it was the only thing that truly mattered.

"What are you thinking?" Reese asked. "A pulse wave maybe?"

Jon Reese had gone through indoc and the advanced course with Sheridan before their posting to ANS *Courageous* and subsequent assignment to Team Valkyrie. He was a bit taller than Sheridan, with chestnut hair that he claimed *was not* thinning in the back. Like Sheridan and the rest of the members of Team Valkyrie, Reese had excelled in team sports all the way through school and had top marks in fitness and weapons qualifications. He was also one of the smartest electronics specialists Sheridan had ever met and possessed an uncanny ability to infiltrate even the most secured system and completely wreck it.

He repeatedly denied accusations that his hacking and technology background was why he'd joined the Marines, but like his thinning spot on the back of his head, no one believed him. Only Sergeant Willard Robalt on Team Two rivaled Reese's expertise with the keyboard.

Sheridan shook his head. "If we get Cole up here with his drones, I'd say we'd have to give it a chance. You have your HX7?"

Reese hesitated for a moment, then said, "I've got some 3."

"It'll work. Actually, that'll work better than the 7. Hand it over."

"Sheridan, you're not thinking what I think you're thinking." Reese reached into a pouch on his tactical vest and produced the small canister wrapped in red and yellow striped plastic wrap. "Please say you're not thinking that. You know we're not authorized for that."

"He never said we *couldn't* use it," Sheridan corrected, grinning. He took the cylinder. "Get ready to move."

Sheridan crossed the corridor, crouching in an alcove next to a small mechanical access panel. He pulled the seal off the top end and began drawing a line of pale pink foam across and down the slate gray bulkhead. When he'd marked a large enough area, he set the canister aside and pulled a two-inch plastic case from one of the pouches on his chest. From the case, he produced a single fingernail-sized cap which he pushed into the foam, then opened his link and synced it with the detonator.

"You're going to be in so much trouble," Reese said.

"By any means necessary," Sheridan said, quoting what their team commander, Captain Eric Chambers, from their pre-mission briefing.

Reese winced. "Eh, I'm not sure that's what he meant."

Technically speaking, the exercise briefing stipulated that they were to assault the ship "as-is." As with a lot of training sites, some areas were labeled as off-limits even though you could physically see it and it was out of bounds for the scenario. Most of the time, it was understood that there would be no tampering with the training areas, to preserve the locations for further training.

The *Bulalo* however, was a wreck, barely a shell of a ship, used for shipboard assault training. Boarding operations was one of the most hazardous missions Sabers undertook, and because of that fact, they tended to go through training ships on a fairly regular basis. Simulating blowing through a steel hull in zero-gee space wasn't the same as actually doing it, and because MARSOC Marines didn't like to do anything they hadn't actually practiced, the training grounds kept a substantial amount of training vessels on hand for just that purpose.

And blowing through an interior bulkhead is pretty much the same thing, Sheridan told himself, opening the detonator control panel on his link.

"On three," Sheridan said under his breath, backing away.

After the count, Sheridan tapped the trigger. His helmet's automatic sound dampeners activated as the explosive foam detonated, shielding his ears from the blast. He saw the brief flash out of the corner of his eye, and immediately closed his link and made his way to the freshly made oval hole in the bulkhead.

It was a tight squeeze with all his gear and for a moment, Sheridan was worried he wouldn't make it all the way through. The room on the other side of the bulkhead was one of the remote reengineering and mechanical spaces, used to access the ship's many systems. Exposed pipes, conduits, and other electrical units filled the space— equipment that Sheridan knew was integral to the working of the ship, but had no understanding of the actual workings.

He continued through to a hatch on the far end of the room. It was unlocked, and he breached it in a matter of seconds.

The next room was empty, save for a few crew lockers. On the far side of the room, to Sheridan's left, the compartment's exterior hatch was open, the anti-personnel mine hanging from the door frame. He took a moment to trace the device's sensor lines. The conical "danger area" of the mine extended out from the front of the device in an expanding detection radius. The downfall of this particular mine was that it lacked any kind of anti-tamper or detection sensors on its backside, which Sheridan thought that should've been something the egg-heads would've have figured out by now.

But today, he was glad they hadn't. All he had to do was approach it without accidentally crossing the forward detection area, and he was in business. He pushed his MOD27 around behind him on its sling and pulled a pair of simple pliers from a pouch on his belt. Slowly, he reached up, needing only to disconnect the—

A two-tone alarm blared throughout the ship, signaling a ship-wide broadcast. The sudden noise turned Sheridan's stomach. The freighter's dim emergency lighting was replaced by primary lighting panels along the ceiling, providing the operations with amber light. Outside, in the hallway, corridor lights flickered to life along the ceiling and the bottom of each bulkhead.

"What the hell?" Reese said, his voice echoing up from outside in the corridor.

Sheridan eyed the ceiling as if it was going to provide him answers. The same question resonated in his mind. They hadn't failed, he knew that much, and the exercise shouldn't have been called off until they'd met the conditions for either victory or defeat.

They hadn't even fired a round.

"*End ex. End ex. End ex,*" a digitized voice said over the ship-wide. It was Master Sergeant Kline, Team Valkyrie's senior non-comm. "*Exercise Condor Control has been terminated. All Valkyrie Elements report to Bay Two for transport back to* Courageous *immediately.*"

Reese appeared in the hatch, giving the fake anti-personnel mine a cautious side-long glance. "What the hell is this all about?"

"No idea," Sheridan said, shaking his head.

"You really think you could've disabled that thing?" Reese asked. "If it had been real, I mean."

Sheridan slipped the pliers back into the pouch on his belt and grinned. "They would've never seen us coming."

"That's what I'm talking about," Reese said, holding out a fist.

Sheridan thumped it hard. "Come on, let's go find out what the hell ruined our perfect run."

CHAPTER 3

Briefing Room Two
ANS *Courageous*
Detached Marine Training Center - Absolution Market
Location: Classified
22 July 2607

After the short shuttle ride between *Bulalo* and *Courageous,* Master Sergeant Kline met them on the hangar deck and directed Sheridan and the rest of the team to their main briefing room on Deck Twelve.

"And Sheridan," Kline said, pointing to him as the team headed out of the bay. "We're going to have a conversation later."

Reese cleared his throat as Sheridan turned.

"Roger that, Master Sergeant," Sheridan said.

Sergeant Devon Cole, Team One's drone operator, patted Sheridan's shoulder as they left the bay. "What the hell did you guys do?"

Cole was a year younger than Sheridan, though he been in service nearly two years longer. It'd taken him three selection rounds to be picked up by the Alliance Marine Corps' Special Operation Command. He'd gone through initial selection and training with Sheridan and Reese and had taken as much of the grief the instructors had handed out. For some reason, he was just not physically able to keep his mouth shut.

"We worked the scenario," Sheridan said truthfully.

"*We?* Don't you say 'we.' That bit of work was all you, my friend," Reese said.

"*Working* the scenario doesn't generally land you Tops office after it's over," Sergeant Luciana Rocha, Team One's ranking NCO, and element leader, said.

"I didn't do anything they haven't trained us to do already," Sheridan said. "I adapted to the situation and overcame it."

"You cheated?" Sergeant Stephanie Neal asked.

Sheridan turned to face her, walking backward through the corridor. "I didn't cheat, thank you very much. As a matter of fact, I took a page out of your book and cleared an obstacle."

Every member of Team Valkyrie, as was the case with all the teams, was trained in the deployment and use of explosive ordnance to clear obstacles or destroy valuable targets. Sergeant Neal, on the other hand, was trained in their disposal. She was one of two Explosive Ordnance Disposal Technicians on Team Valkyrie. Her counterpart, Sergeant Lewis Oliver took care of the duties for Team Two. She was short, with shoulder-length blonde hair and could match any man on the unit on the range, on the mat, and in the bottle. The fact that she voluntarily wanted to disarm and clear active enemy explosive devices, though, put her in a tier outside of the rest of them.

"He blew a hole through a bulkhead to disable an AP mine," Reese said.

Neal laughed and reached forward to pump Sheridan's fist. "My man."

Sheridan grinned. "I knew you'd be proud."

"You realize that blowing holes in training resources is punished under the MCJ, right?" Sergeant Rocha said. Her tone suggested she was giving him shit, but the Staff Sergeant was sometimes hard to read. She'd been a Marine Saber for longer than anyone else on the team, and while she was Team One's element leader, and it was technically her job to keep everyone in line, she'd never let the position go to her head. Not that Sheridan could tell, anyway.

"I didn't do it maliciously," Sheridan argued. "I was within the scope of the scenario and using the tools provided."

Team One's element leader grinned but shook her head. "You're a brave, brave man, Allen Sheridan."

The team continued to rib him as they made their way through the crowded corridors of the light cruiser, *Courageous*. The warship was nearing the end of its lifecycle and was showing signs of wear here and there, but she still did her job, and her crew loved her. She'd been an asset of Special Operations Command since even before her keel had been laid out; designed from the ground up to be a Saber warship. Ten years ago, when she'd first been commissioned, her stealth systems had been state-of-the-art, and her drive skirted the edge of .7 Lane speed, the fastest ever achieved in its day. Even by today's standards, it ranked in the top ten percent of the fleet.

Word had gotten around though; this would be their last tour. Orders had been handed down by Fleet Command, and the crew would be transferred to new postings after this operational cruise. Some headed off to bigger and better positions. Others took instruction positions at the Naval Academy, and some had simply opted to retire.

Sheridan pressed himself into the bulkhead, as did the rest of the team. Several crew members rushed past, calling apologies over their shoulders as they headed off to whatever post they'd been assigned. They dropped down several decks, using the main stairwell near the center of the ship and again, had to dodge crew. The general understanding aboard any naval ship—when it came to Marines, at least—was that while onboard, their presence was to be as unobtrusive as possible. They were passengers only. And while they were the elite of the elite when it came to their hierarchy of the Marine Corps, as far as the Navy was concerned, they were just glorified passengers.

"What do you think this is all about?" Cole asked after several more crew ran past.

Reese shrugged. "Who knows, man. Maybe the ol' girl is kicking the bucket early."

"That's not funny," Neal said.

After two more decks and another long corridor, the team finally reached the brief room. Sheridan got to the hatch first and held it as the rest entered. Team Two was already assembled, all scattered throughout the permanent seating on the port side of the room. Four rows of bolted-down seats formed a half-circle facing a single podium with the Team Valkyrie patch emblazoned on the front. The color on the winged-skull looking up a wire-framed globe had faded slightly over the years, but the words "Eyes Up"—Valkyrie's motto—were still plainly visible below the patch.

"Shit, it's about time you guys show up," Robalt called from his seat at the back of the room.

"Yeah, some of us have to work for a living," Reese retorted.

Sheridan found Sergeant Nguyen, Team Two's element leader, and nodded. "Nice work, Staff Sergeant."

Ted Nguyen wiped a grin off his face, then held his arms out to either side. "What?"

Sheridan moved to a seat in the second row in front of the Sergeant, shaking his head. "Nothing."

"We did some work," Reese told Nguyen, sliding in beside Sheridan.

Before Sheridan could properly chastise Reese for taking credit for something he'd just all but denied having any involvement in, the hatch opened, and Master Sergeant Kline walked in.

"Room, ten-chun!"

The members of Team Valkyrie all sprang from their seats, or turned to face the front of the room, cutting off conversations mid-sentence, and immediately coming to attention. A moment later, Captain Chambers, Team Valkyrie's commanding officer ducked through the hatch and made for the podium at the front of the room.

"Take your seats," the Captain said without looking up. He stopped at the podium and tapped his link, syncing with the room's holodisplays on the bulkhead behind him. The recessed lights along the ceiling dimmed as their Valkyrie's emblem appeared behind Chambers.

Sheridan settled into his chair as the Captain stepped away from the podium, looking up at the image of a system fading into view. Orbital lines appeared in red, the name 'Centralis' glowed in all caps under the blue star in the center of the image. Rows of text appeared on the left-hand side of the image with pertinent data about the system, population, outposts, and major colonies.

"This isn't a training op," Reese whispered in Sheridan's ear.

"No, Corporal Reese, this is not another training operation," Chambers said, pointedly not looking in the Marine's direction, but focusing his attention on the rotating solar system.

Sheridan jabbed an elbow into his friend's side.

The Captain continued, "And before we get into this, I want to apologize for cutting the training you *were* conducting short. Unfortunately, there has been an incident that requires a measured response, and we're the closest detachment."

A wave of anticipation flowed through Sheridan, and he inched forward on his seat. His first mission as a Saber.

Chambers tapped his link, and the planet grew, taking up all the unused space in the room.

"Centralis, an unaffiliated world along the Alliance/URT southern border. Known for its rare mineral deposits and vast quantities of He3. As you might expect, they've been experiencing a steady stream of raider activity over the past six to eight months, but for some reason, in recent months, those encounters have begun to increase exponentially. They have a small system security force, which I'd be hesitant to call a navy, and it seems as though they've reached the limit of what they can effectively handle.

"Like pissin' in the wind, right, sir?" Cole asked.

"That's one way to put it," Chambers answered. "Another way would be to say that because their defensive forces are so lack-luster, they've effectively lost control of their system and are looking for outside assistance to keep the raiders at bay."

"And they want the navy to come in and clean up all the riff-raff for them," Staff Sergeant Rocha said.

"If that were the case, we would probably be having a different conversation," Chambers said. "No, in this particular case, we are dealing with one specific incident."

The Captain tapped his link, and the planet shrank away, replaced by three large transport barges, their speed, course, crew complement, and cargo capacity listed in glowing text above their hulls.

"These are refugee transports out of Taru, a Pegasi occupied system near their side of the border. You may have heard about it on the feeds, it's been a particularly heated operation, and thousands of people a day are fleeing the system, heading to whatever system will take them in. Their particular ships, however, instead of finding safety and security—they've been attacked by raiders, and are currently being held hostage."

Collectively, the members of Team Valkyrie sat up a little straighter in their seats, their interest now well and truly spiked. Boarding actions and hostage rescue were both things that Marine Sabers excelled at.

"The raiders have denied repeated requests to release the hostages and have since cut off all communication with the Centralis negotiating team. As of twenty minutes ago, they have been commo-dark for three hours. The Centralis government has reached the limit of what they're capable of, and don't have the resources to effectively mount an assault on the ship."

"And the URT Navy?" Master Sergeant Kline asked from the side of the room.

"The URT are either unable or unwilling to assist at this time," Chambers said matter-of-factly.

Kline grunted. "Typical."

Chambers nodded, and though he didn't respond, Sheridan got the impression that the Captain agreed with the Sergeant's sentiments. "We are being tasked with infiltrating the ship and freeing the hostages. Officially, we are being dispatched to observe and report only, however, as the Old Man has reminded me ad nauseam, Team Valkyrie doesn't really do observation all that well."

While the rest of the team laughed, Sheridan gave a half-hearted chuckle and sat back, a knot forming in the pit of his stomach. His first mission—which had also been his last as a regular Marine— had also been an extraction, and that mission had resulted in the deaths of every single Marine in his platoon. He'd witnessed brutal assaults and vicious attacks on his friends and fellow Marines, and despite what he told the psychologists at his monthly evaluations during MARSOC training, he still had nightmares about that place.

The nightmares weren't coming as often now, knowing the man responsible was going to be finally be punished for his crimes. Though, more than the disgraced admiral Young, Sheridan would've much rather seen Sergeant Thomas swinging from the gallows for what he'd done. He didn't think the image of Lieutenant Hastings being murdered in cold blood would even leave him.

You couldn't have done anything to stop it, he'd remind himself every time he woke up in cold sweats, hands shaking, mind racing. *You did everything you could.*

"Again, I know we've interrupted training for some of you," Captain Chambers continued, eyeing Sheridan and Reese. "Unfortunately, it can't be helped. As I understand it, however, some of us were a little looser with the instructions of the last scenario than others."

Sheridan flushed and couldn't help the grin turning up at the corners of his mouth.

"An interesting approach, Corporal Sheridan," the Captain said, cupping his hands behind his back. "I don't believe we've had anyone deviate the course in such a... permanent fashion."

Slightly unsure of how to respond, Sheridan eyed Sergeant Rocha, hoping his element leader might give him some direction. Instead, Rocha raised an eyebrow and canted her head to the side, as if to say. "Hey, you dug yourself this hole, now it's time you dig yourself out of it."

Turning back to the Captain, Sheridan straightened in his seat. "Nothing in the mission briefing specifically stated we couldn't adjust our approach, sir. The briefing confined the area of operation to the interior of the freighter. Several access routes were available to utilize, but did not say we couldn't create new ones, sir."

Captain Chambers considered Sheridan for a long moment without saying a word.

Sheridan cleared his throat. "Unless, I'm mistaken, sir." A little bit of doubt began to creep into this mind.

"You are correct, Corporal," the Captain finally said. "There *was* nothing in the mission briefing that prevented you from blasting through the secondary bulkhead to access and render the obstacle safe."

Sheridan felt a sense of relief come over him that, just a second ago, hadn't been there.

"That being said," Chambers continued. "Special Operations Command only has a finite number of resources when it comes to training, that freighter being one of them. If every Saber decided to take it upon themselves to start blasting holes in every ship we had, we'd quickly run out of ships to train in, wouldn't you agree?"

"Yes, sir," Sheridan said, feeling his face redden once more.

Master Sergeant Kline cleared his throat. "Chief Watson thinks he'll be able to repair the panel without any trouble, sir." He said it with a half-grin on his face like he was in on a joke that no one else in the room but he and the Captain were privy to.

"Very well, Master Sergeant, I guess we'll just have to be a little clearer in our exercise instructions in the future, won't we?"

"Yes, sir," Kline said. "Of course, sir."

The Captain nodded, apparently satisfied, and returned to the podium. "To bring this back home, all training has been postponed until the current situation has been resolved. Corporals Sheridan and Reese, and Sergeant Cole, barring any disagreement from your team leaders, I am tentatively attaching to Valkyrie as full operators until the final paperwork can be completed and sent through to Command."

Reese laughed and pumped Sheridan on the arm.

"Thank you, sir," Sheridan said, beaming. Cole and Reese hurriedly added their thanks as well.

"We'll have a more complete mission assessment once we

arrive in Centralis," the Captain said. "Until then, get cleaned up and grab chow. Master Sergeant Kline will be sending kit parameters to your links within the hour. If there aren't any questions..."

Chambers let the invitation hang in the air for a moment, then nodded. "Very well, I'll leave you to it then."

Master Sergeant Kline snapped to attention as Captain Chambers stepped away from the podium and barked, "Room, ten-chun!"

Before the team had fully risen to their feet, Chambers waved everyone back into their seats. "Carry on."

Richards and Neal both patted Sheridan on the back, in turn, congratulating him and Cole and Reece on their official acceptance to the team. The rest of the team clustered in around their two newest members, shaking hands and punching arms.

After a few moments, a path appeared as team members stepped back, allowing Master Sergeant Kline access. The team's senior noncom was built like a brick shithouse, with broad shoulders and thick arms covered with tattoos. He stood five inches taller than Sheridan, making him the tallest member of Team Valkyrie—his short-cropped salt and pepper hair, the only sign of his age.

Kline stopped two paces away from Sheridan and eyed him, his jaw set. After a long moment, he allowed the slight hint of a grin to form at the corner of his mouth and extended a hand, his Marine Corps class ring proudly displayed on his finger. Congratulations, Corporal."

Sheridan took the offered hand and squeezed hard. "Thank you, Master Sergeant."

With his free hand, Kline pulled a patch from his pocket. It matched the design on the podium at the front of the room. "You've earned this. Don't let anyone tell you different."

Sheridan took the patch and ran his thumb over the stitching. "Thank you, Master Sergeant. I appreciate it."

After Kline had presented Reese and Cole with their own patches, he stepped back. "Just do me a favor, would you?"

"What's that, Master Sergeant?"

"Don't blow up any more fucking freighters, would you? Please?"

Sheridan laughed. "Roger that, Master Sergeant. I will do so my best."

CHAPTER 4

Office of Fleet Admiral Hunter
Alliance Naval Station Phoenix
Solomon System
22 April 2607

Fleet Admiral Gary Hunter was tired. It wasn't that he needed sleep, just some much-needed rest. Looking over the walls covered with plaques and awards he'd earned over the years, holos of people he'd met, gifts from friends and family, he realized not only how much he'd accomplished with his life but almost how much his career had taken out of him.

He'd lived a very blessed and fulfilled life, done things he'd never imagined himself ever doing, done things he wished he hadn't had to do, but he's always tried to do more good than bad. And that was how he wanted to leave the office—in better shape than when he'd accepted it all those years ago.

Thirty-five years didn't feel like a long time when he looked back after the fact. An eye blink and his career was over. It felt like just yesterday he was serving in at the Naval Academy in Hollow. Thirty-five years, fifteen of which he'd spend right here in this office—an office he was preparing to hand off to someone else. It didn't feel right. A part of him felt like he couldn't leave, that it was his responsibility to stay and serve, that no one else could do the job as well as he could.

But that wasn't the case at all, was it? It was just his ego trying to keep him from admitting that the was tired, that after years of selfless service, it was finally time for Gary Hunter to enjoy doing something strictly for himself.

Now it was time to *enjoy* life. Hunter chuckled to himself and slipped another book into the box on the table in front of him. He'd never understood the idea of "finally" enjoying life *after* you retire, when so much of your life has already passed you by. He'd made a conscious effort to ensure that every day in uniform was a gift, and he'd promised himself a long time ago that, as long as he wore the uniform, he'd make sure that it wasn't wasted.

He finished packing his current stack of books, then moved across the office to the bookshelf for another. Only two more shelves to go, then it was on to the next bookcase.

He gazed over the collection and sighed. "Whose bright idea was it to get printed copies? Who in their right mind reads on paper anymore?"

He shook his head and grabbed an armful. Halfway back to the table, the entry alert chimed, it could only be one person.

"Now what?" Hunter muttered to himself, then louder, said, "Enter."

The hatch to his left slid open, and Captain Ellis Reynolds entered, carrying a stack of datapads under one arm. He crossed the expansive office to Hunter's desk, which sat in front of a panoramic view of Solomon and the traffic lanes around Phoenix Station. The system was teaming with warships, something to be expected near the fleet's headquarters, but this week, the number of ships floating in the void outside Hunter's office had almost doubled. Something that both thrilled and dismayed him.

"You know, I can have a couple of ratings up here and get all this packed away for you in an hour," Reynolds said, setting the stack of pads on the desk.

Hunter chuckled. "That's the third time you've mention that in as many days, Ellis. How many times do I have to tell you, I don't want any help."

The admiral's executive aide shrugged. "Just trying to make life easier for you is all, sir. I hate moving."

"Oh, I'm not a fan either," Hunter said, putting a couple of the books in the crate. "But this is something I need to do. Call it... closure."

"Closure, sir?"

"That's right."

Reynolds gave Hunter a crooked smirk. "Whatever helps you sleep at night, sir."

Hunter put the rest of the stack into the box and straightened, pressing his palms against the small of his back. "When did packing books become strenuous work anyway?"

"Well, you aren't exactly a spring chicken anymore, sir."

Hunter shot his aide a look of mock indignation. "And what exactly is that supposed to mean?"

"Nothing at all, sir."

"I'll have you know, Captain, I'm in my prime, thank you very much."

"Of course you are, sir. My apologies, sir."

"Anything in there I need to take a look at?" Hunter motioned to the pads.

"Couple ship transfers from 2nd Fleet, a request from New Tuscany about the *New Washington*, two requests from Senator Beilman on our current logistical needs and requirements, and a report on the Centralists debacle. Nothing too pressing, sir. Just a day in the life."

Hunter laughed. "And what a life it is. What about Centralis? Those bastards release their hostages yet?"

"No, sir. The raiders are still holding them. The Centralis planetary governor has made several very loud threats to use his military to take the ships back by force, but they're just words. They have no weight behind them at all, and the raiders know that."

"Well, it's not like he really has anything to throw at them, does he?" Hunter asked. "Otherwise, he wouldn't have come begging for our help."

"Very true, sir."

"And our response?"

"The orders have been dispatched, sir," Reynolds said. "It's my understanding the *Courageous* will be underway shortly."

"Good." Hunter crossed to the bookshelf for another stack of books. "And I assume Beilman is still going on about the drawdown?"

"Yes, sir." Reynolds sighed. "Despite the best efforts of Vice Admiral Ling and Vice Admiral Evans. Even now, with this Centralis thing, and the increased raider activity along the border, he's still pressing them for answers. His oh-seven budget items are really pushing for a reduction in military spending. His latest proposal was eight percent lower than the last one."

Hunter shook his head, his hands full of books. "How do we make him understand if we don't maintain our operational readiness and current strength numbers, we'll lose our advantage. The problem with the raiders is only getting worse, this most recent incident in Centralis only proves that."

"Not to mention that the media has been screaming for military intervention since the whole thing began," Reynolds added.

"You'd think the last few incidents would have pushed him off his soapbox for a little while."

"Don't give them too much credit, Ellis, I've seen a couple of those broadcasts. Yesterday, some fool was campaigning for what amounted to a complete military takeover of the Talu system, and locking it down until we could kick the Pegasi occupiers out and make it safe for the natives again."

"Ah, yes, that's a bit of an extreme response, sir. Despite how much I would like to kick some Pegasi ass at the moment."

"Extreme? Hell, it's downright illegal. But that's the thing, those people screaming for us to do something are the very same that tie our hands behind our backs when we actually have the ability to act."

"I can't disagree with you on that particular point, sir."

Hunter clenched his fists, fighting off the growing wave of anger and frustration growing inside of him. "See, this is precisely why I wanted to pack *alone*. This is supposed to be an enjoyable experience—a time for me to relax and not fret about what a horrible life decision I'm making."

Reynolds laughed and stepped around the desk. "Absolutely horrible, sir. Another week and you'll be waking up the aroma of fresh bread and pastries every day. A truly miserable life, sir."

"Indeed." Hunter took a sip of water from a cup on the table. "You mentioned New Tuscany?"

"Yes, sir. Another request from Admiral Halstead about the *New Washington,* wanting to know when the ship would be available as his flag."

Hunter frowned. "ASI still hasn't released it?"

"No, sir. Not as far as I'm aware. The last update I received was they were going to hold it until the hearings, which I believe are starting within the next few days. Admiral Cartwright wanted to postpone the Tribunal until after your retirement but decided against it."

"And it'll probably be another week or so after that before they're done with the ship," Hunter said, more for himself than for Reynolds.

The Young case had made headlines and broadcasts throughout the Alliance within minutes of his arrest three months ago. He'd been immediately stripped of his command and put in confinement, but somehow, his influence had continued to make life difficult for everyone involved.

The Admiral had been at the forefront of a conspiracy to push the Alliance into a war with the Pegasi, which, the more Hunter thought about it, the more he was shocked that Young's plan hadn't worked, even after the Stonemeyer mission went to shit. Until Cartwright had issued a gag order on the former commander of 2nd Fleet, Young had been extremely vocal about his lack of involvement in the operation and that it had all been the brainchild of Ambassador Tobias Delaney. A convenient allegation, considering Delaney had been killed during the rescue, along with the entire platoon of Marines sent in to extract him.

For Young's part, it had been a decent plan. Set up a conflict that neither the Alliance nor the Pegasi could ignore and wait for the fireworks to fly. Had it not been for the actions of the Marines on the ground and a cunning ASI agent, they might never have uncovered the plot, and right now, the two largest powers in the region would be duking it out over a lie.

"Send Admiral Halstead my sympathies," Hunter finally said. "I know what it's like to be held prisoner by procedure. Let him know as soon as he's cleared by the Station Chief there, he's free to depart, with my blessing."

"Yes, sir," Reynolds said. "You know—"

A soft chime interrupted the captain, his link activating immediately. The holopanels rotated into place over his left wrist, an orange glow illuminating his face. He read in silence, his expression slowly changing from mild interest to obvious frustration, then anger.

Hunter set another stack of books down and approached his desk. "What's wrong?"

"Another raider attack, sir," Reynolds said. "This time in the Ewing system. One of our light cruisers engaged them before they could destroy the orbital refinery there, but they took heavy damage."

"Which ship?"

"The *Vision*, sir. Don Kimball's boat. And, it looks like he was severely injured in the attack as well."

Hunter gritted his teeth and let out a long, frustrated sigh. "What the fuck are we going to have to do to stop these attacks? The bureaucrats want us to fall back and give space, but every time we do, it costs us more lives. How many more lives is it going to take for them to recognize what we're dealing with out there?"

Reynolds didn't respond. He didn't need to. The captain was as much a personal and official aide as he was a sounding board for Hunter's frustrations, and Reynolds was the only man Hunter trusted to listen to his venting and not spread it all over hell and back for personal gain.

Finally, Hunter said, "I think it's time to spin up *Legend*."

Reynolds raised an eyebrow at that. "Do you think that's wise, sir?"

"Wise? No. Necessary? Yes. You still have your list?"

"Yes, sir."

"Who's at the top?"

"Anderson Ward, sir," Reynolds said without hesitation. "He's a straight shooter, really knows his stuff. He's a hard charger, but fair."

"And where is he?"

"Interestingly enough, he's assigned to the *Vision* at the

moment. He's been Kimball's XO for the better part of four years."

"Four years?" Hunter thought about that for a moment. "He'll have the right motivation then. And anyone that can stand Don Kimball for that long deserves sainthood, forget their own ship. That doesn't leave this room."

Reynolds held up both hands, palms out. "From your lips to my ears, sir."

"Send me his jacket. I'll look it over while I'm finishing here."

"Right away, sir."

"Anything else?" Hunter asked when Reynolds didn't move.

The captain grinned. "Just trying to figure out whether or not you're going to be done packing before your retirement ceremony, sir."

"Maybe I'll surprise everyone and actually show up," Hunter replied.

"That would be something, sir."

CHAPTER 5

Fischer's Apartment
Blue Lake City, New Tuscany
23 July 2607

The destruction wrought across the small room was incredible, and Fischer stood at the center of it all, trying to comprehend what had happened. It was almost impossible to see the floor through the mess, and he had no idea where to start. Better to give up now. It was a losing battle anyway.

"I honestly don't understand how one little person can create so much chaos," Carissa said, then laughed and raised an eyebrow at her husband. "No, actually, never mind, I do."

"What's that supposed to mean?" Fischer asked, squatting down to pick up three stuffed animals and a plastic toy datapad. "I'm nowhere near this bad."

"Uh-huh," Carissa said, sounding completely unconvinced.

"It looks like it was a madhouse today."

Carissa laughed. "Today? This is what it's like every day. That girl is a menace."

"Now that's not true," Fischer chided.

JOSH HAYES

"No, it is. I love her, you know I love her. She's the light of my world, best thing that's ever happened to me. But she's a menace. Borderline baby terrorist."

"Best thing?" Fischer raised an eyebrow at his wife.

She eyed him for a moment, then nodded. "Definitely."

Fischer tossed the toys in the basket beside the couch. "You cut me deep."

"I'll do more than that you keep these hours up," Carissa said, dumping an armful into the basket. "I thought you said it was slowing down."

"I'm sorry. Really, I am, but with the Tribunal coming up, and this new piece of evidence, we've been going full speed trying to put everything together."

"You've been going full speed since this whole thing started," Carissa said. "Ever since that ship with the Marines got here and you went to Stonemeyer, this case has become your entire life."

"That's not true."

"It is true, Jackson, it is. When was the last time we went out and did something fun together, with or without Maddie? I can't remember, that's how long it's been."

Fischer opened his mouth to respond, then immediately closed it. He did, in fact, remember their last date, and it was for that very reason he hadn't been inclined to take her on another. The night the ghost had watched him from across the bar, then disappeared into the night.

Despite their best efforts, they hadn't been able to track him, and his face wasn't listed on any known database in the Alliance. Fischer guessed they'd spent more money on trying to identify that one man than some agencies spend on their entire yearly operating budget. For almost a month after the incident, ASI had run scanner algorithms throughout the Alliance, hoping the man would pop up somewhere, but he never had. He'd become somewhat of an anomaly. He'd become a literal ghost.

42

Fischer ground his teeth together, suppressing a sigh. That was a sure way to set his wife on a tirade. She hated his sighs. "Look, I'm sorry, all right? I know it's been a shitty few months. I know that. Yes, I'm worried about you and Maddie. I don't want anything to happen to either of you. But there's some pretty heavy shit going on right now that—honestly—scares the fuck out of me."

Carissa hesitated for a moment, toy in hand. "If it scares you, then why not let someone else do it."

"I can't do that, babe, and you know it. I can't pass this off, no matter how much I want to. This is my case to work. And to be honest, I wouldn't trust anyone else to do it."

"I'm just ready for the long days and late nights to be over," Carissa said, tossing the last toy into a bin. "You can't solve every problem in the universe by yourself, you know?"

"I know," Fischer replied. *But I can try*, he didn't add.

Carissa looked at him for a long moment, then crossed the living room and pulled him close, her hands sliding up under his arms and around to his back. She laid her face against his chest and said, "I love you so much."

"I love you, too." Fischer rested his chin on the top of her head. It felt nice to hold his wife. It felt right. So why was he always in a hurry to leave? The battle between work and home had raged for months now, and he didn't see any clear victor in sight. Or an end for that matter, victor be damned. He loved Carissa with everything that he was, but there were a lot of good people out there battling for justice every day, and he couldn't, and wouldn't, trust anyone else to do his work.

But even if he could, what would he do? Be a stay at home father? Drive a cab? Admittedly, he wasn't the best dad in the galaxy, but he was working on it. Besides, he didn't have any other skills. All he knew how to do was work cases. It was all he wanted to do.

"I love you, too," he said, squeezing her back. He kissed the top of her head.

They held their embrace for a while. Fischer inhaled the scent of Carissa's hair, lavender with a hint of mint. He'd always loved that smell. He could still remember the first time he'd smelled it on their first date, sitting with his arm around her, smiling like an idiot.

He did need to take her out. It'd been too long, and whether he liked it or not, the powers that be had seen fit to bring this case to its inevitable conclusion. It was out of his hands now.

"We should go on a trip," Fischer said.

Carissa stepped back, eyeing him. "Seriously?"

"Yeah. You're right, it's been too long. I've got a shit-ton of leave saved up. After this Tribunal is finished, we should pack up and head off somewhere far away from here. Maybe the Nine or the Solomon Lakes. I know you've always wanted to see those."

Carissa laughed. "I was just thinking something low-key like the Tersay Mountains or something else local. Do you know how expensive a trip to Solomon is?"

This time it was Fischer's turn to laugh. The fact was that his wife brought in more money by herself than anyone else he knew —they could afford trips throughout the Protectorate several times over. They owned a modestly-sized apartment in downtown Blue Lake City and had a more-than-healthy bank account. His pay wasn't even calculated into the family budget, it went straight into an education fund for Maddie, and for any other children they might have in the future.

"It's only money," Fischer said. "You can't take it with you."

"Yeah, but you need it to eat." Carissa turned and moved into the kitchen. She pulled a bottle of wine from the small rack on the counter, opened it, and poured herself a glass. "I have heard the Solomon Lakes are beautiful this time of year."

"It's settled then," Fischer said, selecting his half-empty bottle of Fractal Star bourbon from the cabinet. He pulled the stopper out and smelled the sweet aroma. Coffee in the mornings, a good bourbon in the evenings, that was how Jackson Fischer liked to start and finish his days. "When this is over, we're going."

"You can't say that and back out on it later," Carissa said over the edge of her glass. "You're taking me on a trip, mister. Don't make any mistake about that."

Fischer grinned and rolled the amber liquid around in his tumbler before taking a sip, welcoming the burn on his gums. "Yes, ma'am."

"Now, let's go finish cleaning up after this baby terrorist of yours."

"Mine?"

"Yes, yours," Carissa said. "When she does *this* like *this*, she's all yours."

CHAPTER 6

Alliance Security and Intelligence Regional Headquarters
Blue Lake City, New Tuscany
24 July 2607

"Did you run cross-reference checks on the com laser logs?"

Fischer folded his arms across his chest. He was standing behind one of ASI's technical workstations, watching Riley Davis perform her magic. More to the point, trying his best to keep up with her. "Why would we do that?"

Fingers danced over the keys. "They're logged separately," Davis explained. "A lot of times, the laser frequency, duration, and tracking ID could be traced back to the relay itself. Has to be, right? Otherwise, there'd be a lot of people out there getting a lot of information they shouldn't be."

"Or shit they didn't want," Eliwood said. "Can you imagine some housewife trying to access a message from her dear old mom and some sick porn shit comes through instead?" She laughed. "Actually, I'd pay to see that."

"The registries are usually embedded in the burst code and

independently recorded. If we run a comparison scan..." Davis trailed off as she worked, swiping through multiple screens faster than Fischer could follow. "There."

A message panel appeared on the holodisplay, and Fischer leaned forward to read it. "Alistair Communications."

Eliwood chuckled. "Why does that not surprise me."

"Well, they are one of the largest communication companies in the Protectorate," Davis said. After a moment, she glanced over her shoulder, frowning. "Wait, do you think they had something to do with that file?"

"We're not sure," Fischer said. "But they've come up before." He tapped his link, sending Carter a message. "Can you track down the buoy location?" he asked Davis.

"That's a little complicated," Davis said. "I might be able to track down the registry number, but specific location coordinates —that's something you're going to have to get from Alistair itself. And good luck on that."

The door to the room slid open, and Division Chief Carter walked in. "What's up?"

Fischer motioned to the holodisplay. "Take a look at this."

"Alistair?" Carter glared at Fischer. "Please, don't tell me you're looking into Alistair as a focus again?"

Fischer held out both hands. "Boss, I have to look where the information takes me."

"The fucking thing is going to get way worse before it starts to get better," Carter said. He pointed a finger at Fischer. "And you know damned well JAG isn't going to go anywhere near anything with the name Alistair unless you've got something solid. And I mean fucking concrete. No, scratch that, steel. Tungsten."

"Right now, it's just their property I want a look at," Fischer admitted. "It could've been anyone's."

"But it wasn't," Carter said. "Regardless, do we really have the time to chase it down? And is it going to be worth the time investment? This thing is going to kick off in a few days."

Fischer pointed to the holodisplay. "Someone sent this message. Someone read it. Someone deleted it. One or all didn't want anyone else to know anything about it. In my mind, that makes this important. It could be the thing that puts this all together. This could be the piece that puts Young right in the middle of everything."

"And what if Young's just the tip of the iceberg, what then?" Carter asked. "How far up the ladder are you prepared to go?"

Fischer hesitated for a moment, considering what his boss had just said. He'd thought about that a lot after getting back from Stonemeyer and arresting Young, and he kept coming up with the same answer. "As far as it takes."

"And what if it takes to you to a place no one likes?" Carter asked. "We aren't talking about a supply lieutenant slipping extra supplies under the table for kickbacks, or insider trading or anything like that. We all know this thing is bigger than Stone-meyer. It's bigger than Delaney; it's bigger than Young."

"I don't want anything less than the truth," Fischer said. "Anything less than that and I'd be dishonoring everyone who died to get us here in the first place."

Carter hesitated for a moment, eyes flicking to everyone in the room. "I have to be honest, Fish, this thing scares the hell out of me, and it should scare you too."

"Oh, it does," Fischer said. "It should scare everyone. But being scared doesn't mean we shouldn't act."

"The higher up this shit goes, the more delicate we need to be. We're talking life and death here, Fish. And I don't mean that rhetorically either. I mean it. We're talking serious, like you walk out to your gravbike and instead of the repulsors kicking on, the thing just goes bang, serious."

Eliwood rolled her eyes. "Oh, come on, Boss. You don't really believe that shit, do you? That's crazy. That kind of shit doesn't happen."

"It does, happen," Carter countered. "You just don't ever hear about it. Some politician somewhere has an accident and no one's the wiser. And that's fucking child's play. No one gives a shit about politicians when it really comes down to it. They're bought and sold like stocks on the open exchange. You start looking at something like Alistair..." Carter shook his head. "...you're talking about real money players there. We're talking trillions and trillions of credits. Those are the people that actually run the universe, not the politicians. You start threatening their money, the dead bodies will start to pile up."

Fischer had never known Carter to be a conspiracy junkie. In fact, he's always considered the man to be one hundred percent grounded most of the time.

But now...

"Do you know something you're not telling us, Dan?" Fischer asked.

"You know, I actually wish I did," Carter said. "Maybe this case wouldn't give me the shits so bad, if I did. But I don't. Just doesn't smell right is all."

"That's for damn sure," Fischer agreed.

"The longer this thing goes, the deeper we dig, the worse it will be for everyone involved. Including us. I'm not telling you to stop," Carter said quickly. "And I'm not telling you not to follow the facts, either. I am, however, telling you to be aware of what is going on around you. All the time."

"I have to tell you, Boss," Eliwood said, "you're starting to scare me a little bit here."

"Good," Carter said. "That's the point."

"It's not going to make me stop asking questions though," she said.

Fischer smiled. "Me neither."

Carter chuckled. "I'd expect nothing less from either of you."

"Listen," Fischer said, "we might be able to trace the signal that brought the message in. All the quantum lasers have a unique signature so their transmissions can be kept secure. If we can determine which signal relay it comes from, we can track it back to its point of origin."

"You're going to need a warrant," Carter said.

Fischer nodded. "That's right."

"All right, so what the hell is Cardinal?"

Fischer shook his head. "I don't know. Maybe he's the one behind all of this? My guess it's a code name for someone."

"And Anon Four Two One?"

"It's obviously Young," Eliwood said.

"Probably," Carter said. "But you don't have any proof of that. In fact, you really don't have anything that links this message to our case at all. Just your suspicions."

Eliwood crossed her arms. "I'd say they're a little more than suspicions, Boss."

"Okay, then let's see the evidence. Connect the dots for me and put it on Young."

"Dan…" Fischer said, understanding where Carter was coming from.

"I'm not trying to be a hard-ass here, Aniyah. Truly, I'm not. But if we don't have any evidence linking Young directly to that message, I'm going to have a hell of a time presenting it to the Magistrate and asking for an extension that I know he's not going to give."

"We *can* link it to Young," Fischer said. "We just need—"

"Time," Carter said, cutting Fischer off. "I know. But it's time we don't have. Young's transport dropped into the system twenty minutes ago."

"What? He's here?" Fischer asked.

"They're bringing him down as we speak. Full military escort. Nemesis fighters—the works. They should be planetside shortly."

CHAPTER 7

Airspace above Blue Lake City, New Tuscany
24 July 2607

First Lieutenant Craig Norris adjusted his course, banking the VAF11 Nemesis fighter back to the left, keeping pace with the modified Albatross shuttle ahead. The twin EE3 microfusion drives situated directly behind the cockpit thrummed, vibrating his couch. Three holopanels were arrayed in front of him, half as tall as they were wide, giving him an unrestricted view through the cockpit's windshield.

A two-tone alert chimed softly inside Norris's helmet as they passed one of the mission's waypoints. He reached forward and tapped the blue trajectory line in the center of the main display, causing it to flash green. The two secondary options vanished.

"Flight Control, Cinder Lead, we've passed Waypoint Charlie and are proceeding on primary route."

"Roger that, Lead," the flight operations controller answered through Norris's cochlear implant. "We have you on approach. You are clear to proceed to LZ Gold."

"LZ Gold, confirmed," Norris said.

Ahead, the Albatross and the forward escort Nemesis fighter closed on Blue Lake City. They'd made re-entry over the body of water for which New Tuscany's capital was named, and were now approaching the coast. At five-thousand feet, Blue Lake City stretched out to the horizon, spreading out along the coast, and inland as far as Norris could see.

The city was beautiful, the modern high-rises reaching thousands of feet into the air. The Pont-Newman buildings, three glass-walled structures that spiraled around each other and joined together at their peaks, dwarfed the surrounding buildings on this part of the coast. Atop the buildings was an expansive luxury resort covered by a massive glass dome. Patrons received a full, unobstructed view of the cityscape in all directions. Norris made a mental note to check the resort prices. Regardless of what they actually were, they'd probably be well outside his price range, but Trace would love something like that.

Most, if not all of the air traffic, had been automatically rerouted for their arrival, though the majority of the citizens would never even know. Blue Lake Air Traffic Control had simply fed their navigational computers with alternate course information, taking them away from the flight. Their arrival hadn't been announced, and with the amount of regular military traffic into the city, their appearance probably wouldn't have been noted by anyone.

That didn't change the fact that two Nemesis escorts and the platoon of Marine guards onboard the Albatross seemed like overkill. Young was a bastard, everyone knew that, and the asshole deserved everything he got for what he'd done, but New Tuscany was in the heart of the Alliance. It wasn't like he was going anywhere. Right at that moment, there were no less than thirty warships in orbit, including the carrier *Archimond*. No one in their right mind would even consider attacking them here. It'd be a suicide mission.

Another alert chimed as the flight crossed the coast and entered the city. Two-thousand-foot-tall residential towers lined white-sand beaches. Mirrored windows lining their exteriors reflected golden sunlight and blue waves. Rooftop pools were filled with residents and their guests, splashing in the water and laying out, soaking up the sun.

That's what I need, Norris though, trying to remember the last time he'd just laid out and relaxed. It'd been a while.

The life of a Navy combat pilot was an exciting one, there wasn't any doubt about that, but it definitely was not where the money was at. Trace didn't mind, in fact, he'd said several times that he absolutely detested the "high life," but Norris had never experienced it for himself, and wanted to be able to have the option at least.

One day, he told himself, adjusting course slightly. A lot of old fighter jocks landed jobs with the big interstellars, chauffeuring executives around. That was where the money was, that was when he'd be able to afford a lake-front condo.

Six more years.

"Cinder Lead, Cinder One, Passing Waypoint Delta," his wingman, Lieutenant Kendra May said over the taclink.

"Copy that," Norris responded, bringing his attention back to the operation at hand. Daydreaming about the afterlife could wait.

His eyes tracked to the panel by his right hand, confirming everything he already intuitively knew; weapons systems, power, engines, communications, sensors, defense systems, were all active and functioning. The fighter's sensor suite had been active since departing the *Archimond*, identifying every vessel within range, and logging the information without any input from Norris. Trader ships, freighters, personnel shuttles, cabs, orbital skiffs, all documented and tracked.

Blue Lake ATC and local law enforcement had been tasked with securing the ground routes to and from their destination, the

Regional Alliance capitol building and the readout on his main display told Norris they were just over halfway there.

"Homestretch," he told himself.

A proximity warning appeared on his primary display—two aircabs moving into the convoy's airspace. Sensor data populated additional panels, showing Norris they weren't anything other than what they appeared to be.

"Son of a bitch," Norris muttered, tapping the communications panel next to his left hand. "Flight Control, Cinder Lead, be advised, we've got civilian aircraft encroaching on our designated flight path. You might want to put a boot into those local ATC guys."

"Stand by, Cinder Lead, we're attempting to establish contact now."

Another proximity warning flashed. On his tactical display, a heavy cargo shuttle appeared, on re-entry vectors that would converge on their current course. It was descending toward the city, two thousand meters above them. A little too close for comfort.

Norris looked over his shoulder and saw the large vessel descending, its hull partially obscured by the sun. "What the hell? How hard it is to—"

A third alarm sounded: a mid-size personnel shuttle, coming in on an opposite heading. It would cross Cinder Two's flight path in another three minutes.

"Flight Control, Cinder Lead, it's getting awfully crowded up here. What's the story with ATC?"

"Cinder Lead, Control, we haven't been able to reach them on comms. We're contacting Blue Lake emergency response right now."

"Can't reach Traffic Control?" Norris asked. Their pre-mission flight briefing had explicitly stated they'd have a dedicated line throughout the operation. The hairs on the back of his neck stood. Something about this didn't seem right.

"Flight Control, change of plans. We're going to Flight Profile Falcon, do you copy?"

"Copy that, Lead, changing alternative flight path."

Norris switched to his direct link with Lieutenant May. "Cinder One, Cinder-Six-One, Cinder Lead, we are switching: Profile Falcon, confirm."

"Roger that, Lead. Falcon confirmed," Lieutenant May answered without hesitation.

"Cinder Lead, Cinder-Six-one," the pilot of the Albatross said. "Confirming Profile Falcon."

Ahead, May's fighter banked left, pulling off their primary flight path, and heading to the new one. The larger Albatross turned slower, banking and pulling up behind the Nemesis fighter, engines flaring, aerofoils folding up and down.

Norris flipped through the growing number of targets currently being tracked by his fighter's computer. Five new target profiles had appeared in the last ten seconds, all approaching from different directions. It was as if the local air traffic control had lost their grasp on the lockdown they'd supposedly instituted.

He gritted his teeth, trying to keep a lid on the anger he felt rising in his chest. "Flight Control, Cinder Lead, what the hell is going on? The sky is filling up fast."

"We've lost all contact with Blue Lake ATC," the controller said. "The local authorities have personnel en route to their operations center now."

"That's not gonna help us right now," Norris said, barely managing not to curse. "Request additional escort units on station ASAP. I don't like the way—"

Lieutenant May's icon flashed on his main display, her communication request overriding his link with Flight Control."

"Cinder Lead, Cinder One, I'm reading a power fluctuation in the—"

The transmission cut out.

Ahead, May's Nemesis fighter at the lead of their formation exploded. Flames engulfed the fuselage as streamers of burning debris arched away. The Albatross banked left, flaring to avoid the explosion.

"May!" Norris shouted, slamming the control to port, and moving to shadow the Albatross.

Alarms wailed through his cockpit as warning panels appeared, identifying hazards and debris.

"Flight Control, Cinder Lead, Cinder One is down! Cinder One is down!"

"Cinder Lead, Flight Control, say again."

"Control, my wingman's spacecraft just fucking exploded!"

Norris twisted around, trying to visually locate the enemy that his sensors hadn't detected. He hadn't seen the tell-tale sign of a missile's contrail cutting through the sky and hadn't received a launch detection from his tactical computer.

"Cinder Lead, Flight Control, are you under attack?"

He swiveled the other direction, craning his head, trying to see, but there wasn't anything to see at all. He turned back to his displays and started swiping through warning panels, looking for anything that would explain what was going on.

"Cinder Lead, this is Flight Control, are you under attack?"

A shadow passed over his cockpit, and he looked up to see the underbelly of the heavy cargo shuttle he'd seen just minutes before. It held course, flying parallel to him and the Albatross, and seemed to be slowing down. Norris banked to the left, pulling away from the new ship, and allowing him to see the entire fuselage. The cargo hatch on the port side was open, just aft of the craft's stubby wings, several figures silhouetted in the opening.

"What the hell?" Norris said.

"Cinder Lead, Flight Control, what is your status?"

Without taking his eyes off the open hatch, Norris said, "Control, Lead, I… I don't…"

A yellow and orange panel appeared on his main display:

INTERNAL   RELAY   FAILURE.   POWER   LEVELS
CRITICAL.

"What the fuck?" Norris asked, his pulse pounding. Additional diagnostic warnings appeared, one right after another. Then a power fluctuation in the fighter's main drive coil.

Before he'd even known he was going to pull it, his fingers wrapped around the ejection handle and Craig Norris pulled with everything he was worth. Canopy bolts blasted away, followed by the explosive separation of canopy from fuselage, and a second later, Norris's couch shot out of his fighter.

CHAPTER 8

Alliance Security and Intelligence Regional Headquarters
Blue Lake City, New Tuscany
24 July 2607

Fischer held his breath, watching the VR playback, as two Alliance Marines in tactical vests and combat gear, planted themselves at the front of the Albatross's cargo bay, blocking the hatch to the secured cabin and cockpit at the front of the craft. Both had their LR27s up and ready.

Sparks sprayed into the bay. A bright orange line drew itself around the personnel access hatch on the Albatross's starboard side, a plasma torch cutting through the shuttle's hull. Thirty seconds later, the hatch was torn free from the fuselage and a torrent of wind whipped into the bay, nearly throwing the two Marines off their feet.

A second later, the maelstrom subsided, and three figures dressed in black combat uniforms, helmets, and tactical vests swung through the opening, their Modified KGA17s up and firing before they'd even got their feet set. The short-barrel automatic gauss carbines were usually carried by Pegasi special forces, though the weapon itself was for sale throughout the URT and the independent systems.

The Marines never stood a chance. Only one of the two managed to even get off a shot, though it did nothing more than put a hole in the shuttle's ceiling. The fury of fire dropped them where they stood.

"Son of a bitch," Eliwood muttered under her breath.

Fischer looked on without saying a word, fury burning inside his chest.

The attackers stepped aside as two more came through the behind them. Then, they all moved forward to the hatch the Marines had been guarding. Their size and gear suggested they were male, but the masks and helmets they wore made it impossible for any kind of identification.

Two of the attackers pulled the dead Marines aside, giving the others room to work. Two more pulled out plasma torches and each traced even lines around the hatch. They were through in seconds, pulling the metal back and letting it fall to the deck. The three waiting attackers flowed through without hesitation, weapons up, hunting for targets.

A single Marine, kneeling at the far end of the short passage, had his rifle up and fired, hitting the lead attacker in the chest. The impact knocked him into his companions. The third man in the stack shoved his way past, pushed his rifle around them, and returned fire. The rounds smacked into the fully armored Marine, throwing him back against the hatch he was guarding. The Marine fired several more times as he fell, all the while taking more rounds from the attackers until he finally collapsed on the deck, unmoving.

The attacker who'd taken the first rounds lay still on the deck, obviously dead or dying. One of his companions grabbed him and pulled him back into the cargo bay, getting him out of the way while the other four pressed on.

They stopped at the secured cabin on the port side of the passage, again using laser torches to slice through the hatch. After cutting it free, they heaved it aside, clearing the way for the others to enter the small compartment. Not a full minute later, they re-emerged with their prize.

Marcus Young walked out of the compartment, his hands bound in front of him with electrocuffs. He held them out and looked away as one of the attackers cut through the bindings with a laser. The restraints fell to the deck, and Young was free. He rubbed his wrists, smiling broadly.

"Mother fucker," Fischer said, clenching his fists tightly, fighting the urge to turn off the playback.

One of the attackers held out a black harness and helped him slip it around his waist and chest. Young clapped the man on his shoulder. Then they led him back through the passage, into the bay. They picked up their fallen comrade, carrying him to the open hatch where six cables were waiting for them. They attached the dead man to one and eased him out of the Albatross. The forcefield covering the opening flashed blue as the man's body slipped out and swung free.

Young went next, though he hesitated before stepping out of the shuttle. When he was clear, the rest of the attackers followed in short order. The cables they were attached to retracted into the open underbelly of the large sprinter hovering above the Albatross, and the bay doors folded shut behind them.

Almost immediately, the sprinter changed course and punched its engines, racing for orbit. After breaking atmo, the sprinter broke every safety regulation in the book, pushing its drives to their max and shooting up the gravity well, away from the Navy ships which were just learning of the attack. They'd barely had time to dispatch the active patrol birds, much less the Ready-Five fighters. It reached a translation point for the JumpLane before any of its pursuers were given a chance to catch up.

The Nemesis pilot, Craig Norris, had been picked up shortly after he'd touched down and was immediately escorted to ASI headquarters to be debriefed. The remains of Lieutenant Kendra May was being collected by the Blue Lake coroner's office for examination. ASI scene techs, assisted by some of the local investigators, were en route to process the multiple scenes.

The playback ended, cutting to black. Then after a moment, the VR started again, starting from the beginning.

Fischer clenched his fist so hard his fingers ached. As the footage played again, the urge to double over and vomit almost overwhelmed him. He opened his mouth to speak but couldn't find the words.

"The *Kilo* class shuttle wasn't on any inbound registry," Carter said finally, breaking the silence. He was checking through the dispatch they'd received just a few minutes before they the video downloaded. "The tactical data from our orbital sensors and fleet records is being compiled as we speak. Navy units are being dispatched to all the systems along the Lane's route in hopes we will be able to catch them when they come out."

Fischer slammed a fist against the table, rattling the data pads and glasses. "Son of a bitch! We should've been ready. If we would've had some kind of warning, we could've stopped this."

"You don't know that," Carter said.

Fischer bared his teeth, his chest tightening. He pointed at Carter but managed to contain his outburst to a controlled growl. "That bastard should've never left Blue Lake. We should have kept him in our custody and never released him to Navy Security."

"Now isn't the time to play what ifs or what we could've dones. We need to focus on what we *can* do to fix this."

"I knew Young was just the tip of the iceberg," Fischer said, pacing. "I fucking knew it. And now that mother fucker's out again."

"Jesus," Eliwood muttered, leaning back in her seat, eyes locked on the multiple holopanels replaying the abduction. "The number of resources it must've taken to pull something like this..." She trailed off, looking at Fischer. "I mean, who can do that? They looked like special forces, right?"

"Those were Pegasi rifles," Fischer said. "How much you want to bet the drives on that *Kilo* were Pegasi military? Because they sure as shit weren't standard. There's no way a sprinter like that would've outrun those gunboats. No way."

"We're not betting anything," Carter said. "And we need to clamp down on any rumors about Pegasi involvement until we know more. Eliwood, I want you to contact Blue Lake ATC, I want all the flight records and registry data they've got. Everything. I want the entire area locked down. Call anyone we need, get them in there."

"Play the second fighter explosion again," Fischer said.

Davis cycled the feed, queueing it up at the appropriate time, then let it play. The tag above the fighter read "Cinder Lead." The fighter banked slightly to the left, then the explosive bolts holding the canopy to the fuselage blew, sending little geysers of white compressed air spraying. The transparent canopy blew a second later, immediately grabbed by the wind and thrown backward along the fuselage toward the tail. The pilot ejected a half-second later, his seat arcing out of the cockpit, protective blue forcefield flashing.

"Freeze it," Fischer said.

The emerge froze just as the rear of the fighter began exploding. The titanium alloy fuselage ripping open, the fireball just starting to expand.

"There's no rockets," Fischer said. He turned to Davis and motioned to his link. "You mind?"

"No, go ahead."

Fischer moved around the table, tapped his link, and began

manipulating the image. He rotated the view around the fighter in all directions, zooming out, then back in. He played the footage forward, then backward. None of the angles he saw showed any sign of a rocket, missile or other projectile striking the fighter.

"These fighters weren't shot down," Fischer said, through the frozen image of the Nemesis explosion.

"What the fuck?" Eliwood said.

"We need to keep that pilot in here and isolated," Fischer said. "He's the only eyewitnesses to this thing, him and the Albatross pilots."

"I don't understand why they didn't kill the shuttle pilots," Eliwood said.

"Because they would've had to deal with a shuttle maybe?" Davis offered.

Fischer shook his head. "No, the onboard safety controls would have kept it in the air. They didn't go after the pilots because they didn't need to. It would've been a waste of time. They were after Young. Once he was theirs, staying on the shuttle any longer than necessary was redundant. They got what they were after and left."

"And you think the pilots are going to be able to give us something not shown on the videos?" Eliwood said.

Fischer pointed to the frozen image of the exploding Nemesis. He knew something was wrong, or else he wouldn't have ejected. We need to know what that was."

Eliwood shook her head. "You think those fighters were sabotaged?"

"Not saying that," Fischer admitted. "But just looking at the information available, there aren't a whole lot of alternative options. If they weren't destroyed by an outside attack, they were destroyed from within."

"We'll have plenty of data points for a forensic recreation of the event," Carter said. "Maybe that'll give us something. Could be the image renders we have now aren't complete."

"It's possible, but I doubt it," Fischer said.

"Probably won't do any good, but run those attackers through profiling," Carter told Davis. "Might get lucky and one of those bastards could be in the database."

The tech nodded. "You got it, Boss."

Eliwood pointed to one of the holodisplays beside the main display. "Look, the mayor's making a statement."

"Son of a bitch," Carter said, swiping a finger across his link, activating the broadcast's sound.

"...still in the very early stages of this incident, and we're still trying to understand it." The mayor of Blue Lake City, Lin Wu, stood behind a podium emblazoned with the city's seal. "I must implore our citizens to allow the authorities to do their jobs. Please stay away from the affected areas. City crews are already being dispatched to deal with the cleanup and reconstruction of damaged buildings.

"At this time, the Alliance Military is heading up the investigation. However, I have pledged to provide any and all resources available to assist their investigators. Rest assured, the evil men who perpetrated this attack on our city will not go unpunished. They will be found, and they will be brought to justice."

The image shifted to a man dressed in a burnt orange suit and black shirt and tie. His ear-length white hair was combed to the side and his beard trimmed to mere stubble. Footage of the second Nemesis fighter exploding played on a loop in a panel next to him. "The footage, brought to you exclusively from BLN, shows a first-hand account of the devastating attack. The reports we're getting from our sources on the ground suggest as many as a hundred people have been affected by these explosions and the subsequent destruction caused when they crashed. Of course, we will continue to update you as the information becomes—"

Carter shut down the feed and looked around the table, meeting the gazes of each of his people in turn. "Start making your calls. We're going to be burning the midnight oil on this one."

Fischer unclenched his fists and leaned forward, palms on the table. "We need to trace that fragment, Dan."

CHAPTER 9

Valkyrie Six-One
Centralis System
24 July 2607

With the shuttle's engines powered down and the rest of her systems running in stealth mode, the bay was still and quiet. Eerily quiet, like something was wrong. The sounds of his own breathing echoed inside Sheridan's helmet, his eyes locked on the stars outside. The Albatross's main bay door was open, and the atmospheric forcefield turned off, requiring the members of Team Valkyrie to endure the ride sealed within their void suits.

It's like a sea of diamonds, Sheridan thought. The infinite dark making him feel insignificant.

Captain Chambers' icon appeared on the bottom left of Sheridan's HUD. *"Time to target, two minutes."*

Sheridan felt the Master Sergeant Kline's hand on his shoulder. He met the man's eyes and nodded. "Two minutes."

Team One was sitting on the aft side of the bay, Team Two, starboard. Both element leaders, Sergeant Rocha, and Sergeant Nguyen stood near the open bay door, looking out over the edge of the ramp as if staring into oblivion. The shooters of Team Valkyrie were silent as they approached their targets, putting themselves into the right headspace for what they were about to do. They were professionals, and Sheridan felt more than a little intimidated by them.

As he looked around the bay, Sheridan couldn't help but remember his first and only combat drop he'd made as a regular Marine. The platoon had been cutting up the entire way down, making jokes, poking fun at each other like they didn't have a care in the world. As if the idea of something bad happening was so far outside the realm of possibilities, it wasn't even worth the time to think about.

Of course, thoughts of that drop led to thoughts of the drop-ship spinning out of control and crashing into the street, thoughts of panels exploding and bullets chewing through the fuselage. The jarring impact launching his friends' bodies into the air, the flames and smoke filling the compartment.

Thoughts of Biagini. And Hastings.

He squeezed his eyes shut, gritting his teeth against the memory, trying to push it from his mind. The gunshot rang in his ears, louder than anything in the world, and he jumped in his seat.

Cole, sitting next to him on the bench, turned. "You okay?"

Sheridan nodded. "Yeah, fine."

This is different, Sheridan told himself. *That's not going to happen here.*

Kline's icon flashed on a private link to Sheridan. "Doing all right, Corporal?"

"Yes, Master Sergeant. Fine."

"You sure?"

Sheridan was careful to keep the anxiety out of his voice. "Yes, sir. One-hundred percent good to go, Master Sergeant."

"Good," Kline said. "Eyes up, right?"

Somehow, Valkyrie's motto gave him a renewed sense of

confidence. As if those words had solidified the fact that he wasn't on Stonemeyer, and this was not the same mission that had failed all those months ago. Sheridan nodded. "Eyes up."

"One minute," the pilot reported over the taclink.

Sheridan steeled himself, adjusting his grip on his MOD27. The modified weapon was a recoilless rifle, firing six-millimeter case-less ammunition, and its optical sight synced with Sheridan's combat information display, showing him capacity, remaining rounds, and targeting. His helmet's battle computer used information from the team's taclink, feeding data to the weapon's optics, and vice versa, allowing targeting information to flow seamlessly between team members.

Their void suits were bulkier than regular body armor; individually armored sections linked together and sealed against the vacuum. The suits did inhibit their movement somewhat, but not nearly as much as standard issue, and they'd spent weeks learning how to move in ones twice as restrictive as these. To Sheridan, it almost felt like wearing a second skin, something he wouldn't have thought impossible when he'd first been introduced to them.

"Coming up on the tail section," the pilot said. The red light over the open hatch blinked to orange, and Sergeant Nguyen motioned to this team. They stood in unison, shifting toward the exit with slow and practiced precision.

"Up," Sergeant Rocha said to her team, waving them out of their seats.

Sheridan stood and shuffled toward the exit.

At the top of the ramp, Sergeant Nguyen put a hand on the rail and peered out over the edge. The glow of the freighter's engines appeared below. Nguyen turned, nodding to his team. "Go! Go! Go!"

One by one, the members of Team one left the shuttle bay and disappeared over the edge. Sheridan and the rest of Team Two moved closer to the ramp. Sheridan had to crane his neck but after a moment, he could see Team One touch down on the hull and begin securing their entry point.

"Fifteen seconds to secondary jump," the pilot said.

"All right," Chambers said. "By the numbers. These refugees are counting on us to get this job done quickly and quietly. Eyes up, Valkyrie."

"Eyes up," Sheridan and the rest of the team responded.

An alarm sounded, and the deployment light flashed to green.

"Go! Go! Go!" Chambers shouted.

Sheridan, at the back to the stack, followed the rest of the team. Orange trajectory lines appeared on his HUD as he stepped off the ramp, providing him with course information to the freighter. He activated the small thrusters on his upper back and flew more than fell toward the freighter.

The slate gray hull wasn't streamlined like most modern space-fairing ships. The fuselage was covered in modified sections bulging out from the main structure in several locations and was peppered with discolored silver, and black patches where repairs had been made and the maintainers hadn't cared enough to match the original paint. Sensor clusters that would have been located internally on most newer vessels extended out in clusters of antennas and dishes.

Sheridan's flight computer flashed a proximity warning, and he flipped over, firing his thrusters, slowing his descent. He touched down, bending his knees to absorb the impact and activated his mag-boots. He looked up, which a moment ago had been down, and watched the shuttle bank away on its maneuvering thrusters.

"Valkyrie Six-One, Valkyrie Actual, we are down and locked. You're clear to orbit."

"Roger that, Actual. Will maintain orbital pattern Two-Delta."

"All right," Chambers said over the taclink. *"Secure Entry Point One. Reese, you have the bypass."*

"Roger that, sir," Reese said, moving to the access panel just aft of the emergency airlock. He tapped his link on his left forearm, and the holographic display appeared over his armor. The suits paired directly with their link implants, with the same functionality and capabilities.

Reese swiped through a few menus, shaking his head. "Security software is outdated by about ten years. Installing the redirect. Shouldn't take more than... Oh, ha! That was fast." He looked up from his link display. "We're in. I'm syncing with their core now. Rerouting to *Courageous.*"

Sheridan stood two meters away at the opposite edge of the airlock's hatch, his weapon held across his chest, eyes scanning the length of the freighter's hull. He could just barely make out the other team, positioning themselves near a similar airlock over the engineering section. The expanse of stars above was incredible.

"Internal feeds coming through now, sir," Reese said. Additional display panels appeared over his link, showing feeds from multiple cameras throughout the freighter.

"The bridge?" Chambers asked, stepping closer to Reese, looking over his shoulder.

Reese nodded and tapped one of the panels. It expanded to take up the entire display. Red outlines flashed around five figures; two near the flight control systems at the front of the room, three standing around a group of kneeling hostages in the center.

"Five hostiles," Reese said. "Looks like seven hostages."

"That'll be the bridge crew," Chambers said. "Tag targets. Can you ghost the hatch?"

"No problem, sir," Reese said. "Just need a second to load the program."

"Ghosting the hatch" would trick the freighter's internal sensors into thinking the airlock remained closed and sealed while the Marines entered the ship. Since blowing or cutting through the hull, in most cases, led to explosive decompression, the ability to bypass the ship's internal systems was the preferred method of entry. It might not have been the quickest way in, but it would allow the team to maintain the element of surprise.

"Right," Reese said, stepping away from the access panel. "Got it. Cycling the lock."

There was always the possibility of the airlock rupturing and blowing atmosphere into space, so the Marines gave the hatch a wide berth. Thirty seconds later, the airlock completed its cycle and the outer hatch slide open,

Sergeant Rocha went through first, followed by Neal and Cole. Sheridan brought up the rear, floating through and sealing his boots to the deck. Chambers came in next, followed by Reese and Hanover. Reese tapped his link, and the airlock hatch slid shut behind them. Another command from the electronics specialist and the compartment pressurized.

The airlock's anteroom was an octagon filled with lockers mounted on most of the exposed bulkheads. Each would be likely to contain survival suits and emergency kits. The room was lit by two recessed lights on either end, providing minimal illumination.

The team's footsteps echoed as they shuffled out of the airlock. Cole and Rocha immediately moved to the opposite hatch, their weapons up and ready.

"Want a drone or two?" Cole asked.

"Negative," Chambers said. He turned to Reese. "How's your eyeball? Do we have a clear path?"

"Primary and secondary routes to the bridge look clear, Captain," Reese said. "I'm marking potential threat areas now. But I'm not seeing any movement.

"That can't be all the crew on the bridge, can it?" Neal asked. "Not on a ship this big."

"One thing at a time," Chambers said. "Rocha, our objective is the bridge. Make it happen."

"Roger that, sir," Sergeant Rocha said. "Smooth and steady, people. Zero signature until we reach the bridge. Hanover, you have point. Sheridan, on his six. The rest of us fall in after."

Sergeant Kirk Hanover, Team One's sniper, shifted his HR91 sniper rifle around behind him and drew his MP10 ten-millimeter pistol from the holster on his thigh. For this operation, the team's weapons were loaded with condensed plastic projectiles, intended to cut through light body armor and eliminate enemy threats, but wouldn't puncture the hull. Hanover held the pistol close to his chest, barrel pointing straight out in front of him and climbed up through the hatch as Cole pulled it open.

Sheridan followed him through, keeping at least half a meter of distance between them and half even that to the sniper's right side. They moved steadily forward, clearing hatchways and inter-sections as they went. The dim lighting of the corridor actually worked in their favor, partially concealing them while their HUDs provided significantly enhanced vision through its imagining filters.

They followed directions laid out by Reese, overlaid onto their HUDs, blue markers leading them through the ship's interior.

"Hold up," Reese said over the taclink. "I've got movement. One hundred meters ahead."

Hanover slowed, pressing himself to the left side of the corridor. Sheridan did the same on the right, pulling his rifle tighter into his shoulder, eyes shifting between the corridor in front of him and the HUD on his helmet's visor.

"Seventy-five meters," Reese said.

"Friendly?" Hanover asked, taking a knee and pushing his pistol out.

"Unknown."

Ahead of them, the corridor came to a T-intersection. On his HUD, Sheridan watched as a red dot appeared on the right side of the display, moving toward the junction. It wasn't moving very fast, but it was definitely moving with a purpose.

"Assume it's hostile," Sergeant Rocha said.

"Roger," Hanover said, his voice barely above a whisper.

Sheridan followed the sniper's example and went to one knee, the sights of his weapon locked on the intersection ahead. Focusing on steady breathing, he slowly slide his finger onto the rifle's trigger as the dot approached. It wasn't the first time he'd been in combat, but fighting for his life was something completely different than waiting to kill someone who didn't even know you were there. Wasn't it?

The dot reached the intersection, and a male figure appeared around the corner of the bulkhead. He wore a black jacket and pants. His face was clean-shaven, his auburn hair pulled back in a ponytail. The MAR12 he held across his chest was a clear indication of which category he fell into.

Without warning, Hanover squeezed off a single round. His pistol jerked, barely making a pop, and a moment later, the plastic penetrator smacked into the man's face, punching through the top of his nose. The man's head snapped back, and his feet stumbled backward. He bounced off the bulkhead, the impact jarring the weapon from his hands, sending it clattering to the floor.

"Tango down," Hanover said, already moving forward, and keeping his pistol trained on the man. Once on top of him, Hanover knelt and confirmed the kill.

Sheridan moved around the corner. He read the location identifier on his HUD and said, "Corridor Two secure."

"In another fifty meters, take the hatch on the starboard side;

it's the main ladder," Reese advised over the taclink. *"The Bridge is two decks down."*

"Any more surprises?" Hanover asked.

"Looks clear," Reese said.

One of the first things Sheridan had learned about MARSOC combat rules was to not become reliant on their advanced combat systems and equipment. *"Systems and equipment fail. Eyes never lie,"* his instructors had said. *"Always go into a fight with the knowledge that your equipment can and will fail. Then, when it does, you won't hesitate; you'll just act."*

Eyes Up, Sheridan thought and pressed forward.

CHAPTER 10

Freighter *Orphaned Star*
Centralis System
24 July 2607

Sheridan held his MOD27 close to his chest with his right hand and balanced himself on the ladder rail with his left.

Hanover reached the landing first and stepped over to the hatch. Sheridan stepped off the ladder and moved quickly to the opposite side. There was only enough room on the landing for two more; Sergeant Rocha and Neal filled those spaces, and the rest held their positions on the ladder.

"The main bridge hatch is open," Reese said. *"Through the hatch to the left, ten meters."*

Hanover made eye contact with Sheridan through their visors. "Remember, slow is smooth and smooth is fast. You stay right on my six when we go through. I've got corners one and two. You take three and four."

Sheridan's heart thumped hard in his chest. "Got it."

"All right." He looked back at the rest of the team. "We're moving."

Hanover opened the hatch and immediately moving out into the corridor. Sheridan followed on his heels, shifting to the far-right side. The bridge's main entrance spanned the entire four-meter width of the corridor, its double steel-alloy doors stuck open, edges protruding from the bulkheads on either side.

"Body on the ground," Hanover said. A male who looked like he was in his fifties lay face down in the corridor several meters in front of the entrance to the bridge, blood pooling beneath him.

An angry male voice echoed through the open doors. "... then what the fuck is that Alliance cruiser doing out there?"

"I don't fucking know," another voice said, this one female. "Maybe Centralis called them for help."

"No way they would've done that," the first voice said. "Not with their cargo."

"Don't stop," Hanover said through the taclink, his voice low. "Watch your shots."

Hanover slipped through the entrance, immediately moving left. Sheridan moved right, clearing the area just inside the door before turning his attention back to the rest of the room. Two quick pops echoed through the compartment, and he saw two of the hostile contacts drop, their outlines flashing to yellow as they hit the deck.

Ten meters ahead, one of the armed raiders pushed himself to his feet from one knee, struggling to get his slung rifle off his shoulder. Sheridan didn't hesitate, firing a burst from his MOD27 center-mass. His rounds punched into the man's chest, knocking him off his feet. His body collapsed to the deck with a metallic *thud*.

"Stay down!" Sheridan shouted to the three captive crew members sitting cross-legged on the deck. He passed them, moving to engage another raider.

Drawn by Hanover's first shots, the pirate didn't see Sheridan until it was too late. He'd just swung his rifle around, getting a bead on Hanover when his eyes flicked back to Sheridan, widening in realization. Whichever target he picked, the other would best him. He opened his mouth to shout, and Sheridan squeezed the trigger, putting a round in his throat.

Blood fountained out. The man's eyes bulged as bright red sprayed out of the hole in his neck. He dropped his weapon, both hands reaching up to cover the wound as he collapsed to his knees. His mouth opened and closed, making gasping noises as he attempted to speak, but no words come out. He remained on his knees for a short time, eyes locked on Sheridan before finally falling to his side and dying.

More shots echoed around the chamber as the rest of his team came through the opening, dropping the remaining hostile targets.

Sheridan scanned the rest of the compartment but didn't see any more contacts. "Clear."

"Clear," Hanover confirmed.

"All clear," Sergeant Rocha said, standing at the bridge's center, near the hostages. "It's going to be okay, you're safe now. Richards, check them out."

"Roger that, Staff Sergeant," the medic said, moving over to begin triage.

Sheridan looked down at the raider he'd shot in the throat, his blood still pumping onto the deck. The brilliant red arterial blood flowed from the wound as if from a garden hose. The man's lifeless eyes were still wide in surprise and confusion.

Staff Sergeant Luciana Rocha let her MOD27 hang from its combat sling across her chest and opened her helmet's visor with a tap of a finger, revealing the face of a relatively young hispanic woman. Her jet-black hair was cut short and sweat beaded on her face. She was shorter than Sheridan, but even so, she could go toe-to-toe with any of the males on the team, and probably best most of them.

She extended a hand to the closest man. "Staff Sergeant

Luciana Rocha, Holloman Alliance Marine Corps, we're here to help. Are all your crew accounted for?"

The man, dressed an olive t-shirt and brown pants, nodded and held out his bound wrists. Rocha pulled a tactical knife from its sheath on her belt and carefully slid it between his hands slicing the plasticuffs apart.

"Thank you," he said, rubbing his wrists together. "We were beginning to think no one was going to help us. We are grateful."

Reese stepped up and helped Rocha cut away the rest of the crew's bounds.

"These bastards are filth," the man said, "but we know what do to with them. Please, my executive officer will see you to the airlock."

Rocha frowned. "I'm sorry?"

"I'm sure you understand, this entire affair has severely delayed us. We have some very precious cargo that needs to get to its destination as soon as possible." As the man spoke, he was attempting to escort Rocha back toward the bridge entrance. He hesitated when Captain Chambers entered.

"Is there a problem here?" Chambers asked. He tapped his helmet, opening his visor.

The man backed up a step, shaking his head. "No problem at all. I was just telling your... comrade here that we are very thankful for the Alliance's assistance in getting our vessel back on course. But our schedule is very tight, and we are considerably behind, thanks to this debacle. Time is money, you know."

Chambers was silent for a moment, obviously considering the man's words. "We need to ensure there aren't any more hostiles on board, sir. Are you the captain?"

The man frowned, then nodded to the corpse lying facedown outside in the corridor. "No, they killed him as soon as they boarded."

One by one, the rest of the crew began to spread out, moving to check various consoles and ship's systems, seeming completely oblivious to the dead pirates around them. Sheridan watched them work as if they hadn't just been held captive for days.

Not too concerned with people dying.

"Valkyrie One, Valkyrie Actual, what's your status back there, Sergeant?" Captain Chambers asked over the taclink.

Kline answered, sounding calm and collected as always. *"We're clear here, sir. Four hostile targets engaged and pacified. Looks like they were trying to make the reactor overload."*

But he said there weren't any more, Sheridan thought, looking at the man in the olive shirt. He was sweating and pale, but that could've been from his time in captivity, or from the brutal assault that had just occurred right in front of his face. Civilians weren't accustomed to seeing violence on that scale unless it was in holos, and even then, the reality of death was watered down.

Chambers frowned. "Overload?"

"Looks like that way, sir. I'm having Robalt shut it down."

"Very well. We need to sweep the rest of the ship. Bring your people forward, and we'll alternate decks."

"Roger that, sir," Kline said. *"En route now."*

"Captain..." The man paused, reading the nameplate on Chamber's chest. "... Chambers, with the captain dead, I am now responsible for the ship and its cargo. And regardless of what has occurred, this is now my ship and my crew. I have an obligation to both them and the shareholders of this vessel to try and salvage what I can from this horrible trip."

"What's your name, sir?"

"Acario Nasca. I was the executive officer, but it appears now, I am the captain of the *Orphaned Star*."

"The raiders who attacked you were trying to blow up the ship by overloading your engines." The man's eyes went wide. Chambers continued, "Any idea why they would do that?"

Nasca shook his head. "None. But, as I have said, if the

danger is gone, then I'd like to kindly ask you to leave our vessel. Our customers are extremely private people, and they wouldn't appreciate their cargo being disturbed."

"Sir, I have no interest in the ship's manifest, but we must make sure *all* of the hostiles have been eliminated. I'm sure you can agree with that."

"Mister Captain, I'm sure you can understand that our clients have been expecting their shipment for quite some time now. A shipment which is now four days late. I can't, in good conscience, force them to wait any longer; we must get underway."

The Captain tilted his head to the side, considering the man. The newly-promoted ship captain had a week's growth on his beard. His black hair was matted with sweat, and his eyes were red from lack of sleep. His shirt had been torn, and his wrists were bruised and bloody from the restraints, and despite all that, he didn't seem the least bit relieved that the Alliance Military had saved his life and the lives of the rest of the crew. In fact, he seemed more than a little irritated about the whole thing.

"Captain Nasca, I understand you and your crew have been through a traumatic experience here, I'm not discounting that at all. But my orders explicitly state the removal of all hostile forces. And I'm sure you would agree, if we, for whatever reason, missed some of the hostiles, you and your crew would be right back in the same situation you were in before we got here."

"We will clear the ship," another one of the bridge crew said. The woman was in her fifties, her gray hair cut short. One eye was severely bruised and swollen, and blood trickled down her cheek. She moved to the bulkhead, reaching for an unmarked panel.

The hairs on the back of Sheridan's neck stood up as her fingers pulled the latch. Something about the way she was moving, maybe the way she'd said the words put him on edge, the way the new captain was trying to push them off the ship as fast as he could. Something wasn't right. He adjusted his grip on his rifle, heart pounding in his chest.

The woman opened the locker and pulled out a pistol.

"No!" Sheridan yelled, bringing his MOD27 up.

"Whoa!" Reese shouted next to him, raising his own rifle. "What the fuck, lady? Put that shit down."

The woman didn't point the pistol at anyone, just held it at shoulder height, muzzle pointing it at the ceiling. "The fuck you pointing your guns at me for? I didn't do nothing!"

"Celesta, please," Nasca said, raising his hands.

"It's my ship," the woman countered. "I'm allowed to have a gun if I want."

Nasca turned to Chambers, pleading. "Captain, please take your men and go. We are fine now, I promise you. We can handle sweeping the ship. My crew knows this ship better than anyone."

Sheridan kept his rifle on the woman, but let his eyes shift to the Captain, watching to see how he was going to handle this new situation.

To his credit, Chambers stood stone-faced, his gaze locked on the ship's captain. He spoke slowly and deliberately. "Tell your friend to put that weapon down, Captain. I will not argue that point. I know you and your crew have been through quite an ordeal here, but we can't have non-military personnel running around the ship with guns, not while my team is on board. We don't need any accidental discharges or anyone else getting hurt."

"Alliance bastards," the woman snarled, "Think you control everything you touch."

"What the fuck is your problem, lady?" Reese repeated.

Sheridan's finger lightly rubbed against the rifle's trigger. *Just put the damn thing down*, he thought.

Finally, Chambers looked at her. "Ma'am, I don't know to

whom or what you're referring to, but I can assure you the only thing my people and I want is to secure this ship and go back to ours."

"Then go," she said, lifting her head. "No one's keeping you here."

"Ma'am, I—"

Master Sergeant Kline's icon flashed on Sheridan's HUD, his transmission coming through the taclink. *"Sir, we might have a problem here."*

Chambers gave Hanover a sidelong glance. With his visor up he wouldn't be able to respond without the freighter's crew overhearing.

The Sergeant gave him an almost imperceptible nod and said, "Captain's slightly occupied at the moment, Master Sergeant. What can I do for you?"

"We're at the main cargo bay, but the crew is refusing to open the hatch. They say the area is strictly off-limits to unauthorized personnel."

"Yeah, that seems to be a trend here," Hanover said. "Stand by, One, we're working things out up here."

"There's two ways this is going to go down," Captain Chambers said to the woman. "Either you're going to put that weapon down on your own, or we'll make you put it down."

Blood pounded in Sheridan's ears. The weapons stash on Stonemeyer. Sergeant Thomas pointing his pistol at Lieutenant Hastings. The heavy stillness that filled the room as the Marines held their breath, waiting to see what Thomas would do. His finger tightening on the...

CRACK!

Sheridan started, the room coming back into focus around him. He looked past the muzzle of his rifle and saw a red stain on the gray bulkhead. His finger let off the trigger.

Screams echoed around the bridge as two of the hostages

scrambled toward the woman's body, now lying in a heap on the deck, blood spilling from a hole in her head.

"Stand down, Corporal!" Sergeant Rocha shouted.

"What the fuck did you do?" the freighter's captain shouted, his eyes wide with terror and confusion.

Sheridan barely heard him.

One of the crew knelt next to the woman, hand reaching. His curly blonde hair fell across his face, partially concealing the fury behind his gaze. His cheeks were flushed, his teeth bared as he reached for the woman's pistol.

Sheridan lowered his rifle, but only enough to center the optic on the man's skull. "Don't!"

"Back away!" Reese shouted, moving forward, his rifle up. "Don't you fucking touch it!"

The man froze, his hand centimeters away from the gun. His eyes flicked from the Marines to his captain.

"Sir, back away from that firearm," Chambers ordered, pointing. "No one else has to die here today."

Sheridan replayed what he'd seen in the fraction of a second before he'd pulled the trigger. She'd been lowering the gun. He could see the barrel of the pistol leveling at him. If he hadn't fired...

He glanced at Chambers. "Sir, I—"

"Murderer!" the curly-haired man said, still crouching over the woman's body, hand still hovering near the pistol.

He's reaching for that pistol, a part of Sheridan's mind told him. *Don't let him get that weapon.*

"Back up!" Reese repeated.

Captain Chambers raised both hands. "All right, lock it up. Everyone calm down."

"She was going to fire, sir!" Sheridan retorted, his voice breaking slightly. *She was. I know she was.*

"Cole, secure the firearm," Chambers ordered. He pointed at

the curly-haired man. "This probably should go without saying, but you decide to make a move for that firearm, it will go badly for you."

The man's eyes darted from Chambers to Sheridan, and then back down to the pistol.

"Don't," Sheridan said again.

Cole approached slowly, reaching for the weapon. "Easy now." His fingers wrapped around the grip, and he backed away.

"Corporal Sheridan," Kline said. "Stand down."

Sheridan swallowed hard, then lowered his rifle.

"You're going to fry for that," the curly-haired man said through clenched teeth.

"Enough!" Nasca shouted. "Captain Chambers, as captain of this vessel, I am ordering you to leave. Under interstellar law, you have no right to be here."

"Well, Captain, I can't do that," Chambers said, sounding like he was on the verge of losing his cool. "This area is now under Alliance Military jurisdiction and will be until such time as our investigators have the opportunity to sort this situation out."

"Ain't nothing to fucking sort out," the curly blonde-haired man said. "That mother fucker shot Celesta. She wasn't doing nothing but arming herself against the raiders. He shot her in cold blood."

"That's not what happened," Sheridan countered, feeling panic rise inside his chest. "She pointed the gun at me, she was going to shoot me. Didn't anyone else see it? Play my link recording back, you'll see it. She was going to shoot me."

"*Lies!*" Curly screamed.

Reese raised his rifle again. "Step back!"

Master Sergeant Kline's icon flashed again. *"Sir, you're going to want to see this."*

This time Chambers answered, obviously not caring who

heard him. "Sergeant, we're in the middle of something up here. Can it wait?"

"Are you secure, sir?" Chambers asked.

"Negative."

Hanover spoke up. "I'm secure, go ahead Valkyrie One."

"If you haven't done so, Sergeant, as quickly as you can, take those crew members into custody."

The Captain's eyes shot to Hanover, eyebrows knitting together.

"Yeah, we're kinda having an issue with that, Sergeant," Hanover said.

"What's wrong, Kline?" Chambers asked.

"They're slavers, sir. We just found their cargo, locked up down here. About a hundred souls."

Chambers turned back to Nasca, red-faced with growing anger. When he spoke, his voice was cold as ice. "Sheridan."

"Yes, sir," Sheridan replied.

"Keep your weapon trained on this man. If he moves, shoot him."

"What is the meaning of this, Captain? I told you, I want you off my fucking ship right this minute. You have no right to hold us here. None."

"Staff Sergeant Rocha, take these people into custody," Chambers said, ignoring Nasca's words.

"You have no authority here, Captain!"

"You got 'em," Reese asked Sheridan.

Sheridan nodded, holding his rifle ready. "I got 'em."

Reese pulled a pair of electrocuffs from a pouch on the back of his body armor and secured Curly's hands behind his back. "Sit on your heels."

Sheridan took a breath, lowering his rifle as Sergeant Rocha stepped up behind Nasca and secured his wrists.

"Captain Nasca," Chambers said. "You and your crew are under arrest. Your best option is to shut the hell up."

CHAPTER 11

Nemesis Crash Site
Blue Lake City, New Tuscany
25 July 2607

"It's chilly this morning," Eliwood said, holding out a coffee for Fischer.

Fischer nodded, accepting the steaming drink. He held it and inhaled the aroma of the cheap, burnt coffee. It was caffeinated at least, and right now that's all that mattered. His eyes burned from lack of sleep and his back was stiff from sleeping on the living room couch. He hadn't wanted to wake up Carissa last night.

No, Fischer corrected himself. *It'd been this morning.* He'd managed to get two hours before heading back in. It was better than nothing.

"You look like shit," Eliwood said.

"Thanks," Fischer said.

They'd spend the entire night reviewing the Blue Lake Air Traffic Control logs and their network security procedures, trying to figure out why their control links had all dropped out at the same time. From everything they'd been able to find, the system had been working correctly until thirty-seven seconds before the ships began to encroach on the convoy's flight path. After that, the primary control system dropped offline, replaced by a ghost program which directed seemingly random aircrafts off their intended paths and into the convoy's primary route.

After running its course, the program shut down as the *Kilo* disengaged and made for orbit. The program code had been patched into the system two months ago, during a routine system update. The contractor assigned with the job was no longer working for the organization, but Davis and Campbell were working on tracking him down.

Neither was optimistic about their chances.

Carter's request for the fighter maintenance logs had been routed up the chain, but by the time they'd left—after finally deciding they could no longer see straight—they'd yet to receive a response from Lexington, the Naval Shipyards where the fighters had been serviced.

Carefully, Fischer sipped the coffee, eyes sweeping over the scene, watching tech crews catalog and collect evidence. Blue Lake PD had actually done a fairly decent job securing the scene after the incident. They'd shut down the area for a three-block radius and, so far, had maintained a perfectly secure cordon. To their credit, the citizens of Blue Lake were very accommodating to the investigators, leaving them to do their work, not making it any harder than it needed to be.

The media on the other hand—what an entirely different story. Every news outlet in the city had reports and camera crews on scene, trying to get a new soundbite or image for their broadcasts. Fortunately for Fischer and his team, BLPD were handling all the press briefings, which amounted to an hourly update of, "We are still investigating, and we will let you know when we know something."

A large holodisplay on the side of one of the office buildings across the street lit up with the image of Senator Julius Kramer sitting behind a desk, talking to a female anchor dressed in a red business suit. The tagline at the bottom of the image read, "Never again." Fischer tapped his link, bringing up the audio feed from the broadcast.

"...maintain that we need additional resources so this kind of thing can never happen again," the senator was saying. "When we're talking about real human lives here, are we really going to trust that people are just going to treat us justly and peacefully of their own free will? The number of threats against the Alliance is only growing, and at an exponential rate. This fact made evident by this most recent attack on New Tuscany. Not to mention the countless other attacks against hard-working people throughout the region that are happening every day that never get reported.

"Our military needs to be given the tools needed to protect us, no matter what. We're talking about the security and safety of our children, and not only them, but their children's children as well. We cannot continue to let people chip away at our way of life and threaten our very existence. What will we have to give our children when it's their time to take the reins?"

"Yes, but isn't what you're arguing for encroaching on the very rights the Alliance guarantees its citizens?" the anchor asked, leaning forward on the broadcast desk.

Kramer shook his head, not bothering to hide the dismissive smirk on his face. "The argument over security and personal rights is a responsible conversation to have, sure, but not while our security is in jeopardy. First, we need security, then we can work on everything else. We need to push back against these terrorists who think they can operate with impunity and threaten our citizens. I mean, what good are rights if you're not alive to exercise them?"

"And what about Senator Beilman's stand that our way of life is built around rights and freedoms that should not be infringed upon for any reason whatsoever?"

"Listen, my friend Senator Beilman and I are definitely two sides to a very distinct coin. But to him and all the rest of the politicians who disagree with me, I just have one question to ask: What if it had been your loved one who'd died today? And for that matter, what will you say to the families of the victims there in Blue Lake City, or around the Alliance who are suffering at the hands of these outlaws? Because I'm sure they'd be willing to put up with a little more inconvenience in their lives if only to have their loved one back today."

"But aren't the things you're suggesting, a little more than simply inconvenient, Senator?" the anchor asked.

"How about this," Kramer said and turned to face the camera. "I challenge any one out there that thinks my suggestions are over the top or overreaching—go and talk to the family of Lieutenant Kendra May and Staff Sergeant Hindrick, Corporal Kendoshi, and Corporal Bewer. Ask them if their lives are worth it. Ask the parents that are going to be burying their babies in the coming days, ask them if their lives are worth it. Because I guarantee you, they will say they are."

The feed switched to a full shot of the anchor, who smiled. "That was Senator Julius Kramer, chairman of the Senate Security Committee, thank you for—"

Fischer killed the link.

"Laying it on kinda thick, don't you think?" Eliwood asked. She took a slow sip of her coffee, sucking in a quick breath as the hot liquid touched her tongue.

Fischer blew on his coffee, eyes drifting down to the smoldering wreckage on the street. "He's not wrong."

"About?"

"About the need for security. We've been living in a dream

world for far too long. People have forgotten that there're a lot of people out there that don't like us."

"Yeah, I get that," Eliwood said. "But come on, Fish, you really think this was the work of random terrorists? I mean this isn't some renegade Stonemeyer militia or URT privateers, this is real high-level shit. I mean, who has the ability to bypass air traffic control nodes? Not to mention blowing up a Nemesis class fighter without so much as firing a shot? Who could do something like that? Not any raider I've ever come across."

Fischer sighed. "I don't know."

"This whole thing is starting to give me the fucking creeps again. There are some people you just don't want to mess with. Carter said it too."

"And those are exactly the people we need to stop," Fischer said, feeling his determination grow stronger even as he said it. "They're the real threat to our way of life. When they can manipulate whole planets and governments to do what they want, and no one even realizes it, that's the kind of power that's pure evil. That has no business being allowed to thrive."

"I agree with you." Eliwood closed her palms around the coffee. "But we're only two people. We can't fight this whole thing by ourselves and you definitely can't do it alone."

Fischer chuckled, and Eliwood raised an eyebrow at him. "What?"

"Oh, I've just heard that from more than one person recently," Fischer said.

"Great minds."

"Something like that," Fischer said, taking another sip.

Fischer led Eliwood into the street and nodded to the local cop posted on the inner cordon. They stepped through the glowing yellow and black holographic scene markers, their links automatically sending biometric data to ASI's central mainframe. Identifying and recording everyone who entered and left the scene had always been something the Agency required when dealing with any high-profile investigation, but considering the events of the last few months, Fischer knew it was even more imperative now.

Two blocks down, rows of reporters screamed questions, each trying to outshout the other.

"Do you have any updates?"

"Have you found anything useful?"

"Do you have any suspects?"

"Who did they kidnap?"

Eliwood laughed, shaking her head. "I really hope they run with that story."

"What's that?" Fischer asked.

"A kidnapping. I mean, when the truth gets out, they'll be pretty embarrassed."

"You assume they won't just point fingers at ASI and blame us for everything like they always do. I'm surprised they haven't started already."

"Eh, you're probably right," Eliwood conceded.

"I know I'm right."

They approached the wreckage, where teams of lab techs and service bots were picking through the pieces, rendering and collecting. The lead technician looked up from his datapad.

Frances Hoskins wore a pale blue disposable jumpsuit and matching booties. Black hair tied back in tight braids, her ebony skin glistening with beads of sweat.

"Morning, Fischer. Eliwood."

"Frances," Fischer said. "In early or still here?"

"Are you kidding? Do you have any idea how much physical evidence there is? This place is a disaster. We'll be picking up detritus and wreckage for the next month."

Fischer knew she wasn't exaggerating. If Frances Hoskins was anything, she was meticulous. He'd worked with her on several high-profile cases since she'd been assigned to the New Tuscany office a year before and hadn't been disappointed once. If anyone was going to put this mess back together, it would be her.

"I even called in all of our reserve crews, and we've barely made a dent." She shook her head. "Can't ever get ahead."

Fischer looked over the heap of twisted metal and steel alloy, charred by heat and stained by fire suppressant. Four bots floating above the tail section held a tarp between them, providing relief from the New Tuscany's blazing afternoons, especially during the summer months when the temperatures rose into the one hundreds.

Rows of metal containers hovered on repulsor pads around technicians going through the various components scattered across the street. Six-legged sensor bots climbed over the wreckage, taking detail scans of the fuselage; the data would be used later for their reconstruction.

Fischer moved past Hoskins, giving the tray of tools and pads a cursory glance before stopping in front of the wreckage. He slipped his hands into his pockets, surveying the damage. Jagged pieces of the ship curled out from where the explosion had ripped apart the hull. Inside, the fighter's drive had been rendered into so much slag. The frame had fused with engine components. Cables, and steel lines were cut and frayed.

"So it *was* internal?" Fischer asked.

"As far as we can tell," Hoskins answered. "We've already sent off residue samples for testing, and we've been scanning the debris for components, but so far we've come up short."

"No device?" Fischer asked.

The technician shook her head. "We've had scour-bots in there all night, so far nothing. Not even a casing fragment."

"And nothing from Lexington?" Eliwood asked, sipping her coffee.

"Last I knew, they were still trying to track down the tech who performed the last maintenance check on the fighters in question."

"Wait." Fischer turned. "Track down?"

Hoskins shrugged. "Apparently, he's on leave—been for about a week."

"Better recall his ass," Eliwood said.

"Like I said, they've been trying to track him down since the incident occurred. Apparently, he packed up his family and left. No one has seen him or heard from the family since."

"Great."

"Have you had any luck tracking the sprinter?" Hoskins asked.

"We've got people out looking for it," Fischer said. "But no, not yet."

A grin turned up at the corner of Eliwood's mouth. "You say 'people' like it's not Jones."

Fischer did his best to conceal his surprise. "I don't know what you're talking about."

"Come on, Fish, I know you talked to him last night. I don't have any problem with it, but do you really think he's going to be able to turn anything up, and not get himself killed in the process?"

"Jonesy, can take care of himself," Fischer said, knowing it was one hundred percent true. "If there's something out there to find, whether it's this Cardinal or not, he's going to find it."

Eliwood crossed her arms. "He's not a spy, you know that, right? Regardless of what he thinks of himself. You don't think you're asking too much of him?"

"I didn't ask him to do anything," Fischer said. "He volunteered. Jones hates Young just as much as I do. It'll be fine, he knows how to handle himself. He'll be fine."

CHAPTER 12

Office of the Armed Services Committee
The Pressfield Building, Regional Government Building
Solomon System
25 July 2607

The briefing began with the usual rhetoric Hunter had come to expect from Senator Marcus Beilman. The senator had been on record numerous times about his desire to start a massive draw-down of all Holloman Military Forces, beginning with the "overblown and over-armed" Navy. The fact that there wasn't any media in the room for Beilman to play to compounded Hunter's frustration, because that meant he was truly just talking to hear himself talk. Everyone present in the room was, no doubt, well aware of the senator's opinions on the state of the Alliance Military apparatus. They didn't need to listen to a ten-minute diatribe of regurgitated campaign speeches.

Hunter sat at the far end of the elongated oval table, next to the Vice Commander of the Marine Corps, General Wilford Maddox and the Secretary of Defensive, Jeffrey Obergarten, two men he respected, both for their level-headedness, and for their ability to speak their minds with absolutely zero regard for the repercussions of those statements. The fact that they were usually both correct in their assessment usually played well in their favor.

"Do you think he'll ever run out of breath?" General Maddox whispered in Hunter's ear.

Hunter held a glass of water in front of his mouth as he spoke. "Doubt it."

"…and not only that," Senator Beilman was saying. "The example we set for ourselves should be…"

"A beacon for the rest of the galaxy to follow," both men muttered under their breaths, mimicking the Senator signature sign off. Hunter kept his glass up, hiding a smirk.

At least that means he's done, Hunter thought. *Hopefully.*

"I know the Diplomatic Corps has a lot to say about what's happening throughout the URT right now, but what's happening in the URT is not what's happening here at home. That is where we need to be focused. Especially after the Stonemeyer incident."

At the far end of the table from Hunter, Samantha Owens, Senior Advisor to the President, cleared her throat, and leaned forward in her seat, resting her elbows on the table. "Senator Beilman, I think we're all aware of your feelings on our current foreign affairs policies, but with all due respect, they are working."

"Working?" Beilman asked. "By whose standards?"

"We've made more progress in the last eighteen months than we have in the last five years," Owens explained. "But the URT is at a boiling point, and if we increase our response to these events, they will boil over, and when that happens, we're not going to be the only ones trying to pick up the pieces. The New Tuscany incident is just the most visible of a long list of attacks that have occurred throughout the Alliance."

"We are not the galaxy's police force," Beilman said. "Even if we doubled our military expenditures and put ship after ship into the URT, it wouldn't make a difference. Because they have to *want* our help. And not only that, but there are more than a few systems that, simply, flat-out hate the Alliance and everything we stand for. I don't see how we can force ourselves on anyone for any reason."

"And this situation on Centralis?" Sean Kingston, the President's Foreign Affairs Advisor asked, raising an eyebrow. His skin, the color of freshly brewed coffee, blonde hair and bright, almost crystal, blue eyes, exposed his Del Raycan heritage. "Yet another system that has devolved into a cesspool of complete corruption and a haven for criminal activity. There were over five thousand slaves en route to government-sponsored work camps on those ships. And those are just the ones we know about."

The Secretary of Defense raised his hand. "Senator, if I may."

"While the actual specifics of the operation are classified, our forces were able to stop those unfortunate people from lives of slavery, and I don't think that's a small thing." Obergarten nodded at Hunter. "But this is only one operation in one system, and the increase in raider activity is concerning on a number of levels, not just from an Alliance perspective. We're talking about billions and billions of people that are being affected by these attacks and right now, we seem to be the only nation willing and able to do something about it."

"That is correct," Hunter said. "And I can tell you that the longer we let this kind of activity go, the worse it will get. I guarantee you that. In all my years of dealing with these kinds of people, it never gets better on its own. It requires swift and sometimes harsh action."

"Ah yes," Beilman said, standing. "This is exactly what I want to avoid. These kinds of black ops missions that inevitably lead to the deaths of most involved. I don't like the idea of government-sanctioned kill teams."

Hunter clenched his teeth. This was always the argument from people who didn't have the first clue about what his people actually did. "We are not, and have never employed the use of kill teams. But I can tell you for a certainty, that if we don't act, people will die. That's not hyperbole; it's the truth. And despite what you think, sir, we are all safer in our beds at night because of the work these men and women do day in and day out."

Beilman leveled his gaze across the table and Hunter, staring him down for several long moments.

If you're trying to intimidate me, you're going to have to do better than that, Hunter thought, returning the senator's stare with equal determination. He'd never been one to back down from a fight, especially if it genuinely needed fighting, but caving to bullies simply because of their position wasn't something he'd ever done, and he wasn't about to start now.

"I know what you're talking about Admiral," Beilman said. "And I don't like it. We need to be extremely careful with something like the Legend Project, especially now. Our treaty talks with Corwynn are in the very beginning stages, they're delicate and tentative, and the Alliance needs this treaty to happen if we're going to have any chance at winning a war with the Pegasi. I'm sure you haven't forgotten about them."

"I have not forgotten, sir." Hunter inhaled slowly, careful not to let his irritation show. He wouldn't give Beilman any ammunition to use against him.

The President's Advisor cleared her throat, obviously trying to cut through the tension of the room. "Let's not forget why we're here, gentlemen. The President needs a response to this situation. New Tuscany and Centralis aren't going to go away any time soon, they are too big. He needs to be able to say that we're doing something to combat this growing raider situation."

"So our first response is to let the Navy have a free pass to do whatever they want, with no oversight and no repercussions?"

"The Legend Project is not a free pass, sir," Hunter said. "It is a tool, nothing more. And the people responsible for using that tool are professionals. They will do their duty within the scope of the law and the orders we give them."

Obergarten nodded. "The Legend Project could be a real game-changer for our operations along the border and in the URT and I, for one, wholeheartedly support its implementation."

"Well, I don't," Beilman said flatly.

Owens chuckled. "Yes, Senator, we're all aware of your feelings on the matter." The comment brought a round of chuckles around the table, and before Beilman could respond, the President's Advisor continued, "I want to be able to go back to the President today and tell him we have a plan. Something we can put into operation right now, not a promise to discuss options, not a plan to institute studies, something that will produce results. And from what I understand about this project, it does seem like the most ideal response."

"It is," Obergarten said.

"How soon can you put it into operation?" Owens asked.

"Most of the assignments have already been made," Hunter said. "Those people are either on board or en route as we speak. Conservatively, I would say active operations could start within the next week or two."

"All right," Owens said. "By a show of hands, who supports this project?" All but Beilman raised their hand. "That's what I needed to know."

The President's Advisor tapped her datapad closed and stood. The rest of the room, save for Beilman, stood. "I'll take this to the President this evening. Admiral Hunter, please proceed with preparations. I expect you will have the green light within the next twelve hours."

Hunter nodded. "Yes, ma'am."

"Gentlemen." Owens turned and left the room.

Beilman stood, glaring at Hunter, but to his credit, he kept his peace and followed Owens out without another word.

Obergarten turned to Hunter with a grin and extended a hand. "Congratulations, Admiral. You've got your own little war now."

CHAPTER 13

ASI Sprinter *Sam's Justice*
Cathcart Station, Del Raycu System
27 July 2607

"We're on final." The pilot sitting just forward of the sprinter's passenger compartment called back. "You ever seen Cathcart close up, sir?"

Fischer tapped his link, clearing the file he'd been reading and unbuckled his harness. "Years ago, when I was a kid." He stood and moved past the rows of empty seats, stopping just inside the cockpit.

The pilot sat behind an array of translucent holographic displays that cast an orange hue throughout the cockpit. Approach data was splashed over the main holodisplay, showing the shuttle's course projected through the lines of traffic.

The pilot nodded to the empty seat to his right. "Help yourself."

"Thanks." Fischer sat, opting not to secure the harness. "Oh, wow."

"Darius Stedman, by the way." The pilot leaned over, extending a hand.

"Fischer." He shook the man's hand and turned back to the view.

Outside, the enormous bulk of Cathcart Station loomed in the void. It was an amalgamation of spherical sections, clustered together around the three main cylinders in the center that made up the original station. Additional sections were added as the need grew. Cathcart was, by far, the largest single space station in the Holloman Alliance.

Thousands of ships and billions in material and commercial goods, not to mention people, moved through the station daily. Everything that was produced, grown, or sold in the Alliance passed through Cathcart at some point on its journey to the consumer. The station itself was a landmark that attracted visitors from as far away as Thresh, on the far side of Alliance space, several weeks away.

The sprinter—one of hundreds of similar spacecraft coming and going in long, highly organized lines—dipped under an enormous freighter and a soft chime sounded, and the notification panel flashed on the pilot's holographic display.

"Just passed the inner beacon," the pilot explained. He tapped it, and it vanished. "We'll be getting our bay assignments here in a minute or so. Hopefully, they don't stash us in the boonies."

Fischer raised an eyebrow. "The boonies?"

"Yes, sir," the pilot said with a laugh. "I mean, you can see how big the station proper is, some sections are a couple dozen kilometers away from the rest. I've heard of people taking forty-five-minute rides to get to their next connection. It's kind of a clusterfuck, if you don't mind me saying."

"Guess it's a good thing I don't have a connection."

"How long are you staying, sir?"

Fischer sniffed. "Who the hell knows?"

He'd asked himself that very same question throughout the trip from New Tuscany. The only good thing about the journey was that he'd been forced to take a sprinter shuttle, which meant the usual four-day trip took only two. Still, he'd had plenty of time to review the file of the naval technician who'd worked on the Nemesis fighters during the flight. Martin Gorges's file, however, hadn't revealed anything negative about the man other than his apparent gambling problem. He had a wife and daughter, modest savings, small apartment, and by all accounts was a brilliant technician.

Fischer had entertained a dozen theories as to why the man had sabotaged the fighters, but none of them seemed to hold much water. Gorges didn't have a record, aside from a few minor traffic infractions in his teen years, and his military career had been about as good as it could've been; high markers from his supervisors, recommendations for early promotions, citations for exceptional work performance. The list was extensive.

So, why did you become a murderer? Fischer asked himself every time he closed the man's file.

Another alert chimed on the pilot's console, and a new panel appeared on the screen. Darius Stedman let out a breath, chuckling. "Well, it's not the boonies, but it's not much better. Obsidian Ring, Bay Sixty-Seven. Could be worse."

Ten minutes later they'd cleared the protective forcefield covering the entrance to the expansive bay and were floating through the interior of the docking area. Several landing pads were arranged at varying heights and spacings throughout the easy chamber, connected by wide metal walkways and service tubes. Each level had a central platform where the main mag-lev tubes connected them all, then branched off to the various sections of the station proper.

A series of holographic marker lines displayed across the cockpit window guided them through the maze of platforms.

Fischer shook his head. "No way I could do your job. I'd crash into something for sure."

Stedman tapped the controls. "She does most of the work for me. Docking is probably one of the most boring parts of the job. Here at least."

"Oh?"

"Station control is fanatical about control inside their bays. Unless you've got some kind of waiver, they slave your controls to their station pilots. All we have to do is sit back and enjoy the ride."

"Nice."

The shuttle flared as it descended to the indicated pad.

"Looks like you've got a welcome party," Stedman said, nodding to a lone figure standing just on the outside of the yellow and black safety lines that bordered the circular pad.

Fischer leaned forward in his seat. "Huh? Wasn't expecting anyone. I'm not even supposed to be here until tomorrow."

The man wore a navy-blue jumpsuit, with what looked like the Cathcart station logo on both shoulders. He was too far away to read the name tag, but the pistol holstered to his hip told Fischer everything he needed to know.

"So much for a low profile," Fischer muttered, slouching back in the couch.

The shuttle settled onto its landing struts, pistons and hydraulics hissing as the engines powered down. Several messages appeared on the screen, advising the pilot his landing sequence had completed, and the struts were locked in place.

"Thanks for the lift," Fischer said, standing.

"I'm here for the duration. I've got a steady diet of caffeine and alcohol in my future, I think."

"I know the feeling." Fischer shouldered his bag as he ducked out of the cockpit. The hatch chimed and slid sideways, disappearing into the bulkhead as the ramp outside extended out of the fuselage.

The man waiting on the platform smiled as Fischer exited through the shuttle's hatch and walked down the ramp. He appeared in his fifties, a full head taller than Fischer and solid. His broad shoulders pressed the fabric of his Cathcart jumpsuit, the sleeves rolled up just under the elbow, exposing muscular forearms covered in intricate tattoos. His salt and pepper hair was combed to the side, his matching beard neatly trimmed. The patch on his right breast pocket identified him as Tannis, Chief of Security, Cathcart Industries.

"You're early," the man said, extending a hand. "Greg Tannis."

Fischer pumped the security chief's hand. "Jackson Fischer. I was hoping to keep a low profile."

Tannis grinned. "Why do you think it's just me?"

"I was surprised to see this hadn't already hit the networks," Fischer said. "Your doing?"

"That's right. Ten years Marine Corps CID before I retired. This place was supposed to be my ride off into the sunset spot."

"It's not?"

"Shit," Tannis drew the word out as he turned to lead Fischer off the platform. "I've done more work here in the last few years than my entire career. And I'm not dealing with sailors bound by regulations and military justice. First thing I learned after I took this job: the civilian world is a much different world than we're used to. Took me all of fifteen minutes to get my first middle finger and uncooperative victim. All these bastards think their shit don't stink."

Fischer's stomach turned a bit as he followed Tannis onto the walkway between the platform and the main deck. The expanse of the hangar stretched for hundreds of meters below and above. A metal railing was all that kept him from falling into the abyss.

"Not scared of heights are you?" Tannis asked, looking over his shoulder.

"You know, I can fly a gravbike all day, doesn't bother me at all. Put me on a ledge like this, I don't want anything to do with it."

Tannis laughed. "Well, stay away from the arboretum then."

"Noted."

They reached the lift at the end of the walkway, and the double doors slid open automatically. Tannis led the way onto the platform, then swiped his link over a small gray box. A holopanel appeared, the words "Priority Tasking" glowing in orange.

"Section 83, Frame 6," Tannis said.

The holopanel flashed from orange to green. The doors slide shut, and the lift started moving.

"Priority tasking?" Fischer asked.

"Allows us to skip regular boarding, re-routes us through the tubes, giving us a best-time path. Otherwise, it'd take us an hour to get there." Tannis held up his hand, wiggling it like he'd just performed a magic trick. "One of the perks."

Fischer nodded. "I can see where that would come in handy here."

Small, oval portholes gave them a view of the interior of the transit tube. Three minutes into their trip, the solid bulkhead disappeared, replaced by a transparent plastiglass shell. The expanse of the station—multiple spherical docking sections interspersed with long rectangular residential and commercial sections—stretched away from them. Hundreds upon hundreds of shuttles crisscrossed each other on their way to various ships and station areas.

"Damn, that's a nice view," Fischer said, stepping closer to the viewport.

"You know, I tell myself I'll get used to it someday. Doesn't ever happen." Tannis pointed. "So, you think this Gorges guy is connected to your investigation?"

Fischer nodded and said, "As to what extent, that remains to be seen."

"Yeah, well, I don't know the guy, and I don't know what your case is about, but whatever it is, no one deserves to go out like he did."

"That bad?"

Tannis shook his head. "I've seen some messed up shit before, but this... this really over the top. Just who did this guy piss off?

"That's what I'm here to find out."

CHAPTER 14

Short-term Residential Cabins
Cathcart Station, Del Ray System
27 July 2607

Fifteen minutes later, the lift doors opened, and Tannis led Fischer into a long narrow corridor flanked by several uniformed Cathcart security guards.

"The bodies are in the morgue. Our lab techs are working those and still processing the scene," Tannis said. "The remodel's done, but I have to tell you though, that's one sim I'm not going to want to review."

"And your guys found the body?" Fischer asked, following him toward an open hatch fifty meters away from the lift's exit.

"That's right," Tannis said. "Well, technically, the crew did. Came to service the room and couldn't get it. Had to call us to bypass the security locks."

Tannis stopped outside the door, nodding to one of the guards who stepped away without a word. "After you."

Fischer took a deep breath, then entered the apartment. An entryway opened to a combined living, dining, and kitchen space.

Two sofas set perpendicular to each other, with a small table in the corner. The dinner table on the far side of the unit, kitchen area off to the left. A short hall branched off the living area leading to a latrine and two bedrooms.

The body—or rather, the simulated body—of Martin Gorges lay face down in the middle of the living room on top of a carpet soaked through with blood. The TruSim was good. If Tannis hadn't told him about the sim, Fischer might not have immediately recognized it for what it was. As Fischer slowly moved toward the image, it flickered almost imperceptibly, and the coloring wasn't quite right—just a bit too dull.

Gorges' head was only attached to his shoulders by the thin strip of flesh that looked like it, too, was on the verge of tearing. He was naked, his ankles bound, wrists tied behind his back, the cords having dug deep gouges into his skin. Blood had pooled around his corpse, covering almost the whole living area. It ran under the couches and halfway through the shadow of the dinner table.

"And no one's been in here since your people found them, right?" Fischer asked, both knowing the answer and wanting the Station Chief to confirm it for him.

"That's right. I sealed it off personally right after my guys called me."

"And the sims… they were set up before anyone touched the bodies?"

"That's correct. The entire scene is being set up in our VR lab if we need to enhance anything in particular."

Fischer squatted down, turning his head to the side, inspecting the man's gaping neck wound. It had not been a clean cut. Whoever had severed this man's head had done it with several vicious thrusts of a blade. He'd been angry, or at the very least, emotional about it. Which made sense, considering everything else that had happened. This wasn't "strictly business." This was personal.

"And the other two?" Fischer asked, following the flow of bright arterial blood with his eyes.

"Family's in the other room," Tannis said. "Far as I know, he didn't have any family or friends here. He only ever went out one time, the day he was murdered. Went to a local bar, ran up a fairly big tab."

"Going to the bar doesn't sound like something a man on the run with his family would do on a whim," Fischer said, stepping over a line of blood, entering the hallway to his left.

Recessed lighting in the ceiling came on automatically, revealing bloody shoe prints in the tan carpet. Fischer paused and pointed at the floor. "We're going to want scans of the prints."

Tannis nodded. "Our tech people are already running them. We've got some of the best in the business."

In addition to simply providing security for the station, Cathcart Security Division also doubled as the station's police force, complete with special response teams, patrol officers, detectives, and explosive disposal unit. For a station with an average daily population of over half a million transients and half that number in permanent staff, they needed all the local resources they could afford. Which in Cathcart's position, was probably more than most planets.

Fischer glanced into the latrine as he passed. Blood was splattered everywhere; the floor, mirror and sink, and the shower. Hands had smeared blood on the walls and swirl marks on the floor indicating someone had slipped or was struggling against someone.

He moved on, stopping at the first bedroom. Again, the lights activated as he stepped through the doorway, illuminating a little girl's room, complete with pink sheets and comforter on a bed covered with stuffed animals of all shapes and sizes. The TruSim

Lauren Gorges lay in the middle of the floor in the fetal position, a bullet hole plainly visible on the side of her head. Her long brown hair was matted with blood.

She hadn't been tied up. Probably because it would've taken longer than to simply throw her down and shoot her. Fischer inhaled slowly and ground his teeth together as images of Maddie flashed into his mind. This girl was several years older than his daughter, but that didn't keep him from imagining Maddie in her shoes. He couldn't even imagine what might have been going through the poor girl's minds as the bastards dragged her away from her parents to end her life, in her room, alone and scared.

Blood boiling, he backed out and moved on to the last room. Shelly Gorges lay spread eagle on her back, legs dangling off the side of the bed. Her face was a mangled ruin. Her skin was covered in bruises. It was obvious what had happened to her, probably more than once, and it was obvious that she'd put up one hell of a fight. Her knuckles were torn and bloody, her fingernails covered in dried blood.

Good for you, Fischer told her silently. *Don't ever let them get away clean.*

He leaned forward, squinting. "She's got some skin under her fingernails."

"Also being processed," Tennis said from the hallway.

Fischer nodded, grateful the Security Chief was competent. He'd come across more than a few who weren't.

Alliance biomedical scanners could work wonders on DNA mapping and comparison, but like any good piece of equipment, it was only as good as the data it was given to work with. If the attackers were in the system, it would find a match within a couple days, most likely. If they weren't...

"How deep are your security checks through customs?" Fischer asked.

Tannis chuckled. "If you're wondering if we get DNA scans

on everyone that enters the station, the answer is no. Even if we wanted to, it wouldn't be logistically feasible. You're talking about a half-million people a day, at a minimum, and through over a thousand points of entry. Besides, there's a lot of people that would find the practice invasive—even those who have nothing to hide."

"The prices we *aren't* willing to pay for safety and security," Fischer said, backing out of the room.

Tannis crossed his arms. "You think whoever did this was sending him a message?"

Fischer considered that for a moment but shook his head. "They were sending a message, but if it was intended for him, it was short-lived, they killed him right after."

CHAPTER 15

ANS *Courageous*
JumpLane 8617
27 July 2607

"Two pair," Neal said, tossing her cards onto the table.

"I don't know why you'd even play those," Cole said, grinning. He put his own cards down; three of a kind. "I'm starting to think poker just isn't your game, Neal."

"It's not," Neal admitted. "But it's better than avoiding Robbi for hours on end. I hate chess."

"That's because it's for players of exceptional mental intellect," Sergeant Robalt called from across the compartment.

Sheridan laughed. He stood behind Neal, watching the game unfold. Like Neal, he wasn't great at cards, but he was trying to learn. He'd spent many hours playing on his link, practicing the game, but so far, hadn't been able to master it. He'd watched Cole play almost a dozen games during their cruise back to Lexington, and was sure his friend was cheating—he just couldn't prove it.

Cole maintained that it was just knowing the odds, and watching the other players at the table, but Sheridan thought there had to more to it than that. Or, Sheridan wasn't as good at math as he thought he was.

"Bah," Reese said, throwing his cards down, face-down.

"What'd you have?" Cole asked.

"A whole lot of fucking nothing, that's what," Reese said.

Sergeant Celina Guerrero, the last player and Cole's counterpart on Team One, shook her head in frustration and tossed down her cards; also two pair, but not as good as Neal's had been.

"Ha!" Cole collected his chips, pushing them into his growing pile, then reached for the cards to start shuffling the next hand.

"Oh, no," Neal said. "I'll deal this one."

Cole looked hurt. "What? You don't trust me?"

"It's not that I don't trust you," Neal said, "but I don't trust you."

"That hurts, Neal. Deep."

Guerrero laughed. "But she's not wrong."

Neal looked over her should at Sheridan as she sorted the cards. "You want in?"

Sheridan hesitated for a moment, unsure.

"Come on, Al," Cole said, sliding his chair over, making room at the small round table. "Pull up a chair."

Reese reached down and brought up the small case that held their chips. "Twenty cred buy-in."

Neal flashed him a smile, her white teeth flashing. "It's only money."

Sheridan sighed and grabbed the back of a nearby chair, pulling it around to the table.

"That's the spirit," Cole said.

Sheridan tapped his link and sent the money to Reese, who counted out the right number of chips and handed them over.

"It's dealer's choice," Neal said, "but since you're new, I'll let you pick."

"All right," Sheridan said, considering his options. "What about Hold 'Em, you guys okay with that?"

"Ugh, really?" Cole asked, a look of disgust on his face. "What about something interesting like Black Hole or Star Dancer?"

"It's his choice," Neal affirmed, cutting him off. "When it comes back to you then you can do whatever you want."

Sheridan shrugged. "What can I say, I like the classics."

Cole rolled his eyes. "Fine, do whatever you want."

Neal dealt two cards each to the players then set the deck down in front of her. Sheridan gave Cole a sidelong glance as he picked up his cards; a Jack and a Ten, both Hearts.

Not bad, Sheridan thought.

"You start the bet," Neal told Fischer. "Ante is ten."

"Oh, right." Sheridan found the correct chip and tossed it into the center of the table along with another.

"Heavy bettor, I see," Cole said, and matched the bet.

The other three also matched and Neal dealt the next the cards on the table, face-up; Jack of Spades, Three of Hearts and Six of Diamonds. Not extremely helpful.

"Check," Sheridan said.

Everyone checked except Neal, who bet ten with a smile at Sheridan. He was really starting to appreciate that smile. He tossed in ten, and after the others had followed suit, Neal dealt the fourth card. A Jack of Diamonds.

It was everything Sheridan could do *not* to smile. He forced himself to recheck his cards and purposely didn't look at the other players. Three of a kind was a good hand, but it wasn't the be-all and end-all. The key here was not to overplay, he wanted to make a little bit of money and not push anyone off who might be willing to play with him.

He eyed his chips, considering his bet. "Fifty." Half the pot was a safe bet.

Cole raised an eyebrow and pressed his tongue into the inside of his cheek. "Interesting."

After a few seconds of holding Cole's gaze, Sheridan turned away, both unsure of how long he'd be able to hold without cracking and to give Cole the impression that he might not be as confident about his hand as he appeared.

"Call," Cole said, tossing in his chips.

Reese laughed. "Now we're talking." He tossed in chips as well.

"I'm out," Guerrero said.

Neal hesitated for a moment, looking from the cards to Sheridan, staring into his eyes as if reading his soul. He felt himself blushing slightly, and Neal gave him a half-grin. "Call."

As she reached for the last card, the hatch to the Valkyrie rec room slammed open.

"All right," Master Sergeant Kline shouted, coming through the hatch. "Eyes up, people."

Captain Chambers followed the Sergeant in, holding a datapad in one hand, his face giving off no signs as to whether the impromptu briefing was good or bad. They were still in the Jump-Lane to Lexington, en route to be decommissioned, it couldn't be another mission.

Or could it? Sheridan thought, standing from the table and moving toward the captain, taking his cards with him.

"Sorry to interrupt your downtime, people," Chambers said. He lifted the datapad. "But we've just received our orders, and I wanted to share them with you as soon as possible."

The team pressed closer, everyone eager to find out where they were going. There'd been rumors of splitting the team up, though both Kline and Chambers had repeatedly dismissed them as that... just rumors. Being combined with another MARSOC was also a worry, as Special Operations Command was in the process of downsizing their operational scope in order to centralize the management of the Teams.

"As of thirteen hundred today, Team Valkyrie is now officially attached to ANS *Legend*. After we are done transferring the refugees at Cathcart Station, we will offload our gear and take a sprinter to our final destination. And before you ask, I don't know where that is."

Hanover frowned. "Sir, I'm not familiar with that ship. The *Legend*?"

Several others shook their heads, looking to the others as if someone in the group *should* have known the name.

"According to the orders, it's brand new, but I don't have any other information than that. We will be attached to First Fleet, Task Force Phoenix, for the duration of the assignment."

The anxiety everyone had been feeling quickly left the room in a collective sigh. Task Force Phoenix, despite the intriguing title, was responsible for the security in and around the Solomon system, home to the Alliance Naval Headquarters. The fleet was generally considered to be glorified babysitters.

"So much for high-tempo," Sergeant Robalt said, folding his arms across his chest.

"What could we possibly have to offer TF Phoenix that a detachment of regular Marines couldn't handle?" Hanover asked.

"I don't know," Chambers said. "And when I asked for further clarification, I was told it was classified."

"Wait a minute," Sheridan said, almost before he knew he was going to speak. "Sir, Lexington is on the way to Phoenix Station, why wouldn't we just stay on *Courageous* for the duration?"

"I asked about that as well, Corporal. I'll let you guess what the answer was."

"Isn't that a little strange, sir?" Staff Sergeant Rocha asked. "I mean, we've all been cleared through Ultra Top Secret. Anything above that requires Presidential authorization."

Chambers gave Team One's leader a grin. "You're absolutely right, Staff Sergeant. But like I said, I was not given an overabundance of information, and for that, I apologize."

"Working on less than no intelligence is something we're used to, sir," Kline said, eyeing a few key team members. Everyone laughed.

"We'll be arriving at Cathcart in another twelve hours," Chambers said. "I want gear stowed, and weapons checked in an hour. I want to be able to move as soon as we're feet dry. The faster we can get the refugees secure, the quicker we can proceed with our next mission."

"We'll make it happen, sir," Master Sergeant Kline said.

"Questions?" Chambers asked. There were none. "All right, let's get to it."

"Eyes up!" the team members said in unison, separating as the captain turned to leave.

Cole gave Sheridan a confused look. "What the hell is that all about?"

"Your guess is as good as mine."

"All right, people you heard the man," Master Sergeant Kline said. "Gear check and weapons inspection in forty minutes."

Cole moved around the table, eyeing the cards still laid out. "Hey, Master Sergeant, what do you say the winner of this hand gets a hard pass on the inspection?"

Kline crossed his arms. "And what exactly do I get out of this?"

Cole thought about that for a moment then said, "Ten percent sound about right?"

"Make it twenty-five, and everyone has to go all in, and you've got yourself a deal, Corporal."

Cole looked to the rest of the players for confirmation.

"Sure why not," Guerrero said, sitting back down at the table.

Sheridan almost laughed, but just managed to keep it bottled up. He stood behind his chair, eyeing the cards in his hand again. "I'm in."

The other two agreed, and Neal reached for the last card. Jack of Clubs.

Sheridan laughed.

The Majestic
Lucent Station, Ulara System
27 July 2607

The Majestic was definitely the worst place they'd been in over the last few weeks. It was dirty, and the air had the persistent odor of stale beer and bad decisions. A haze of smoke floating through the room made it apparent that the air circulators didn't seem to be working either.

"Ugh, I can't. I just can't." Tensley Jones pushed the glass full of amber liquid across the table. "You call that beer? It's literal shit."

Greg Loomistripoli lifted his glass, considering its contents. "I don't know, I don't think it's that bad. Maybe a little flat, but other than that…"

"A little flat?" Jones shook his head, there was no use arguing with Loomis, the man was an idiot. He looked up at the waiter bot. The blue and red emblem of the bar on the side of its chases had faded with time, much like the rest of the bar had. "You got anything harder?"

The waiter bot's cylindrical torso rotated atop a four-legged chassis, its four waldo arms moving to punch its customer's order into an archaic-looking datapad. The thing could have easily just relayed the order to the cook automatically. For the life of him, Jones couldn't decide whether the attempt at appearing to actually take his order was intriguing or just plain ridiculous.

Of all the places they'd visited over the last few weeks, Jones had been particularly intrigued to return to the Majestic and see how the place had held up over the years. Twelve years ago, when he'd first visited the station, the Majestic had been a truly one-of-a-kind bar—upscale drinks, knowledgeable staff, and the type of customers that weren't liable to shoot you in the face if you looked at them wrong.

Like the waiter bot standing beside their table, the Majestic had not aged well. The clientele, however, was just the sort of people that they were looking for. Dressed in a myriad of outfits ranging from oversized coats to unbuttoned vests over bare chests. One woman, whose head was shaved on one side, with bright pink on the other, wore a thin piece of fabric across only her nipples, exposing breasts that were two or three times too large for her petite frame.

Jones had on the same old leather flight jacket he'd worn for years. The patch on the sleeve where his Holloman Alliance patch had been removed was still a couple shades lighter than the surrounding well-worn leather. The fur around the collar was stained grayish-brown from years of sweat and grime. He washed it regularly—even had it done professionally once or twice—but it never seemed to help. Underneath, his Montgomery Sentinels shirt was also several shades lighter than it had been when he'd first picked it up, but one of the things he'd grown to appreciate about being a freelancer, was the need *not* to have to impress anyone.

"We have a long list of liquors to suit any taste, sir." The bot's high-pitched voice was digitized and filled with static, obviously in need of maintenance.

"I'm sure you do," Jones said. "Just give me a gin, straight up, no ice, no nothing. Can you do that? Just crisp, clear gin."

"Yes, sir, I can do that. Thank you for your patience. I'll have it right out."

The bot's leg assembly turned, but the optical sensors and its torso remained facing Jones. It moved away, steel feet clanking against the gunmetal deck.

Jones held the bot's gaze for a long moment before looking away, shaking his head. "This place has really gone to shit."

Loomis laughed mid-gulp, spilling some of the beer on the table. "You say that like this was ever a classy place, to begin with."

"Well... relatively speaking."

"Relative to what? A trash dump?"

"Hey, back in the day, this place was actually pretty nice."

"Uh, huh."

"You know, you're really negative, Loomis. I don't need that kind of negativity in my life, okay?"

"The beer's not that bad." Loomis took another long pull, and Jones grimaced.

He gazed around the bar, taking in the scenery while he waited for the waiter bot to return with his drink. Beyond the bar, the rest of Lucent Station could be seen. It too had once been a welcome respite for long haulers, but now, it looked like it was barely hanging on. The station was on the verge of not being able to service ships like the *Doris* and her crew, and once they lost that ability, the Lucent Station would likely close up shop for good.

At least the dockmaster had been a real person. Whereas, the staff of the Majestic—which had once taken pride in being one-hundred percent human—appeared to have been affected by the apparent downturn in clients. Sure waiter bots were cheaper over the long-term, but in Jones's experience, most patrons preferred a living, breathing human to bring them their drinks and laugh at their horrible jokes. Jones didn't care much either way, he just wanted a drink he could pallet and enjoy. Preferably not piss.

A group of men laughed two tables away, apparently over-joyed at their companion's lack of progress with a certain female bartender—this one human—at the far end of the bar. Jones leaned over, craning his neck to see what the target of is ill-fated affections looked like and chuckled.

Not a chance, he thought, shaking his head. The woman behind the bar was in her sixties, and judging by her distinct lack of clothes, she believed she was still in her twenties.

"What's so funny?" Loomis asked, twisting in the booth to see.

"Nothing," Jones said.

The waiter bot reappeared with his gin. It swirled in the glass as the bot's three-fingers set it down on the table. "I hope this is more to your liking, sir," the bot said without any hint of annoy-ance or malice.

Jones didn't respond, only flicked a finger across his link, sending over payment for their drinks. He took a sip and let out the breath he'd been holding in a sigh of relief. "Finally."

The crisp, clean alcohol burnt slightly, but it was worth it.

Jones pulled out a small case from inside his jacket and opened the lid. He kept it under the edge of the table while he worked, tapping on the backs of three tiny microbots. The six-legged spider-bots weren't much bigger than a fingernail, completely black, with no external markings. He'd paid a fortune for them, and so far, they hadn't yielded anything but juicy gossip.

At least the drinks are free, he thought. While it wasn't techni-cally accurate, Fischer had assured him that ASI would ultimately be footing the bill. He took comfort in knowing the bureaucracy he hated was contributing to this well-being.

One by one, the tiny bots activated, scurrying out of the case, across the underside of the table, and down to the floor. From there, they made their way to various locations within the bar, one each to opposite corners, the third climbed up to the ceiling and positioned itself in the very center of the room. Even right under the lights, the spider-bots were virtually invisible. Even Jones had trouble picking them up, and he knew what he was looking for.

Synced with Jones's link, the bots listened to every conversation within range, running them against an exhaustive list of trigger words Jones and Fischer had come up with together—filtering out ninety-five percent of the noise, allowing him to focus on things most likely to contain the information he was looking for. He stored all the recordings in a secure data vault aboard the *Doris*, which he backed up every week to his encrypted hub on Montgomery.

Over the last six weeks, they'd overheard a number of interesting conversations. Interesting enough, that if he'd been so inclined, Jones could've made a fortune selling the information to the various law enforcement agencies and increase his market share at the same time by eliminating the competition.

And I still might do that, after this is all over with, Jones thought.

They sat there for a time, sipping on their drinks, watching the people come and go, order drinks, laugh and crack jokes. One drunk, barrel-chested man threw an empty glass at the waiter bot, shattering it on the bot's cylindrical torso. His friends laughed, urging him to throw another one, but the bar's broad-shouldered bouncer appeared just as he was picking up the second glass and put a stop to it. It hadn't been so much the words he'd used, but the large caliber pistol tucked into his waistband. A glimpse of the weapon, and a sneer that told everyone around that he wouldn't hesitate to use it, had brought the festivities to a screeching halt.

Jones tapped his link, tweaking his cochlear implant to pick up the audio feeds from the spider-bots, picking up several of the conversations around the bar. Most were nothing, some were couples fighting about ridiculous relationship issues—of which Jones was glad he'd never succumbed to—but there was one booth...

Two men, three tables to their left, were talking about shipments into Pegasi controlled territory, arguing over the best way to get food and supplies to the underprivileged and needy. Altruistic, yes, but it was also a very lucrative undertaking, if you could get the right contract. Contracts out here, though, were few and far between, even for quasi-respectable businessmen such as himself and Loomis.

The problem was that those profitable contracts were becoming fewer as the price for the insurance bids on regular contracts was rising. And it wasn't just the backroom contracts either. He'd found himself locked out of long-standing open contracts due to an undisclosed bidder, which in and of itself wasn't that uncommon, but the fact that it was happening all over the URT was troubling.

If I'm not careful, I could find myself out of work and without a ship, Jones told himself, taking another sip of gin.

"Can you believe that guy just scammed eight thousand for some vitrostims? That's at least a two-week round trip," Loomis said.

"Money means different things to different people," Jones said. "Eight thousand to a super freighter is peanuts, but to a guy who'd visit this place, it's a fortune. It's really just science."

Loomis laughed. "Science, eh? I think you and I have pretty different interpretations of what 'science' means."

"Sure we do, the wrong one and the right one, and we both

know which is which." Jones set his glass down and rubbed his face with one hand. "Meh, I miss the good ol' days, man. You know, when a crew could make an honest living and not have to worry about getting it from both ends."

Loomis raised an eyebrow. "Honest?"

"Semi-honest."

Loomis grunted and kept drinking. "You don't really think this guy is actually going to show up here, do you? With all the cloak and dagger stuff he's pulled, you'd think he'd have been a little more care setting this up. I mean, we don't even know what he looks like."

"No, but I know his type. Dark, brooding, I bet he has a scar over one eye."

"A scar, huh?" Loomis asked, one eyebrow raised.

"They always have scars."

"Uh, huh."

Besides," Jones let his gaze sweep around the bar, "We know Fero and Danva are already here. Hard to miss the *Firestorm*."

Loomis nodded agreement.

The *Firestorm*, a medium-sized freighter, had been parked at the station's outer docking ring when the *Doris* had arrived. It was like most other freighters in its class, small enough that it didn't require a large crew, and just large enough to be capable of bulk hauling. But, unlike most freighters, *Firestorm* was painted bright orange, accented with red and yellow paint along the various outcroppings of equipment along the hull.

"And you think this is where they'll be?"

"It's where I would be," Jones said simply. "Someplace out of the way, where everyone is up to no good, where even the cops don't go. The Majestic fits all those descriptions. Isn't that one of the main reasons we're doing this?"

"What—so we can sit around in filthy bars, drinking lukewarm beer and listening to the dredges of humanity plot its demise?"

Jones smiled. "Exactly."

Loomis shook his head. "I didn't think Fero was smart enough not to get involved in something like that."

"Well, there's your first mistake. Fero isn't the brains of the operation, Danva is. I've never had any dealings with them, but I've talked to several who have, and Fero is pretty much a figurehead."

"Oh, kind of like you, then."

Jones grunted and tapped on his link, redirecting the bots.

"You know, speaking of contracts," Loomis said, setting the half-empty glass down. "We've been out here for weeks and haven't found anything yet, don't you think we should be lining up some backup jobs to cover the spread? I mean, we're not exactly flush with credits."

"We've got plenty of reserves. And Fish is set to cover the rest."

"We have some, not plenty," Loomis corrected. "Listen, I know he's your friend, but have you considered the fact that he doesn't have that kind of authority?"

"Jackson Fischer has never failed me," Jones said with more determination than he felt. "If he says the Agency will cover, they'll cover."

"And Cardinal?" Loomis asked under his breath. "What if Fischer's wrong."

"Even if he is, which I don't think he is, we're not out anything. Just think of all the inside information we've picked up out here. That stuff alone could net us a fortune in the hands of the right people."

"His theory is pretty fucking thin, Boss. And the longer we're out here, the thinner it gets."

"It's thin, sure," Jones said. "But it's really the only thing that makes sense."

"Or Young could be responsible for everything."

"If that bastard is the son of a bitch behind all of this, then when this is all over, I'll fly back here and drink every one of those god-forsaken beers."

Loomis laughed. "I'm going to hold you to that."

"Hold me to it then. It's never going to happen."

Not that he would ever tell his friend, but Jones had actually been considering those points just a few days before. But the idea of Young being the catalyst for everything that had gone down just didn't seem likely. When he laid everything out and looked at it objectively, it really didn't add up. And now with his escape…

"Fish is right," Jones repeated, not knowing whether the words for him or Loomis. "I know he is."

"I guess we'll see."

Loomis nodded, finishing his drink and setting the glass back on the table. Movement at the bar's entrance caught his attention. A man and woman entered, hesitating just inside the arched doorway. The bartender looked up and gave them a curt nod.

"Sit wherever you'd like," she said, her words coming through Jones's implant.

They both ignored her, looking around the bar, obviously sizing up the place.

Jones averting his gaze as the male of the two glanced his direction. Nudging Loomis's leg under the table, Jones said, "They're here."

CHAPTER 17

The Majestic
Lucent Station, Ulara System
27 July 2607

The woman was taller than the man by at least five centimeters, dressed in a gray jacket and matching slacks. Danva Del Garo was in her thirties, with long brown hair that framed her angled jaw and high cheekbones. The man, Fero Yazdani, was in his fifties and wore a light-blue, long-sleeve shirt. The dim light hanging above reflected off his bald scalp. He motioned to a booth along the back wall, and the woman nodded. Fero led her through the bar, then waited until she'd sat to slide into the booth next to her.

Very gentlemanly of you, Jones thought.

Their booth was illuminated by a dull yellow bulb hanging from the ceiling, the partitions on either side decorated with fake greenery. It was situated in the corner, with clear lines of exit through the front and unmarked exit in the back. Fero looked over his shoulder, sweeping his gaze around the bar before turning back to Danva and nodding. His mouth moved, but it was too low for the spider-bots to pick up.

Immediately, Jones redirected one of the bots to the table, positioning it on the ceiling next to the anchor for the hanging light. A small optical sensor captured images of their faces for Fischer to log later, and the audio feed came through Jones' implant.

"This place stinks," Danva said.

"Yeah. That's sort of the point, isn't it?" Fero asked.

The waiter bot stepped up to the table and asked for their drink orders, then retreated after they'd ordered, slinking back through the service entrance next to the bar.

"When he shows up, let me do the talking," Danva said.

Fero shrugged. *"Don't think there'll to be that much talking on our end."*

"Probably not, but still."

Loomis leaned across the table. "I take it back."

"Can't take it back now," Jones said. "They showed and the bet stands." He was relieved he didn't have to drink any more of the piss-water.

The waiter bot returned with their drinks, then disappeared again. The woman lifted her glass, a rosy-pink colored liquid with a frothy top. She took a sip, testing. Her eyebrows raised and she nodded appreciatively.

"Not bad," she said.

"Ugh, this tastes like piss," the man said, pushing away a glass of the same beer Jones had tried.

Jones give Loomis a knowing look. Loomis rolled his eyes but said nothing.

Fero called the waiter over and ordered another drink, then they sat in silence for a time, sipping on their beverages. They were on their second drink when Danva froze, locking eyes with a man who'd just come through the bar's entrance.

"Heads up," Jones said. He'd expected a formidable, perhaps imposing man—a kingpin—but the man crossing the bar to their table was anything but. Everything about him was average; his hair, what he was wearing; a plain gray long-sleeve shirt and black pants, even the way he walked.

He didn't appear nervous and stepped up to their table with a confidence that suggested he was a pro. He sat without invitation, sliding into the booth next to Danva.

"I'm Davna," the woman said. "This is—"

The average man held up a hand. "I'm very aware of who you are are, Miss Danva."

Fero and Danva exchanged curious looks, and the average man continued. "Time is critical, and my instructions are not to waste a second. We understand our transaction, yes?"

Fero leaned forward, giving their surroundings a cursory glance. "That's—"

"We're aware," Danva said, interrupting Fero. He bit his lip and sat back. "We pick the items up and bring them to you. Couldn't be any more simple."

The average man nodded. "However, there's been a slight change in plans."

"What the hell do you mean, change of plans?" Fero hissed, leaning forward again.

"I will be traveling with you."

Fero and Danva exchanged confused glances. Danva set her glass down. "That wasn't the arrangement."

"No," the average man said. "It wasn't. However, it was deemed necessary."

"Deemed?" Fero asked. "Deemed by who, Cardinal?"

Again, Jones and Loomis exchanged looked. Jones' pulse quickened at the mention of the name. No one—not even Fischer —seemed to know what the name meant, or who it referenced, but it was important enough for Fischer to send him out here looking for it, and that was enough for Jones.

The average man held Fero's gaze for a long moment, then said. "That is correct."

Fero frowned and sat back.

Danva gave Fero an irritated look. "And payment?"

The man held Fero's gaze as he activated his link, the orange glow of the holodisplay illuminating his angled face. "As we discussed. Half now and half on arrival at our destination."

"And where exactly are we going?" Fero asked.

The man smiled. "When we arrive at the pickup point, I will give you that information. Not before."

"And where exactly are we going to pick up this…" Danva hesitated for a moment, then said, "cargo?"

"There are multiple pickup points," the average man said. "An order in the size we require would not go unnoticed by the authorities, no matter how inept or how high the bribes." He tapped his link.

Danva brought up the information on her own link. "Esperon?"

The average man nodded. "And we should leave as soon as possible. We are on an extremely tight schedule."

"And what is our final destination?" Fero asked.

"I will give you that information after we have successfully picked up the entirety of our cargo. Not before."

"You sure are asking a lot of us without giving us much in the way of information," Fero said.

The average man cocked his head to the side. "You have our money, the information will come when it is necessary, or when you prove yourselves."

"Prove ourselves?" Fero asked. "Hey, you came to us with this job, not the other way around. It seems to me like we've already proven ourselves."

"Your reputation for fast and reliable service is what garnered you this assignment," the average man said. "However, reputation and loyalty are not the same things, and above all else, we desire loyalty. When you have proven that, you may be privy to more."

Fero grunted. "Just seems kind of disingenuous is all."

The average man didn't seem fazed at all. "This is how he does business. I'm sure you're aware of his capabilities."

Fero opened his mouth response then closed again, saying nothing.

Danva nodded, "We're aware."

"Good, then it requires no more explanation." The average man stood up. "Wait seven minutes, then leave. I have another meeting to attend to before I join you on *Firestorm*. Please make arrangements to leave within the hour."

The average man didn't wait for a response before sliding out of the booth and leaving the bar. He never even looked back.

Danva looked like she wanted to rip Fero's head off. "I fucking told you to keep your mouth shut."

"What? I asked a question. Is that a crime?"

"You piss him off, and it won't matter," Danva said.

"Come on, you don't believe all that crap they say, do you?" Fero asked.

"It doesn't matter what I believe."

"It's a bunch of bullshit if you ask me," Fero said. "Just some stories thought up to keep people who don't know any better terrified into doing what they want them to do."

"Yeah, well, even the biggest lies are based in truth," Danva said. "And I'd rather not find out if they're true or not. Come on, get the fuck out of here."

Loomis raised an eyebrow at Jones after the two had disappeared through the bar's exit. "So, should we call Fischer?"

Jones shook his head. "We need to make sure this is what we're after first. Fischer's got enough on his plate right now.

Don't want to risk sending him on a wild goose chase if this isn't the real deal."

"Oh, come on, after all that, you don't think it's the real deal?" Loomis asked.

Jones recalled the drones and brought the case out of his pocket again, holding it open for them to retreat inside. "It probably is, but I want to know what this cargo is before we do anything. Won't do any good if we tell Fischer we found something if we can't tell him what we found."

Loomis put a hand on the table as Jones stood. Jones stopped halfway out of his seat and frowned. "What?"

"We're not spies, Tensley," Loomis said. "You remember that, right? I think we're getting into something bigger than anyone thinks and it scares the shit out of me."

"I know what we are," Jones said. "But there's no one else I can ask to do this. If it gets too deep, I'll call for help."

Loomis gave Jones a doubtful look.

"I will, I promise." Jones straightened and nodded toward the exit. "I'll even let you decide when to make the call."

The dark expression on Loomis's face lightened slightly as he stood. "Yeah? Okay, let's call him now."

Jones raised a finger. "I'll let you make the call later. Come on. We have some spying to do."

CHAPTER 18

Main Security Office
Cathcart Station, Del Raycu System
28 July 2607

"There, that's him," Tannis said, pointing over Fischer's shoulder to the holodisplay in front of him.

The security footage froze, showing the image of the Martin Gorges, stepping off a transport shuttle's ramp in one of Cathcart's massive hangar bays. The man was dressed in plain clothes; a brown jacket and gray pants. He hadn't shaved in a few days, his hair was disheveled, and he had dark circles under his eyes.

"Hasn't been sleeping well, has he?" Fischer asked.

"He's worried," Tannis said. "Why else would he sneak his family all the way out here?"

"I think 'worried' is an understatement. He's probably terrified, and with good reason."

Tannis straightened. "You really think this guy caused those fighters to explode?"

"In the absence of any other explanation, it's the only thing that fits," Fischer said. "Add that to the fact that he went AWOL and brought his family out here to disappear, and was then murdered for his efforts, I'd say it's a pretty good possibility."

Tannis grunted. "You know, generally speaking, people come to Cathcart to get away from their troubles and most of the time, it works."

"He was close," Fischer said. "But the kinds of people that can orchestrate something like this, aren't the type of people that are just going to let you walk away."

Fischer tapped the display, starting the recording again. He spread both hands over the panel, enlarging the image, letting it expand around him. The actual room Fischer was standing in faded away, replaced by the virtual recording. Crowds flowed down the ramp, spreading out around Gorges, heading out to various mag-lev platforms. Exhaust pumped out from ports on the shuttle's hull, flowing over the side of the platform and vanishing into the open expanse of the bay.

Shelly Gorges, a tall brunette, wearing a blue jacket, white skin-tight pants, and a pair of blue flats, followed her husband. She held their daughter's hand, leading her down and keeping her close. Gorges hesitated, scanning the landing platform, obviously looking for threats. It was painfully obvious he didn't have the first clue about tradecraft or keeping a low profile, the three of them stuck out sore thumbs. The family picked their way through the crowds, careful not to lose touch of one another.

Fischer followed them away from the shuttle. The security feeds throughout the station were all linked, enabling him to observe his target from almost every angle. The information the computer lacked from the feeds, it extrapolated and reconstructed in real-time, giving Fischer a seamless record.

As they moved, Gorges' eyes darted around the bay, eyeing the mass of the people with a mixture of suspicion and fear, but he never stopped scanning.

"He's scared shitless," Tannis said.

Fischer nodded and rotated the image.

"What are you doing?" Tannis asked.

"We know the Gorges'," Fischer said. "What we don't know is who killed them. At some point, their killer had to have made at least visual contact with them. My guess is the killer was either on the shuttle with them, or arrived here after the fact, but my money would be that he was on the shuttle."

"Why do you say that?"

"Because they had to have eyes on him at Lexington," Fischer said, panning through the crowds, occasionally slowing to check faces. The computer was running recognition scans at the same time, scrutinzing every face and running it against his ASI database. "They wouldn't have wanted him to get away from them, and killing a family on a transport shuttle is a lot more difficult than on a station with over a million people processing through every day."

Two message panels appeared, hovering over a pair of heads moving quickly through the masses as if on a mission. The red warning text advised they both had extradition warrants out of Solomon for theft, assault and a long list of other charges.

"Those guys?" Tannis asked.

Fischer shook his head, swiping the panels away. "No."

"How do you know?"

"Well, for one thing, they're heading in the wrong direction. For another, the people behind this thing aren't the type of people to farm jobs out to amateurs. I'm sure if you scroll through their files, you'll see they've been in and out of correctional facilities and courtrooms their entire lives. In fact, I'd be willing to bet they've got about five years of total freedom between them."

Tannis had already opened the files and was scrolling through the data. He laughed, shaking his head. "How'd you know?'

Fischer smiled but didn't answer.

Tannis closed the panel. "All right, so what kind of person are we looking for?"

"The kind that doesn't show up on facial recognition scans."

"Is that even possible any more?"

"Oh, it's possible," Fischer said. "It's just not very common. But for this, yeah, we're looking for ghosts. People that haven't ever been and will never be processed through any system anywhere."

"That's some pretty high-level shit."

"High-level doesn't even begin to describe it."

Tannis crossed his arms. "So what—we're talking like big, galactic-spanning conspiracies here?"

"To be honest," Fischer said, "I don't know. But my gut tells me this isn't small. It also tells me that whatever is going on here has implications that I haven't even thought of, and would probably scare the hell out of me if I did."

Fischer adjusted the view back to the family. They walked along the platform for several minutes, seeming unsure of where they were going. Gorges kept checking his link, then back to the crowd, head on a swivel.

"Why doesn't he just sync with the station's navigational array and tap in his destination?" Tannis asked.

"Stress does strange things to people," Fischer said. "He's so concerned with being followed, he can't comprehend anything else, even simple everyday things."

It took Gorges another ten minutes to locate the correct mag-lev platform where he and his family huddled together at one end of the capsule as if hurtled through the station. The image flickered around them, occasionally losing resolution. At one point, whole sections of the image winked out, and it took a minute for the computer to reconstruct them again.

"Feeds lose signal strength in the tubes," Tannis explained. He raised a hand as Fischer turned. "We know it's an issue, but there's over two thousand kilometers of track running through the station and installing enough redundant sensor clusters would cost Cathcart billons. I'm not saying it's a great excuse, I'm saying it's the truth."

Fischer couldn't fault the man. Those kinds of decisions were made well above his pay grade. And if he was being honest with himself, ASI—along with all the branches of the Alliance government for that matter—all ran on exactly the same principle: good enough is good enough. Nothing was ever perfect. The truth was, Cathcart probably had a better security array that most military installations.

Fischer turned back to the flickering image. "We all work with what we have, right?"

Tannis chuckled. "Story of my life, man."

They followed the family from the mag-lev track, through the station to another junction where they took a second mag-lev to another of the section. There they finally found the temporary residence cluster and checked in. After receiving their room assignment, Gorges led his family to their room and locked the door behind them.

Fischer tapped his link, freezing the feed and swiped a hand through the air in front of him, collapsing the images. The room lights brightened, and Fischer rubbed his eyes. He stretched and rolled his neck, feeling the vertebrae pop.

"I'm getting too old for this shit," Fischer said. "Surveillance is a young man's game."

"You know, we have techs that can break the footage down for you," Tannis offered.

"Thanks, but I prefer to look at everything myself. And that's not a slight against your people, it's just my process. I don't mean to offend."

"No offense taken," Tannis said. "I completely understand."

Fischer moved away from the observation platform, taking in

the rest of the office. Rows of holopanels floated over the walls of the octagonal space, displaying feeds from multiple corridors, hangar bays, exterior feeds, and communal areas. A massive real-time display of the station and surrounding JumpLanes took up the majority of the vaulted ceiling, multi-colored dots represented the thousands of ships coming and going from the station.

Cathcart security was actually extremely good. One of the best Fischer had ever had the opportunity to work with. At any given time, he could select one of the feeds, enhance it, and experience it as if he was walking right in the middle of it all, like he was a spectral being walking among mortals. It wasn't perfect—no security system ever was. From misinterpretation of data and faulty equipment to simple human error, there were a thousand ways the system could fail.

Fischer stopped at a collection of holodisplays labeled 'Restricted.' They showed multiple neighboring platforms, all occupied by medium-sized transports. Hundreds of tired-looking people were being herded down the ramps, rows of Navy ratings directing them onward across the platforms to where processing stations had been set up.

"What's this?" Fischer asked.

"Refugees," Tannis explained. "Came in with ANS *Courageous* a few hours ago. All of them full of human trafficking victims from Centralis. You hear about that shit?"

Fischer nodded. "Hard to believe that shit still happens on this kind of scale."

"I hope those bastards get what they deserve. Those people look like they've been through hell."

"What are they doing here?"

Tannis laughed. "For all the grief everyone always gives Cathcart for being a stuck-up, asshole, trillionaire, he's got a soft spot for people going through hard times. He offered to put them all up here while the government figured out the best way to handle them."

Fischer raised an eyebrow. "Out of the goodness of his heart?"

"For a small fee of course," Tannis added with a grin. "But hey, the Alliance is footing the bill so…"

"So, it's not going to be a small one."

"That's the beauty of government spending. Why buy one when you can buy two at twice the price."

Fischer enlarged one of the images. A squad of Marines stood near the edge of the one platform, watching as lines of refugees streamed by. One of the Marines looked familiar. He zoomed in closer and chuckled. "Well, I'll be damned."

CHAPTER 19

Entertainment Cluster 21
Cathcart Station, Del Raycu System
28 July 2607

"So, you're a Sabre now," Fischer said, motioning to Sheridan's black uniform. "Corporal stripes look good. Congrats on the promotion."

"Thank you, sir," Sheridan said.

Fischer grinned. "I told you before, you don't have to call me sir. In fact, I'd prefer if you didn't. Makes me feel old."

Sheridan chuckled. "Right, sorry."

"Don't worry about it." Fischer sipped his water. He would've preferred bourbon, but he was still on the clock, and he needed to stay sharp.

They were sitting at a table on an elevated ledge overlooking one of the station's enormous concourses. Levels upon levels stretched up from the main deck, open-air shops and rows of luxury apartments and hotel rooms. Each level had an expansive walkway that doubled as an observation deck, allowing patrons to look down on all the lower levels.

Fischer chose a bar across from the section's main mag-lev terminal. Every few minutes, a new capsule would arrive and disgorge a few dozen passengers as another group boarded from the opposite side. The capsules traveled the length of the concourse on an elevated track, then disappeared through a tunnel at the far end.

It was an endless sea humanity. Shop owners held up their wares. Men and woman weaved through the masses, swiping link invitations to clubs, bars, and whore houses; all vying to entice tourists for creds. Tall holos of the latest technological device twirled above their heads, neon-colored, half-naked women flickered above businesses, some merely trying to get you to buy something, others trying to sell themselves.

The massive "City in the Stars," Cathcart Station was home to every vice known to man, and as Fischer's eyes swept over the concourse, he couldn't help but think of the nightmare security would be. Just on this concourse alone, he could see three or four things he'd want to follow up on as an investigator. He had to remind himself that Cathcart was truly its own entity. Sure, it was located in Alliance space, and even though it still technically had to submit to Holloman Alliance legal jurisdiction, there was clearly a demarcation line separating the two at the station's airlock.

At first, Fischer had been mistrustful of Tannis' assertion that they'd been able to keep the murder quiet. After all, in most station atmospheres, once one person knew, everyone knew. But now, looking out over the crowds, and imagining the number of creds that passed through here every day, Fischer understood why. No one cared about one family's death, much less one man's. They'd locked down the residential block under the guise of a maintenance issue, and had, so far, kept any mention of the murdered family from hitting the media.

"What is it?" Sheridan asked, his brow knitting together.

"Huh?" Fischer asked.

Sheridan tilted his glass toward Fischer. "You looked like you were contemplating the meaning of the universe there for a second."

Fischer chuckled. "No, no, nothing like that. Sorry, forget about it. I heard you've had an interesting couple days."

"Interesting is one way to put it."

"I've come across a few slaver ships like that. They're never fun."

"Can't understand how anyone can treat people like that," Sheridan said. "It just doesn't make any sense to me. You know?"

"Trust me, I get it." Fischer took another drink.

"Bet you see a lot more fucked up shit than that in your line of work."

Fischer shrugged, but couldn't help seeing the Gorges family in his mind. "Yeah, but it all becomes background noise, right? I see it and process it, then I dump it. It's why cops have the worst sense of humor—besides nurses and Marines, of course. You know what I'm talking about. I know you're no choir boy."

Sheridan laughed. "Guess you're right about that. It's just..." His smile faded.

"What?" Fischer prompted.

"I killed one of them." Sheridan looked down at the water glass and ran a finger around the rim. "I mean, she was a horrible person, right? Selling people for thousands of credits apiece. Making a living off other people's misery. And I shot her. Just didn't figure I'd feel this... off about it."

"It's normal. You're a Marine right? That's what you train for."

"Killing in combat—that's one thing. Blowing a hole in someone's face that's standing in front of you, that's something else. Isn't it?"

"What happened?"

Sheridan shook his head. "She had a gun. Probably would've shot me and my team if I hadn't taken the shot."

"Then you saved lives."

"Yeah." Sheridan looked away, gazing out over the crowds. "I can't get the image of Hastings being shot out of my head. Saw Thomas sneering at him as he pulled the trigger. I've seen the footage from HyperTrans Blue Lake; that look he had on his face right before... well, you know. That was the same look he had right before his shot Hastings. And I can't get it out of my mind."

"You have to give it time," Fischer said. He wasn't actually sure if he even believed that. He still wasn't completely over Corporal Biagini's death. It didn't matter that he couldn't have pulled her off that ledge even if he'd wanted to, her death weighed on his conscious regardless.

"Yeah," Sheridan said. He took a drink, then set the glass back on the table. "Most of the guys on my team, they probably wouldn't think twice about pulling the trigger. They're on it. I don't know if this is some kind of... I don't know, imposter syndrome? But I feel like if they'd be okay with it, I should be, too. Like you said, that's my job."

"You can be a good shooter and still not like killing very much," Fischer said. "It's when you *stop* thinking about it. When you start *liking* it, that's when shit's a problem. That's when I'd be worried."

"I guess you're right about that." Sheridan waited a moment, took a breath and said, "So what brings you all the way out here? They finally get sick of you on New Tuscany?"

Fischer frowned. "You haven't heard?"

"Heard what?"

"Young's escaped."

Sheridan's face darkened. He leaned forward, grabbing the edges of the table, knuckles going white. He spoke through clenched teeth. "The fuck do you mean, he's escaped?"

"The convoy bringing him to his tribunal was attacked. Pro team too. Blew up two Nemesis class fighters and conducted a mid-air extraction. Like something right out of the holos. I wouldn't have believed it myself if I hadn't seen it first hand."

"I don't understand," Sheridan said, leaning forward. "How the hell did they get out of the system? Where was the Navy?"

"Oh, they were there," Fischer said. "The mercs' modified sprinter outran the gunboats."

"It out*ran* them?" Sheridan repeated, obviously still trying to process. "How the hell do you outrun them? They should have been right on top of them the whole time. Who the hell was it? Do you know?"

Fischer shook his head. "Not a clue. Ex-military probably, but other than that, we don't have a lot to go on."

Sheridan clenched his fists. "How in the fuck did Young pull this off?"

"Trust me, there isn't anyone who wants to know that more than me. He had help, that much is obvious. There's no way he could have managed this on his own. Not from a jail cell. As far as we know, he didn't have any contact with anyone except the staff and his JAG lawyer."

A thought hit Fischer, and he looked away, disgusted with himself. "Son of a bitch."

"What?" Sheridan asked.

"Just something I should've thought of right when his whole thing kicked off. I was so preoccupied with where that bastard went, I ignored where he'd *been*. We should have pulled his lawyer in first thing."

"You think is JAG lawyer set this up?" Sheridan asked.

"To be honest, I don't think any *one* person set this up," Fischer said. "Whoever it was had access to highly classified information that even our ASI office wasn't provided, and I'm not sure what disturbs me more: the fact that we weren't trusted with it, or that there's someone in a position to receive it that shouldn't be."

Sheridan's eyes widened slightly as he recognized what Fischer was saying. "You mean a traitor. Another one? Jesus, how many of them are there?"

Fischer winced and held up a hand, eyes darting around. "Right now, it's just conjecture, but it is based on conclusions drawn from the available evidence. There's not a lot of other options at this point."

"That sounds like an attorney's response," Sheridan said.

"That's because I don't have anything concrete to back it up," Fischer said. "It's a hunch right now, albeit a strong one. But, like I said, there were only a few key people that knew the route and schedule. The pilots hadn't even been told. They were just flying the route given."

"So Young gets away scot-free?" Sheridan asked.

"I'm out here, aren't I?"

"What are you doing out here?"

"Looking into the death of the maintenance tech that performed the work on the Nemesis fighters that were destroyed in the attack," Fischer said. "He left with his family and ended up here."

"Death?" Sheridan tilted his head to the side, frowning. "You mean he was murdered?"

Fischer sighed. "Yes. I'm working through the station's security logs to see if I can develop any suspects."

"Have you?"

"Not yet," Fischer admitted. "But we've only just started running this case down."

"No?" Sheridan asked. "I thought you Intel guys had all the dirty tricks up your sleeves and access to all the super-secret, big-brother shit?"

Fischer laughed. "Yeah, well, it's not as great as all that.

Mostly, it's just a shit-ton of leg work. We'll figure it out, it'll just take some time."

"Time doesn't sound like something you have in abundance."

"It's not," Fischer said. "Every second we aren't on him puts Young that much farther away, and that much more difficult to catch."

"And you don't have any idea where he's going?"

"None. Navy checked out all the systems along the route they took when they left New Tuscany, but honestly, it's like searching for a needle in a stack of needles. Once they made it to the URT, that was all she wrote. He could be anywhere by now."

"Son of a bitch needs to fry," Sheridan muttered.

"I don't disagree," Fischer said.

"So, what—now you chase down leads here to figure out who killed this maintenance tech, hoping that'll lead you to Young?"

"Whoever caused those explosions is involved. Even if it's just that one thing, it all connects. Has to. In something like this, all the roads lead somewhere."

"And you think it's Young?"

"He's definitely a big part of it, but whether or not he's the brains behind the whole operation... I just don't know."

Sheridan glanced around them, looking down across the masses flowing through the concourse. "How high do you think this goes?"

"Before a few days ago, I thought Young was pretty damn high, but now..." He trailed off. The implications of a high ranking Admiral being in something like Stonemeyer was bad enough. This though... this was something on a scale that Fischer didn't even want to consider.

Sheridan held his gaze for a moment and nodded, obviously picking up on what Fischer hadn't said. "Kind of mind-blowing to think something like this is actually going on."

"Yeah," Fischer said.

"They all need to burn for what happened on Stonemeyer," Sheridan said. "And anything else they've done."

"Well, I can promise you one thing…"

"What's that, sir?"

Fischer glared at Sheridan who took a sip of his water, grinning. "I'm not going to stop until I find out the truth. If this thing takes my entire career, Young and everyone else involved will pay for what they've done. Whatever it takes."

Sheridan nodded. "Good."

CHAPTER 20

Alliance Naval Sprinter
Undisclosed Location
30 July 2607

"Finally," Sheridan said, unbuckling his harness as the sprinter settled onto its rails. "I thought that flight was never going to end."

"You and me both," Cole said.

At the rear of the compartment, the ramp was folding down and an officer in charcoal gray utilities was walking up to greet them.

"Hey, Captain, Three Rings inbound," Hanover said from the back of the bay. When Chambers looked in his direction, the sniper nodded to the approaching officer.

Chambers set his gear down and moved aft, meeting the man at the top of the ramp. He saluted for the team. "Commander."

"At ease, Captain Chambers," the man said, extending a hand. "Lieutenant Commander Stinson, Operations."

"Eric Chambers, Valkyrie Team Commander" the captain said, shaking the man's hand.

"Glad to have your team aboard, Captain. I assume you're wondering what you're all doing way the hell out here in the middle of nowhere?"

Chambers offered him a half-smile. "Actually, sir, waking up in strange locations is half of MARSOC's mission."

Stinson laughed. "I believe it. Permission to address your team, Captain? There's just a few things I need to brief before we can allow you to disembark."

"Absolutely, sir. Valkyrie, eyes up."

"There's just a few things I have to cover with all of you, so if I can have your attention for a few minutes, we'll get on with in-processing."

Cole leaned close to Sheridan and muttered, "The hell's he talking about, *allow* us to disembark?"

Sheridan allowed the hint of a smile but said nothing.

"First, I apologize for the distinct lack of operational information available thus far," Stinson said. "However, the nature of the assignment and its mission requires it. And trust me, I know how that sounds pretty vague. I was suspect myself when I was brought on board, but believe me when I say, our mission is unlike anything you've ever participated in.

"That being the case, this mission is strictly voluntary. Yes, even for you Marines. And when I say voluntary, I do mean, voluntary. You have the right to refuse this posting if you wish without any negative repercussions on your career, whatsoever. That's not lip service. It's one hundred percent true. We've had a few back out and received not so much as a note in their file."

A murmur went through the team at that. Sheridan frowned. MARSOC itself was strictly voluntary, you didn't join without knowing full-well what you were getting into: long deployments, not knowing when you'd see home, not knowing if you'd *see* home. It was a decision that every Marine put a lot of thought into. Though for Sheridan, it hadn't been a hard decision at all.

Stinson continued, "Once you step off this shuttle, you will be subject to a complete communications blackout. I cannot stress this enough—you will have absolutely no contact with the outside world. None. Not to your spouses, not to your parents or children, not to your girl or boyfriends your spouses don't know about."

The team laughed.

"You will not be able to talk about anything you see, hear, or experience once you step through this hatch. Everything that happens from here on out is strictly classified. Is that understood?"

"Yes, sir," Sheridan and the rest of the team answered in unison.

What have you gotten yourself into? Sheridan asked himself.

He didn't have any intention of staying on the shuttle, and the communications blackout didn't bother him in the slightest, but it added another layer of strange to an already strange operation. They'd been told their orders were classified, and the team had discussed the ultra secrecy surrounding their new assignment at length during the sprinter ride out here, but now it was real.

"If anyone wants to head back, please let me know now."

No one said a word.

"All right," Stinson said, "If you'll all come with me."

"What the hell are we doing out here?" Cole asked Sheridan. "Wherever *here* is."

"I don't know, but this doesn't seem like the usual 'classified' nonsense I've seen before. This seems like legit important shit."

"Don't get your hopes up," Richards said, shouldering his pack. "How much you want to bet this is going to wind up being some kind of glorified listening and observation post watching the Pegasi or some stupid shit."

Cole laughed. "Aw man, come on, don't jinx us like that. That shit's not right."

"Been in worse postings," Richards said.

"In Special Ops?" Sheridan asked, genuinely curious.

Richards hesitated. "Eh, maybe not in MARSOC, but definitely when I was a grunt, sure."

"You're always a pessimist," Neal said, slapping Richards on the back. "Could be a kick-ass assignment."

"It's gotta be if we can't talk about it, right?" Cole asked.

"Talk about what?" Richards asked with a wink.

Sheridan followed the rest out of the shuttle out into a relatively empty hangar bay. Four Nemesis fighters were arranged at the far end, along with three Albatross shuttles and a sprinter. The bay could've held ten times that.

A repulsor trolley waited on the deck. Two outward-facing benches stretched back from the driver's bench at the front, where a crewman in a black uniform waited behind the wheel. A second trolly, this one with a flatbed on the back, waited behind the first.

"Ramp-side service," Cole said. "Nice."

"Toss your gear on the second trolley, we'll make sure it gets to where it needs to go."

The trolley took them out of the bay and into a system of wide tunnels that cut through the station. The corridors were painted space gray, lighted by a single row of panels that ran down the center of the ceiling. There were no markers or section identifiers on any of the bulkheads, just blank, unfinished corridors. The entire place looked like it had been constructed with only the barebones, no money at all spent on amenities.

"Does this place seem a little... empty to you?" Cole asked Sheridan as they turned into another corridor.

"You know, I was just thinking the same thing," Sheridan said.

Most military outposts were bristling with activity. Considering the cost that went into simply constructing the bases, not to mention staffing and running them, generally, every spare centimeter of a station was utilized. Here though, it appeared as though entire sections of the station were empty.

They passed an empty repulsor trolley, headed back toward the bay they'd just left, but aside from that, and the two escorting them now, they'd seen no one.

Five minutes later, the trolly stopped in front of two gray blast doors, the edges marked with yellow and black stripes. Large red letters, painted across both doors read AUTHORIZED PERSONNEL ONLY.

The thought of anyone being *not* authorized at this point made Sheridan grin. Even with the lack of obvious security, this place seemed more secure than the Phoenix Battle Station.

At the front of the trolley, Stinson stood and faced the Marines. "What you're about to see is the Alliance's best-kept secret, most powerful weapon, and your new home."

Despite himself, Sheridan leaned forward as heavy bolts thunked, unlocking. Steel groaned as the two doors slid apart and the trolley floated between them.

"Holy shit," Sheridan said, taking in a breath at the vast bay.

Where they'd landed earlier had been expansive, but this one made that look like a small locker by comparison. Where the first could house ten vessels, this could fit a hundred and still have room for a game of blastball.

The deck came to an end fifteen meters ahead, looking out over a domed chamber a thousand meters in diameter and at least that high. As the deck stretched away from the entrance, it became an observation platform that encircled the entire space.

Floating in the center, surrounded by walkways and floating maintenance craft, construction bots, and workers on repulsor platforms was a giant warship. Bold black letters, painted on the aft section, wouldn't have stood out against the gray hull without the two spotlights illuminating the words from below:

ANS LEGEND CFH-001

It was definitely a heavy cruiser, but not a configuration Sheridan had even seen before. Its front section was wrong. On either side of the armored bow, where clusters of antennas and sensor domes protruded, were openings that led into twin hangar bays, like a carrier, with quick-out launch tubes arrayed in a line along the ventral spine of the ship. The aft section, where most ships sported two drives, *Legend* had three. Something else Sheridan had never seen before. All along the hull, open panels were exposed where crew and bots were working, some spraying sparks from large welding cranes.

Six missile emplacements were extended along the dorsal spine, ordnance floating on platforms next to them waited to be loaded. Sheridan counted ten visible railgun turrets and guessed there were probably more on the far side. It was one of the most heavily armed warships he'd ever seen.

The repulsor trolley floated to a stop and the Marines hopped off, all moving to the rail at the end of the platform.

"She's the first dual-purpose heavy cruiser ever built," Stinson said. "A full squadron of Nemesis fighters, two assault shuttles, and four rapid attack craft. She's got twelve missile emplacements, giving her a single salvo launch capacity of one-hundred and eight missiles, not to mention the Mark-VIII railgun batteries. And, of course, a dedicated team of Marine Sabers. She's got a crew of about two thousand, all the best in their career fields, hand selected for this mission."

"Well," Cole said, leaning close to Sheridan. "Some are better than others."

A two-tone alarm sounded, echoing around the chamber. A row of lights encircling the chamber began to strobe orange. Blue energy drew a vertical line at the far end of the bay, to Sheridan's right, becoming a wide opening as two enormous blast doors slid apart. The forcefield flickered, streaks of color occasionally flashing up and down its length.

A flight of six Nemesis fighters appeared, slipping through the field, two Albatross shuttles came in next, followed by an armored frigate with a blue stripe painted diagonally across its fuselage, from the top of the aft drive section to the bottom of the ship's nose. Five gold stars were painted in a circle just below the bridge's wrap-around viewport at the bow.

"Holy fuck," Cole muttered. "That's Admiral Hunter's shuttle."

"I thought he was retiring," Sheridan said.

Cole turned to him, a sardonic grin plastered across his face. "Oh, did the Admiral of the Fleet not run his personal itinerary past you for approval?"

Sheridan grunted.

Six more Nemesis fighters passed through the hangar's force-field, and the two-tone alarm sounded again as the bay doors began to close behind them.

"Tell you one thing, though," Cole said, nudging Sheridan with an elbow. "If Hunter's here, this shit ain't no joke."

Sheridan raised an eyebrow. "You didn't get that from the ultra-high security measures and secret base in the middle of nowhere?"

"Touché."

"Commander Stinson," Captain Chambers said, turning from the railing. "What exactly is this all about?"

The man smiled, clasping his hands behind his back. "Let's go find out."

CHAPTER 21

Flight Deck, ANS *Legend*
Undisclosed Location
30 July 2607

It took fifteen minutes to pass through security and board *Legend*. Every person was scanned; every piece of luggage and personal property examined. That they were Marine special operators with the highest security clearances available seemed to make no difference to the master-at-arms overseeing the procedures.

"Least he could've done was buy me dinner first," Cole muttered as the moved away from the station.

The team followed Stinson through the ship, onto *Legend's* flight deck, where a large number of the ship's crew had already been assembled in front of a stage at the far end of the compartment. Two rows of chairs flanked a podium at its center. Behind the stage, a flag bearing the Alliance crest—a ringed planet with wings on either side and a stylized starburst in the background— hung across the bulkhead.

Captain Chambers led his team to the side of the compartment where they fell into the loose formation without a word.

"You have to love a Commander's Call before you've really even started," Sergeant Neal said.

"Oh, it's the best," Cole said. "I was just thinking to myself on the way over, shit, I hope we get to have a Commander's Call before too long."

"Lock it up," Kline hissed from the back.

One by one, officers dressed in black flight suits ascended to the podium, standing in front of their chairs at parade rest. Sheridan immediately recognized Anderson Ward at the far-right side of the stage. Ward had served as executive officer aboard ANS *Vision* during his first assignment. He'd never actually met the man, but from what he'd heard, there wasn't much to complain about. He knew his shit, and by all accounts, he was fair, and that's about the best anyone could say concerning most decent officers.

"Room atten-chun!" a deep booming voice shouted. Sheridan hadn't seen who'd issued the order, but instantly, everyone in the compartment snapped to attention.

When the room was still, the same voice announced, "Alliance Naval Commander, Fleet Admiral Hunter."

Sheridan craned his head and watched as Hunter stepped onto the stage. Instead of his usual dress blacks, the Admiral wore a black flight suit, and Sheridan could just make out the Alliance crest on the left breast pocket. He'd met the man once before, after Fischer had pulled him from the slums of Stonemeyer. Along with his gratitude and respect, Hunter had offered him his choice of assignments within the Alliance Military. Sheridan hadn't had to think twice.

"As you were, please," Hunter said, crossing to the podium. He stopped behind the podium and motioned for the officers behind him to sit. Hunter surveyed the assembled crowd for a moment, then nodded in obvious appreciation. "Thank you. Good afternoon."

A chorus of "Good afternoon, sir!" echoed throughout the compartment.

"First and foremost, I'd like to welcome you all aboard ANS *Legend*. I know some of you are just getting here and I apologize for the expeditious nature of your orders. However, in our current operational tempo, there was no other choice. I can only imagine what you all must be thinking. In your position, I'd be wondering the exact same thing. 'What the hell am I doing here?'"

A murmur of polite laughter rippled through the assembly.

"I know the secrecy and security behind this project has probably put some of you off. Hell, it pissed me off, and I set it all up."

Another round of laughter. This time a little more genuine.

"But the fact is, it is all absolutely necessary. I know every one of you is aware of the need for general operational security throughout the Navy's daily routine, but in this situation, 'general' operational security just isn't enough."

Hunter stepped around the podium and rested a hand on the corner. "You know, in most situations, you all would have the advantage on me; you all would know me, and I wouldn't know you, but in this case, I know each and every one of you, and that says more about you than it does about me. You are all exceptionally skilled and qualified and have all received exemplary marks from your supervisors and commanding officers. And that is precisely why you are all standing here today.

"Ladies and gentlemen, I can say without hyperbole that this ship is *the* most advanced in the fleet and is truly one of a kind. The Legend Project has been a personal project of mine for the last three years. A project which has, despite all odds, remained secret. The only people in the galaxy that know of this ship's existence, besides the people standing next to you right now, are the President and a few key members of the Senate. That's it. In fact, *Legend* itself is listed as a maintenance barge."

Another murmur went through the assembly. Sheridan and Cole exchanged bewildered glances.

Hunter continued, "As I said before, each and every one of you was handpicked for this mission, the details of which will become clear very soon. But know this, I have every faith in your ability to make the project succeed. The Alliance is facing some hard times, and this ship and her crew will be at the very forefront.

"Some of you may know each other. Some of you might not know anyone, but I can guarantee you after this project is finished, you will all be bound by forces stronger than blood. Now, if you'll permit me, I'd like to introduce your new commanding officer Commander Anderson Ward."

At the end of the row, Ward stood and approached the podium. Hunter shook his hand and put his other on Ward's shoulder. "Commander Ward has distinguished himself among his peers as an exemplary officer and has proven time and time again that he has what it takes to command the most capable and well-trained people this Navy has to offer."

Hunter motioned to an officer standing just offstage. The man moved quickly to the podium, holding out a small case. Hunter took it, and the officer returned to his previous position.

""Which brings me to my next point. We all know the phrase, 'rank comes privilege,' yes? Well, the rank of Captain holds a special place in the hearts of all naval personnel, going back to the dawn of sea-going vessels. The long months, sometimes years spent away, outside of the usual chain of command, required rank to which there could be no ambiguity in its role. This ship is one of a kind, quite literally, the tip of the spear, and as such, requires a commander of similar standing."

The officer who'd handed Young the case went to attention and shouted, "Attention to orders!"

The chorus of heels snapping together echoed throughout the chamber. On stage, Admiral Hunter turned to Ward.

"Commander Anderson Ward, you have served the Alliance with distinction and honor for eleven years, the last three of which as Executive Officer about the ANS *Vision*. Your accomplishments, which are many, speak for themselves and are too long for me to recite here. Suffice it to say, this has been a long time coming."

Hunter opened the case.

"Commander Ward, by the authority granted me by the President of the Alliance and Naval Regulations, I hereby promote you to the rank of Captain, with all the rights and privileges thereto." Hunter took a small pin from the case and pressed it against Ward's uniform just above the left chest pocket. congratulations, Captain."

"Thank you, sir," Ward said, smiling.

Hunter started clapping, and the assembly joined in, several whooped and cheered. After several moments, the Admiral held up a hand, calling for quiet. The look on Ward's face was one of complete shock.

"Now," Hunter continued, "*Captain* Ward, had no idea he was going to be pinned today, as you can tell. So I won't pressure him to give a lengthy speech, but," he turned to Ward and motioned to the assembly, "why don't you give a speech, Captain."

The assembly cheered and clapped again as Captain Ward took the podium. Hunter stepped to the side, hands clasped behind his back.

Ward shook his head, obviously still trying to wrap his head around what had just happened. Finally, he said, "Thank you, Admiral Hunter. Words can't begin to express what I'm feeling right now. I would like to say thank you to all of you. Like me, you've undertaken this journey without knowing the destination, and that takes a lot of courage and bravery. That alone makes this command an honor to hold. I will do my best to ensure I don't let any of you down, and by the end of our time together, we will make sure no one forgets the name *Legend*."

The audience roared.

"Thank you," Ward repeated, then stepped away, motioning for the Admiral back to the podium.

"Well done, Captain," Hunter said. "Now, for all of you still wondering what the hell you're doing way out the middle of nowhere, let me say this. I didn't give you that biggest and best weapons platform in modern naval history to just sit around on your assess and wait for war. When I say *Legend* is the tip of the spear, I mean it quite literally. Your mission will be to bring the fight to the enemy, wherever they might be. And you *will* win this fight, is that understood?"

"Yes, sir!"

CHAPTER 22

Captain's Office
ANS *Legend*
Undisclosed Location
30 July 2607

"That was an excellent speech, sir," Captain Ward said, stopping just inside the office door. He stepped aside, allowing Admiral Hunter to follow him in and the hatch slid shut, separating them from the entourage that had followed Hunter since he'd come on board.

"Thank you," Hunter said. He stopped and turned, motioning to the desk. "I believe that's your seat, Captain."

Ward hesitated for a moment, then continued across the office, moving behind the desk, but not sitting. He ran his hands along the back of the chair as if unsure how to proceed.

Like most captain's offices aboard ship, the cabin was small, but large enough to conduct business. Life aboard warships wasn't supposed to be a luxury cruise.

"You hear that?" Hunter asked, touching an ear.

Ward listened for a moment. "I don't hear anything."

"Exactly. No aides talking on links, no one handing you data-pads to skim and sign, no reporters asking questions, no politicians breathing down your neck. Oh, to be in your shoes, Captain."

Ward smiled.

"You know it's not very often in an officer's career that they have the opportunity to christen a ship on her maiden voyage," Hunter said. "I was lucky enough to captain two, but it's exceedingly rare."

Ward's gaze scanned the room. "To be honest, I'm at a loss for words, sir. I never, in my wildest imagination, pictured myself in command of a ship like this."

Hunter smiled. "And you're just getting to know her. Wait until you know all her secrets. Then you'll really be impressed."

"Thank you, sir. I..." Ward trailed off.

"What is it, Captain?"

"Sir, it's just... I don't understand."

"You're wondering why I picked you for this command?" Hunter asked. "Why you out of all the other candidates?"

"Yes, sir."

"And why is that?'

"Well, sir, I can think of at least fifteen captains right not that have, not only seniority, but experience over me. In fact, I hadn't expected to receive a CO's position for another four years, at least."

Hunter frowned. "Are you saying you're not ready for the job, Captain?"

"Well, to be honest, sir, aside from what you said back there, I'm not really sure what the job actually is or if I have the experience for it."

"This may come as a surprise to you, but I have never selected a commanding officer based on their experience. Would you like to know what my qualifications are?"

"Yes, sir."

Hunter laughed and waved a hand through the air. "Relax, Anderson. The door's shut." He moved to one of two chairs facing Ward's desk and sat. "Sit, please. Let's have a conversation for a bit."

Ward hesitated, then finally sat. He leaned forward in the chair, obviously still uncomfortable to be having a conversation like this with the highest-ranking officer in the Alliance Military. Hunter could remember how he'd felt as a junior officer dealing with higher ranks, especially Admirals. They always felt like mythical beings, untouchable and all-knowing.

Oh, how the truth shines a pale light, Hunter thought. "Where were we?"

Ward cleared his throat. "Qualifications for—"

"Ah yes," Hunter said, crossing his legs. "When I look at putting someone into a command position, I don't look at what they've done, I look at the potential for what they *can* do. Experience can be measured, written down, quantified. Potential, though, that's something that no one can put a marker on. It's the very reason why you were picked for this job over all the rest."

"My potential, sir?"

"That's right. Have you ever heard of the expression, 'can't teach an old dog new tricks?'"

Ward nodded.

"The Alliance has a lot of fine, experienced commanders, some with combat records that could put mine to shame. But all of that experience is built on a very specific set of rules, rules they've spent their entire lives programming into their subconscious. Everything from routine ship functions to battle plans are built around those rules, and in most cases, those rules have saved more lives than you or I could ever count."

"With this, though," Hunter motioned around the cabin with a finger, "with *Legend* we re-wrote the rules. Threw out the old rules almost entirely, actually. *Legend* comes with her own, brand new rules, specific to her and her alone. We're taking the Navy in a completely new direction with this girl, and in my experience, the only way to make those kinds of transitions go smoothly and hassle-free is to use new blood."

Ward opened his mouth to respond, but no words came.

Hunter laughed. "I know, I'm sorry. Reynolds—my aide—says I get a little carried away sometimes, I apologize. My point is you're the perfect candidate for the job Captain Ward and don't ever let anyone tell you differently. I want you to come at this thing with a completely open mind. I want you to try new things, experiment, figure out was works and what doesn't. Nothing is off the table."

"Yes, sir."

"There's only one stipulation, and it's non-negotiable. If you can't abide by it, then I'll have your ass running logistics at Lexington for the next twenty years, got it?"

Ward straightened. "What is it, sir."

"You have to succeed. You cannot fail, Captain. That's an order. The concept of a multi-capable ship built for any engagement is going to be what the Alliance Navy will become over the next ten to twenty years. Oh sure, we'll still maintain carriers and capital ships, but more and more, those ships are being relegated to the mission of deterrence. They're defensive more than offensive. *Legend* and the ships that follow will be the enforcement arm of the fleet, and they will be a force to be reckoned with."

"I won't fail you, sir."

"Good man."

Hunter pulled the datapad he'd been holding in the cargo pocket of his flight suit and set it on Ward's new desk. Hunter knew the empty surface would soon be full of similar pads, all awaiting his signature and blessing. For now, though, the pad he slid toward the warship's new captain was the only thing that mattered.

"I wasn't kidding when I said your mission is going to be one of the most aggressive operations we've ever launched. You, your crew, and this ship have been given a blank check. Your orders are to be as aggressive and ruthless as you deem necessary to disrupt, destroy, and remove this rising raider threat. By any and all means at your disposal, Captain, and I don't say that lightly."

Hunter tapped the pad with a finger. "This is your trump card. A golden ticket, if you will. Executive Orders, signed by the President himself. You will report to no one but the Fleet Admiral. You will operate outside the bounds of the regular Navy, with authorization to go wherever the mission dictates. And yes, I do mean anywhere. This is the closest anyone in the history of the fleet has ever come to complete and total autonomy."

Ward picked up the pad and turned it over in his hand. His face showing no sign of emotion at all.

"I want you to hunt down and kill every last one of those mother fuckers, Captain. By the end of this thing, I want anyone even considering raiding, here or anywhere else, to know the name *Legend* and think twice. I want those bastards to spend every day looking over their shoulder, scared out of their minds that any second, you and your crew will be dropping out of a Lane and sending them straight to oblivion. Sanction with extreme prejudice."

A grin formed at the corner of Ward's mouth.

"Ah," Hunter said, also smiling. "That's the spirit."

Ward considered the pad for a moment, running a finger over the edge. "So we're hunters, sir?"

"That's right. Hunters with the sharpest damn spear in the galaxy."

"It's a big responsibility, Admiral."

"Your damn right it is," Hunter said. "Are you up to it?"

"I think so, sir."

Hunter raised an eyebrow. "You *think* so?"

Ward nodded. "I *know* so."

"Excellent." Hunter stood. "I want weekly reports on your progress."

Ward stood as well. "Yes, sir, but... my apologies, sir, but aren't you retiring?"

Hunter laughed. "You want to know what the best-kept secret in the whole Alliance Navy is, Captain? Fleet Admiral's don't actually get to retire."

The look on Ward's face suggested Hunter's explanation hadn't answered his question. "Admiral Gulliver has already been briefed on the project, and not only is fully aware of your capabilities but stands behind your mission one hundred percent. And remember," Hunter pointed at the pad on Ward's desk. "So is the President. You won't get any grief from them, I guarantee it."

Ward eyed the pad and Hunter could tell the man wasn't exactly one hundred percent satisfied.

"No one's going to leave you out to dry on this thing, Anderson," Hunter said. "I can promise you that. This project has been my baby from the get-go. It's my legacy. No one is going to forget that. Least of all me. I might not be wearing this for much longer," he pointed to the star on his collar, "but I'll never take it off."

"Yes, sir," Ward said. "Thank you, sir."

Hunter smiled, stepped forward, and extended a hand. "Thank you, Captain. I have all the confidence in the world that you and your people will do this operation proud. I know you will do everything in your power to make the name of this ship a true legend."

CHAPTER 23

Cathcart Security Office
Cathcart Station, Del Raycu System
30 July 2607

"Right there," Fischer pointed to the holodisplay. "Freeze it. Who's that?"

Behind him, the technician's fingers danced across his terminal, and the image froze. Red outlines drew themselves around Gorges' figure and another woman sliding onto the barstool next to him. The image rotated around, showing the woman's face as she made eye contact with Gorges, her mouth open, saying something.

Her blond hair was cut short, not quite reaching her ears, combed to one side, the other side buzzed. She wore a red tank top and gray slacks. The computer isolated her face, enhanced it automatically, and began running recognition protocols.

Tannis moved around Fischer and shook his head when he got a look at the woman. "Don't need facial recognition to identify her."

"You know her?" Fischer asked.

"Lenora Piner," Tannis said. "Called Cathcart home for a number of years. Left, oh, going on three years ago now. Better prospects elsewhere, I gather. But she comes back through every now and then. She's in big with the slum lords around here, a kind of all-around enforcer—you know the kind. Does a little bit of everything."

Fischer nodded. "Yeah, I've met a few."

"Her specialty is getting people places quietly and under the radar."

"Human trafficking."

Tannis laughed. "Eh, not quite. More like a sort of underground railroad for people who can't go to the authorities."

"She doesn't look like the kind of person that's out to help people out of the goodness of her heart."

"Oh, it's not cheap," Tannis said. "Takes years to pay off. But that's never stopped anyone from using it if they really need to. We had to shut it down here because it was getting a little out of hand. Last I heard, she was working for an outfit around Solomon, but who knows. These types—even they don't know where they're going to be from day to day."

"Have to go where the work is," Fischer said.

"In a nutshell."

"So what's she doing back here?" Fischer asked.

"Why don't we go ask her."

Fischer raised an eyebrow. "You know where she is?"

"If Piner is here, there's only two places she might be: Rings or Dusters. No doubt about it. Hell, she'd probably be in the station registry."

"Got her," the tech said from his station behind the two men. "Still checked into 184B-154. Gamma Section."

Tannis laughed. "See?"

"Isn't that kind of odd?" Fischer asked. "Just walking around the station without a care in the world. In her position, I think I'd want to keep as low a profile as possible."

"Eh, even if she tried, she wouldn't be able to." Tannis swiped a finger across his link, throwing a personnel file onto the holodisplay. She's known here; does business with everyone. I'm surprised we didn't know she was here sooner."

"Do you think she'll talk to me?" Fischer asked.

Tannis laughed again. "Man, if you can get her to say anything you can use, I'll give you a free spin at Dusters. She's as tight as a vault. Trust me, I worked her for years. She's as professional as they come. Knows all the tricks. Doesn't flinch under pressure. Hell, she probably knows the law better than you do."

Fischer doubted that, but he didn't say anything. Most criminals only thought they knew the law better. And knowing the law and breaking it were two completely different things. Even the smartest criminals made mistakes.

He peered at the image for a long moment, memorizing her face. "They're obviously talking about something serious. You can't get audio in there?"

Tannis shook his head. "Privacy, man. You know people here go crazy over that shit. Frankly, I'm surprised the cameras fly, but Cathcart wouldn't budge on those. Audio though, that was a harder sell."

"Privacy?" Fischer asked. "In a place like this? The entire station is one giant public venue, right? There's no expectation of privacy here, is there?"

"Technically, this entire station is private property. We have the absolute right to refuse service to anyone for any reason. Not that I can think of anyone we've ever refused service to, not counting some pretty violent criminals we've banned. But other than that, it's a pretty open market. That's part of the reason he can charge such astronomical docking fees; an almost one hundred percent guarantee that you can come here and do business and not have anyone interfere."

"Haven for criminals and villainy."

Tannis laughed. "I mean it's not the Wild West of Old Earth, there's law and order, at least."

"Is there?" Fischer asked, not quite believing the security chief.

"When it comes to enforcing station regulations and Alliance common law, yes, we police, but for the most part, we aren't out trying to run our ticket count up. We don't have quotas or saturation patrols or contraband inspections. All that's handled by Alliance Customs at the ports of entry. Once they're actually inside the station, that's a completely different ballgame." Tannis tapped a panel on the display. "Last place she swiped in was her room."

The door opened, and one of Tannis's security officers stuck his head in. "Hey Boss, another agent is here. Wants to talk to him." He nodded to Fischer.

"Another agent?" Tannis asked, giving Fischer a confused look.

"Didn't know anyone was coming out," Fischer admitted.

Tannis waved to the officer. "It's all right."

The officer disappeared, and Eliwood stepped through the door.

Confused, Fischer asked, "Woody? What the hell are you doing here? Did you find him?"

"Still working the node location," Eliwood said. "But no, didn't find him." She tapped her link. "Got something else you might be interested in though."

"Greg Tannis, Aniyah Eliwood," Fischer said by way of introduction. "My partner at the New Tuscany office."

Tannis moved across the office, hand extended. "Good to meet you."

Eliwood smiled and shook the man's hand. "Any relation to David Tannis, on Montgomery?

"My Uncle."

"Hell of a cop," Eliwood said. "Knew him before I joined ASI. Worked with him a few times on some local stuff, nothing big. He's a machine though.

Tannis nodded. "He's retired now, but still a worker. I don't know if he'll ever stop. Doesn't have anything else to do now that his wife died."

"Ah, shit, I hadn't heard that."

"Two years ago," Tannis explained. "Lung cancer. Caught it too late; wasn't anything they could do."

"That's horrible."

"That's life right?"

Eliwood shrugged. "I guess."

"What did you find?" Fischer asked. "And why couldn't you send it through the net?"

"Didn't want to risk the wrong eyes looking at the data," she explained. "Not with everything that's going on."

Fischer raised an eyebrow at that. Anything important enough for her to hand-carry all the way out here was definitely something he wanted to see.

Eliwood pointed at the main display. "You mind?"

"No," Tannis said. "Go right ahead."

She tapped through a few menus on her link, then swiped a finger across the screen, flicking an image onto the main display.

Fischer frowned as he took in the image, then his blood ran cold. "Holy fuck."

"Exactly what I said." Eliwood tossed two more images on either side of the first. "These were all taken on different days, all at the same location. As you can see, you and our man Gorges have a mutual friend."

Fischer stepped forward, not really believing what he was

seeing. The image was from a high angle, looking down on a table in a dimly lit bar. Two men sat across the table from each other, there was one glass of beer in front of Gorges, nothing in front of the other man.

"I don't believe it." Fischer clenched his teeth, thinking back to the first day he'd seen the man's face. It'd been in Del Monico's, on a much-needed date with Carissa. He'd made eye-contact with him several times before he'd run out of the restaurant. Fischer had followed him but lost him in the crowds outside. He'd disappeared into the New Tuscan night, vanishing from sight and invisible to the planetary security network.

"Who's that?" Tannis asked,

Fischer raised an eyebrow at his partner. She shook her head.

"Still coming up zero on a name," Eliwood admitted. "He left Lexington right after their last meeting. Boarded a silk merchant freighter registered out of Del Raycu."

"We have a lock on the ship?" Fischer asked.

Eliwood nodded. "It's still in Del Raycu, our people apprehended it getting ready to leave the system. No joy, though, our mystery man wasn't on board. I didn't have high hopes anyway, not with the time delay on the information. He had too much of a head start."

Fischer blew out a long breath, frustrated, but he wasn't surprised. With everything he'd seen over the last six months, the thought of anything coming together seemed like a far and distant dream.

"We're interviewing the crew and all the passengers still on board," Eliwood continued. "The local police are tracking down the passengers that disembarked, but…"

"They won't find him," Fischer finished for her.

"They won't find him," Eliwood repeated.

"Son of a bitch," Fischer said, feeling his cheeks flush. He'd almost forgotten about that man, the Ghost, but seeing again only reinforced his belief that they were dealing with something more significant than any of them could imagine.

"Who's Gorges talking to there?" Eliwood asked, finally seeing the image they'd been discussing before she'd arrived.

"Lenora Piner," Tannis told her. "We were actually just talking about going to have a chat with her."

"You think she killed our boy?" Eliwood asked.

"No way," Tannis said. "Piner's a lot of things, but a killer isn't one of them."

"Thought you said she was a jack of all trades," Fischer said.

"Yeah, but listen, I've known Piner a long time. Trust me, she didn't do this. Talk to her yourself, she'll tell you the same. I'm not trying to defend her. She's the last person that needs anyone to defend her, much less me. I'm just saying, there's no way she's your killer."

"Let's go find out."

CHAPTER 24

Short Term Residential Units, Gamma Section
Cathcart Station, Del Raycu System
30 July 2607

It took fifteen minutes to get to the unit were Piner was registered. The corridor was empty, save for several faux trees and bushes positioned at regular intervals along the plain gray bulkheads. This was definitely where the more affluent visitors stayed when they were aboard. Light panels along the ceiling and recesses ambient light along the base of each bulkhead gave the passageway a very *rich* feel.

This is a place Carissa would want to visit, Fischer told himself as they made their way toward Piner's unit.

There were two other security officers with him, which he had watching the corridors, making sure no one snuck up on them while they were working. Tannis stopped outside the door, drawing his pistol from its holster on his hip.

"I thought you said you knew her?" Fischer asked, putting a hand on his own weapon.

"I do," Tannis said. "But I'm not crazy."

He tapped the panel. "Piner, it's Tannis. You in there? Saw you were back on board, thought we talked about checking in the last time you were here?"

Fischer and Eliwood waited a few meters away. Fischer couldn't help but imagine the hatch flying open and the woman rushing out, guns blazing, making a violent last stand. It was a habit he couldn't shake, no matter how hard he tried. He wargamed everything, from high-risk apprehensions to simple interviews. There was just no way you could be entirely sure about someone, or know everything that was going to happen.

Tannis waited for a few moments, and when she didn't respond, he said, "Lenora, come on now, I know you're in there."

Fischer felt the little hairs on the back of his neck stand up when the woman didn't answer. He tightened his grip on his pistol, thumbing the break.

The security chief backed away from the panel. "I can override the security code, but I'm going to need a damn good reason."

"Is she a fighter?" Eliwood asked, hand moving to the small of her back, where her duty pistol was holstered.

Tannis shook his head. "Not with me, she's not."

"But she's not opening the door."

The security chief hesitated. "Could mean anything."

"Maybe she can't answer," Fischer offered. "Welfare check?"

Wincing, Tannis said, "Pretty thin."

"How about an official ASI request to talk to an important witness," Fischer offered.

Tannis grinned. "Actually, that just might work."

Fischer and Eliwood exchanged apprehensive looks as Tannis swiped his link access over the panel. Priority access routines bypassed the internal security and the hatch unlocked. Fischer drew his pistol, keeping it down by his leg, then he and Eliwood inched closer to the security chief.

As Tannis pushed the hatch open, his link flashed a message alert, which he quickly swiped away without reading and brought his pistol up, keeping it at chest level. He moved in first, Fischer following on his heels, Eliwood behind him.

A small entryway opened up into the round common area of the suite, consisting of two lounge sofas and a cylindrical holo-projector hanging from the center of the domed ceiling. A small kitchenette on the backside contained a small refrigerator, an oven, and sink. Two doors led to the right, one to the left. There was no sign of the woman.

Tannis inched forward into the room, side-stepping to the left to allow the agents to enter. Fischer swept the room, moving right, toward the first of the two doors.

"Piner?" Tannis called again, slowly continuing left.

No one answered.

Fischer exchanged a knowing look with the security chief and paused by the first door. Both were closed. He nodded to Tannis. "Go. We'll cover."

Tannis returned the nod and slipped through the open door. A second later, he reported, "Clear. Coming out." He continued around the far side of the suite, passing through the kitchen and stopping on the other side of the doors.

Fischer pushed the first door open, revealing a small latrine. A set of toiletries was arranged on the sink, neat and orderly. Tooth-brush lined up parallel to the little white tube of paste; brush next to that. A container for soap and shampoo were arranged in a similar condition on the edge of the tub. Whoever this woman was, she was neat and orderly beyond anything Fischer had ever seen before.

He moved to the second door. Tannis twisted the handle from the far side and pushed the door open. Fischer stepped in and stopped just inside the entrance to the bedroom.

"Goddammit," Fischer said, lowering his pistol and stepping aside as Tannis and Eliwood came in.

Lenora Piner lay face down, her upper half on the bed; feet, and legs resting on the floor. Blood stained the bedding around her head, short blonde hair matted with scarlet.

"Son of a bitch," Tannis said.

"Seems like your station isn't as safe as it's reported to be," Eliwood said.

Tannis glared at her. He was obviously upset, but Fischer didn't know whether it was because they'd been two murders on his station, right under the security chief's nose, or because he'd seemed to like the woman. He'd seen that kind of friendly rivalry before.

"She deserved better," Tannis said, shoving his pistol back into its holster.

"So, what—she was killed for trying to help Gorges?" Eliwood asked. "Is that what you're thinking?"

Fischer sighed. He really didn't know what to think. He knew he wanted the trail of bodies to end at some point. "Maybe."

"They certainly are tying up a lot of loose ends," Eliwood said.

"Problem is, you start killing everyone involved in thing, eventually, there won't be anyone left to work with," Fischer said.

Tannis tapped his link. When a woman answered, he said, "Lockdown Section Gamma and put a temporary hold on all departures. I want link scans of everyone leaving the station."

There was silence for a moment before, "Uh, yes, sir. I—who are we looking for?"

"I don't know," Tannis growled. "Just do it." He terminated the connection and let out a long, frustrated sigh.

"We're not going to find them," Fischer said. "If they're still on the station, which I highly doubt, they won't be leaving through controlled channels. Not if you put a lockdown on them. These people are too good for that."

"I have to do something," Tannis said, sounding more than a little frustrated. "We can't let them get away with this."

"Trust me, I know what you're feeling," Fischer said. "But she's been dead for at least a couple of days, judging by rigor mortis and lividity. Whoever did this is probably long gone by now."

"I can't *not* try."

"I know," Fischer said. He understood the man's need to do something. Were their positions swapped, he might've been doing exactly the same thing.

"Whoever did this had to have known her," Tannis said. "Piner wouldn't have let anyone into her suite, much less her bedroom, without trusting them implicitly."

Fischer pointed to the body. "She was walking to the bed. I'd say you're probably right. Either she knew the person, or whoever it was surprised her."

Tannis shook his head. "Piner would've have let anyone get the drop on her like that. I'm telling you, she was a pro."

Fischer scanned around the small bedroom. A hard, plastic, square case sat open on a stand at the foot of the bed, women's clothing folded neatly inside. The small closet was ajar, hangers even spaced, one light blue jacket hanging from the middle rack.

"Sounds like you admired her, Chief," Eliwood suggested.

"I didn't admire what she did; I admired *who* she was and how she operated. Like I said before, we had a good working relationship. Can't say that about most people in her line of work."

"You mean criminals," Eliwood said, head tilted.

Tannis flushed. He pointed a finger and took a step toward Eliwood. "Hey, you got a fucking problem or what?"

Eliwood never budged. "Just calling it like I see it, Chief. That woman was a criminal, plain and simple. She chose her life, and it bit her in the ass. Sooner or later, it happens to everyone in the game. I don't admire anyone that feels the need to prey on others to make a living. Regardless of how they are in bed."

"I never—"

Fischer raised a hand. "Enough. This isn't going to get us anywhere. We need to run the feeds from the room and corridor outside. We're back at fucking square one, and I'm sure we're going to find the same fucked up feeds as the first time."

Fischer moved around to the woman's side, examining her body. Her left arm hung partially off the bed at the elbow, fingers purple from postmortem lividity. He squatted down on the balls of his feet and tapped the back of her hand.

"Hey, what the hell are you doing?" Tannis asked. "Shouldn't we wait on the lab?"

Fischer didn't answer.

The link activated, its orange holodisplay rotating into view over the back of Piner's hand. Fischer swiped through several menus, but after a minute of searching, stood and said, "It's been wiped."

"Wiped?" Tannis asked.

"Same thing they did to Wallace, Thomas, and Biagini," Eliwood said.

Fischer nodded.

"Who?" Tannis asked.

"An old part of this case," Fischer said. "More dead waiting on justice."

"Maybe the lab can pull something from it," Tannis offered.

"They can try," Fischer said, "but I doubt they'll find anything. If it's the same people responsible for this whole damn mess, and I'm fairly confident it is, they won't have left anything behind."

"You talk about them like they're boogeymen or something," Tannis said.

"They are." Fischer stood and left the room. He slapped the door frame on his way out. "Goddammit."

Eliwood followed him out. "Maybe we'll find something on the freighter."

"We're fucking chasing our tails here. There's nothing on the ship to find." He looked around the room. He was sure whoever had killed Piner hadn't left anything behind. They were obviously good at their job. Attention to detail was paramount, not only in law enforcement but also for the people that made a living outside the law last for longer than a few years.

In the other room, Fischer heard Tannis relaying instructions to the rest of his security team, locking down the sector and making sure all the feeds for the last week were backed up.

"I'm sorry, Fish," Eliwood said.

Fischer shook his head. "Nothing to be sorry about. This is a shit case."

"We're going to find him."

"Yeah," Fischer suppressed a snort. He'd been telling himself the same thing for months, it'd become a kind of mantra. If he said it enough times, it would come true. But it was becoming increasingly apparent that he might never solve this case, much less find Young. Whoever was behind this operation had reach, far more than Fischer would've ever thought possible; from the lowest criminal enterprise and middleman to the highest-ranking admiral in the Alliance Navy. It was truly astounding.

"Hold up," Tannis said from the other room.

Eliwood moved out of the way as the security chief came back into the living area, his link on, eyes locked on the screen.

"What is it?" Fischer asked.

Tannis shook his head. "It's a message from Piner."

"You mean the dead woman lying in the next room?" Eliwood asked, jerking a thumb at the door.

"I don't understand," Tannis said. "It looks like an automatic message, sent when my security access override triggered the door. "It's her ID stamp all right, but I don't understand the message."

"What's it say?" Fischer asked, stepping closer.

"It's just one word: Cardinal."

CHAPTER 25

Landing Pad
Nebulous Interstellar Mining Outpost
Verikus System
31 July 2607

"All right, eyes up," Captain Chambers said from the head of the Albatross's bay. He stood in full kit, his visor up, rifle slung across his chest, barrel down. He held tight to the rail above him, fighting to keep his balance as the assault boat rocked around him. Sheridan couldn't help but see Lieutenant Hastings there.

You're not on Stonemeyer. He had to keep repeating it to stay grounded in the present and not back on that hellhole of a planet.

After receiving the original distress call from the miners, *Legend* made a max-speed run to the Verikus system and dropped into what Captain Chambers had described as a shitstorm.

The He3 mining facility was actually multiple orbiting stations that extracted the gas from the Verikus-Two. Then it was transported to a central refinery built into an asteroid the size of Ceres from Sol. The asteroid had been moved into its orbit by

Nebulous Interstellar, and they owned almost eighty-percent of the fuel produced by the station.

The question that was on everyone's mind was, where were the Nebulous security flotillas? While not likely to ward off attack from superpowers like the Alliance or Pegasi, it should've been more than capable of defending the outpost from raiders. Their initial briefing had been sparse on details, but after they'd made the translation, their assumptions of a large hostile force were confirmed.

Over twenty ships were actively engaged with the Nebulous defenders—ten of them ranging from a small, single-turret corvette to a lone destroyer that looked like it should have been decommissioned a decade before. The holo-image floating in front of Chambers showed a relay of what the command crew was seeing; a multi-ship battle. One in which the defenders were not winning.

"Since dropping into the system," Chambers said, "CIC has received multiple additional distress calls from the orbitals, and while the fighters and *Legend's* guns are clearing out the riffraff around the refinery, it's our job to clean up the inside. We don't have any idea if the workers are still alive down there, but we're going in under the assumption that they are."

The team listened intently, the collective mood, all business. This was their first engagement since departing on *Legend*, and they were all eager to prove the team's worth. The fact that there hadn't been any spin-up time surprised most of the senior members of Valkyrie, but Sheridan didn't mind it at all. They'd already been training together for months. It wasn't like they needed more time to acclimate to each other.

Much like Sheridan had experienced during the majority of their training ops over the past few months, the team's ability to flip a switch and be "on" was impressive. That wasn't to say that regular Marines couldn't do the same, but this was on a different level, one that Sheridan was proud and excited to be a part of. He'd definitely had his moments of doubt, but now, sitting in the cramped bay, waiting to go into combat, he knew in his bones that he'd made the correct decision joining the Legend Project.

The Captain continued, "Do not shoot unless your target is shooting at you, one of your teammates, or civilians. Command is interested in prisoners to question, but not at the expense of our safety. Check your backgrounds. There are things on board this station that don't like being shot. Don't shoot those."

A collective chuckle went through the bay.

"I don't need to remind you that our entire mission out here is to find and eliminate the continued pirate threat," Chambers said. "This is the first step in that mission. Don't forget that. And make no mistake, Valkyrie is already on the map. Otherwise, we wouldn't have been called up for this operation, we don't need to prove anything, we just need to do our job and do it as well as we can."

Behind Chambers, the co-pilot in the left couch turned. "Sixty seconds out, Captain. Sensors are picking up some movement on the deck. Could be the raiders. They still have birds on the ground."

"Roger that," the Captain said. "Master Sergeant Kline, we're going in hot."

"Yes, sir!" Master Sergeant Kline stood from his seat at the end of the row, his MOD27 held in one hand. "All right, you heard the man! Eyes up! We are inbound on a hot LZ. You know the drill, people."

Sheridan stood, adjusting his footing against the rocking of the Albatross. He tapped the backside of his helmet, activating the visor's internal HUD. The system only took a second to initialize, syncing with his own MOD27 and the rest of his body armor. An orange dot appeared at the center of this screen, then quickly expanded across the visor, populating it with various icons and data panels. Vitals, gathered from multiple sensors embedded in his armor, showed heart rate, blood pressure, body temperature, even lung function.

His rifle's magazine level showed in the top-right corner, along with the total number of rounds available to him based on his current loadout. Six extra magazines, secured in pouches on the front of his vest, combined with the one seated in Sheridan's rifle, made for a total of four-hundred-and-twenty rounds. A second number, below his rifle load, displayed the sixty rounds he had for his MP10 pistol holstered to his right thigh.

"Ten seconds," the co-pilot said again. "We're inside the station's atmospheric shield. Oxygen levels and gravity are nominal."

"Roger that," Captain Chambers said.

A metallic *clank* echoed through the bay as the Albatross's ramp unlocked at the rear of the compartment. Outside, stars dotted the blackness of space, the orange and gold orb of Verikus-Two just visible to the left. The refinery complex rose up around them as they descended, completely surrounding the shuttle in a matter of seconds. Tall metal scaffolding stretched up away from the surface of the asteroid like skyscrapers.

The shuttle flared, the back end dropping, revealing more of the flat, gray tarmac. The engines outside roared as the Albatross settled onto its landing rails, kicking up clouds of dust that curled around the open ramp.

A string of high-pitched twangs echoed through the Albatross's bay.

"Heads up, we're taking small arms fire from hostiles at our one o'clock," the pilot called back.

"Move!" Kline shouted. "Out! Go! Go! Go!"

Sheridan slipped past Cole, who was pulling two reconnaissance drones from his kit. His link screen appeared over his left arm, glowing orange, and his fingers danced along the display. "Two-Bravo, I have eyes in the sky."

"Roger," Kline said.

Sheridan followed the line of Sabers down the ramp. He turned right at the base of the ramp and ran for a row of rectangular cargo containers situated at the side of the landing pad. Red squares appeared on a bird's eye map, identifying the enemy one hundred meters ahead of their position, giving the Sabers a real-time advantage of knowing exactly where the enemy was. All they'd have to do was figure out the best way to shoot at them.

"Valkyrie Six-One, Actual, we are clear!" Chambers shouted.

The shuttle's engines roared as it lifted off, kicking up waves of dust and dirt.

Sheridan knelt at the edge of one of the containers, looking around the corner, getting a visual on the enemy. Two corvette-sized ships were sitting on the far end of the pad. The Albatross lifted away, revealing the smoking wreckage of a transport shuttle in the center of the pad. Fires burned from several exposed panels and smoke curled out through the multiple holes blow out of the hull.

"Nguyen, take your team to that shuttle. Team Two will cover," Master Sergeant Kline said.

"I've got seven confirmed targets," Cole advised over the taclink. Data from his drones populating the battlenet.

Sergeant Rocha was already moving, keeping low. She reached the end of the row of containers, found her first target, and fired. *"One down."*

The rest of Team One took up positions behind the row of containers, moving to the best engagement positions they could find. For Sheridan, that meant the third container back from the first. He took a knee and pressed around the edge, scanning the area with his optics. One of the marks appeared, moving from behind the cover of his corvette, his rifle up, also searching for a target.

"Gotcha," Sheridan said and squeezed the trigger. The rifle jumped twice, and his target dropped to the deck. "Two down."

"Moving," Nguyen said over the taclink.

Two more hostiles crossed between the corvettes, obviously looking to get a better angle on the Sabers. A barrage of gunshots rang out, but the rounds went wild, twanging off metal containers. Sparks erupted from the edge of the container Sheridan had just ducked behind.

Shit, he thought, blowing out a relieved breath. He straightened, identified his target on his HUD, then stepped up the edge and peered around. He found him—her... a woman kneeling behind one of the right corvette's landing struts, her rifle bucking as she fired in Team Two's direction, each muzzle flash briefly illuminating her face.

Sheridan fired again, taking the woman high in the chest, almost through the neck. She fell back, her hands and arms flying to the side, and hit hard, bouncing once, then lying still. "Three down."

"Moving," Hanover said.

Out of the corner of his eye, Sheridan saw the sniper pressing forward on the other side of the row of containers, his rifle pulled tight into his shoulder.

"Four down," Rocha said. *"Neal, Cole, watch that right side."*

"Roger," Cole answered, shots from his rifle echoing in the background.

"Five down," Hanover said. *"Six."* His voice was calm and steady like he was relaying his grocery list over the radio.

"Seven down," Nguyen said. "All clear."

"All clear," Cole confirmed.

Sheridan, like the rest of them, waited for several moments, before emerging from behind their cover. Just because the drones said it was clear didn't necessarily make it so.

"Reese," Kline said, pointing. *"Get the hatch."*

"Roger." The specialist jogged across the landing pad, immediately going to work on the security while the rest of the team cleared the hostile corvettes.

"We're in," Reese said, opening the door.

"All right, Team Two, secure those corvettes," Chambers ordered.

"Copy that," Nguyen answered.

Rocha led the rest of Team One across the pad to the refinery's entrance as Nguyen's team filed forward, covering off the dead hostiles and their ships.

Inside, the narrow corridor was lit by a series of flickering panels on the ceiling. The bulkheads were lined with exposed conduits, pipes, and cables, and the deck was a simple metal grating that echoed under their boots.

Sheridan followed Cole, moving single-file, deeper into the facility. A map, overlaid on the left side of Sheridan's HUD, showed them the most direct route to Operations, the central control room for the complex and where the distress calls had originated. Progress was slow but steady, clearing each intersection they passed, briefly scanning the additional corridors leading into various parts of the station.

"Valkyrie Actual, Two-Alpha," Nguyen said over the taclink. *"Hostile birds clear."*

"Roger," Captain Kline answered. *"Establish a perimeter and hold the LZ."*

"Copy that."

It took Sheridan's team another five minutes to reach Operations. They paused at the end of the corridor where it formed a T-intersection, one branch leading to the control center, the other leading off toward the residential section. Cole motioned for Sheridan to take the lead so he could back up and work his drones.

Sheridan peered around the corner, then pulled back. "Clear."

"Sure is quiet," Reese said.

"Goddammit, Reese," Neal said. "You don't say that shit."

"Drones aren't picking anything up yet," Cole said, checking his link. "But it could be because there's a shit-ton of interference from the complex. Signal strength is only forty-seven percent. The hatch to the control center is open though. Doesn't look like there're any hostiles."

"All right," Staff Sergeant Rocha said. "Standard sweep and clear. Reese is Number One, Neal, you're two. Remember, intel says there are civvies in there. Watch your fire."

Reese slid past Neal, his rifle's stock pulled into his shoulder, barrel pointing at the deck. The rest of the team stacked up behind him. Sheridan found himself fourth back, behind Richards. Cole, Rocha, and Hanover made up the back of the stack. The team's sniper had his pistol out, his HR91 slung across his back.

Captain Chambers and Master Sergeant Kline hung back. While they weren't technically part of either element, they attached themselves where-ever the need was, and despite their rank, allowed Staff Sergeant Rocha to work her element as she saw fit.

"Go," Rocha ordered.

The team moved around the corner in one smooth motion, weapons up, sweeping the corridor ahead. Reese reached the door and pushed it without hesitating. The rest of the team pressed into the room behind him.

The operations control center was a large circular room with a high, flat ceiling. Workstations were positioned in two circular rows, facing inward to a central station in the center. Under normal conditions, Sheridan was sure every exposed inch of space was covered with holodisplays, showing everything from internal system pressure to what was for lunch that day. Now, however, all those screens were dark. The compartment lit only by a handful of amber emergency lights.

Sheridan moved away from Cole, heading left after Reese, then side-stepping between to banks of computers. He swept his rifle back and forth as he pushed through the rows of workstations, searching for targets, his pulse pounding in his ears. To his right, a group of workers huddled together. They sat with their hands bound behind their backs and gags tied around their mouths, terrified expressions covering their faces.

"Clear," Reese advised as he reached the far side of the compartment.

"Clear," Neal repeated from her side of the room.

Sheridan juked right, angling between another cluster of computers. "Clear."

He lowered his rifle and approached the group of hostages. A few of the men looked like they'd taken a pretty good beating—eyes swollen, faces bruised, lines of blood trickling down their skin. Two of the woman had been crying so hard their gags were covered in snot and tears. All of them watched the Sabers approach with a mixture of fear and confusion.

"Are you all okay?" Sheridan asked.

Rocha slipped between a row of terminals and reached the group just as Sheridan did. "Where are they? Where are the people that did this?"

One of the workers tried to speak, but his words came out as a muffled jumble of syllables. Rocha bent down and pulled the gag out of his mouth.

"They left," he said. "Just a few minutes before you got here.

That way." He nodded to one of the hatches leading out of the control center opposite the one they'd just come through.

"What's that way?" Rocha asked.

A deep, reverberating rumble echoed in the distance, vibrating the deck under their feet. The emergency lights flickered, some going out for several seconds before coming back on.

"What the hell was that?" Reese asked, head swiveling as he glanced around the compartment.

"Oh my god," a woman said as Neal pulled her gag out. She gave the first man a wide-eyed look of horror. "They're not going to blow the reactor?"

Captain Chambers nodded to the hatch where the man had pointed. "What's through there?"

The man shook his head. "Engineering, secondary landing platforms, the refinery. There's no way they can bypass the safety protocols on the reactor though. No way."

The woman stood. "But he if damages the—"

Chambers lifted a hand, cutting her off. "And if the reactor goes?"

"This whole facility goes," she said. "You have to stop them!"

"Are there any other ways off this rock?" Chambers asked.

"Our emergency sprinter," the man said. "It's secured in Bay Three. They forced us to give them the codes, they were going to... they were going to kill us."

"It's okay, you're safe now," Chambers said. "Valkyrie Two-Alpha, Actual, change of plans. Redirect to engineering. Hostiles may be attempting to overload the station's reactor."

"Roger that," Nguyen said. *"Moving."*

"Legend Command, Valkyrie Actual," Chambers said after switching channels to the command net. "Be advised, we have contact with station personnel. The hostile element may be attempting to overload the station's reactor. There is a secondary egress point as well. A company sprinter could be attempting to flee. Advise close air support to be on the lookout; the sprinter is not friendly."

"Copy that, Actual. Advising flights now. Secure that reactor, Captain."

"Copy that, Command, Actual out."

"Please," the woman said, stepping closer to Chambers. "They have Catrin. They said they were going to…" she trailed off, a pained expression on her face. "Please."

Reese moved to one of the terminals, pushing his rifle around behind him on its sling. "The main operating system looks like it's still functional. What's your security system like? Can you shut the reactor down from here?"

Cole cut the restraints on the man, who stood, rubbing his wrists. The collar of his navy-blue jumpsuit was stained black from blood that still glistened on his chin, draining from his nostrils. He grimaced, gently probing his injured nose with his knuckles.

"We don't have camera feeds," he said, helping the woman to her feet.

Cole moved down the line, freeing the rest of the hostages. They helped each other up, staying close to each other for physical support as much as emotional.

"Don't have feeds?" Reese asked, obviously surprised. "What kind of station doesn't have feeds?"

"Not cost-effective," the woman said. She rubbed her bruised wrists.

"Unbelievable," Reese said. He swiped through his link menu's syncing with the station's core. Two additional panels appeared, but from his position, Sheridan couldn't read the data on them. "A lot of the primary systems are offline. Looks like they're fueling the sprinter. No read on progress, though."

"All right," Chambers said, "We work with what we've got."

"If they get away they'll kill her," the man said.

"They won't," Sergeant Rocha said. She pointed to the indi-cated hatch. "Sheridan, Neal, Cole, Hanover. With me."

Sheridan was already moving, slipping through the banks of computer stations, heading for the hatch. The deck shook under his feet, causing him to stumble into one of the terminals. He pushed off and kept going. The idea of this rock blowing up around him was not something he wanted to entertain.

CHAPTER 26

Corridor Twenty-two
Nebulous Interstellar Mining Outpost
Verikus System
31 July 2607

Sheridan stacked up behind Neal and Cole, all hugging the bulk-head. Ahead of them, Hanover looked back, ensuring they were ready to move, then pulled the hatch open and stepped through. Sheridan struggled to control his breathing as Cole and Neal followed the sniper through.

Doorways, or "the fatal funnel" as they'd been called for hundreds of years by operators throughout the galaxy, were the bane to any combat assault. Doorways were where things went bad. They were where people froze. They were where people died.

Cole followed Neal through, and Sheridan brought up the rear. He kept his rifle pulled into his shoulder, the barrel pointing to the deck, his eyes scanning ahead. With three people ahead of him, there would be little to no opportunity for him to engage any targets in front. His job was cover and rear security.

Like the first corridor they'd come through, this one was narrow and unfinished. Every few meters they had to duck a low hanging pipe or twist around a control valve. Sheridan wondered how many had knocked their heads on the ductwork when they weren't paying attention. Several exhaust vents leaked clouds of white vapor that rolled along the deck, seeping through the holes in the metal grating.

Another deep rumble shook the deck. The recessed lights along the ceiling flickered. For some reason, Sheridan thought about all the horror vids he'd seen over the years that had started just like this. Some alien or ghastly creature always crawled out of the ductwork to eat people or devour their souls.

Focus, he told himself, looking over Cole's shoulder.

They're breaking through the primary security routines," Reese said over the taclink. *"They'll probably be through in another seven minutes or so."*

Valkyrie Actual, Two-Bravo, we're nearing the reactor pod," Nguyen advised, gunshots echoing in the background. *"We've engaged several hostile targets and have them pinned down on Level 3."*

"Roger that, Two-Bravo," Captain Chambers replied. *"We're moving to assist."*

Sheridan gritted his teeth, fighting the urge to backtrack and help his teammates.

You have your own mission, he told himself.

"One down," Nguyen reported, sounding slightly out of breath.

"We need to hurry," Rocha said. "Hanover, step it up."

"Roger," the sniper confirmed. He paused at an intersection, peering around the corner, then leaned around the corner, his pistol up covering the rest of the team as they crossed.

"Eyes up. Watch for traps," Hanover said, now bringing up the rear.

Neal, at the head of the stack, pressed on, her rifle up and ready.

Sheridan began sweeping the surrounding bulkheads, mentally cursing himself; he should've been doing already. Not that it was likely he'd spot anything out of place here. He didn't recognize half of the control junctions, and cable outlets as it was anyway, much less an improvised boobytrap or IED.

The map on Sheridan's HUD showed they were approaching the secondary landing pad. It was significantly smaller than the pad their Albatross had landed on when they'd arrived, but there was still a lot of open space.

Rocha turned to Cole. "Let's get eyes in there."

"Roger that," Cole said. He took a knee and tapped his link. Feeds from one of his drones appeared, the corridor zipping past in a blur. The drone flew past them, giving Sheridan a kind of out-of-body experience as he appeared, then quickly vanished on the feed.

"Looks like I can get through one of the vent shafts," Cole said, maneuvering the drone by sliding his fingers across his link's display.

Sheridan watched him work, mesmerized at the ease in which his friend operated the tiny machine. He'd tried his hand on drone-wrangling once. It hadn't gone well. He didn't have the patience for it. While piloting, movements needed to be precise and situational awareness acute to the drone's surroundings, a feat Sheridan hadn't been able to master.

The drone left the corridor, slipping through a metal vent and into the rectangular ventilation duct. The slate-gray conduit took the droid straight toward the hanger by, turned vertical ninety degrees, then came to another vent. Cole brought the drove to a stop, floating just inside the conduit, sensors peering out through the vent slats.

The sprinter sat on its landing rails in the middle of a four-hundred square meter bay. The ramps at the bow and stern were down, and a fueling hose was attached to the intake just behind the starboard engine pod. A woman dressed in tactical vest and black fatigues, a rifle slung over one shoulder, stood by the fuel pod ten meters away from the sprinter's ramp, nervously glancing around the bay. Her hair was pulled into a ponytail. A primitive-looking headset cupped one ear, a mic extending from its base to her chin. The drone's sensors drew a red outline around the woman, tagging her on the team's battlenet as Tango-One.

Cole switched the feed to infrared, and the image changed from regular to shades of blues and grays and oranges and reds. Two orange heat blooms moved in the sprinter's cockpit, obviously trying to get the ship started. He marked the final two targets Tango-Two and Tango-Three.

"I make three total targets," Cole said.

"Looks like they're getting ready to jet," Neal said.

"I've got Tango-One," Sergeant Rocha said. "Hanover, you have overwatch."

The element's sniper holstered his pistol and pulled his sniper rifle off his back. He popped the protective shield of his optics and pulled the weapon into his shoulder. "Roger."

"Cole, Sheridan, you have the bird. Get in fast and neutralize those two, got it?"

They both nodded. Sheridan felt the blood pumping in his ears, his heart thumping in his chest. They stacked next to the hatch, Neal working the panel with her link.

"We're in," she whispered, despite her helmet's sound dampening system being all but soundproof. Short of full-on yelling, she could say whatever she wanted, and unless a person was standing right next to her, they wouldn't hear a peep. She swiped away the panel on her link and put a hand on the door. Then, holding up three gloved fingers, she waited for each member of the team to hold up a matching set.

They pushed through the hatch, Rocha through first, followed by the rest. Sheridan and Cole were a quarter of the way to the open ramp when Sheridan heard the soft report of Rocha's MOD27. Two shots in quick succession, followed by a muffled thud. He never took his eyes off the ramp, didn't need to see what Neal had done. He—like the rest of his teammates—knew she'd done her part. Now it was time to do theirs.

"... and tell Ingram to hurry the fuck up!" A male voice shouted from inside.

There was a sharp smack, followed by another male yelling, "I said, stay the fuck down!"

Sheridan reached the ramp first, crouching and using the top end for cover. He only hesitated a fraction of a second before pushing up the ramp, into the sprinter's passenger compartment. The spacecraft was a hybrid—the rear reserved for but devoid of cargo, the forward half for passengers and crew.

Sheridan slowed as he closed in on the back row of seats, his rifle aimed toward the bow, through a short passageway to the cockpit beyond. Two figures stood in the cockpit, facing the sprinter's holodisplays which wrapped the forward end of the compartment.

On the deck, just inside the open hatch, Sheridan saw what he thought was a woman, cowering on the deck behind the two men. She whimpered, pushing herself against the passage's port-side bulkhead. Now fully visible, Sheridan could see blood trickling down the side of her face from a small gash above her right eye. Tears streaked her cheeks.

Biagini being dragged away. Her screams. Their laughter.

Sheridan shook himself, pushing the images aside. *You're not on fucking Stonemeyer!*

Cole's voice came over the taclink, quiet. *"I don't have a shot."*

Sheridan ground his teeth, peering through his optics, trying to convince himself that he could take both, but he couldn't. The passage was too narrow. He'd be able to hit one, but there wouldn't be enough time for the second. Once the first went down, the other would become aware of the team's presence, and that would put the hostage at risk.

Don't have a lot of options, Sheridan thought, rubbing the tip of his finger lightly on the trigger.

"I've got eyes on," Hanover's voice came over the taclink. "Number one, portside, black shirt. Number two, starboard, red vest."

Sheridan adjusted his sights, centering the crosshairs on the man in the red vest. "I've got number two. Be advised, there is a hostage on the floor by the cockpit's hatch. Portside."

"Roger that," Hanover replied.

"Where the fuck is Ingram?" the first pirate shouted again. The man in the black shirt threw up his arms. "If he stopped to fuck with those damn Marines, I'm going to rip his fucking throat out."

Sheridan flinched, hesitating before ducking low behind the seat. He peered over, keeping his rifle trained on the cockpit. "We're running out of time."

"Son of a bitch said it would take five minutes," Black Shirt continued. "We're topped off, tell Yasmin to get up here."

"Number two is moving away," Hanover said as Red Vest turned.

The pirate stepped back to the hatch, and squatted over the woman, touching her face. She flinched away from him, tried to scream, but the gag in her mouth kept her voice muffled.

"Relax, sweetheart. We're going to have a nice little ride out of here," the pirate said, running his hand roughly over her cheek and through her hair. "No one's going to hurt us. Not while we have you." He stood.

"I have a shot," Sheridan said, blood pounding in his ears.

The pirate turned. "We're going to—"

"Take it," Hanover said.

Sheridan pulled the trigger. His MOD27 spit out two rounds. The bullets punched into the pirate's chest, knocking him back. He bounced off bulkhead then stumbled forward out of the cockpit before collapsing to the deck.

The woman scrambled away from the falling man, pulling herself through the short passage, away from the cockpit, eyes filled with terror. She was trying to scream around the gag.

"Go!" Sheridan shouted.

Cole moved first, rushing up the aisle, keeping his body low and his rifle up. Sheridan followed on his heels, keeping his sights just above the woman, watching the raiders.

Nothing is dead until you see it dead, the instructors at MARSOC had drilled into them. *Everything is a threat until it's not.*

Cole reached the woman and pulled her the rest of the way out of the passage, then hauled her to her feet before helping her back into the passenger compartment. Sheridan angled around them, slowing as he approached the raider he'd shot. The man groaned, rolling from his chest to his side.

"I've got a live one!" Sheridan shouted.

He quickly glanced into the cockpit and saw Hanover's target, the body sprawled on the deck, blood pooling around it. Sheridan hadn't heard the shot, or the plastiglass shattering for that matter, but the headless corpse was proof enough of the sniper's marksmanship skills.

Sheridan kicked the man's rifle away and put himself between it and the raider. "Don't do anything stupid. I won't hesitate to put a bullet right through your skull."

The raider glared up at him, teeth bared. It took him a moment to realize what he was looking at, his eyes widened with recognition. "Fucking Alliance."

"Yeah," Sheridan said. "I get that a lot."

Sergeant Rocha appeared with Cole and Neal in tow. "Status?"

"He's not going anywhere," Sheridan said.

"Cardinal lives," the man said. He worked his tongue inside his mouth then bit down on something. There was a high-pitched whistle, and the man's head jerked, eyes bulging out.

"What the fuck?" Cole said, stepping forward.

"Don't touch him," Rocha said, pulling him back.

Sheridan stood there, shocked. "What the hell?"

"Team One what's your status?" Captain Chambers asked.

Rocha looked from Cole to Sheridan to the dead man between them. She shook her head. "Team One up. Shuttle secure."

Sheridan continued to stare down at the now-dead man, trying to process what he'd seen. What had he said? Cardinal. Why did he recognize that name?

Hanover appeared, sniper rifle in hand. He looked past Rocha to the dead raider and made a tsk sound. "Cranial charge. I hear deep-cover spies all have them attached to their cochlear implants. A tiny charge, probably wouldn't sever a finger, but its enough to wreck your brain."

"He killed himself rather than be taken prisoner?" Reese asked, squeezing through the group. He carefully stepped over the headless corpse in the cockpit. "Shit, Hanover, nice work."

The sniper didn't respond.

"You got anything up there?" Rocha asked.

"Yeah, one sec," Reese said, fingers flying over the controls. "Looks like they were heading for a system in the southern end of the URT. Anyone ever heard of Astalt?"

"Nope," Cole said.

Sheridan shook his head. "Me neither."

"Pull the data," Rocha said. "Captain wanted intel, let's bring him some."

CHAPTER 27

ANS *Legend*
Verikus System
31 July 2607

"That's it," Sheridan said, snapping his fingers. "I got it."

Cole pulled his helmet off and ran a gloved hand through his sweat-drenched hair. "What the hell are you talking about now?"

Neal, who was pulling off her tactical vest across the compartment, laughed. "Oh, crap, is Sheridan finally going nuts for real this time?'

They were back aboard *Legend*, doffing their gear in *Valkyrie's* private locker room. The rest of the team were all in various stages of undress, all looking forward to a hot shower and meal after leaving the mining outpost. Not only were they all hot and sweaty, but a fine black powder had seemed to permeate everything, through their clothes in some cases, leaving a dirty, grimy feeling on their skin.

Chambers and Kline were absent, as was Reese, all of whom were presenting the information they'd found on the sprinter's navigational computer to *Legend's* CO. Knowing that information was likely to lead them straight into another battle, the team was determined to get refreshed and refitted as quickly as possible. It was something about being a Saber that no one could impart to someone not on the team. The work is either feast or famine. When it's famine, you train hard for when the shit inevitably does hit the fan. And when it's feast, the work never stops.

"Cardinal," Sheridan said, unclipping his vest and pulling it over his head.

"You're a weird dude, Sheridan," Cole said, shaking his head. "And I mean that sincerely."

"No," Sheridan said, unbuttoning his uniform shirt. "That's what the guy said. Back on the shuttle, before he blew up his head. It finally clicked."

"Alright, you lost me. What did he say?"

Sheridan suppressed a frustrated sigh. "I told you, 'Cardinal.' He said 'Cardinal lives' right before he triggered his charge and killed himself.

"Okay, so who's Cardinal?" Neal asked.

"I don't know," Sheridan admitted. "But it was something that Fischer mentioned back on Cathcart. He said Cardinal was the only clue they had to the whereabouts of Young. He was frustrated because it didn't mean anything to him. They couldn't find anything to reference it with."

"And you know what it means now or what?" Cole asked.

"Well, no… no, I don't. But I know it means something. I'm sure Fischer would be able to figure it out."

Neal pulled an olive-green towel from her locker and tied it around her naked body. Sheridan tried not to look, but in trying not to look, he couldn't help but turn and look. It wasn't anything he hadn't seen before, the teams were unisex. He'd seen Rocha and Neal and the rest naked before, and so far, it hadn't been a big deal. So why was now any different?

Neal arched a single eyebrow at him and smiled. "Yeah, well, good luck getting a message to him. We're on comms blackout, remember? No one's getting any calls out for any reason. Period."

Sheridan pulled his old uniform off, pulled a towel off the rack in his locker and began wiping the sweat from his body. After a quick once-over, he pulled a clean uniform out and started putting it on.

"Where the hell are you going?" Cole asked, pulling his own towel out and wrapping it around his waist.

"I need to talk to Chambers."

Neal laughed. "You might want to wait until he gets back. You know he's talking to the Old Man right now."

Sheridan shook his head. "This means something, I know it does."

"Maybe it does, but maybe it doesn't," Neal said. "Trust me, you don't want to go interrupt the command staff meeting with something like this. Bring it up to the Captain when he's back here, and he'll think about it before presenting to Command. I'm telling you, you don't want to blindside him with this."

"Fischer said he was running out of time," Sheridan said, starting to feel a little desperate. He needed these people to be on his side about this. He knew he was right, he just needed them to back him up. He gave Cole a look, almost pleading for his help.

"I don't know, man," Cole said, shaking his head. "I mean, believe you, but Neal has a point. You don't really know what you know. Don't you want to have some kind of answer or at least something more than a word?"

"Right now, that's all I have. There might not be any more."

Cole held his gaze for a long while, sighed, unwrapped his towel, and started wiping himself off.

"What are you doing?" Sheridan asked.

"Can't very well let you go all the up there on your own. If you're going into the lion's den, I guess I'm going to go in with you."

Sheridan almost told him no, then stopped himself and nodded. "Thanks."

Neal laughed. "You two fuckers are crazy. You call me when you need your asses reattached."

———

Ten minutes later, Petty Officer Second Class Vickers, the master-at-arms on duty outside the conference room, was verifying their link IDs and shaking his head. "Look I'm sorry, guys, but I just can't let you in without prior authorization. I'm sorry."

"Come on, man, you've got to help us out here," Cole said, leaning on the security desk Vickers sat behind.

It wouldn't do any good to argue with him, Vickers was just doing his job.

"I'll call Sarge," Sheridan said. He swiped his link open and keyed in the comm ID for Sergeant Rocha.

She answered a second later. "Sheridan, what's wrong?"

"Sarge, I need to talk to Chambers. It's important," Sheridan said, feeling somewhat foolish. The request made him sound like a schoolboy asking for more ice cream for dessert.

"What the hell are you talking about, Sheridan? Where are you?"

"Outside the Captain's office."

"You're where?" There was a brief pause. "For shit's sake, hold on a second."

Five seconds later, the door to the conference room opened, and Sergeant Rocha stepped out. "What the hell's going on, Sheridan? We're in the middle of Command Staff."

"I know. I'm sorry," Sheridan said. "But listen, that thing that raider said just before he killed himself, I think it means something."

"Yeah, Cardinal, okay. So, what does it mean?"

"I don't know."

Rocha's eyebrows knitted together. "You're killing me, Sheridan."

Cole stepped forward. "In all fairness, Sarge, I told him the same thing."

"No, seriously, I know it means something," Sheridan repeated. "And I think I know someone who can tell us."

"I'm listening," Rocha said.

Sheridan told her about what he and Fischer had discussed during their stopover on Cathcart Station. The entire team knew their history; pretty much everyone in the armed services knew their story for that matter. But Sheridan mentioned it anyway, trying desperately to give credence to his story. He knew in his bones that there was something to this. He just needed to make everyone else see it as well.

Sergeant Rocha crossed her arms as she listened without interruption. When he'd finished, she said, "All right."

Sheridan opened his mouth to press his argument, then caught himself as the Sergeant's words hit him. "What?"

"I said all right. Let's talk to the man." She waved the to master-at-arms. He looked like he was on the verge of refusing to let them pass, but finally relented and pressed the lock for the hatch. It opened with a click and Rocha led them in.

Inside the Captain's conference room was much like every other compartment onboard, bare and utilitarian. However, because of the nature of the space, it was larger than most, complete with a twelve-foot long oval table surrounded by high-backed leather chairs. A table-wide holodisplay showed the Verikus system, along with images of the *Legend*, her squadron of Nemesis fighters and the enemy fleet, all engaged in close-in combat.

Captain Ward sat at the head of the table at the far end of the compartment, Commander Manchester, *Legend's* XO, to his right, and Lieutenant Commander Stinson to his left. There were two or three other officers that Sheridan recognized as command officers, but couldn't place faces with names. Captain Chambers, Master Sergeant Kline, and Sergeant Nguyen sat at the foot of the table. Their vests and armor were sitting on the deck next to their chairs.

The officers around the table looked up as the three stepped into the room. Chambers looked over his shoulder and stood when he realized who'd entered.

"Sergeant Rocha?" Chambers moved around his chair. He stepped closer, and Rocha kept her voice low.

"I'm sorry, sir, but I believe Sheridan has some information you need to hear."

Chambers looked surprised. "Right now?"

"Yes, sir."

Chambers considered Sheridan for a moment, then nodded. "Corporal?"

He'd run through his breakdown in his mind during their trip up, but now that he was here, Sheridan was having trouble finding the words.

Chambers leaned forward, arching both eyebrows. "Sheridan?"

Sheridan shook himself. "Yes, sir. I'm sorry."

"Captain Chambers?" Captain Ward asked. "Is there a problem?"

Chambers straightened and turned back the to table. "No, sir, sorry, sir. If I can have a moment with my man?"

Ward's eyes drifted to Sheridan, curious. He nodded.

"What is it?" Chambers asked Sheridan.

"Cardinal, sir—it has something to do with what Agent Jackson Fischer is working on. He's the agent that found me and arrested Admiral Young."

Chambers nodded. "I'm aware."

"Yes, sir. He mentioned on Cathcart that something about Cardinal was frustrating him. That it had something to do with finding Young like maybe Young was working for this Cardinal person."

"All right, you've lost me," Chambers said, holding up a hand. "Who's Cardinal?"

Sheridan barely suppressed is sigh, but couldn't keep his shoulders from slumping. "The raider I shot today, sir, in the sprinter. He said, 'Cardinal Lives' right before he killed himself."

"Yes, but what is it?"

"I don't know, sir. I don't even think Fischer knew really what it was, but it definitely had something to do with Young."

"What about Young?" Ward asked. He'd stood and moved around the table, obviously listening in to their conversation.

"Sorry, sir," Chambers said. "Corporal Sheridan believes he might have found a connection to Admiral Young's disappearance."

"*Former* Admiral Young," Manchester said, leaning back his chair.

"Of course, sir," Chambers said.

"What about Young?" Ward asked again, this time to Sheridan directly.

I'm beginning to sound like a VR stuck on repeat, Sheridan thought, and repeated his story a fourth time. When he'd finished, he said, "I might not know what it means, but I'm sure Fischer will know what to do with."

Ward considered Sheridan for a long moment, then looked over his shoulder at Manchester who was still reclining in his chair. "Have we verified that navigational data from the sprinter?"

Manchester sat upright again, tapping the table's black mirrored surface with one finger. A panel appeared, glowing orange and hovering over the table. His fingers tapped through several more screens until a holographic star chart appeared, replacing the combat replay from Verikus. Next to the system map, a larger map manifested, showing the systems position relative to the rest of the sector.

"Astalt is a barren system," *Legend's* executive officer said, "listed in our charts as Class Three, uninhabitable, no viable resources. It's well outside any known JumpLanes, the closest system is Siren. About seven days out from that. Two weeks outside of Alliance space, sir."

"Two weeks," Ward repeated, moving closer to the table to look at the map. "Long time to be outside the major Lanes."

"Especially for raiders, Captain," Manchester added. "Logistically, it doesn't make a whole lot of sense. Fuel costs alone make it extremely unfavora…" he trailed off, realization dawning on his face. "Son of a bitch."

Ward was nodding, eyes still tracing the lines of the star map. "That's a hell of a long way to go on a hunch." He sighed, grinding his teeth together.

Sheridan felt the urge to say something but knew he was already in way over his head. It hadn't been his intention to brief Ward. Captain Chambers was one thing, *Legend's* commanding officer was something else entirely. He'd already pressed his luck enough.

And what else do you have to say? Sheridan asked himself.

He really didn't have any information. Cardinal meant absolutely zero to everyone in this room, himself included. And the Captain was right, a two-week roundtrip was an incredible amount of time to dedicate to something so enigmatic.

"And this… Fischer," Manchester said, leaning back in his chair again to see around Ward, "Do you think he'll be able to shed some light on this for us, Corporal?"

Sheridan cleared his throat. "To be honest, sir, I don't know. But I think if anyone will, it'll be him. He's one of the best investigators ASI's got, and besides me, he wants Young more than anyone in the galaxy." He flushed slightly, realizing he might have taken his candor just a fraction to far.

Manchester grunted and leaned forward again. "Orders implicitly state: total comms blackout for the duration unless deemed critical to the continued success of the mission."

"Our mission is the complete destruction of any and all raider ships, fleets, and bases," Ward offered, folding his arms across his chest. "We all know that with the intelligence we've seen over the last few months, the raider attacks have become increasingly frequent, and by all accounts, more organized. That could be a raider base, or it could be a red herring, intentionally left by that raider to throw us off."

"They have been more organized," Manchester agreed. "We saw evidence of that today. The attack fleet they used here in Verikus is proof that they're moving away from smaller two and three ship raiding parties, to larger more sustaining targets. If they'd managed to get away with those tanks of He3, they would've been able to fuel their operations indefinitely."

"Agreed," Ward said. "And knowing what Admiral Hunter expects out this ship and her crew, I'm not sure we have a lot of options here."

Sheridan felt a sinking feeling in the pit of his stomach.

"Break comm silence," Ward said, then he looked back at Sheridan. "Get me Admiral Hunter. Let's see if this theory has merit."

CHAPTER 28

Main Security Office
Cathcart Station, Del Raycu System
31 July 2607

Fischer was getting tired of VR sims. He stretched his neck out and tried to shake the stiffness from his hands. The timestamp on the video told him he was interacting with images one hour before Lenora Piner had been murdered. He'd spent the last few hours walking through Piner's final hours, watching her eat, watching her talk with Gorges, watching her walk through the station as if reliving some treasured childhood memory. Watching her.

The VR sim almost made him feel like he was reliving a person's life, knowing that every step they took was one more step toward their last. When he'd first started working cases like this, after joining ASI, he'd found himself trying to warn the victims, all but pleading with them to make another decision. Now though, he watched with a detached sense of finality, knowing the end was quickly approaching, and only interested in how it actually happened.

He couldn't decide whether that was extremely morbid or not.

He'd only made the mistake of sharing such experiences with Carissa once. After, she'd left the room disgusted, Fischer decided that when Carissa had told him she wanted to be involved in every aspect of his life, she really hadn't thought that particular request all the way through.

Fischer started the feed again, following Piner through one of the many entertainment plazas on board. Every now and then, he'd change the angle, swiping his hands left or right to look at the people around her, watching them to see if they were doing anything suspicious. There'd been a couple times he'd thought someone was watching her, but after several minutes of back-tracking their movements, determined it was just coincidence and moved on.

But every time you're wrong, you lose more time, he told himself. Unfortunately, there wasn't any way around it. If he didn't follow up every hunch or suspect, he might end up ignoring the one that mattered, and he would never forgive himself if he missed something vital.

After another ten minutes of walking, Piner finally reached a mag-lev exchange and rode a pod to her quarters. She entered without issue and locked the hatch behind her.

"Son of a bitch," Fischer said, backing away from the image. The feed was still running, only now it was just an image of the door. He flicked his wrists, pausing his control of the simulation, and rubbed his eyes.

"It's going to happen soon," Tannis said, nodding to the time stamp on the holodisplay in front of him. He was sitting at one of the perimeter consoles, keeping an eye on the program and also watching to make sure Fischer didn't miss anything.

And with our luck, we aren't going to see a thing, Fischer thought, stretching again.

"I'll punch it to time and a half," Tannis said.

The image flickered slightly as it streamed. Occasionally,

Tannis would slow the feedback to regular speed when someone approached, only to speed it back up after they'd moved on. Fischer ground his teeth as the feed progressed, frustrated to once again be stuck in this office, watching VR feeds, waiting for the inevitable.

At some point, you're going to have to get ahead of the curve, Jackson, Fischer told himself as Tannis slowed the feed again.

A man in his fifties came into view, holding the hand of a much younger woman. From the look on their faces, he appeared to be much happier with the situation than she was.

Tannis sped it up again.

"Coming up on fifteen minutes," the security chief said.

Fischer nodded. Fifteen minutes and Lenora Piner would be dead.

You can't stop this one, but maybe you can stop the next one.

It was a lofty ambition, Fischer knew, but he could feel himself slipping into a dark place, and he needed to remember what he was doing all of this for. He was the voice for the people who couldn't speak for themselves, that were unable to stand up and call out their attackers because the worst had been done to them. They couldn't fight for themselves now, so he had to do the fighting for them.

"Here we go," Tannis said, slowing the feed to normal and leaning forward in his chair.

The current angle of the VR showed Piner's door from the direction of this sector's main lifts. A woman approached, her hair dyed blue, done into a bun. She wore a loose-fitting white jacket, and skin-tight, gray leggings tucked into knee-high boots. Even wearing the jacket, Fischer could tell the woman was athletic and fit.

This is her, Fischer thought, lifting his hands to manipulate the VR. He rotated the image as the woman approached Piner's door and touched the panel next to it, giving him a clear view of her face. She was in her thirties, fair skin, and bright green eyes. He captured the image with the wave of a hand and sent it to his link.

"Don't open the door," Tannis murmured behind Fischer.

That's not the way this works, Fischer thought but kept it to himself.

Next to the door, the panel blinked to life. Piner's face appeared, and after a moment, her expression seemed to change. She smiled, and the panel went dark again just before the hatch to her room opened, and the blue-haired woman stepped in.

"She did know her," Fischer said as the hatch closed behind the blue-haired woman.

"Son of a bitch," Tannis said, moving closer to the image. He tapped a control on his link and the image fast-forwarded again. The visitor came out ten minutes later, eyes darting down both sides of the corridor. Then, she headed for the lifts.

"Follow her," Tannis said.

Fischer was already ahead of him, moving the VR to follow on the woman's heels.

"Goddammit," Tannis said. "How could she been so stupid?"

Eliwood shook her head. "She obviously knew whoever that was. Probably didn't have any reason to suspect anything. Old lovers probably."

"How the hell could you tell that from five seconds of VR?" Tannis asked.

"Because she was killed in the bedroom," Fischer said before Eliwood could answer.

Tannis frowned. "That doesn't mean…"

"You're right," Fischer said. "It doesn't necessarily mean that. But, you know Piner better than anyone else here. Do you think she would let her guard down in front of someone she wasn't one hundred percent comfortable with? Much less turn her back on."

Tannis inhaled deeply, jaw muscles flinching. "No."

"Running her biometric data and facial recognition now," Eliwood said.

With the luck they'd had so far, Fischer doubted she'd find anything. He adjusted the view of the VR as Blue Hair descended in the lift, feed becoming spotty as it made its way through the station.

God knows we could use some luck right about now, Fischer thought.

"Fuck," Tannis said, kicking one of the consoles. "It's too fucking late anyway. That bitch is long gone now. She's damn sure not on the station anymore. Even if we do find out what ship she left on, it isn't going to matter."

"It's another piece," Fischer said.

Tannis leaned forward, eyeing Fischer, both hands pressed on the edges of the console. "Pieces of a puzzle that's forever a jumbled mess, Agent Fischer. A case like this... it's not meant to get solved."

Fischer tapped his link, letting the VR run automatically as the lift continued to move through the station. The security chief was upset, and Fischer couldn't blame him. This case was pushing them all to a place none of them wanted to be. Fischer could feel it, and he knew everyone else was feeling it, too.

"We're going to see this thing to the end," Fischer said, trying to come up with something encouraging to say. He needed to keep the morale up, regardless of how he personally felt about it.

"That's fine for you," Tannis said. "But your end isn't my end. Your case is bigger than Cathcart. I get that, but I'm still responsible for those bodies down there. They were killed on my watch, and regardless of how this all turns out, that's still something I have to answer for."

Fischer hesitated for a moment, wanting to argue but also knowing the man was right. These murders had revealed some pretty glaring deficiencies in his station's operational security network and Fischer had no doubt Tannis's bosses would have something to say about that. Hell, for that matter, Fischer's bosses were going to have something to say about it. He was fairly sure Carter would see these events as something beyond their control, but Fischer knew the higher up the chain it went, the more and more unlikely that was to be the case. Someone somewhere was going to have to answer for what was happening, and Fischer was under no illusions about who that someone would be.

His link chimed, the ID surprising him. "Now what?" He accepted the message and waited while it loaded.

"What's up?" Eliwood asked.

"Looks like a message from Jones."

Jones's face appeared on a holopanel above Fischer's wrist. "Fish, you're not going to believe this. Have you ever heard of someone named Cardinal?"

Fischer's pulse quickened as Jones explained everything he'd learned and about the weapons *Firestorm* was in the process of picking up. They'd stopped off at three locations so far, and each time they'd picked up a large number of sealed cargo containers.

"So far, these are the people I've tagged as being involved," Jones said, and three images appeared on Fischer's link.

"Holy shit," Eliwood said.

"This is it," Fischer said, blood pounding in his ears as he stared at the face of the average-looking man who'd followed Fischer at Del Monico's.

The mysterious man stared back at Fischer, taunting him.

"From what I've been able to figure out," Jones continued, "We've got another three stops before we're done and it sounds like Ulara is going to be the last pick up, but I have no idea where we're going after that. That's the one thing they haven't talked about during this whole thing. This ghost-man has been extremely tight-lipped about that. I give us six, maybe seven days, before we get to Ulara. After that, it's anyone's guess. I'll keep you up to date. Jones out."

Fischer slapped his palm down on the console next to him. "This is it!"

"So, I'm just going to play devil's advocate here," Eliwood said. "This thing with the weapons buying, it might not be directly related to Young. It could be something completely different, and we're just going to go racing off after it?"

Fischer shook his head. "There's no way it's a coincidence. Not when people are throwing around the name Cardinal. Not if he's involved." Fischer pointed to the average man.

"But we still don't have any idea who he is," Eliwood said.

"But we know *what* he is. And just look at what he's doing— buying weapons. That's the interlocking piece here."

"The weapons?"

Fischer nodded. "It was exactly what they were doing on Stonemeyer. How much do you want to bet that the stockpile Sheridan and his old platoon found would've been part of this shipment? Hell, it might very well have been the shipment and the Marines messed up their plans when they destroyed it. So, now they have to start all the way back at square one."

"I don't know, Fish," Eliwood said. "That's really thin."

"It's not thin at all," Fischer argued. "It makes sense. This is the break we've been looking for. I need to call Carter."

"And what are you going to tell him? 'So we know where this asshole is going to be. Can we actually do anything about it? I mean, the places these people are going aren't exactly the places we can just walk right into, you know? We can't just take a sprinter out there with an arrest them. We're going to need some firepower."

She was right, Fischer couldn't argue that, but it didn't change anything. They had to do something. He tapped his link. "I'm not going to let that bastard get away."

231

CHAPTER 29

Office of Fleet Admiral Hunter
Alliance Naval Station Phoenix
Solomon System
1 August 2607

"Sheridan and Fischer," Hunter mused, shaking his head. "Those two are a recipe for trouble."

"I don't disagree with you, sir," Special Agent Dan Carter said, the holo-image of his face floating above Hunter's desk. "But I can't fault Fischer's logic on this. And if you put that together with what you've told me from Captain Ward's report…" Carter let the implication hang in the air.

Hunter nodded. "Agreed. However, we need to approach this very carefully. If Fischer is right and this damn thing is bigger than just Young, we can't know who to trust with the information."

"If there's one gun, there's probably two," Carter said.

"I'm sorry?"

The agent shook his head. "Just an old saying in law enforcement, sir. It's common practice while searching; if you find one weapon, you don't relax because you've found it, you proceed like there's a second one, always on your guard."

"It's a good analogy," Hunter said, though the thought of his Navy being infiltrated by traitors and turncoats made his blood boil. *That* was something he couldn't leave behind. "But Young and these weapons aren't the only thing that bothers me, Agent Fischer. They are major objectives, yes—but they aren't the end game. We know Young isn't the only double agent in our midst, we need to be able to root out the rest of them."

"I agree, sir. This is a giant first step, however, and it's closer than we've ever been to putting this whole mess to bed. But I agree, it should be handled very delicately."

"What do your people want to do?"

"Sir, Jackson Fischer knows more about Young and this case than anyone. So, before I get too far into this thing, that's something you should understand. He's worked on nothing else since this whole thing started. He thinks, and I agree, if we charge in, guns blazing, there is a very real chance that we'd destroy evidence or, worse, lose Young again.

"The best chance we have is to grab *Firestorm* and infiltrate whatever defenses these bastards have before taking any action. The closer we can get to Young without him knowing anything, the better. Once we have hands on him, everything else is bonus."

"Bonus is not the word I'd use to describe the situation," Hunter said, trying to keep from thinking the worst about the people he'd served with for his entire career. The thought of those people actively working against him turned his stomach.

It can be that bad, can it? He asked himself. *But what if it is? Can you afford to do nothing?*

Carter pursed his lips. "Of course, sir. I only meant—"

"I know what you meant, Agent Carter," Hunter said, interrupting him. "That wasn't a slight against you, but what we're talking about here is extremely unnerving.

"Yes, sir, it is."

Hunter sighed, looking through the holodisplay at his aide, Captain Reynolds, standing in front of his desk, hands clasped behind his back, patient as ever.

Could you be one of them? No, not a chance.

But still, the thought persisted, and Hunter knew it was only going to get worse. Trust was something not easily earned, but knowing that there were people who'd been able to gain his trust and were also plotting against him cut deep. Hunter hadn't ever been close friends with Marcus Young, but he'd worked with the man for the better part of twenty-five years. Never once had he questioned the man's loyalty and commitment to service.

"Where is your man now?" Hunter asked.

"Fischer and Eliwood are at Cathcart currently," Carter said. "The last information I had on Jones was that he was on his way to Entane following *Firestorm* on her route. As to his exact location, I'm not one hundred percent sure."

"Seems to be the trend with this whole damn operation," Hunter said. "I've never been one to orchestrate from the office, Agent Carter. We need to put these elements together. This thing needs to be handled in real-time, not by old men lightyears away, sitting behind desks or bogged down in committees."

A slight smile crept onto Carter's face. "I agree, sir."

Hunter tapped his link. "All right, Agent Carter, what you're about to be read into is Eyes Only. Do you understand?"

CHAPTER 30

The *Doris*
Clarena System
3 August 2607

The galley on board the *Doris* was small, but the coffee maker worked, and after a rough sleep, it was something of a necessity for the four passengers. Jones sat at the small table at the forward part of the compartment, back against the bulkhead, feet propped up on the table in front of him, steaming mug in his hands. Fischer stood across from him, his own mug in hand, and Eliwood sat longways on the bench, legs stretch across its blue-padded surface. After a warm greeting and handshakes, Loomis had retreated to the cockpit, preferring to nap while they waited for *Legend* to arrive.

Jones and Loomis had dropped in system seven hours after the ASI sprinter delivered Fischer and Eliwood. After transferring the *Doris*, the sprinter which had brought them a day and a half from Cathcart into the middle of the URT, immediately departed, leaving the *Doris* alone in the barren system. Two naked rocks orbited an M Class star well outside the habitable zone and what little astrogation data the Alliance had on them suggested they were less than optimal in available resources.

Which, for their purposes, was perfect. The likelihood of anyone coming across their rendezvous point was slim to none, and it put them within two days of Ulara, the last system on the *Firestorm's* route. Of course, the downside was it also put them out of reach of any Alliance backup forces, until *Legend* arrived, anyway. Not the most exciting position to be in.

"So," Jones said, resting his head against the bulkhead behind him. "What's your big master plan here, Fish? I hope you're not planning on charging in headfirst like you always do."

"I don't *always* do that," Fischer said, looking up from his coffee.

"Yes, you do," Jones said.

"Yes, you do," Eliwood echoed.

Fischer grunted. "You know, to be honest, that's pretty much what I was thinking. Run in, grab Young and get the hell out."

"*If* he's even there," Eliwood added.

"He's there," Fischer said.

"Whether he is or isn't, I don't think you understand what exactly you're talking about doing," Jones said. "This kind of operation... it's not just a rag-tag band of thugs and mercenaries. This is the real deal here. The number of weapons they're shipping, they can arm a damn army and still have some left over."

"Which is why we need to stop them, now," Fischer said.

"And you think you and a bunch of jarheads are going to be able to pull this off?" Jones asked.

"They aren't regular Marines, Jonesy," Fischer said. "They're special ops guys that know their shit. If anyone has a shot in hell to pull this off, it's those guys."

Jones closed his eyes. "All right, I'll take your word for it. Just remember, this isn't like Feringer or Stonemeyer. Stonemeyer was a shitting piece of business, but it was manageable. Been in plenty worse. This though..." He trailed off, leaving the implication hanging in the air.

Fischer shook his head. "I don't think Sheridan would blow smoke up my ass, and I know Admiral Hunter wouldn't. The fact that he suggested this says a lot about what he thinks about them too."

"Not to mention the fact that he's got his own little private warship that no one knows about running around kicking over rocks and burning down houses out here," Eliwood said.

"Yeah, what the hell is up with that?" Jones asked.

"He's doing what needs to be done," Fischer said. "Someone's got to make the tough calls. I, for one, am glad they're out here. We should have done it years ago."

Jones laughed. "You know, that surprises me coming from you."

"Why?"

"Are you kidding? Mister Justice-For-All over here is celebrating what basically amounts to a free-for-all against criminals. I mean, don't get me wrong, I think it's been a long time coming, but don't think for a minute that there won't be people out there that will shut them down and hang them up by their ears once they find out what's going on."

"Not if they can show it's working," Fischer argued. "Unfortunately, some people you just can't reason with."

"Don't have to tell me," Jones said. "Met plenty of those kinds of sons of bitches. I'd rather pick my teeth with a rusty needle than deal with some of these low-life bastards out here."

Eliwood chuckled. "That's ironic."

"What is?" Jones asked.

"Well, I mean, you're one of them, aren't you?"

Jones sat forward, arm on the table in front of him. "I beg your pardon. I'll have you know that I've never been anything but—"

A two-tone alert chimed through the compartment, and Loomis's voice came over the intercom. *"Heads up, boys and girls. The big dogs are here."*

"It's about damn time." Jones pushed himself to his feet and ducked through the forward hatch, heading for the cockpit.

Fischer and Eliwood followed him through the short corridor and into the cockpit where Jones was pulling himself into his elevated flight couch. Loomis sat in his own couch at the nose of the compartment.

Outside *Doris's* wraparound windshield, loomed a warship unlike anything Fischer had ever seen.

"Now, that is a sexy beast," Jones said, fingers dancing over his console. Sensor data populated his screens, identifying various sections of the ship—weapon emplacements, the opening hangar bay doors at the bow. Multiple contacts appeared, immediately streaking off in multiple directions.

"What's this?" Loomis asked. "Fighters? Since when do cruisers have fighters?"

Jones laughed. "Hunter doesn't do anything small, does he?"

"They're hailing us," Loomis said.

Jones glanced around the edge of his flight couch. "This is your party, brother."

Fischer laughed. "The party's just getting started."

CHAPTER 31

ANS *Legend*
JumpLane 4194
1 August 2607

"Your plan," Captain Ward said, standing with his arms crossed in front of *Legend's* main holoplot, "isn't the most ideal."

"Never said it was," Fischer said. "Unfortunately, we don't have a lot of options."

Fischer, Eliwood, Jones, *Legend's* command crew, Captain Chambers, Master Sergeant Kline, and Sheridan were all present in the warship's Command Information Center, which made the already small room feel practically claustrophobic. Fischer had just finished laying out the pieces he and Eliwood had discovered over the last week and fitting those put together with everything the *Legend* had encountered. It painted a pretty bleak picture, indeed.

Above the holoplot in the center of the room, the Ulara way station slowly rotated on its axis, surrounded by several message panels identifying the sections. It was a small station, by Alliance standards anyway. Nothing this small would've been profitable to run outside the Alliance. There just wasn't enough real estate to handle the enormous shipments that came in through places like Cathcart. But in the middle of the URT, a station like this was a haven for operations like Jones'.

"And from what I understand, even if we did, we don't have any time to consider them," Ward said.

"That's true."

Legend's captain sighed, rubbing his chin. "If time is the issue, why wait until all the weapons are loaded? Why not just take the *Firestorm* as soon as they land? It's not like we need them."

"Well," Jones drew the word out with a grimace. "I wouldn't say you don't need them."

"What do you mean?" Ward asked.

"I could be wrong, but I doubt these people are going to be extremely interested in small talk. They're going to want to get right down to business."

Fischer scratched at his beard. "They're going to want to see the weapons, first thing."

"You can be damn sure if they find an empty cargo hold, they're going to know pretty damn fast something's up," Jones added.

"All right, we keep the weapons on board the freighter," Ward said. "But that's an awful lot of responsibly we're taking on here. If those weapons somehow make it out…"

"That won't happen," Fischer said. "We'll make sure of it."

"Even so, I think we're getting a bit ahead of ourselves here," Ward said. "We don't even have custody of the damn ship, much less the weapons inside. And what you're talking about isn't a simple snatch-and-grab. We're talking about nabbing a ship without anyone on the station—or anywhere else in the system, for that matter—noticing, then infiltrating hostile territory for a man that may or may not be there. There are a lot of variables to unpack here. First and foremost, is how do we even get out people onto that station to be in a position to take *Firestorm*."

Jones leaned forward, elbows on the glowing holoplot table, the orange hues casting a strange tint on his brown skin. "You're not going to want to go in guns blazing, I know that. You're going to want to handle this with a bit of finesse. I've been to Ulara once or twice, and while it's no raider stronghold, they're definitely not friendly to outsiders. Especially not outsiders in an Alliance warship."

"Well, unfortunately, Mister Jones, we don't have a lot of other options," Captain Ward said.

"Ah, it's Captain, actually," Jones said, raising a finger. "But, you're wrong. You've got other options; you're just not thinking far enough outside the box."

Ward's eyebrows lifted. "Please, educate us then, *Captain.*"

"Well, for one thing, you drop into system in this thing, it'll be like turning a light on in a dark, filthy room. The roaches are going to scatter everywhere. I'd be willing to bet you won't even get a glimpse of *Firestorm* before you lose her for good. It's the same argument Fish is making for catching Young."

"What are you suggesting?" Ward asked.

"We leave your ship in the Lane and take Doris. We grab *Firestorm*, and we both rendezvous with you back in the Lane.

Next to the captain, Commander Manchester snickered. Jones frowned at him, but Ward ignored it.

"Your ship isn't exactly up to military specs, sir," Ward said. "And while I appreciate your willingness to assist us, I cannot, in good conscience, order my people to carry out such a highly dangerous mission with substandard equipment."

"What are you calling substandard?" Loomis blurted out, stepping forward.

"Hold up a minute, Loomis." Jones put up a hand. "What the hell *are* you calling substandard, Captain? The *Doris* is a pristine piece of craftsmanship. She'll handle anything you can think to throw at her and then some. Hell, I'd be willing to put her up against any of the Nemesis IIs you got out on your deck right now."

A surprised look came over the Captain's face.

"Yeah," Jones said, his expression filled with righteous indignation. "I can tell they're second generation, it's not really that hard, the intake manifolds for the plasma modules are drastically different from the originals and the triple micro fusion is a nice touch, though I don't know that it's all that more effective. What —you don't think an old, worn-out merchant trader is smart enough to pick up on something like that?."

"I never said anything of the sort," Ward said. "The specs on the Nemesis II's are classified top-secret. Have been for years. I'm curious about how you came into possession of those particular pieces of information."

Jones laughed. "Are you serious?" He shot Fischer a sardonic look and pointed. "Is he serious? I've never seen the specs. I could tell that just by looking at the chassis size. Jesus, you guys really think you have everything figured out. Hey, that's fine. You don't want to use my ship, fine. I'd like to see how you get on board that freighter though."

"I—" Ward started.

"And not to mention the fact that you wouldn't have even known about this damn ship if it hadn't been for me and my *substandard* ship—"

"And crew," Loomis put in.

"—and substandard crew," Jones added. He snapped. "How about I just go ahead and bounce on out of here, because you guys obviously have everything figured out."

Fischer held up a hand. "All right, Tensley, you made your point."

"Have I now?"

"Yes," Fischer said. "And you're right, we can't just go in there guns blazing. There are too many variables to the situation. Some we don't even know about."

"What about reprogramming the transponders on the assault boats?" Manchester asked.

Ward chuckled, and Fischer knew why. It'd been the same thing that Lieutenant Meyers had used when he'd rescued three Marines from Stonemeyer after their mission had gone to shit. Fischer remembered standing in the bay, listening to the pilot recount his story. He hadn't been able to take his eyes off the blood on the deck. The smell had almost been overwhelming. And when he thought about what those Marines had been through, and what they'd done, he couldn't help but be revolted all over again.

Fischer quickly pushed the thought away, bringing his mind back to the task at hand. "Won't work."

"Why's that?" *Legend's* executive officer asked.

"Because once we land, they'll know. Hell, once we get into optical range, they'll know who we are. If we're going to take that freighter with the least amount of resistance, we have to be able to get on board and make it out of there without tipping our hat. The *Doris* isn't the entire answer, but it's a start. It'll get us in the door."

Jones didn't say anything, but his smile suggested he was thinking something along the lines of, "I told you so."

Fischer made a point of not looking at his friend, not wanting to give him the satisfaction. Instead, he continued with his break-down. "We're going to need to get close enough to the ship without anyone seeing us coming. How busy do you think this place is going to be, Jonesy?"

Jones shrugged. "I don't know, maybe ten or twenty ships a day, give or take."

"So, not extremely busy but not empty either. That's good, we can use that." Fischer pointed to the station's main docking bay. "We have to operate under the assumption that someone is watching that ship, so we're going to have to figure out a way to get on board without causing a scene, then keeping everything moving like there isn't anything wrong. That's going to be the hard part."

"And do you have any ideas on how we'd pull that off?" Captain Ward asked, crossing his arms.

"We're going to have to wait until the deal is done and they're getting ready to leave," Fischer said. "That'll be the best window for us to make a move. Once they're finished, I'd imagine that if someone is watching, they'll be satisfied and move on. But that's just a guess."

"And what about the takedown, Captain Chambers?" Ward asked, turning to the Marine commander for the first time since their discussion had started.

"My people have trained for these scenarios, yes, but in my experience, battle plans as complicated as what we're talking about here tend to not hold water as well as you think they will. I also don't like sending my team into theater with little to no intel about the objective. We don't know the layout of the ship, nor do we know how many crew she may have. Not to mention what their weapons capabilities are. I don't like that."

"Neither do I," Ward added. "And we'd have to assume that most arms dealers and smugglers are generally ex-military of some kind. Even if they aren't, they'll definitely have weapons."

Chambers motioned to Jones. "You said the crew numbered about ten? Are you sure about that?"

"Hey, I can only go off of what I saw with my own two peepers." Jones used to fingers to point at his eyes. "I saw seven, but there could be more inside that never bothered to show their faces."

"And what do you suggest we do with the crew after we've

taken them into custody?" Ward asked, turning back to Fischer. "I don't think it would be prudent to bring them along with us."

"We'll off-load them as soon as we can," Fischer said, thinking the answer was obvious. "We can have another ship rendezvous with us at a pre-determined location and get rid of them."

"The problem with that is I'd have to clear it through Fleet Command. *Legend* is a top-secret project, the knowledge of her existence is limited to a few select people who aren't on board right now. Before we make any arrangements, I need to get authorization."

"And again," Chambers said, "you're talking about taking an untested ship into a situation which, by all accounts, is probably going to be a cluster-fu—" Chambers's eyes darted to *Legend's* captain.

Ward chuckled and motioned toward the Marine. "No, please, continue. I think that description is very appropriate in this situation. A cluster-fuck is right." He gave Fischer a stern look. "I remember you from the Stonemeyer mission, Agent Fischer, and I remember how determined you were to get the truth. I admired it. But this… this seems like it's something bigger than us."

Fischer felt a flare of irritation swell in his chest. Both men had legitimate gripes, he couldn't hold it against them. If the positions were reversed, Fischer wasn't sure he'd have acted any differently.

"This *is* a cluster-fuck," Fischer said. "I one hundred percent agree. Unfortunately, there isn't anything I can do about it. And while I sympathize, we aren't exactly going up against a hardened military target here, and Jones is the furthest thing from an amateur I can think of. I have no reason to believe that he wouldn't report his observations accurately and succinctly."

"I don't think anyone is calling into question the Captain's assessment of the situation," Ward said. "But as the commanding officer of this vessel, the responsibility for its crew and its mission resides squarely on my shoulders. Knowing that, the decision to proceed is entirely mine, a fact that I'm sure Admiral Hunter will concur with."

"Captain," Fischer said, "I know this may very well be a long shot, but it's a long shot at completing both of our objectives. Your mission is to get rid of the raiders; mine is to find Young. All the evidence I've seen suggests the endgame for both is at the same point, and our window for getting there won't be open long."

Neither men argued. Grateful, Fischer let out a slow breath. It seemed that the tense atmosphere that had been building in the room was quickly dissipating. He didn't like the idea any more than they did, but they didn't have a choice. *He* didn't have a choice.

"All right," Captain Chambers finally said. "Let's say we get aboard the station without any issues—how exactly are you going to acquire this freighter without making a scene?"

"Simple," Fischer said, crossing his arms. "I'm going to walk right up and ask him for it."

CHAPTER 32

The *Doris*
On Approach to Ulara Way Station, Ulara System
2 August 2607

The civilian clothes the Marines wore made them looked like a ragtag band of misfits, which was, Fischer realized, the point. They'd been ordered to select plain clothes for the mission to make their approach less conspicuous. Their body armor stretched their shirts, though several of them had found jackets to help cover their equipment. There was no way to conceal their rifles, but armed raiders wasn't exactly a rare occurrence.

The other half of their team was kitted out in their assault gear: tactical vests, body armor, helmets, weapons. True to form, their gear looked significantly more advanced than regular Marine issue, their reflective, golden visors hiding their faces. They would act as a quick response team in case the first team became engaged and bogged down. If the operation went south, it wouldn't matter how the Sabers were outfitted.

Of course, looking at the team now, Fischer guessed that the rouse wouldn't last under close scrutiny; there was just no way to not see the operator underneath the clothing. Fortunately, Fischer had already been wearing plain clothes and not the suit he typically wore. But as with the Sabers, he couldn't see anything but an investigator staring back at him in the mirror.

The trip in system had been relatively quiet. The way station maintained a high orbit around Ulara-Two, just above the rings that wrapped around the planet's equator. They cleared the outer beacon with no issues, Jones's flight record and ship ID had still been in the station's central net from his last visit to the station.

"We're coming up on the bay now," Jones advised over the *Doris's* internal comm. *"There was an open spot near* Firestorm. *Station control didn't even bat an eye at the request. Externals are up."*

Well, that's one point for us at least, Fischer thought.

He tapped his link, opening a large panel displaying one of *Doris's* external feeds.

The docking bay was expansive, but still small when compared to those on Cathcart. They passed over a group of smaller ships, three corvettes and five frigates, arranged almost like ready fighters prepared to launch and defend the station if the need arose. The frigates dwarfed the *Doris* but wouldn't stand a chance against a warship like *Legend*. But out here, in the middle of the URT, the most common issue was raiders, and Fischer didn't think they were likely to have an issue with that in a place like this.

"There she is boys and girls," Jones said.

A red outline appeared around the medium-sized freighter in the rear section of the bay. *Firestorm* was flanked by two smaller frigates on its port side and a small collection of cargo containers on the starboard side.

"Our landing area is just on the other side of those frigates," Jones said.

"Roger that," Captain Chambers said. He turned to his team,

already assembled at the front of *Doris's* cargo bay. "Eyes up, people. We're inbound."

Together, the Sabers moved closer to their commander—plain-clothed on one side, uniformed on the other. Weapons in hand, visors down, and minds focused. There was no joking or pre-mission jeering. Every Saber seemed to be focused one hundred percent on the task at hand. Calm, collected, and ready to kill.

Fischer envied them. They didn't really have to contemplate the nature of their mission. It was straightforward and to the point. Get in, take the objective, and get out. They didn't have to consider the further ramifications of what would happen to those caught up in the case. For them, this wasn't a potential turning point in their careers. It was just another op. For Fischer, though, this was the beginning of the end for his mission to bring down Young and everyone else associated with him. He didn't even want to consider what would happen if they failed.

Keep that negative shit out of your mind, Fischer told himself. Like the Sabers, he needed to get his head in the game. His fingers brushed against the grip of his pistol. *This is going to work.*

"Looks like our friends are inspecting the last bit of cargo," Eliwood said, pointing to the display floating above Fischer's arm. "Wonder what she's not happy about."

The two arms dealers stood at the base of a wipe loading ramp. Fero had a pad in one hand, obviously double-checking the manifest as the deckhands pushed the large crates of weapons into the ship's hold on gravcarts. Danva stood beside him, her arms crossed, shaking her head, her expression frustrated.

"Maybe they don't serve her kind of caviar here," Jones suggested, his voice echoing around the *Doris's* bay.

"If she's frustrated about something it might give us an advantage," Fischer said, ignoring his friend. "Her mind might be on other things and not fully on her surroundings."

"Doesn't matter what her mind is on," Kline said. "We'll handle her, irregardless."

For a brief moment, Fischer almost corrected the Saber's word use, but quickly decided against it. From the look on the sergeant's gruff face, he probably wouldn't take too kindly to Fischer's thoughts on his grammar.

"All right people, everyone knows their assignment," Captain Chambers said. "We're going to move fast and with a purpose. Agent Fischer will make initial contact. After he's done that, we'll move in and secure the ship. Master Sergeant Kline and the QRF will be here on standby. If anything goes wrong, we retreat to the *Doris* and exfil. Any questions?"

There were none.

"Touch down in thirty seconds," Jones said.

The group of Sabers separated. The assault force shifted to the back of the bay, near the still-closed ramp. The quick response force marched out of the way, staying near the front. A small workstation had been set up where Reese and Robalt, the team's two electronics specialists were already working, attempting to infiltrate the station's security network.

"Robbi, how are we looking on the intrusion?"

The Saber didn't look up from his screens. "The network node shell is pretty straightforward, Cap, but the framework is more complex than I'd anticipated."

"Can you do it?" Master Sergeant Kline asked.

"Can I do it?" Robalt asked. "Sarge, do you know what's cool about being a Marine Tech Specialist?"

Beside Fischer, one of the plain-clothed Marines rolled her eyes, "Oh, shit. Here we go."

Kline crossed his arms and tilted his head to the side. "What's that, Robbi?"

"I can ruin your credit score, change your security rating, and reroute your savings account to your ex-girlfriend who's soaking up the sun on the Nine with her new boyfriend without you even knowing a thing. Oh, and I can put a bullet through your ankle from five-hundred meters and really fuck up your day."

Kline laughed. "Only problem is, I've seen your range reports, and I know that's bullshit."

A ripple of laughter went through the team. Robalt shook his head, "It was fucking windy that day. Damn."

"We're through," Reese said, tapping on his screen, then spreading his hands apart over its surface, expanding the panel he was working on. "We'll have the primary security routines isolated in a few seconds."

That seemed to satisfy Kline. He nodded, and he moved away, giving his people room to work. Fischer had served under countless supervisors over his career, and both Kline and Chambers seemed like they'd be the decent sort you'd want to be under. No micromanagement Trusted their people. As simple as that seemed, in Fischer's opinion, that trust was the single most valuable aspect of being a good leader. If trust were an issue, everything else would be as well.

"Rails down in ten seconds," Jones said.

Fischer and Eliwood approached the ramp opposite the Marines and Fischer grabbed the railing above the door, holding on as the *Doris* flared for landing. The sound of the engines reverberated through the hull and the deck rumbled under his feet.

A series of mechanical clanks announced the ramp's opening, and the pistons on either side whined as it lowered. Fischer bent, scanning everything he could, looking for any sign of trouble. Aside from a few deckhands here and there, the bay was relatively empty. He didn't see any sign of security personnel anywhere.

Guess when it comes to criminals policing criminals, they

figure everyone will just take care of their own, Fischer thought, slowly descending the ramp. Eliwood followed, staying close.

The frigate between *Doris* and their target was a bulky, rectangular ship that had obviously been built with capacity in mind and not aesthetics. They gave the ship's flat bow a wide berth, not wanting to incur any undue ire from the ship's crew and draw more attention to themselves. A couple of crew looked up from around one of the landing rails where they were working on something, but they looked away after a few seconds, disinterested in the new arrivals.

And who would ever want to come here and cause trouble? Fischer thought.

The whole station was crawling with criminals who'd sooner throw someone out an airlock than deal with the possibility of capture.

As *Firestorm* came into view, Fischer saw Fero and Danva standing at the base of one of the ramps, supervising the loading operation.

"No sign of Target One," Fischer said.

"Roger," Chambers responded.

The man Jones had dubbed 'Average Man' had been with them throughout the operation, according to Jones, and Fischer hoped that not seeing him on the deck was just a sign that he thought himself above the operation and was stuck inside the ship.

But what if he's not? Fischer asked himself, momentarily slowing his gait. But there wasn't anything they could do about it now. They were committed. *He's going to be here.*

Five crates, all floating on gravcarts, waited on the deck for their turn to be loaded into the ship. A group of deckhands jogged down the ramp, moved to the two nearest containers, then tapped links, obviously accessing the gravcart's controls. Within seconds, they were connected and running, maneuvering the containers up the ramp and disappearing inside the ship.

"How're we looking on that interference?" Fischer asked under his breath.

Robalt answered him over his link's implant. *"You're clear, Agent Fischer. They're not seeing anything we don't want them to."*

"Fantastic."

Fischer approached, using the remaining containers to conceal his approach as long as possible. He slowed as two more deckhands came down the ship's ramp, both caught up in conversation, not paying any attention to what was going on around them. They moved to collect their containers, oblivious to Fischer and the team a dozen meters behind him, acquired their containers, and maneuvered them toward the ramp.

Here we go, Fischer told himself, stepping out from behind the final container, approaching the two smugglers.

"Nice looking ship you got there," Fischer said as Fero looked up from his datapad.

Danva, who'd been reading the pad over his shoulder, looked up, her brows knitting together, hand casually moving to the small of her back.

Don't do anything stupid, Fischer thought, mentally willing the Sabers behind him to keep their cool. Marines, in general, were naturally distrustful of anyone they didn't know, and Fischer had no doubt that the men and women behind him were no exception. He just needed everyone to keep their cool for a few more seconds.

"Get the fuck out of here, man," Fero said, waving Fischer off. "We ain't offering rides."

"Oh, sorry," Fischer held up his weak hand, his gaze flicking from Fero to Danva as he twisted his body ever-so-slightly, his right hand slowly moving back. "Don't want any problems, friend. Don't need a ride. Just being friendly is all."

"We don't need any more friends," Danva said. Her hand was now on her weapon, ready to draw at a moment's notice. "Get lost."

"What type of ship is that anyway?" Fischer asked, motioning to *Firestorm's* bow.

"Are you fucking deaf?" Fero asked, lowering the datapad to his side.

"I can hear just fine," Fischer said. "Just interested in the ship is all."

Fero hesitated for a moment, obviously confused as to why this stranger was approaching him about his ship. "What the hell do you want?"

In one smooth motion, Fischer closed the distance to the dealer, drew his pistol and held it to the man's stomach. "Don't fucking move."

"What the—" Fero grunted as Fischer pushed his pistol hard into his gut, cutting him off.

Eliwood stepped up beside Fischer, her own weapon leveled at Danva's nose. "Don't even think about pulling that thing."

Danva froze, her eyes locked on Eliwood, filled with hate and anger.

"Now, slowly, move your hand away from that gun," Eliwood told her.

Two Sabers slinked past, stepping behind the two dealers and relieving them of their weapons.

Danva's face flushed red. "Do you have any idea who you're fucking with? This isn't just another cargo run. Do you have any idea who you're stealing from? You really fucked up."

"Yeah," Fero sneered. "Cardinal doesn't take too kindly to people fucking with his shit."

Fischer couldn't help but smile. "Cardinal, huh? As a matter of fact, I'd very much like to meet with this Cardinal."

"You don't know what you're talking about," Danva said. "He'll kill you just for interfering this much. Your best option is to drop that fucking gun, walk away and forget you ever saw us or this ship and its cargo. He might only come after you and your immediate family."

"This Cardinal doesn't scare me," Fischer said. "Just another asshole, trying to make life difficult for the rest of us."

"You're mistaken," Danva said, her voice calm and steady. Her anger diminished somehow. "You literally just walked into your deaths."

Fischer said, motioning up the ramp. "Let's talk about it inside."

CHAPTER 33

Commercial Freighter *Firestorm*
Ulara Way Station, Ulara System
2 August 2607

"Keep your hands up," Sheridan ordered, his pistol leveled at a crew member as she stood from her station. It felt wrong somehow to be taking action like this without being in uniform, like it was underhanded or illegal. It almost felt like they were actually stealing the ship, like they were the pirates.

The woman, dressed in dirty gray overalls, her hair pulled back in a messy bun, glared at Sheridan. "What the fuck is this?"

"Just get up," he said, motioning with his MOD27.

Cole and Neal edged by, each taking an arm and securing her wrists behind her back with electrocuffs.

The woman shook her head as Neal pulled her away from the station. "You're insane. Do you know what happens to people for jacking a ship like this? You guys are totally fucked."

"Since when is a criminal like you concerned about the law?" Sheridan replied.

"Law?" she laughed. "Who said anything about the law? I'm talking about the one who owns all of this."

"We don't really give a shit about your boss, lady," Neal said, ushering her out of the compartment. She toggled her taclink. "We've got one in custody. Moving to control."

"Roger that," Reese said.

The team had split up into three small squads, searching the ship and arresting the crew. Fortunately, Chambers and Reese had been able to make it to *Firestorm's* command deck and take it over before anyone had realized what was going on. This woman was, as far as they could tell, the last one.

Sheridan brought up the rear as they left the compartment, glancing over his shoulder as he stepped through the hatch, conducting one last scan of the room before leaving. They hadn't missed anything—the compartment was clear—it was just a feeling he had. He hesitated in the hatch, then turned to follow the others through the dimly lit corridor.

Like everything else aboard the freighter, the corridor was unfinished; lined with conduits and cables, exposed lighting panels and air ducts. The grated metal decking echoed under their boots. It was three times the width of most of the corridors on *Legend*, a result of needing space to move pallets of cargo around the ship to various bays. Despite the larger corridors, *Firestorm* had less than a quarter of the operating space *Legend* had, the rest dedicated to cargo capacity.

Several of the over-sized corridors branched off from the central passage, occasionally interconnected by smaller ones—that would be standard size aboard any other ship—leading to other cargo bays and sections of the ship. Cole paused before the intersections of each, working his drones, clearing the corridors ahead of them, then continuing. The glow of his link reflected off the bulkheads on either side, the holodisplay leading them through the bowels of the ship.

"Goddamn Alliance thugs," the woman growled. She pulled against Neal's hold but didn't fight. It was more posturing than anything.

"Take it easy," Neal said, pulling her back.

"Oh yeah, such big bad Marines," the woman said.

"Shut up," Neal told her.

"Hey, I've got movement ahead," Cole said, stopping. "No visual yet, just movement, maybe someone heading to the crew berths. I'm going to—Whoa, what the hell?"

"What's wrong?" Sheridan asked.

Cole's fingers frantically tapped on his link. "Just lost the drone."

Sheridan stepped closer to get a better look at the screen and immediately felt foolish. He wasn't going to know anything more than Cole did about the data. "Ship interference?"

Cole shook his head. "Not a chance. The drones have multiple redundant operational connections. Not only that, but they're designed to operate independently should I ever lose telemetry. This one just dropped off completely. Like it's just not there." He tapped his link, cycling through several diagnostic panels, but having no luck.

"Someone took it out?" Sheridan suggested. He knew it was unlikely, but it was the only thing that made sense.

"Gotta have some pretty decent gear to drop a drone like that without any warning," Cole said. "Maybe it's Fischer's mystery man."

Sheridan tapped his taclink. "Valkyrie-One, Seven-Alpha, be advised, one of our drones was just taken offline."

"Not so tough without your gear, are you?" the woman said. "You're fucked now."

Neal pulled the prisoner across the corridor, away from Cole and Sheridan. "Shut the fuck up!"

"Roger that, Seven-Alpha," Master Sergeant Kline said. *"We've got two heading to the crew berths now from Control."*

"Copy that—"

A loud crack echoed down the corridor, and Neal's body jerked to the side. She grunted in pain but never lost her grip on the woman's arm. She pushed herself up from a knee and pulled the woman to the opposite side of the corridor, pressing them both behind one of the steel ribs separating the sections of the ship.

"Son of a bitch!" Neal shouted.

"That's what you get, you bitch," the woman shouted.

"Shut the fuck up," Neal shouted and slammed an elbow into the woman's jaw. The woman's head snapped back, thudding against the bulkhead, and her eyes rolled back into their sockets as she slumped to the deck. Neal grabbed her side, wincing.

Sheridan took a knee across from them, bringing his rifle up but not finding a target. "You okay?"

Neal pulled her hand away, her gloved fingers red with blood. "Fuck."

"Six-Alpha, Valkyrie One, we're under fire. Corridor Three-Two, Section Eighteen," Cole said over the taclink.

"Son of a bitch," Neal said through gritted teeth. "That stings."

"Four-Alpha is hit," Cole continued. "GSW to the right side."

"Six-Alpha, One. Can you rally on our location?" Master Sergeant Kline asked.

"I can move," Neal said.

"No, don't," Sheridan said. "Stay there. Six-Alpha, we need a medic here, ASAP."

"Richards is on his way," Kline said.

Cole pulled out another drone from a pocket on his thigh, thumbed the activator and tossed it into the passageway. He tapped his link to access his drone's feed. "Clear to fifty."

"I'm fine," Neal said. "Go get that son of a bitch."

Sheridan hesitated. "You sure?" He looked at the unconscious woman on the deck.

"If she wakes up again, I'll fucking thump her good. Go!"

Sheridan nodded and keyed his taclink. "Seven-Alpha, we're moving to pursue."

"Copy that, Seven, proceed with caution," Kline said.

"How's it look," Sheridan asked Cole.

"Clear to a hundred," Cole said without taking his eyes from his link's display. "Looks like someone is heading toward the crew berths.

"Come on," Sheridan said. He stepped in front of Cole, his rifle up, one eye peering through the optical scope, the other open and watching the corridor ahead. Without his HUD there was no battlenet display to identify targets or show him the ship's layout. He would have to rely on his own eyes and the weapon's enhanced holographic sight. The square optic would highlight and range any target in its field of view.

"Seven-Alpha, Valkyrie-One, Two-Bravo, and Three-Bravo are heading to your position," Master Sergeant Kline advised.

"Roger," Sheridan muttered, slowing as he reached the end of the corridor where it branched off through the length of the ship. He peered around the corner, then rolled quickly into the corridor, keeping himself pressed close to the starboard bulkhead.

He glanced down at his link, checking his position. The crew berths were another hundred meters forward.

What the hell does he want there? Sheridan asked himself, steadily advancing through the corridor, trying to keep the sound of his footfalls to a minimum. In the empty passage, however, it was nearly impossible. Every step sounded like a herd of charging elephants.

Sheridan stopped just aft of the hatch on the port side and waited for Cole to cross to the other side. Sheridan tapped the hatch control panel, which glowed to life, blue light illuminating the dark passage around them.

"Hold up," Cole said, crouching. He pulled another drone from his pocket and nodded to Sheridan. Sheridan tapped the control, and as the hatch slid open, Cole tossed in the drone, immediately taking control from his link and piloting the tiny device into the compartment.

Sheridan pulled his rifle in close to his chest, barrel down and lifted his chin to his partner. "Why don't you just let those things free-fly?"

"You kidding?" Cole whispered, tapping his link. "You know how temperamental these things are?"

Sheridan tapped his own link, bringing up the feed from the drone. The crew section was designed around an ample common space that took up two full decks. The fifty-meter-long compartment contained several tables and chairs and two counters for serving food at the far end. Five hatchways on either side of the space led to the crew cabins on the main level and on the higher second level, accessed by a metal walkway and stairs at either end.

The room was empty.

"Bastard's holed up somewhere," Cole said. "Switching to thermal."

The feed floated slowly around the room, rising to just below the ceiling, then panning its sensor suite across the space in a slow, methodical motion. A blue hue saturated everything in the image, the indigo tables and chairs outlined in a slightly lighter shade of navy. A path of lavender footprints weaved through the space—residual heat left from their quarry.

"You see that?" Cole asked.

Sheridan nodded.

The path led up the stairs at the far end of the compartment, then backtracked to the second-to-last cabin on the port side.

"Valkyrie One, Seven-Alpha, we've located the rabbit," Sheridan said. "Break, Seven-Alpha, Two-Bravo, can you guys come in from the bow?"

"Stand by," Sergeant Trevion, Team Two's medic, said. *"Checking."*

"Two-Bravo, that's affirm," Reese said. *"Keep heading forward, I'm sending you the path now."*

"Copy that," Trevion said.

"Looks like there's a camera on that hatch," Cole said, pointing at his screen. "As soon as we get close he's going to see us."

Sheridan saw it, too—a small module centered on the top of the door frame.

The hatch to the cabin their attacker had entered was closed, but the heat around the handle still glowed orange. It hadn't been long since it'd been touched. Cole cycled a new spectrum, turning the display black, it showing the occupant inside in an outline of orange and red. The figure was standing at the back of the room, hands and fingers moving over a keyboard.

"Gotcha," Cole said.

"What the hell is he doing?" Sheridan asked.

Cole shook his head, then toggled his taclink. "Reese, you got an eye on what that asshole is doing in there? He's going to town on his terminal."

"Yeah, stand by. Looks like he's trying to access the engineering routines," Reese answered, *"I'm going to try and lock him out."*

"Engineering?" Sheridan asked. "He can't fly the ship from his room, can he?"

"No, but he can overload the reactor core and blow it up," Reese said. *"He's got some fairly powerful programs running. Not sure I can crack his connection."*

"We need to get in there," Sheridan said. "Reese, can you access that camera feed?"

"Negative, it isn't tied into the main system. It's gotta be a local set up, no way to access it."

"And there's no way of telling what kind of weapons he's got in there either," Sheridan said.

"Seven-Alpha, Two-Bravo, we're in position at the bow side," Trevion said.

"Copy that, Two-Bravo, stand by there," Sheridan said.

The bow hatch was on the opposite side of the compartment from their target's room. They'd have a clear shot, but so would he.

"Back your drone off," Sheridan told Cole. "Can you give me an overall?"

"Yeah, one sec." Cole moved the drone to the corner left of their hatch, and high up on the bulkhead, almost touching the ceiling.

Sheridan studied the image, visualizing various approaches, running through options in his mind.

"What about shutting down power to the section?" Cole asked.

Sheridan shook his head, but Reese answered before he could. *"I shut down power; it kills everything, including life support."*

Without their gear, Cole and Sheridan would have to evacuate before Reese could even start the shutdown process. Powering down would take time, not to mention the time it would take for both Marines to reach a safe area, and time was something they didn't have in excess.

"Reese," Sheridan said over the taclink, "do you have door control access?"

"Wait one." There was a brief pause, then Reese said, *"Negative, looks like he's either disabled the hatch controls or taken them off the main system. I have no access."*

"We've got to get in there and stop him," Sheridan said, inching closer to the door.

"As soon as we step into that room, he's going to know we're in there," Cole said.

Sheridan nodded, thinking. Finally, he said, "Trevion, you have your dazzlers with you?"

"That's affirm," Trevion answered.

Cole stepped closer to Sheridan, looking past him through the hatch. "What are you thinking?"

"I'm thinking they can distract the asshole while we make entry and take this guy out," Sheridan said.

"All right, good plan. Except for the part about how we're going to take him out? He's behind a sealed hatch with eyes on."

Sheridan slipped his pistol back into its holster and tapped his link display off before bringing his rifle back around to his front and pulling the stock into his shoulder. "I'm counting on it."

CHAPTER 34

Crew Berths
Commercial Freighter *Firestorm*
2 August 2607

"On three," Trevion said over the taclink.

Sheridan tensed, his left hand on the partially open hatch in front of him. "Stay close."

"I'm there," Cole replied.

"... one, go!" Trevion said.

The hatch at the far end of the compartment opened and three seconds later, Trevion's dazzler went off with an earsplitting crack. Light flashed around the edge of the hatchway, the steel vibrating in his hand.

Sheridan pushed the hatch open and ducked through, immediately shifting right, keeping close to the bulkhead. He scanned the space, seeing a small line of smoke curling up from the floor where Trevion's dazzler had exploded.

With his rifle up, Sheridan reached the starboard edge of the room and pressed forward, passing the closed hatches on the lower levels.

"Heads," Trevion said over the taclink. *"The hatch is opening."*

Five shots rang out, the flashes barely visible to Sheridan from his position below the second level walkway. Sparks jumped from the bulkhead around the open forward hatch, sending resounding clangs echoing around the compartment.

"Come out!" Sheridan shouted. "There's no other way out of this!"

Five more shots rang out. Sheridan slowed, inching out from the bulkhead slightly, trying to see around the edge of the walkway above him. He caught a brief glimpse of a weapon, then it was gone, and the hatch slammed shut again.

"He's gone back in," Sheridan advised. "Guerrero, you got your Ramsey launcher?"

"You're goddamn right I do," Guerrero said.

"All Valkyrie elements, this is Actual, hold. I say again, hold," Captain Chambers ordered over the taclink.

Sheridan froze. He glanced over his shoulder as Cole came up behind him and mouthed, "What the fuck?"

Cole shook his head.

From beneath, Sheridan eyed the walkway above him, his rifle up and ready for the bastard to make another appearance. Two side steps to the left and he'd have a shot. He could end this with two or three well-placed rounds to the chest. The longer they waited, however, the closer whoever it was got to blowing up the ship.

He hadn't made any demands, hadn't ordered him back, hadn't said anything. In Sheridan's mind, that meant the man didn't have any intention of leaving. This was a murder-suicide mission, and he was dedicated to accomplishing his assignment.

"What are we waiting for?" Cole hissed behind Sheridan, pressing close to his back.

"I don't know." Sheridan adjusted his grip on his rifle and

eyed the hatch across the compartment. Trevion and Guerrero were slipping through the opening. Trevion moved to the forward bulkhead and took cover behind one of the tables, crouching as low as he could. Guerrero slipped around him, and her Ramsey launcher unpacked and held in both arms, her rifle slung behind her back.

Sheridan ground his teeth and shook his head. "Seven-Alpha, Actual, we are in position. Requesting permission to go."

"Negative, stand by one." There was a pause, then Captain Chambers spoke again. *"All Valkyrie units, be advised, the subject is a high-value target. I say again, he has been identified as a priority. Our instructions are to apprehend if at all possible."*

"What the fuck is he talking about?" Cole asked. "How the hell could they know that?"

"Roger that, Actual," Sheridan responded. "Break, Reese, any luck with that hatch?"

"Negative, I have no access."

For fuck sake, Sheridan thought.

"How the hell are we going to *apprehend* anyone?" Cole asked. "We blow that door, he's just going to come out shooting. We'll have no choice but to shoot back."

"Agreed," Sheridan said. He eyed the hatch on his right. "Reese, can you open the hatch next to me, third up from the stern, starboard side."

"Roger, stand by," Reese said.

A moment later the hatch slid open, and Sheridan got a look inside the cabin. Like sleeping berths on most ships, the cabin was small and longer than they were wide. A single mattress hung from the aft bulkhead, and a private latrine and wardrobe took up the bow side.

"Whatever we're going to do, we need to do it fast," Reese advised over the taclink. *"He's just broken through the first layer*

of security around the engine core. I estimate another five minutes before he's all the way through. Ten at most."

"We can cut through the hatch," Cole suggested.

"It'll take too long," Sheridan replied. "And then there'll be no question of our position."

"What about mechanical access?" Cole asked. He'd sent his question over the taclink as well.

Reese answered. *"No dice. Looks like there's about a foot of bulkhead, conduit, and cabling along the backside and overhead."*

The idea hit Sheridan like a freight train. "What about between the rooms. The top and bottom, I mean?"

"About fifteen centimeters of space, some power conduits and water and air ventilation."

Sheridan thought about that for a moment, trying to picture it in his mind. Finally, he pushed his rifle around behind him on its sling and said, "Shouldn't be a problem. Cover me."

"What are you doing?" Cole asked, moving forward, lifting his rifle.

"You remember the *Bulalo*?" Sheridan looked up at Cole, who's eyes widened in disbelief.

They hadn't worn all of their tactical gear, but he'd brought his modular pack. The small kit was affixed to his belt at the small of his back. He reached behind and opened the pack, searching the contents with his fingers until he found what he was looking for. He pulled out an eight-inch cylinder sealed in plastic wrap, marked with red and yellow alternating lines.

"You're kidding, right?" Cole asked. "Tell me you're kidding."

Sheridan peeled off the protective wrapping. "Cole, you still have your eyeball? I need to see where this guy is."

Cole hesitated, shaking his head as Sheridan stepped onto one of the mattresses.

"Come on," Sheridan said.

Cole opened his link without a word and went to work. Sheridan tapped his own link, accepting the feed from the drone as it neared the exterior of the room above. The man was working on his terminal at the backside of the room again, almost directly above where Sheridan now stood.

Sheridan put one foot on the counter along the back of the cabin, then popped the cap off the can of HX-7, reached up, and drew a line across the slate gray ceiling. The pale pink liquid, sealed in vacuum inside the can, turned to foam once it contacted the oxygen in the cabin, adhering to the ceiling, expanding slightly, and becoming an adhesive resin.

He worked his way around the ceiling, creating an oval shape. He pulled a cap out and pressed it into the gel.

"That's not going to work," Cole said.

"It'll work," Sheridan said, stepping down off the bunk. He tapped his link, syncing with the detonator he'd just implanted into the foam and nodded for the hatchway. "Come on."

"You're a crazy son of a bitch, you know that?" Cole asked on his way out.

Sheridan ducked through the hatch and pressed his back against the bulkhead. "I've been told that on occasion." He toggled his link and kept his voice low. "Seven-Alpha to all Valkyrie elements. Fire in the hole, fire in the hole, fire in the hole."

Before anyone could countermand him, he tapped his link and turned away from the hatch.

The explosion shook the ship around him and sent a cloud of smoke and dust shooting into the common area. Sparks shot from light panels along the ceiling as their circuits overloaded and blinked out. Pressure lines burst all along the compartment blowing out panel covers and sending debris spinning. Half of the chamber went dark, illuminated only by the flickering emergency lighting and the occasional burst of sparks.

Without the sound dampeners in his helmet, Sheridan's ears rang, a high-pitched noise that drowned out everything around him. He worked his jaw open and shut, shaking his head, trying to relieve the ringing, but it did no good. Then, he remembered what he'd been trying to do in the first place.

Sheridan pushed off the bulkhead and ducked through the hatch, into the room, pistol up and ready. He squinted, trying to see through the haze of dust and smoke, holding his breath as he stepped further in. He saw the vague outline of a man lying on the deck, face-up, his arms spread to either side, eyes closed. Sheridan knelt down beside him, pressing a finger to the man's carotid. There was a pulse.

Cole appeared next to him, shaking his head. "He okay?"

"Hey's alive." Sheridan pulled a pair of electrocuffs from his thigh pocket and slapped them on.

"Holy shit, man," Cole said. "Blaster is right."

"He's alive, just unconscious," Sheridan said. "Help me get him out of here."

They dragged him into the common area, carefully laying him on the deck between two tables. Trevion and Guerrero jogged up, their helmets and visors obscuring their faces.

When Trevion spoke, his voice was muffled and digitized by his helmet's external speakers. "You're one crazy son of a bitch, you know that?"

Sheridan grinned at Cole, who grinned back, still shaking his head. "That's the rumor." He keyed his taclink. "Valkyrie Actual, Seven-Alpha, be advised, VIP secure, and alive."

"Roger that Seven," Captain Chambers said. *"All Valkyrie elements, rally in control."*

"Copy that, Actual," Sheridan said. "We're en route."

The Bridge
Commercial Freighter *Firestorm*
2 August 2607

"His vitals are fine," Corporal Richards said. The medic rose and stepped away from their prisoner, packing his handheld field scanner and setting it on the small cart next to the cot. "Some bruising, possibly a concussion, but other than that, he came away fairly unscathed."

Fischer crossed his arms, trying not to fidget. The Average Man— the man who'd followed Fischer on New Tuscany, who'd killed at least one of their witnesses, and who was likely behind the deaths of several more—lay secured to a cot, hands bound to the sides, chest strapped down. His breathing was shallow, and his fingers twitched occasionally. He was alive, and it was everything Fischer could do *not* to shake the bastard awake.

You're mine now, you son of a bitch, Fischer thought.

"Any damage to the ship's internals?" Chambers asked. He stood on the other side of the cot, hands resting on the pistol grip of the rifle slung across his chest.

Corporal Reese looked up from his terminal. "Blaster here took out most of the terminal, but I managed to segregate everything he was using to infiltrate the system and quarantine the malicious code. Scrubbers'll have it completely deleted in a few minutes. Shouldn't have to worry about the engines blowing up around us now."

"Shouldn't?" Master Sergeant Kline asked.

"Yeah, well, unless there's another mysterious suicide bomber on board I don't want to say for certain. Then again, we can just put Blaster on it."

Kline shook his head. "Blaster, huh?" He put a hand on Sheridan's shoulder. "It does have a certain ring to it, doesn't it?"

Sheridan winced. "Eh, I'm not sure about it, Sergeant."

"I like it," Kline said. "Nice work, Cole."

Cole chuckled. "You got it, boss."

"That was some quick thinking, Corporal," Chambers said. "Good work."

"Thank you, sir."

"You're creating quite a reputation for yourself."

Sheridan rubbed his chin, covering a smirk. "That wasn't my intention, sir."

"The best nicknames are the ones you earn," Master Sergeant Kline said. "I can't remember the last time we had a rookie who had such a fascination with bang. Can you, Captain?"

Chambers shook his head. "I cannot."

They were obviously having some good-natured fun with him, but Fischer couldn't have been more grateful for Sheridan's quick thinking. Regardless of the method used, he finally had the opportunity to ask the questions that had been burning inside him for months. He'd all but convinced himself that he might never actually find this man, that he was truly a ghost and that there would be no answers. Now, it seemed, all of his months of waiting were about to pay off.

"It's a good thing he does," Fischer said. "This could've very easily gone the other way."

"We'll rendezvous with *Legend* in about an hour. Once we offload the rest of the prisoners, we'll get you into a secure room with our friend here," Chambers said.

The crew had all been rounded up, and were being held in the cargo bay at rifle point. No one had said anything about the Average Man. In fact, everyone had denied knowing him at all, even knowing that he'd been on the ship in the first place. Instead of getting answers to his questions, Fischer had just ended up with more questions.

More than anything, Fischer wanted to get this man back to New Tuscany. He wanted to get him in a room, with access to the Agency's advanced bio-neural sensor suite, retina scanner, brain activity monitor. He wanted to be able to see, without a doubt, whether or not his man was telling the truth.

Unfortunately, Fischer didn't have that kind of time. He needed answers yesterday. If this ship was going where Fischer thought it was, they didn't have much time at all. They needed to get the answers en route to their destination, and they needed to make sure that this ghost was nowhere near that place when they finally got there. Too many things could go wrong with this plan as it was, they didn't need to introduce any unknown elements if they didn't need to.

"Can you wake him up now?" Fischer asked the medic.

Corporal Richards winced, giving Captain Chambers a side-long glance. "I'm not sure that's a great idea, sir. I mean as long as he's unconscious he's not a danger to himself or anyone else if he wakes up and causes a ruckus…"

"I'm sure it won't come to that," Fischer said, hoping it was true.

Captain Chambers cleared his throat. "Agent Fischer, I understand your desire for information here, but we have to be cognizant of our situation. If we can delay bringing him to until we have him secured on *Legend*, it would probably be safer for all parties involved. After all, this man did just try to kill himself and everyone else on board without even a second thought."

"He has information that is pertinent to my investigation," Fischer said. "I need to know what he knows."

"I understand your concerns," Chambers said. "However, while he's in our custody, I'm responsible for his well being, and I will not be responsible for his death should something unexpected happen."

"This is an Alliance Intelligence priority, Captain. My investigation supersedes your rank, sir, no disrespect. I have authorization from Fleet Command to take this case where it needs to." Fischer looked at the medic. "Revive him."

Richards looked at Chambers, obviously conflicted. The captain's jaw worked back and forth, glaring at Fischer. Finally, eyes hard, Chambers nodded to the medic. "Do it."

Across from Fischer, Eliwood held up a hand. "Just a sec. We might want to flash copy the data core in his link before you wake him. I wouldn't want him to come to and delete any helpful information there before we get a chance to look at it."

Fischer silently cursed himself for not thinking of that sooner. He'd been so focused on actually having the guy in custody, he'd forgotten one of the most valuable tools he had in his arsenal. Links were integral to everyone's life throughout the galaxy. From communication to identification to personal finances and entertainment, the link was, quite literally, a person's connection to the world around them.

In most cases, access to the information stored on a person's link was private, and tapping into them without a warrant was illegal. They were afforded the same privileges as a person had within their home—complete and total privacy. It was easier to get authorization to put video and audio taps on someone than it was to connect to someone's link.

Captain Chambers shook his head. "Without a warrant? Not a chance. Again, we *don't* have the authority to do these things."

"Admiral Hunter gave my office complete operational authority, Captain. There is a documented case pertaining to data-syncing links of unconscious or incapacitated persons in order to preserve evidence. In this case, we don't have any idea what kind of safeguards this man may have implemented to keep the information he has stored from being accessed. Considering his history and the case we've built around him so far, I don't see any reason he wouldn't have something like that in place for just this situation."

"I don't like it," Chambers said. Like most people, he was obviously concerned about the sanctity of a person's link. It wasn't just a piece of technology used on a daily basis, it was a part of a person. Asking for link access, for some, was like asking them to get naked in front of a roomful of peers.

"Like it or don't like it," Fischer said, trying to keep the frustration out of his voice, "we need that data. We can't take the chance, however small, that he'll delete it. We just can't."

Chambers turned to his electronics specialists, each looking over a set of holodisplays, anticipation and the orange glow of the screens lighting their faces. "Can you do it, Robbi?"

The man on the right grinned, raising one eyebrow. "Can I do it? Captain, I thought you'd never ask."

Robalt circled the terminal, picking up a rectangular module from his kit on the way. He tapped his link and swiped through several screens as he crossed to the cot. After a few more key strokes on the adaptor, he set it on the small cart holding the medic's supplies. A second holopanel appeared on his link's display, and his fingers danced over the controls.

Eliwood took the place at the head of the cot to look over the

Marine's shoulder at the screens. "That's a pretty fancy piece of hardware you have there, Marine. Not standard issue, I assume."

"No, ma'am," Robalt said. "One of the first things you learn as an electronics specialist is that the Corps doesn't exactly provide its people with the most state-of-the-art equipment available. Most of it is grunt-proof gear will serve its intended purpose, but they aren't as functional as some of the more... advanced gear."

"So it's illegal?" Eliwood asked.

The Marine laughed. "Not technically speaking, no. A couple of us came up with this baby a couple of years back. It's custom made, based on a piece of Alistair tech from a few years ago. Competitors were terrified of the implications a device like theirs could have on the population in general, and fought a pretty lengthy legal battle to have them pulled. Course, no one knows about these."

Fischer chuckled. The fact that the man had built and maintained his own gear wasn't all that surprising, but the fact that Alistair Holdings had been the roadmap for this tech-head Marine to base his module on was more than a little ironic. While he still didn't have much in the way of actual evidence to prove Alistair Holding had anything to do with the Stonemeyer disaster, Fischer knew without a doubt that they were. There were just too many things that pointed in that direction for it to be a mere coincidence. He was hoping the man lying in front of him would have the answers he needed to fill in all the gaps.

"There we go. Transferring now," Robalt said, motioning to the status bar that was now in the process of filling up.

"How long?" Fischer asked.

The Marine pursed his lips. "Mmmm. Hard to say. Five minutes, maybe."

Fischer nodded.

"We're clearing the outer beacon now, Captain Chambers," a

young female pilot said from the controls at the forward-most station on the *Firestorm's* bridge. "Should be another five minutes to the translation point."

"Excellent," Chambers said, moving closer to her station. "And our civvy friend?"

"The *Doris* is right behind us, sir. Cleared station control with no problems."

"You should buy a lottery ticket," Eliwood told Fischer.

"Oh?" Fischer raised an eyebrow at her.

"I don't know that you've ever had an operation go off without out hitch when Jones was involved."

"They don't all go bad."

"Of the three operations that I've personally observed, two of them have gone straight to shit," Eliwood said. "Those aren't great numbers, Fish."

"Two?" Fischer asked.

Eliwood counted on her fingers. "Starmaker, Stonemeyer, Firestorm."

"Oh, come on now, Stonemeyer wasn't Jonesy's fault. That was a cluster-fuck before we even got there. And if he hadn't been there, things might have been a lot worse."

"I can speak to that," Sheridan said, lifting a hand. He was leaning against one of the side consoles, his arms folded across his chest.

"Mmhmm," Eliwood said.

"Besides," Fischer continued, "if it hadn't been for Jones, I wouldn't have even gotten to Stonemeyer, and he…" Fischer pointed to Sheridan. "…would still be camped out with the rest of the homeless."

"Or worse," Sheridan added.

"Or worse," Fischer repeated.

"All right, I'll give you that one," Eliwood said, "But thirty-three percent is still a pretty big number."

Fischer chuckled, and he walked around the small cart next to the bed to look down at Robalt's link display. The status bar was at ninety-five percent. To the right of the status bar, another panel showed the unit's storage capacity. Even after downloading almost all of the Average Man's link's contents, the unit still had over seventy-five percent free space. The custom-built module wasn't, physically, any larger than two standard datapads stacked on top of each other, and from experience, link data took up a lot of storage space. Most people dumped their links every year or so, to clear it out and keep only what they needed. Fischer kept his backup in a secure storage in his apartment. In fact, it'd been a while since Fischer had dumped his own. He made a mental note to clean it out when he got back home.

Whenever that is, he thought.

Robalt looked up and smiled. "Pretty handy, eh? Don't get to use it very often."

"I was just about to ask," Fischer said.

"I tell myself all the time to leave it behind, but I can't ever make myself do it."

Fischer sniffed. "Good thing."

"You're telling me. Ah, there we go." The module beeped, and Robalt's link flashed a completion message. "Done."

"All right," Fischer said. "Let's see what this son of a bitch has to say."

CHAPTER 36

The Bridge
Commercial Freighter *Firestorm*
2 August 2607

Fischer looked up as Sheridan stepped closer to the cot. Both men exchanged silent, knowing glances as the medic worked to bring their mysterious prisoner back to consciousness.

Sheridan had been through hell on Stonemeyer, lived through things most of his old team hadn't. He was the last survivor of the *Darkstar* mission, and Fischer often wondered how that weighed on the man. Survivor's guilt was a real thing, not to mention all of the other mental trauma he'd gone through during his days in captivity. But to his credit, Sheridan hadn't ever used those experiences as a crutch—not that Fischer had seen anyway—and he seemed to be doing just fine.

Fischer had seen more than one man crack under that kind of pressure, military and civilian law enforcement, it really didn't matter. Post-traumatic stress did awful things to people, and despite hundreds of years of research on the topic, humanity hadn't found a clear-cut way of dealing with it. It just affected people in so many different ways, it was hard to predict what it would to do any specific person.

As far as Fischer knew, this was the first time Sheridan had been in a position to confront any of those responsible for the deaths of his fellow Marines, and Fischer was more than a little concerned about what the man might do. After Fischer had found Sheridan on Stonemeyer, the Marine had requested to be present when Young was arrested, but thankfully, his injuries were such that it made that request all but impossible to fulfill.

Sheridan took a deep breath and nodded to the medic.

Richards pressed a pinky-sized injector against Average Man's arms, and pushed the button on the side. A moment later, the man's eyes opened, immediately looking around, confused. He tried to sit up, but the restraints held him to the cot. He lifted his head, looking down at the cuffs.

"What?" he said, eyes flicking up to the Marine standing next to him.

"I'm Sergeant Richards, Alliance Marines. You're alive, but you've got a concussion and several lacerations."

The man's forehead creased. "I don't—"

"What is your name?" Fischer asked, stepping forward. Richards backed away from the cot without another word. Eliwood joined Fischer, arms crossed.

Average Man eyed Eliwood, then flicked to Fischer. For a moment, the confusion persisted, then slowly, his expression began to change. Confusion gave way to recognition. "I know you."

"And I know you," Fischer said.

"But do you really?" Average Man grimaced, trying to adjust his position on the cot, but the restraints held him firm. After several attempts to pull against his bonds, the resigned himself to the fact that he wasn't going anywhere and laid back down. Cocking his head to the side, he gave Fischer a knowing half-grin. "I don't believe you do."

"Why don't you enlighten me then?" Fischer asked. "What's your name?"

Average Man chuckled. He looked past Fischer to the Marines around the periphery of the room. "You certainly came prepared, I'll give you that. How did you find me?"

"It's called police work," Eliwood said.

"Police work? I highly doubt that. You've been working that case for the better part of three months now, and I have it on good authority that you haven't found a single viable piece of evidence."

"Your authority is mistaken," Fischer said.

Average Man smiled.

"What's your name?" Fischer repeated.

"You can call me Gav," Average Man said. "Now, you tell me something—how did you find me?"

"I told you, police work."

Gav sniffed. "Which means that our meeting here happened quite by accident."

Eliwood laughed. "You don't know half as much as you think you know."

"I know more than you'd expect, Agent Eliwood."

"Who are you working for?" Fischer asked.

"Who am I working for?" Gav repeated. "Well, that is an interesting question, isn't it. Some might say that I'm working for wealth or power, or maybe even the love of a woman. Or a man, for that matter. Others might say I'm a narcissistic psychopath working toward his own self-interests. But I tend to think of myself as working for the betterment of mankind."

"You practice that speech often?" Fischer asked.

"Not as often as you might think," Gav said. "There aren't many opportunities for me to speak to someone such as your-selves, and in these conditions." He pulled against his hand-restraints weakly, not trying to break free this time.

"You didn't answer the question, asshole," Eliwood said.

"I did. You just didn't like my answer."

"I'm not sure how murdering people and orchestrating the escape of traitors amounts to bettering mankind," Fischer said.

"No," Gav said, "you wouldn't, would you?"

"The weapons… who are you selling them to?" Fischer asked.

The man laughed. "Selling? I thought you were an investiga-tor? Agent Fischer, you disappoint me. Don't you know that you're only supposed to ask questions you already know the answers to? That's basic interrogation one-oh-one. You're better than that."

Fischer forced himself to suppress the irritation growing in his chest. It was everything he could do to keep his face expression-less. He didn't want to give the man any more ammunition than he already had. He was right, after all. Fischer was between a rock and a hard place and there weren't many options left. Given enough time, Fischer knew he could have worked out the answers for himself, but right now, time was the one thing he didn't have.

The man certainly didn't seem like he was at all disturbed by having been captured. With the evidence that Fischer had collected so far, he had a solid case for at least one murder, but Gav—if that was his real name—didn't seem bothered by that at all. In fact, he seemed more than a little amused at the situation.

"You seem to be in a good mood for someone on their way to a life sentence, or worse," Eliwood said.

"Good mood?" Gav repeated. "No, I'm not in a good mood. I'm actually very sad."

"Yeah, well, you don't have any right to be sad," Eliwood said. "Not after what you've done."

"My work was necessary work."

Fischer crossed his arms. "And what work is that, exactly?"

The man smiled as if he felt bad for Fischer. "Agent Fischer, have you ever been a part of something grand? Like truly grand? Something that is so far above you, personally, that you can't even begin to understand it, and yet, you know it's what your entire life has been leading to?"

He's stalling, Fischer thought. But that wasn't entirely accurate. Besides, what possible reason could he have for stalling? He wasn't going anywhere, and no one was going to get him. In a few minutes, they'd be into the JumpLane and out of reach of anyone who could possibly do anything for him. He wasn't in a hurry to answer Fischer's questions, he if was going to answer them at all. *He's talking at least, and that's something.*

Fischer strolled around the head of the cot, to the other side. Repositioning was an old technique, but here in this uncontrolled area, he really didn't have a lot of tools to work with.

"The oldest tools are sometimes the best tools," Carter used to say.

"Okay, so you're not selling?" Fischer said. "Are you really going to try and tell me you purchased all these weapons for yourself? Or are you bringing them to Young and his cronies?"

A half-smile appeared at the corner of Gav's mouth. "Ah, that was a good one, Agent Fischer. You know, a couple of months ago, I might have fallen for a trick like that."

"Not a trick," Fischer said. "I don't do tricks."

"Everyone does tricks."

"It must have been a pretty big hit to your operation when all those weapons on Stonemeyer were destroyed," Fischer said. "How many months did it put you behind?"

Gav sniffed again, looking around the room. His gaze fell on Sheridan, and they lit up with recognition. "Hey, I know you, too. Sorry to hear about all your friends. Must be tough being the only one of your entire platoon to make it off that pitiful excuse for a planet."

"Sheridan," Fischer muttered as the Marine stepped toward Gav.

Sheridan froze, looking from Gav to Fischer, then back to Gav. "You're going to pay for everyone who didn't make it off that rock. And for Biagini. Count on it."

"Oh, yes, I definitely will. Though I don't think my punishment will be what you had in mind."

Sheridan frowned, eyes flicking to Fischer.

"For the murder of Gorges, you're looking at life, at the very least," Fischer said. "And once I pin you up in the rest of this damn cluster-fuck, you'll be facing a whole lot more than that."

"And what exactly do you need to *pin* the conspiracy on me, Agent Fischer?"

The constant amused expression on Gav's face was starting to grate on Fischer. He knew the man was toying with him, so he decided to play back. "Well, for starters, a confession would be nice."

"A confession? Now, that would be something, wouldn't it?"

"Why were you following me on New Tuscany?"

Gav laughed. "You have a pretty high opinion of yourself, don't you? I mean, of all the people there that night, and you think that I was there for you?"

"You weren't?"

The man shook his head. "If I had been there for you, you wouldn't have seen me. I didn't even know you were there until I saw you that first time. After all, it's not the sort of spot I'd expect someone of your *caliber* to visit. It is ironic though, all this time I thought it might've been the other way around, that you'd been following me that night. Ha!"

Fischer ignored the slight, trying to recall who else he'd seen there, if there had been anyone that stood out in his mind. He couldn't think of any. Del Monico's always catered to the high-class, more affluent crowd. The only reason he'd been there was because of Carissa's job. His wife was definitely the more significant bread-winner of the relationship, a fact that she teased him about often.

Fischer remembered seeing a couple senators, but couldn't visualize their faces. There'd been a musician—a noir-tech singer —but again, he couldn't think of her name. The rest of the place had been filled with business types. Men wearing single color suits, black, white, gray, blue. Women wearing outfits ranging from simple to downright gaudy, but nothing that wasn't the norm.

"So who were you following?" Eliwood asked.

Gav considered Fischer's partner for a long moment, before turning back to Fischer. "You mentioned a confession? All right, I'll give you one."

Fischer's breath caught in his throat, heart pounding. *He can't be serious.* He canted his head to the side, frowning slightly, trying to conceal his surprise. "Just like that?"

"Just like that," Gav repeated.

"I don't believe you."

"You are, of course, free to believe whatever you want to believe," Gav said.

"What makes you think I'd believe anything you tell me?" Fischer asked. "After everything that's happened, everything you've done, you're going to fold just like that? I haven't even put any pressure on yet."

"There's no need to pressure," Gav said. "And how *can* you believe me? Hmmm, that's a good question. I honestly don't know. I've done so many things that it's difficult to decide where to start."

"Starting at the beginning might be a good place," Eliwood said.

Fischer double-checked his link's recorder, making sure it was still active. "You know we've flashed your link, we'll be able to verify everything you tell us."

At the mention of his link, Gav seemed to hesitate. It was slight, but it was there. "Of course you did. You wouldn't be doing your job if you hadn't."

"And you're not getting any deals," Eliwood said. "No reduced sentencing guidelines or immunity clauses. Nothing."

"I have no need for any such deals," Gav said. "My fate is already sealed."

Fischer frowned. "What do you mean by that?"

"Just what I said, Agent Fischer. I've known for quite some time that this is how we would meet. I have to admit though, I wasn't expecting to happen quite so soon."

"You just tried to blow an entire freighter up with you on it," Eliwood countered. "That doesn't sound like the actions of someone looking to come clean."

"I said I was going to confess, I didn't say anything about coming clean."

"Enough," Fischer said, done with the games. "If you've got something to say, say it. Are you a part of the conspiracy that led to the disaster on Stonemeyer and the deaths of fourteen Marines?"

Sheridan stepped forward, his eyes locked on Gav.

"Yes," Gav said.

Fischer straightened. "Did you kill Private Benjamin Wallace?"

"Yes."

"Were you involved in the attack that freed Admiral Marcus Young?"

"Yes."

What the hell is going on here? Fischer asked himself, mind racing, trying to fit all the pieces together. "Did Young orchestrate the event on Stonemeyer by himself, or did he have help?"

Gav laughed. "If you think that self-absorbed oaf has the ability to put something like Stonemeyer together on his own, you're not half the investigator I thought you were, Agent Fischer. I mean, you know how it turned out." He turned his head, giving Sheridan a side-long glance.

"Who else was involved?"

"I can't answer that."

"What do you mean you can't answer?" Fischer asked. "You just said you wanted to confess."

"That is true," Gav said. "I will tell you what I—specifically me—have done for the cause, nothing more."

"Too late," Eliwood said. "You've already spilled the beans on Young."

Gav shrugged—as much as he could be restrained. "He's a known entity. Your case is weak, and you don't have any real evidence. Let's be honest, if you did, you wouldn't have spent the last three months digging through his ship for clues. Well, until recently, anyway."

Fischer exchanged a look with Eliwood. They hadn't exactly made it a secret, but they hadn't been publicly touting their continued investigation either. Even if they had, the hype around the Admiral's arrest, and the Stonemeyer Incident, in general, had dropped dramatically in the media after weeks with nothing new to report. Like anything in modern life, people's attention was short, and there was always some new, juicy scandal or controversy to talk about. Stonemeyer had lasted longer than usual—almost a full month—but after that, it'd just become old news.

That being the case, however, they hadn't said anything about any new leads to the media. The fact that this mysterious man seemed to know they'd found something was more than a little concerning.

"You seem to be well informed about our work," Fischer said.

"It's part of the job," Gav said. "Just like knowing that even after you decrypted the message, it didn't help you in the slightest."

Fischer's blood ran cold. They hadn't put the message fragment in the official report. The only people who knew about it were Carter, the two agents on board this ship and the techs working to piece it back together.

Son of a bitch, Fischer thought as realization dawned.

Eliwood looked as shocked as Fischer felt, her eyes wide, mouth hanging open. He wondered if she'd come to the same conclusion he'd just made.

"Ah, yes. You're starting to see now?" Gav asked. "You see what you're dealing with. This is bigger than you, Agent Fischer. It's bigger than me. Stonemeyer was nothing. It was a hiccup. A mistake. You haven't even scratched the surface."

"A mistake," Sheridan stepped closer to the cot, fist clenched. "A lot of my friends died during that *mistake*."

"Wrong place, wrong time," Gav said casually. "Actually, I won't take the blame for that disaster. The blame for that falls squarely on Delaney's shoulders. He panicked, plain and simple. He should never have been there in the first place. The man was an idiot."

Fischer didn't disagree, but putting all the responsibility on a dead man was too convenient. "He's not the only one that made mistakes."

"Oh?" Gav raised a quizzical eyebrow.

"We caught your sorry ass," Eliwood said.

The man laughed. "That you did." He took a long breath. "Such a pity."

"Oh, yeah, I feel a shit ton of pity for you," Eliwood sneered. "Normally, I'm all for the system working things out, but I wouldn't be surprised if you had an accident on the way back to the Alliance."

Beside her, Sheridan nodded. "Accidents happen all the time."

Reese, Neal, and Cole all stepped up beside Sheridan, obviously putting their support squarely in his corner. Neal winced as she walked, her hand pressed against the biosynth bandage wrapped around her torso. On a certain level, Fischer was glad to see Sheridan had found a place here among the Sabers. The Marine Corps forged bonds stronger than any composite alloy ever designed, and Saber bonds held firm regardless of the stressors thrown against it.

"Oh, I apologize," Gav said. "I didn't mean to give you the impression that I'd be returning with you."

Eliwood laughed. "Isn't like you have much of a choice, asshole."

"We always have a choice," Gav told her.

Fischer found himself shifting his hand to his pistol. Alarms blared inside his mind. Something was wrong. Something about this whole interaction had been off. Gav wasn't concerned in the slightest about having been caught. He hadn't wanted to be caught. He'd tried to blow up an entire ship in his efforts not to be, but even still, he was confident. More confident than he had a right to be.

"Yeah," Eliwood said. "Well, your options are to rot in a cell for the rest of your life or to rot in a cell for the rest of your life. How do you like your choices?"

"I don't like them at all, I'm afraid."

"Good," Eliwood said.

Gav shifted his jaw back and forth, looking at Fischer. His eyes told Fischer everything he needed to know.

"No!" Sheridan shouted hand shooting out, but Gav was already biting down.

A high-pitched whistle resonated from the man's head and Gav's head jerked to the side, eyes bulging. His entire body spasmed briefly, then went limp, blood trickling from his ears and nose.

Sheridan stopped, his hand an inch away from Gav's face. There was nothing he could do. Gav, Average Man, someone who knew everything about everything was dead.

CHAPTER 37

Command Information Control,
ANS *Legend*
JumpLane 4821, En route to Astalt System
2 August 2607

"So, let me get this straight," Captain Ward said, leaning against the main holoplot in *Legend's* CIC. "This *Gav* all but confirmed Young's involvement in the Stonemeyer incident and then kills himself by setting off an explosive charge inside his skull? That doesn't make any sense. Why implicate Young at all? Why not just kill himself and be done with it?"

"The only thing that makes sense is he was trying to figure out what we already knew," Fischer said. "Which isn't much. He'd obviously already made up his mind that was going to kill himself well before the Marines grabbed him."

Fischer stood on the other side of the holoplot, arms crossed, trying to control the rage burning inside him. Every time he made any headway, he was forced to take two steps back. He'd seen it coming a moment too late.

You couldn't have done anything to stop it, he told himself, as if that made the death of his only lead any better.

He wanted to kick something, break something, to scream at the top of his lungs that this whole damn case was beyond him and anyone else. But he didn't. He couldn't. He wasn't any worse off than he'd been when he woke up this morning, and they still had the freighter and the coordinates for... for whatever was out there waiting for them.

Commander Manchester, *Legend's* Executive Officer, shook his head. "You're damn lucky that charge only killed him."

Fischer nodded. That'd been the second thing that had gone through his mind after Gav had killed himself—if that had been his real name. But he still didn't understand why he'd done it. The man obviously had connections. And as much as Fischer wanted to think differently, he knew Gav could've weaseled his way out of the case somehow. Young's escape was a prime example of that.

"Bastard sure was committed," Eliwood muttered, pacing around the CIC, shaking her head. The red lighting bathing the compartment indicated the ship was still at battle stations. Every station was double-manned, and tensions were high.

Captain Chambers, Master Sergeant Kline and the rest of *Legend's* command crew were spread throughout the compartment, the mood heavy. Sheridan and the rest of the Sabers were refitting their gear and preparing for the next assault. Reese and Robalt, the two electronic technicians, had also remained behind in the CIC, working on decrypting the data retrieved from Gav's link. They'd made some progress, but the likelihood of them gaining anything noteworthy by the time they reached their destination was slim to none.

But what are they doing all the way out here? Fischer wondered, staring at the red icon that represented the Astalt system.

Raiders were known for taking the "back roads," navigating through less traveled systems, but they usually didn't stray too far from the major shipping lanes. It just wasn't cost-effective to go much farther than one or two systems out, and when you were making a living one raid at a time, you couldn't afford to be away from the hunting grounds for that long.

"But committed to what?" Fischer wondered aloud.

"What do you mean?" Eliwood asked.

Fischer spread his hands. "I mean, what exactly was he committed to? Raiders don't typically associate with anyone outside of their limited spheres of influence. And with the exception of doing business with syndicates here and there, they usually keep to themselves. The attack on the mining colony is proof that something else is going on here, something more than just some kind of raider co-op. But what the hell could it be?"

"You're thinking the attack on the mining station was more than a one-time coordinated effort?" Captain Ward asked.

"Absolutely," Fischer said. "Without a doubt. If the number of weapons they're amassing isn't enough proof of that, the effort put into protecting the location of this system should be."

"What, you think someone's putting together some kind of raider nation?" Eliwood asked.

"I don't know what to think," Fischer admitted. "But this is clearly bigger than a few coordinated attacks and killings. Your average raider doesn't have the connections to bypass security systems like Cathcart or Lexington, much less have intimate knowledge of classified ASI operations. Hell, your average raider wouldn't be caught dead with an explosive charge in their head, that's for damn sure."

"You don't think that bastard was just talking shit?" Eliwood stated.

Fischer shook his head. "Not a chance. He was too confident.

He didn't just guess about the fragment—he knew. And he knew that despite having it, it really didn't give us anything.

"It gave us Young," Eliwood suggested.

"We already had Young. But even if we hadn't, how in the fuck did he know about the fragment?"

"Can't be Carter," Eliwood said.

"Not a chance," Fischer agreed. But that only left the Davis and her team, and he'd known them for years, and couldn't believe that either had betrayed their planet.

"I can't picture Davis selling information to the enemy," Eliwood said. "I just can't see it."

"Neither can I," Fischer said. He didn't want to believe, but he knew there wasn't any other answer. *No, there has to be something else. Something we're missing.*

The forward hatch opened, and two pilots ducked through, one male and a female in blue flight suits. The man motioned to the FOO, and Lieutenant Commander Stinson nodded. Fischer recognized the pilot from the *Firestorm*. She smiled and nodded as they entered.

"Excuse me, sir," Stinson told Ward and stepped away.

Eliwood stopped pacing and pointed both index fingers at Fischer. "Okay, let's just say, for a minute, he's telling the truth— why the hell would he tell us that there's a double agent within the agency? You'd think he'd want to keep that shit under wraps."

"Maybe he slipped up," Fischer suggested. "Maybe he's just trying to set us against each other. Tear ASI down from the inside."

Eliwood considered that for a moment. "I don't know. He didn't seem like the type of person that slips up like that."

"And why wait to kill himself?" Commander Manchester asked.

"Once he figured out we really didn't know anything, he figured it was safe for him to go," Fischer said.

"He had to have known we were heading to Astalt," Ward said. "But that didn't seem to worry him either."

Fischer nodded. "That's another problem altogether. If it is some kind of waypoint for this raider collective, then one ship won't last long against them, regardless of how advanced she is."

For a brief moment, Captain Ward looked as if he wanted to contend the point, opening his mouth to counter any claims that his command wasn't capable of taking on the challenge. He shut it, however, pursing his lips in thought. Finally, he said, "So, do we call for reinforcements?"

"My initial thoughts are yes, we should," Fischer said. "But our window of opportunity is only growing smaller by the minute. If we wait, we'll be outside of the delivery window. Chances are, if there is a large raider fleet there waiting for us, we'll get blown out of space as soon as we drop out of the Lane. Not to mention that if we don't show up, they're going to assume something went wrong with the shipment, and my guess is they'll start packing their bags."

"And if they disappear now, we might never find them again," Eliwood said.

"Exactly," Fischer said. "I don't see any other option but to continue as we are. We bring the freighter in on schedule and try to bring them down from the inside. It's also the best option if we're going to have any chance of getting Young back. We fly in, guns blazing, those bastards will scatter like cockroaches."

"Your *best option*," Captain Ward said, putting an emphasis on the last two words, "has its own set of problems. Namely, sending our operators into an unknown situation, going up against an unknown entity, with absolutely no intelligence on their capabilities or manpower. Not to mention the fact that we have absolutely no credible intelligence that says Admiral Young is actually going to be there."

Captain Chambers lifted a finger. "Getting in isn't the issue, sir. It's getting out intact after everything's gone to shit—that's the challenge. My team has the ability to infiltration any stronghold. Nothing is entirely secure. And let's say Young is here—"

"Which we don't have any idea that he is," Captain Ward said.

"Yes, sir," Chambers nodded and continued. "But, supposing Young's here, and we infiltrate the base and locate him, we need to have a viable extraction plan. I can tell you right now, if shit hits the fan and we need to make a fast exit, *Firestorm* is not going to handle it."

"That's an understatement," Chambers said. "Depending on what we come up against, *Legend* can create enough chaos that it will turn their shit upside down, but without knowing exactly what we're dealing with, it's difficult to say. And even if Young is in the system, he'll be extremely hard to locate."

"We can track his link ID," Fischer said.

Captain Ward nodded. "True, but your sensor suite would need to be ten times what is available on *Firestorm*. Her systems aren't nearly advanced enough to find anything that wasn't already staring them in the face."

"What about *Legend's* sensors?" Fischer asked.

"*Legend* has the most advanced sensor suite in the entire fleet," Ward said. "If there's anything to find out there, she'll find it. Once we show up, there won't be any time for hide and seek. The situation will devolve into whoever can get the most shots off in the least amount of time."

"And besides that," Manchester added, "*Legend's* sensor capabilities are advanced, but they're not all-powerful. We have the same range limitations as any other ship in the fleet. We need to be within a million kilometers to even have a shot at seeing anything, half that for the processes you're talking about. If we're waiting until we receive the notification from you," he pointed at Fischer, "then none of that matters."

"You know, if getting into the system is what you're worried about, you could always try a shadow jump," Tensley Jones suggested. He sat on the edge of one of the consoles to Fischer's left, hands stuffed in his jacket pockets, ankles crossed. His black leather jacket was unzipped, the collar of his pale blue shirt unbuttoned.

"You're kidding," Manchester said.

Jones took one hand out of his pocket and slid it flat through the air in front of him. "Nah, you just drop in under minimal power and glide right in. You give Fish and his guys enough time to do what they need to do, and then you open up right under their noses."

"You're suggesting we drop in blind with our defenses down and weapons on standby?" Manchester said. "That's beyond crazy. That's insane."

Jones frowned. He pointed a finger at *Legend's* XO. "Pretty sure that's the same thing. But, regardless, it's an option. Y'all are the guys with the big guns; I'm just a humble merchant, trying to do the right thing."

Fischer couldn't help the smile that spread across his face.

"I've heard of commanders using the technique before," Ward said. "But they were using carriers to mask picket ships, destroyers and frigates to hide in the flanks. The *Firestorm* is only slightly larger than the *Legend* in terms of pure tonnage."

"But it could work," Jones said.

Ward shook his head. "I just don't know. It would depend heavily on the enemy's sensor capabilities and if they're looking in the right direction when we drop in. If they see us…"

"The operation will be over before it starts," Fischer finished for him.

Manchester was typing on his link. "Even with our stealth systems active and the remaining systems at twenty-five percent, our signature would only be just under what *Firestorm* puts out running at maximum. If we were looking at that without sensors, you'd have to be asleep or be having your worst day ever to miss it."

Jones snickered and clapped his hands together. "You do realize we're talking about raiders here, right? These aren't highly skilled and disciplined military officers and ratings. These are misfits and criminals. Your worst day is heads and shoulders above their best."

Fischer watched Jones, looking for any hint of his usual mischievousness, but saw none. His friend was typically not so forthcoming with his praise of Alliance military personnel. In fact, most of the time, Fischer got the impression that he'd just assume to have nothing to do with anyone in uniform.

"Even still," Ward said, "We'll still have to be in range for the sensors to be effective, which means we're going to have to approach almost cold. That'll will take time."

"Time we don't have," Fischer said before he could stop himself.

"Exactly," Ward said. "So, we're still left with moving in under power and exposing ourselves to the enemy, which, I might add, we still know nothing about."

"What if you reconfigured the long-range probes to sync together? A sensor matrix would probably be able to detect it if you had enough bandwidth. You could probably run them with an array on the freighter," a new voice suggested.

Everyone in the compartment turned to face the two electronic technicians standing at one of the consoles on the side of the compartment. Corporal Reese was looking at Sergeant Robalt, his eyebrows raised in obvious surprise. Robalt, for his part, stood with an expression of genuine curiosity. Then, he seemed to realized he'd said something aloud that he might not have intended, and his face flushed. "Uh, sirs."

"Sergeant Robalt," Captain Chambers said, taking a step back and turning to face the man. "You have something to add to the conversation?"

Fischer felt a little bit of sympathy for the Saber. He'd been on both sides of the senior/junior spectrum and knew from experience what kind of stress speaking to high-ranking officers put on the lower ranks. Sure, they put their uniform on the same way, but there was always something intimidating about addressing someone who could, in a very real sense, affect your life in either positive or negative ways.

Robalt cleared his throat, his eyes darting from Chambers to Captain Ward. "Uh, yes, sir. I'm sorry, sir."

"Go ahead, Sergeant," Ward said.

"Well, sir," Robalt said hesitantly. "I was just thinking, that if you're going to send *Firestorm* in-system without *Legend's* guns, you might as well give her the eyeballs to see. I know *Legend* is a new ship, but most ships have a couple hundred auxiliary long-range probes in their stores. We can sync them together, they basically give you a massive sensor field."

Fischer grunted, almost surprised he hadn't thought of that in the first place. He'd been the tactical officer aboard *Paladin* back during his days as an Alliance Navy officer before he'd joined the Agency. Long-range sensor probes were generally reserved for high-volume patrol areas where single ships, or small task forces, needed additional eyeballs in multiple areas. Military recon probes were designed to be one-time use and would self-destruct either on command or with a timed delay.

Captain Ward and his XO exchanged curious glances, both with the beginnings of smiles on their faces.

"What's going on?" Eliwood whispered in Fischer's ear.

Fischer had to remind himself that, unlike the rest of the people in this compartment, Eliwood had never served in the military. It was likely that the awkwardness of the moment was lost here. It wasn't every day an enlisted tech, and enlisted Marine no less suggested using multi-million credit pieces of equipment for an operation out of their design specs.

"They're trying to decide if his idea is plausible or not," Fischer said. "Which it is."

"It can work, sir," Robalt said, obviously reading the situation exactly the way Fischer was.

Captain Ward rubbed his chin. After a moment, he said, "XO, how many RSPs do we have in inventory?"

Manchester, who'd anticipated the question, had his link open already. "One-hundred-eighty-five, sir."

"Retask fifty. Work with Sergeant Robalt here to get the most effective spread. I want them ready to go and transferred to *Firestorm* as soon as possible."

"Aye, sir," Manchester said.

Ward shook his head and turned to Fischer. "Shadow jumping and playing hide-and-seek with drones. You'd better be right about this. We're taking an awful lot of risks."

"I'm right," Fischer said, more confident than he'd been ten minutes before. "I'm right."

CHAPTER 38

Main Cargo Bay
Commercial Freighter *Firestorm*
4 August 2607

Sheridan adjusted his jacket again. The team was in plain clothes now, but they are armed appropriately and wearing body armor. With Neal still in the infirmary, Captain Chambers wasn't taking any more chances. A part of him didn't mind being out of uniform, it gave him a sense of freedom, but it also felt... wrong, like it was just a matter of time before someone saw him and reprimanded him for being out of uniform.

A large part of his career, up until this point, had been all about the importance of the uniform, the tradition it stood for. The Alliance Marine Corps could trace its lineage to the inception of the Alliance, and even further back to their roots on Old Earth. The uniform had a history all its own, and it was an important part of being a Marine.

Now though, it was almost an after-thought. Life as a MARSOC Saber meant doing things that would be unthinkable in the regular Marine Corps. Like being armed aboard ship without your cover on, or preparing for combat operations in gray pants and a red Montgomery Spacers shirt. Neal had given him grief about this choice in attire when he'd checked in on her before boarding the shuttle to *Firestorm*.

"I can't believe you're wearing that," Neal had told him, pointing to his shirt.

"I told him the same thing," Cole said, coming up behind Sheridan.

"What?" Sheridan asked, looking down at the shirt. The stylized 'S' and ringed planet logo for the gravball team had worn slightly since he'd first bought it.

"You know they haven't won a championship in like seven years, right?"

Sheridan gave her a knowing half-smile. "What can I say, I'm a Spacer through and through."

"Well, at least you're not a fair-weather fan," Cole said, patting Sheridan on the shoulder. "I'll give you that much, Blaster."

Sheridan cringed at the nickname, then turned to Neal. "You doing okay? You need anything?"

"I just need Doc to give me the green light so I can get out of this damn clinic skirt and back into boots." Neal held up a corner of the light blue medical gown she wore.

Sheridan nodded to her side. "Need to make sure that heals."

"I'm not worried about that," Neal said. "I'm worried about you guys going out there without me. Who's going to watch your asses when I'm not there?"

Cole feigned injury, putting his hand over his heart. "Whatever are you trying to say? We can't take care of ourselves?"

"That's exactly what I'm saying."

"I'm hurt," Cole said. He slapped Sheridan's around with the back of his hand. "I'll have you know that we're the two most dangerous people on the whole team. Why, if we come upon an obstacle we can't overcome, well, good ol' Blaster here will just put some bang on it and make it go bye-bye."

"Hey, it worked, didn't it?"

"Oh, it worked all right." Cole rolled his eyes.

"Seriously, though," Neal said. "Take care of each other out there." She pointed at Sheridan. "After this is over, I owe you a drink."

"Two drinks," Cole said.

Standing next to her bed, Sheridan would have thought a cold beer with her sounded like just the right thing. Now, standing in *Firestorm's* hold, once again counting down the minutes until the fight, a drink in some seedy bar was the last thing on his mind.

Agent Fischer, his partner Eliwood, and Robalt were all working at two stations set up in a small compartment off the main bay. They were in the process of making sure the sensor network was functional and would do everything Robalt said it was going to do. Sheridan was skeptical, but the tech seemed adamant it would work, and everyone seemed to trust that it would.

Like he'd been trained, Sheridan was mentally preparing for the coming fight. Running through multiple scenarios in his mind, visualizing how he'd react to each one in turn. A warrior's mindset—considering every single possibility and working through his reactions so that when the mission inevitably went to shit, he wouldn't freeze when indecision could mean the difference between life and death.

As they did before every mission, Sheridan's thoughts drifted back to Stonemeyer, to just before the mission had gone south. Standing in the embassy's lobby, waiting for Hastings and the rest of the team to come back up from the basement, wondering what the hell was taking so long. The embassy security team relaying what had happened to them during the days leading up to the extraction. They'd been torn apart, just like the rest of Sheridan's team would be over the course of their mission. And for what? So some rogue ambassador and admiral could make a few extra credits on the side.

He wanted to take the image of Ford out of his mind—him spinning around after taking a round in the shoulder just as he'd thrown that smoker, doubling over as more bullets slammed into his hip and back. Sheridan's stomach turned, but now, instead of being horrified, he was angry. He wanted nothing more than to exact the same pain and fear upon anyone and everyone that had any connection to Stonemeyer. He looked around the bay at the rows of crates filled with weapons and was thankful that he was doing something to avenge his friends. He would make them pay for what they did.

"You all right, Sheridan?" Fischer asked, bringing Sheridan back from his thoughts. The agent was standing behind three wide-panel holodisplays, fingers swiping through options and menus, getting the array read to sort through the sensor data. Robalt stood next to him, working on another set of panels, integrating the relay software to work with their taclinks.

"Yes, sir. I'm fine." Sheridan realized he'd been squeezing the grip of his MOD27 and released it, flexing his fingers. Then, he let out a long breath, releasing his memories of Stonemeyer as well, wanting to focus on the present.

"You sure?" the investigator asked, a look of genuine concern on his face. "You don't look fine."

Sheridan shook his head. "I'm good.

"All right. And cut out that 'sir' business. We've had that discussion before."

"Roger that." Sheridan gave the agent a sheepish grin. "Sorry, old habits. Just ready to kick some ass, that's all." There was more to it, but Sheridan didn't think this was the time or the place.

Fischer seemed to consider him for a moment, then nodded, as if he'd read Sheridan's mind and could see the hatred and passion he was feeling. "We'll make them pay."

The ship-wide intercom chimed, and Jones's voice echoed through the expansive bay. *"We're dropping out of the Lane in about ten minutes."*

It'd taken a little bit of convincing, but Fischer had managed to get Jones to leave the *Doris* on *Legend's* flight deck and pilot the freighter. Jones was the best pilot Fischer had ever met, and if it came down to high-tailing it out of a bad spot, he couldn't think of anyone else he'd want behind the controls. And it wasn't like *Doris* would've have added anything to the operation anyway; she didn't have really anything in the way of offensive weapons—none that would make a difference anyway—and she'd just be another target for the raiders to shoot at once the shooting started.

"You really think this is going to work, Robbi?" Sheridan asked.

"It'll work," Robalt said. He tapped his screen, the orange glow illuminating his frown. "I don't know why everyone is so pessimistic about the situation."

"It's not that they're pessimists," Fischer said. "They're just realists."

"It *should* work," Robalt said. He was wearing plain clothes as well, but his tactical gear and weapon were on the deck next to him.

Fischer turned, giving the electronics specialists a questioning look. "Should?"

Robalt laughed. "Come on now, don't get weird. It'll will work. One hundred percent."

"How big an area will it cover?" Fischer asked.

"Depends on how much resolution you want," Robalt said. "You can go wide and far, but your coverage is going to suffer. But, with these probes? With a decent spread, you're looking at anywhere between ten-to-twenty-thousand kilometers. And once we get a general location, we can narrow it down. We'll lose range, but if we know where to look, that won't matter."

Agent Fischer nodded, turning back to his own screen, his expression all business. Fischer was probably the only person in the galaxy that wanted to find Marcus Young more than he did, and Sheridan wanted that bastard more than anything. The investigator had his own reasons for wanting the former admiral, and while Sheridan didn't quite know what they were, he knew it was more than a simple clear mark on his investigation record. It was more than a little personal for both of them.

Sheridan looked toward the hatch as Cole came in, adjusting his vest underneath his long-sleeve olive green shirt. "Man, you think we'll ever be in grays again? I can never get the vest to sit right."

Sheridan laughed.

"What's so funny?"

"Nothing," Sheridan said. "I just know what you mean."

"Rocha said we're going to rally in the personnel access, starboard side," Cole said. "Deck Five. She seemed worried about this one."

Sheridan nodded. "I think everyone is. I'm more anxious than anything really. I really want that bastard to be here."

"Who—Young? He'll be there." Cole punched a fist into his palm. "We'll get that son of a bitch. I promise."

"Thanks," Sheridan said.

A soft chime came through Sheridan's implant, and Staff Sergeant Rocha's voice came over the taclink. *"All right, rally up."*

Sheridan and Cole exchanged glances and Fischer looked up from his holopanels.

"What's up?" Fischer asked.

Sheridan tapped his ear. "Time to load up."

"Are you not synced up on our channel?" Robalt asked.

Fischer shook his head.

"Here, I'll fix that." Robalt opened his link and went to work, swiping through several menus, then tapping in a specific sequence of commands. Because of his specialty he had higher levels of access to the taclink than Sheridan and some of the screens he didn't recognize.

Eliwood looked up from her holodisplays. "You know, I'm kind of sad we're not going with them. I'd kind of like to see the look on Young's face when they snatch him up."

"You don't have to tell me," Fischer said.

The agents were going to be in charge of offloading the weapons to fulfill the contract while the Sabers searched for Young. Fischer hadn't been keen on the idea of staying behind, but Captain Campbell had been firm on that point.

"My team are trained professionals, Agent Fischer," the Captain had said. "They've trained together for months, and they know each other. I can't ask them to go into battle with an untested man. No offense. Besides, someone's going to have to convince these sons of bitches that we're supposed to be here, and that is where your specialty lies. You talk, we walk."

To his credit, Fischer had agreed. The longer they could legitimately remain on the station, the better chance the Sabers had of locating Young without raising an alarm. Of course, that was best-case scenario.

And when the hell does that ever happen? Sheridan asked himself. Never on his watch.

Robalt tapped a final command into the system. "All right, she's up and running. All we need now is a target."

"Come on," Cole said, motioning for Sheridan to follow.

Sheridan stopped next to Fischer. "We're going to find him and bring him back. I promise."

Fischer held Sheridan's gaze for a moment, then extended his hand. "Take care of yourself. I don't want to have to come find your ass again."

Sheridan grinned. "You got it."

Cole led Sheridan and Fischer through the maze of passages to the forward personnel hatch, into an octagonal compartment. The hatches were on exactly opposite sides of the space, the rest of the bulkhead space taken up by lockers with emergence void suits and survival gear. Illumination panels arranged on the ceiling lit the compartment with a dull white light.

The rest of the team was already assembled and ready, all dressed in plain clothes.

We really do look like raiders, Sheridan thought.

Captain Chambers stood near the exit hatch, flanked by Master Sergeant Kline and the two team leaders, Sergeant Rocha and Sergeant Nguyen. Kline looked up as Sheridan and the other two entered.

"All right," Chambers said, stepping forward into the middle of the room. The rest of the team formed a loose circle around him. "Listen up. You know the target. The plan is to stay as close together as possible, but we need to cover ground quickly. The sensor matrix should provide us with enough data that we'll be able to navigate directly to our objective, but we need to be prepared for alternatives.

"Make no mistake, we are going into enemy territory here. If we're discovered there won't be any talking our way out of it, so don't give anyone any reason to give us a second look. Minimal footprint. If we can get to Young without being detected, all the better for us."

"And if we are detected, sir?" Sergeant Hanover asked. The butt of his HR91 sniper rifle rested on the deck between his legs, his hands wrapped around the barrel. He had a MOD27 slung over his back, its muzzle pointing at the deck. Team Two's sniper, Sergeant Vega, stood next to him. They'd both been assigned overwatch duties, providing security for their only escape option: *Firestorm*.

"If we're detected then all bets are off," Chambers said. "Engage as you identify. Until then, weapons cold."

Several heads nodded acknowledgement.

"Young is the target. We apprehend and detain. We need him alive, people. Unless something crazy happens, all other considerations are secondary, including reducing casualties. We will maintain taclink contact with *Legend* and *Firestorm* for the duration of the operation, and a flight of assault boats and fighter escorts will be on standby for extract if *Firestorm* is overrun. Sergeant Hanover, you'll be in charge of demo if it comes to that. Were you able to collect Neal's kit?"

The sniper tapped a pack strapped to his thigh. "Got the bang right here, sir."

"Very good. There's no telling how far into the outpost we're going to have to go, but assume it's at least a few kilometers. Make sure you're paying attention to your surroundings. A raider outpost like this, there's bound to be a lot of weapons out in the open. Make sure we're not seeing threats where there are none. We don't want to start shooting if we don't have to. But if we do have to start shooting, we're going to make sure they know we're Sabers."

Another collective murmur of agreement rippled through the team and Sheridan couldn't help but grin.

"We're about to drop in system. Once that happens, it's go-time until we leave. Keep your heads on a swivel and keep your eyes up," Captain Chambers said.

"Eyes up, sir." The team responded.

CHAPTER 39

Main Cargo Bay
Commercial Freighter *Firestorm*
4 August 2607

"We're passing the inner beacon now," Jones said into Fischer's implant. "We'll be touching down here in about three minutes."

"Copy that," Fischer said.

Entrance into the system had gone smoothly enough. Jones had linked *Firestorm's* communication system through Fischer's link so he could listen in on the traffic. As far as Fischer could tell, the raiders hadn't suspected a thing.

The hope was that none of the raiders here had actually met the two dealers in person and that Fischer and Eliwood would be able to play them during the offload. From what Fero had relayed, they hadn't received any information about what would happen once they got to the station, but he'd said that wasn't outside of the norm for most clients. People in the business of buying illegal weapons didn't like disclosing more information than absolutely necessary.

So law enforcement can't do what we're attempting, Fischer thought, his eyes on the readouts in front of him. Fischer wanted to be with the Marines, hunting Young down in the depths of the outpost, now playing smuggler.

The outpost was built into an irregular asteroid, which at its broadest was just under sixteen kilometers in diameter. The asteroid, which didn't have a name or designation as far as Fischer could find, orbited the star at about one-point-nine AUs, and was the only celestial body within several million kilometers in any direction. The outpost proper was a series of habitats built across its long side; domed structures connected to large hangar bays by long steel alloy tubes. Three enormous transfer stations were tethered to the asteroid, and connected to each other by a one hundred kilometer transit tube.

They had been directed to a building designated "Hanger C" by the crew in *Legend's* CIC. The combination of remote sensor platforms and the warship's own sensor suite had detected over a hundred ships, ranging in size from personal transport shuttles to cruisers, though so far, they'd only detected three such vessels. Most of the ships were at anchor, floating stationary relative to the outpost.

The raiders hadn't given any sign that they'd detected *Legend* dropping in *Firestorm's* shadow. They hadn't even dispatched a scouting patrol to meet them until they were close to the outpost's outer beacon. Apparently, they assumed if a ship had actually made it this far, she was meant to be here. For all the posturing Gav had done, the security around this place didn't seem all that impressive. Lackluster was a much more apt description.

They'd launched their probes as soon as they'd translated, sending them on ballistic trajectories to give them as much coverage on the outpost as possible. Now, as their stolen freighter neared its destination, the majority of the probes were adjusting course, heading in toward the outpost.

"Can you believe this?" Eliwood asked, her fingers swiping

through the ship registry. "*The Hateful Star, The Golden Rose,* and the *Tearful Goodbye.* The bounty on any one of those would set you up for at least a couple years."

"If we could collect them," Fischer said. The regulations on ASI agents collecting financial compensation like bounties were fairly stringent. As in, not allowed. Like most rules, that particular regulation had come into effect after some agents decided it would make sense to only work cases were the bounties were above a certain threshold, ignoring other cases in favor of chasing the credits.

Eliwood made a 'tsk tsk' sound and shook her head. "There's always got to be someone that ruins it for the rest of us."

"Always," Fischer murmured, most of his attention focused on his readouts. So far they hadn't had any sign of Young, but the sensors were just now beginning their detailed sweeps of the outpost. He was trying to remain positive, though, with every passing moment, his thoughts slipped into a negative space.

"Our friends just broke off," Jones advised over the Fischer's link. *"Looks like we'll be making the rest of the trip solo."*

"Good for us," Fischer said. If the raiders had pulled off their fighter escort, it meant they weren't worried about the freighter, cargo, or occupants. It still remained to be seen whether or not the Marines would be able to disembark without being noticed, or at the very least, not draw any unwanted attention. If this was anything to go off, the odds were in their favor.

That's a first, Fischer thought.

"I've got eyeballs on the landing area," Jones said. *"Pumping through your taclinks now."*

Fischer tapped his link and opened the appropriate panel. A live feed from *Firestorm's* bow sensor array showed them closing on the outpost, crawling through the void at a snail's pace. Several ships were flying back and forth and around the base, but it seemed like business as usual.

"Lot of ships out there," Eliwood said.

"Yeah." There wasn't much else he could say. Wasn't anything he could do for that matter. Captain Ward and *Legend* had that responsibility. Right now, his only task was to locate Young's beacon. That's it. The entire mission hinged upon that. In fact, he'd been so set on accomplishing that mission that he hadn't considered what they would do if Young wasn't here.

He's here, he told himself. "We need to bring the probes closer. Need more resolution on the outpost."

"Not sure how much closer we're going to be able to bring them," Robalt said without looking up from his own displays. "They're running on passive, but they get close enough, and someone's bound to pick up their power signature."

"We need to find him. Young's all that matters here. *That* is the mission."

Robalt held Fischer's gaze for a moment, then said, "Roger that, sir."

Fischer winced. "Please, don't call me, sir."

"All right ladies and germs," Jones said over the taclink. *"We're inbound on final. Check the feed. Looks like we're dropping onto a full pad. I'm marking the stall we've been assigned now."*

The designated landing area was near the back of the bay, next to a row of smaller frigates. Their hulls surrounded by racks of parts and tool carts. Supply crates were stacks two and three high, and deckhands crawled over the fuselages, welding, cutting and adjusting.

"Looks like they're retrofitting some old G3s with aftermarket railguns," Robalt said. "See that one in the middle there. Looks like it's almost finished."

"Building warships," Fischer said.

"Like they don't have enough already," Eliwood said.

"Apparently, someone thinks they don't," Robalt said.

Jones rotated the *Firestorm* a hundred and eighty degrees, so her bow faced the open bay doors. Fischer heard the blast of retro engines firing through the hull, and the deck shuttered under his feet as the large ship descended to the hangar deck. Landing a ship *Firestorm's* size took a little more finesse than the *Doris* would have, but Jones handled it like a pro, setting the freighter down on its six landing struts, managing to keep the jolting and rocking to a minimum.

"All right, we're down," Jones said. *"Looks like we've got a little welcome committee coming to greet us."*

On the feed, four figures, three men, one woman, were approaching the *Firestorm's* stern. They all wore black clothing, and all looked more annoyed than anything as if the *Firestorm's* arrival had interrupted some major plans they had for today.

If you're pissed off now, just you wait, Fischer thought tapping his link closed.

"You got this?" he said aloud. "By the looks of those guys, I'd say the odds of things getting dicey are good."

Robalt looked up from his panels, grinned, and nudged the MOD27 leaning against the console in front of him. "Don't threaten me with a good time, sir."

"You don't have to call me, sir."

"Right on," the Marine said with a nod. He tapped his ear, signalling his implant. "We're up on taclink. Hit me up if you need me, okay?"

"Hopefully, it won't come to that."

"Hope in one hand and shit in the other and see which one fills up faster."

Fischer chuckled. "Touché."

Fischer held the hatch open for Eliwood, the shut it behind them, sealing the Saber inside.

"How do you see this going?" Eliwood asked, following him through the maze of weapons containers.

"Well," Fischer said, "they're either going to buy it, or they won't, and my guess is we'll know pretty quick whether all this was for nothing."

"Fantastic."

Fischer swiped his link closed as they started to weave through the container stacks, toward the stern of the ship. He felt a mixture of exhilaration and anticipation. The fact that they'd actually found this place was a testament to good police work, but its actual existence was in and of itself, problematic. Whoever these raiders worked for had deep pockets and a wide reach, further than anything Fischer had ever come up against. If, in fact, they weren't simply a coalition of pirates and criminals working together for the first time in hundreds of years, Fischer guessed this would not be the end of their journey. Regardless of whether or not Young was here.

"Go ahead and drop the ramp, Jonesy, we're almost there," Fischer said.

"Roger that."

"Remember," Fischer told Eliwood. "We're arms dealers. Keep your game face on."

Eliwood nodded but said nothing.

A metallic *clank* echoed through the bay as the ramp's locks disengaged, followed by an audible hiss as the pistons began lowering the ramp to the deck below. Illumination panels and spotlights along the cargo bay's ceiling activated in response to the agent's arrival.

Fischer bent, trying to get a look at the approaching group, only managing to catch a glimpse of their feet and legs before straightening back up. He blew out a long breath, working to calm his nerves and slowly started making his way down the ramp. He moved with a kind of nonchalant gait he'd seen others use, giving off the impression that he thought he was better than the people he was descending to do business with. As if leaving the sanctity of his ship to speak with them was beneath him.

The man leading the group was a short, pudgy, balding man, whose cheeks were bright red. A telltale sign of a man who'd spent years drinking hard. He looked more like an aged politician than a raider, like he'd spent the majority of his adult life hunched over a glass of alcohol in a seedy bar at the back end of the galaxy. He tucked his jacket behind the holstered pistol on his hip, obviously trying to draw attention to it. This man wanted everyone to know he was carrying.

But as Fischer eyed the three others, he noticed they all had weapons, too The man and woman directly behind him had at least one pistol each, and the last man had an old model R6 slung over his neck, muzzle pointing at the deck.

The pudgy man waved a hand at Fischer, hastening him down the ramp. "Eh, Fero, yeah? You're fucking late."

"Yeah," Fischer said without changing his pace. "What do you want me to say? Traffic."

The man stopped at the bottom of the ramp, a hand on each hip, like he was a parent getting ready to scold a child. "The contract listed very specific pick-up and delivery times, Fero. I don't know what you want me to say."

Fischer knew a prolonged argument wasn't going to do them any favors, but he also knew this man was sizing up him and his crew, trying to determine how far he could push Fischer around.

"We're here now," Fischer said. "We going to do business or not?"

"Business is already done," the man said. "We just need the shit of your ship, yeah?"

Fischer frowned. Danva had told them they'd only received half of the payment upfront.

"Don't give us that shit," Eliwood said, stepping past Fischer. "The deal was half now, half on delivery. We're here, so where's our money? And don't give this 'you're late, you're not getting full price' bullshit. We're here with all the product. You short us, we'll short you. That's just how it's going to be."

The man was either surprised at Eliwood's outburst or feigning it. He held his hands out to the side. "But you are late. Five hours late."

"We're two hours late, and we had delivery issues," Eliwood said without skipping a beat. "But fine, you want to argue about payment? You'll pay for what you get. Stiff us on cost, you're not getting all the product."

"You're hardly in a position to negotiate," the man said. He eyed his companions. "I appear to be holding the better cards."

"You *think* you are," Eliwood said. "But you aren't. You might only see two of us, but we're not stupid. Do you think we'd come all this way without making sure we had some kind of insurance plan? Right now, there's four auto-cannons pointed at you and your friends there, and the man at the trigger has been itching to fire them ever since we had them installed."

The man laughed. "Auto-cannons? Come on, give me a break. At least come up with something original."

"Hey, don't believe us," Fischer said. "That's fine. That's your mistake."

The man considered both agents for a long time, then sniffed. He wiggled a finger at Eliwood. "I see you live up to your reputation, that's good. I've met so many piss-babies that fold under the slightest bit of pressure. Always good to see that there are still people in this business that can handle proper business."

He stepped onto the ramp and extended a hand as he neared. "Sanderman's the name, but everyone just calls me Sandy."

Eliwood hesitated for a moment, then shook Sanderman's hand. "Danva. You ready to do business or what?"

Fischer shook the offered hand, suppressing the urge to smile at Eliwood's performance. She'd surprised him with just how forceful she came on but was glad that it had worked.

Sanderman looked passed them. "Thirty-six, eh? That's the biggest load so far. Cardinal's going to be happy."

"Damn straight he is," Eliwood said.

Fischer motioned up the ramp. "Shall we get started?"

Emergency Egress Compartment #1
Commercial Freighter *Firestorm*
4 August 2607

"Drones out," Cole said, the glow of his link reflecting off his face in the dimly lit compartment.

"Drones out," Guerrero repeated.

Sheridan and the rest of the team watched as the two operators deployed their individual fleet of drones. At maximum capacity, both operators could control twenty drones each, either as a cohesive group or as single units. The drones launched from external housings they'd mounted to *Firestorm's* hull right before they'd dropped from the JumpLane.

Immediately, images and data began flowing into the taclink, populating information the entire team drank in like cold crisp water on a hot afternoon. Sheridan tapped through various angles of the bay, noting the locations of the vessels parked on the deck below and watching the people moving between them.

"Doesn't appear to be any guards," Hanover observed, looking up from his link.

"I'm not reading any IR signals either, and their network doesn't look like it's set up as a security device," Cole said. "I don't think they have any active security programs running."

"Confirmed," Robalt said over the taclink. *"The only inter-linked systems they're running are life-support, communications, power, and gravfield. I'm not picking up any kind of security channels at all."*

"It's like they don't expect any trouble at all," Sergeant Rocha said, eyeing her feed from the drones.

"Don't have a lot of reason to, do they?" Captain Chambers asked. "They're hidden in a remote system off anyone's radar. They've got dozens of combat-ready ships out there that aren't governed by any kind of regulations or rules of engagement. They don't have any reason to worry about internal threats, because anyone that gets through that web of destruction out there most obviously belongs here."

"And the fact that they're pirates," Sheridan muttered before he'd even realized he was going to say it. His gaze flicked to the Captain, who'd turned to him, grinning. "Uh, sir. Sorry, sir."

"No need for apologies, Sheridan. We're all on the same team here," Chambers said. "You know my expectations. If you have an assessment, make it."

"Yes, sir," Sheridan said. "Like you said, they don't have rules or regs to follow. Even if they have a chain of command, we've seen from experience that that chain is extremely loose. Most of these people have been doing this kind of thing for a long time—they all know the game. If you screw up in their ranks, it isn't just a simple reprimand and a week's pay. They're looking at going out the airlock without a void suit. The likelihood of breaking whatever rules they do have in place is probably very slim."

Chambers nodded, though whether or not he'd entertained that line of thought wasn't clear. Sheridan hoped he hadn't over-stepped his bounds, despite the Captain's invitation to speak.

He'd know many officers whose "open-door" policies were merely token gestures.

"Seems logical," Chambers said. "Actually, the more I think about it, it gives me an idea. There's probably too many people out here for everyone to know exactly who everyone is. I was anticipating having to dodge security teams and cameras, but if those aren't issues, we might very well be able to walk right through the front door."

"We'll just have to convince the others that we *belong* here," Master Sergeant Kline said.

"Exactly," Chambers said.

"The probes have begun structure mapping," Robalt said. *"Streaming it to you now."*

"Roger that," Kline said. He tapped his link, and a three-dimensional holo-image began to drawn itself above the sergeant's arm.

The three transfer stations appeared first, followed by the tubes to the outpost proper, one hundred meters between them. That would be the most exposed area for the Sabers. With nowhere to run, they'd been so many fish in a barrel until they exited the other side. The outpost proper began to appear on the far end of the tube, multiple sections separated into ten decks and broken down further by compartments.

"Big bitch," Cole said.

Sheridan nodded in agreement. If the locator beacon didn't highlight the admiral—former admiral, he reminded himself—the likelihood of finding him was next to nothing. Even if everything with Fischer and the weapons went off without a hitch, there wouldn't be enough time to search the entire complex.

Chambers was marking points on the floating holo-map of the station; checkpoints from which the team could identify and coordinate movement. "Alpha, Bravo, Charle, Delta, Echo. If we haven't located Young's beacon by the time we've reached Alpha, we're going to spit to cover more ground. Once we've located our target, we converge and then fall back to the *Firestorm*, understood?"

Everyone nodded.

"Our number one goal now is to make it off the ship without anyone observing a large group of armed mercs disembarking." Chambers motioned to the image of the bay we were in. "I'm sure that'll raise some flags, regardless of the lack of security. We'll depart in teams, Sheridan and Cole—"

"I can vent the exhaust from the coolant system," Jones said over the taclink, interrupting Chambers mid-sentence.

Everyone in the compartment exchanged looks. For a brief moment, Master Sergeant Kline looked like he was about to lose his mind on the pilot, but kept silent at a hand from Captain Chambers. Jones had been given access to the channel because of the needs of the operation, but it was apparent Kline wasn't happy about the pilot listening in on their discussion.

"Mister Jones," Chambers said, "you have an idea?"

"Eh, it's not my idea, per se," Jones said. *"I mean, I don't know who originally came up with the idea, probably some dumb kid hit the wrong switch and—"*

"Mister Jones, we're a little pressed for time here," Chambers said.

"Right. It's simple: the exhaust steam ejects through ports along the hull. Usually, this is done in space, but sometimes, people get button punchy, and it happens in dock. I've seen it a few times, though it's a little uncommon. If you're quick, you can make it down and out, and nobody will be the wiser."

The barest hint of a smile turned up at the corner of Captain Chamber's mouth. "Very good, Mister Jones."

"Hey, I'm here for you," the pilot responded.

A handful of Sabers laughed at that. Even Kline cracked a smile.

The captain nodded. "Jonesy it is. As soon as we're rails down, vent the exhaust. I want to be off this bird before the landing cycles complete."

"No problem," Jones said. *"We'll be on the deck in about sixty seconds."*

"Understood." Chambers nodded to Cole and Guerrero. "How's the view?"

"Lots of workers looks like," Cole reported, eyes on his link's display, fingers tapping and swiping away, sending instructions to his drones. "Difficult to distinguish between yard dog and merc. But I count about twenty-seven so far, marking them on the battlenet."

Without their helmets, the team would have to rely on their feeds from the links to locate the targets he'd tagged but watching your arm when you were supposed to be sweeping for enemy targets wasn't an ideal situation. The team would have to rely on their two drone operators to be their eyes. Knowing the geographical layout their operational area was one of the least appreciated skills of Sabers controlling the eyes in the sky but was easily one of the most important. It required a large amount of situational awareness and the ability to know where the team was in relation to a threat so the operator could give them accurate information about the threat.

"From our target LZ, we should only run into about two or three," Guerrero said. "And they haven't looked up from their repairs since I spotted them."

"Very good," Captain Chambers said.

"Thirty seconds," Jones advised.

"Sergeant Rocha, your team has point," Chambers said. "Eyes on that first group of workers. Take us straight to the transit tube. Robbi, how're we looking for a signal on our target?"

"Still working on it, sir," Robalt answered. *"Probes are*

almost finished mapping the station, then we should be able to get an accurate read."

"Ten seconds," Jones said.

Hurry up and wait was something of a known standard for all military operations, but waiting while in the middle of an assault was not something anyone wanted to do. Much less behind enemy lines, trying to maintain a low profile. Five for six people moving together through the station might not be noticed, but five or six people standing around waiting for directions would definitely not go unnoticed.

Please let him be here, Sheridan thought, grinding his teeth. The worry that Young wasn't actually here weighed on him, but he wanted to stay positive. It was the only thing he could do now. *He's here.*

The deck shifted under him, and the pitch of the engines changed as *Firestorm* flared before touching down. The mechanical whine of the landing struts folding down, reverberating through the hull. The freighter rocked ever-so-slightly as it settled.

"All right, you're clear," Jones said over the taclink. *"Venting exhaust."*

Master Sergeant Kline nodded to Oliver, who cranked the manual lock and pulled the hatch open. There was a hiss as white clouds of exhausted filled the air outside, concealing the rest of the bay from view. Visual countermeasures worked both ways.

Kennedy and Richards stepped forward with the coils of polymer cable they'd been holding and tossed them through the open hatch. The thin wire was a centimeter in diameter, but strong enough to tow an Albatross. Both were connected to anchor points above the hatch.

Kennedy already had his grapnel handle out and ready, latching it onto the cable and stepping through the hatch. Richards followed suit on his own cable, and the rest of the team stepped forward, waiting for their turns.

Sheridan stepped up to the hatch and reached out, slipping his grapnel handle around the thin cable above his head. He thumbed the handle's activator switch on the top of the handgrip, and the device clamped down. On the edge of the hatch, he pulled, testing the handle's grip then stepped out, thumbing the control. The grapnel's lock disengaged, and he slid smoothly down the cable.

It was a short five-second drop, and the still-venting exhaust did mask their arrival, but Sheridan still felt exposed and vulnerable. Even with one hand on his rifle, there wasn't anywhere to go, he was captive to the ride until it was over.

Once on the deck, he left his handle attached and immediately moved away, following the Sabers ahead of him. It was everything he could do to not bring his weapon up to bear. The operational instructions called for slung weapons. Even carrying them at low-ready would've been painting them with a big sign that said "We're military and we're not supposed to be here." So, he let his MOD27 hang from its sling in front of him, muzzle pointing toward the deck, partially covered by his jacket.

"On the ground," Chambers advised in a low voice over the taclink.

"Moving to eyeball," Hanover said, stepping away from the rest of the team. He'd slung the black, canvas case concealing his HR91 slung over his back, but even without the weapon in his hand, Sheridan knew the man was as deadly—or more so—with his sidearm than anyone on the Team. He peeled off to the left, heading to find a perch by which he could observe the bay as a whole, but remain unseen. They'd identified over twenty different locations that would provide them such a platform, but like the rest of the mission, those were dependent on whether or not he could reach them without being seen.

"Same," Vega said. She adjusted the rifle's black, canvas carry case over one shoulder and headed off in the opposite direction.

The hangar bay seemed to materialize around them as they edged away from the freighter—walls that reached up a hundred meters to the ceiling and stretched away from them for almost twice that on either side.

The row of frigates to their right blocked much of the hangar from view. A couple were in pieces, with parts strewn across the deck around them. Sparks shot out from the near side, where two workers were busy welding what looked like additional armor plating onto the ship's fuselage. Neither man looked up as the Sabers passed by.

So far so good, Sheridan thought. He looked over his shoulder and saw the faint outline of *Firestorm's* stern cargo ramp lowering. Fischer would be contacting their raiders any minute now. Soon they would know whether or not their cover was going to hold, or whether or not this mission would be over before it even got started.

CHAPTER 41

Main Cargo Bay
Commercial Freighter *Firestorm*
4 August 2607

"I've got a signal," Robalt said over the taclink. *"Patching it through to your links now. Not one hundred percent on the ID yet, but I'm not sure who else it could be."*

Fischer's pulse skipped a beat, and it was everything he could do to keep from immediately checking his link to verify what the Marine was saying. The notification had come through his implant, and as he made eye contact with Eliwood. He knew she'd received the same message. She gave Fischer an almost imperceptible nod, and he turned back to the balding raider.

"Moving," Captain Chambers said.

Sandy was scrolling down a panel on his link, counting the crates on the manifest. The others had moved off, inspecting the first few containers, obviously making sure everything was in order.

Sandy shook his head and smiling. "Goddamn, we really hit

the jackpot here, you know it? I didn't think they were going to pull this shit off."

They? Fischer thought.

"What you think, Jade?" Sandy asked.

The lone woman in their party, who'd leaned over inspecting one of the seals near the bottom of one of the crates, straightened. "Seals are intact." She gave Eliwood, standing next to her, a side-long look. "These first ones, at least."

"They're all sealed," Eliwood said, putting just the right amount of exasperation into her voice. "And they're all ready to be moved, too."

The woman, Jade, crossed her arms. "What's the big hurry?"

Eliwood let out an overdramatized sigh, putting both arms out to her side. "What's the hurry? Nothing, I just don't like being this far out in the middle of nowhere. Do you know how long it took us to get out here, and there's no return haul? I think it's the first time we've ever not had a carry-on run."

"That's very sad for you," Jade said, deadpan, obviously unfazed by Eliwood's frustrations.

"Sorry about that," Fischer said under his breath to Sandy while jerking a thumb at his partner. "She gets cabin fever on these long runs."

Sanderman laughed. When he spoke, he didn't bother keeping his volume down. "The great Danva, cabin fever? I never would've guessed."

Eliwood put both hands on her hips. "The hell did you say?"

"Nothing," Fischer said. "Don't worry about it."

"Don't be talking shit about me." Eliwood pointed at him. "I'll fucking kick your ass again."

"It's him," Robalt advised, his voice low despite speaking through the implant. *"One hundred percent match. He's on level six, section thirty-seven."*

Fischer listened as the Sabers relayed messaged back and forth between themselves, but didn't hear any of the words.

Young was here.

He hadn't felt this much anticipation for taking someone into custody since the day he'd arrested Young on the platform after returning from Stonemeyer. He would make sure the man received justice this time, by any means necessary.

"...I said, when can we start unloading?" Sanderman said, his words bringing Fischer back from his thoughts.

"Right now," Eliwood said for him. "And the faster, the better."

"Yeah, yeah." Sanderman waved at his other cohorts, then headed down the platform.

"Just stay out of our way," Jade told Eliwood as she passed her. "Wouldn't want anything to happen to your pretty little face."

Eliwood shot her a grin. "I hope that's a threat."

"Oh, don't worry. It is."

When the four raiders were out of earshot, Fischer said, "Laying it on kind of thick, don't you think?"

Eliwood shrugged. "It worked. Besides, they expected it. You saw how they acted."

"I'm impressed."

"I know you are."

Fischer doubled-checked that the mercenaries weren't looking, then tapped his link. "Did you hear?"

She nodded. "Son of a bitch is as good as caught."

The images feed from *Legend's* probes were being supplied through Robalt and forwarded to the team. For the purposes of communication and tactical direction, the hangar bay where they'd landed had been labeled south. Right now, the Marines were moving north through Deck One, five decks above their target. The outpost had four main lifts at the center of the complex, and stairs leading down to every deck at each of the corners. Corridors crisscrossed in a grid pattern, cut out of the very rock the outpost was built on.

A red triangle on the second-to-last deck down, in the northern section, marked their target's location. A cluster of red dots represented the Marine team. They'd just exited out of the main tunnel connecting the hanger and the outpost and were in the process of spreading out in teams of two and threes. The five rally points, Alpha, Bravo, Charlie, Delta, and Echo, glowed orange.

"Valkyrie Actual to all Valkyrie Elements, proceed to Delta," Captain Chambers said over the taclink. *"We need to make sure there are no alternative exits out of that compartment."*

A chorus of acknowledgments came back over the link. A small group of dots branched off, moving east, heading for the southeast stairwell. The two groups split off at an intersection, then made their way through parallel corridors, toward the north end of the complex.

Eliwood hung back as Fischer reached the hatch to the sensor room. "I'll keep an eye out. Make sure no one sneaks up on us."

Inside, Robalt looked up from the screens. "We got the son of a bitch."

"We don't have him yet," Fischer corrected. He gazed over the myriad of screens Robalt was working with, almost over-whelmed by the amount of information pouring into the console. He focused on the outpost schematic. "It's pretty damn tight out there."

"Set up like a starship interior," Robalt said. "Looks very utilitarian."

"There isn't a direct route to the bay from there," Fischer said, pointing. "If they get into trouble down there..." He trailed off.

"They can handle themselves," Robalt said. "We're Sabers—it's what we do."

"Can we make contact with *Legend*?"

"We *can*. The question is, should we? They don't have any active security sensors set up that I can see, but that doesn't mean that their computers wouldn't pick up a comm signal, even an encrypted one. Hell, an encrypted signal would probably raise more alarm than a regular connection."

Fischer nodded. "Especially Alliance Military encryption."

"Exactly."

Fischer inhaled deeply and let it out slowly. He had to make sure he wasn't going to make bad decisions. Not now. He couldn't lose his mind and let everything unravel when he was so close to the end. There wasn't much he could do from here other than watch, and as much as he wanted to rush out and be the one to grab Young, he knew it wouldn't work.

You have your job, and they have theirs, Fischer told himself, watching the dots move through the outpost. It kicked himself mentally. He always seemed to forget that he wasn't dealing with regular grunts here on their first mission, with no real experience. These were all hardened veterans of the special operations community, and they knew their business. Every shot extremely qualified and trained.

But at the same time, he wanted to reach out to *Legend* and get them moving. The faster they got here, the better. Because as much as Fischer wanted to believe that Young was an inept fool, the former admiral was anything but. He was competent, cunning, and ruthless. He would stop at nothing to win. He didn't have any sort of moral compass, there were no lines he wouldn't cross.

Fischer had known that from the day he'd first met Young, and yet, the man had always stayed ahead of his downfall, if just barely. Even after Stonemeyer, when Fischer had thought the man was finally finished, he'd managed to escape. Not a small feat considering the circumstances. And whatever happened here today, Fischer was not about to let Young get away again.

"Valkyrie Actual, Overwatch One. Be advised, I have eyes on

a uniformed military officer. He appears to be Pegasi," Sergeant
Hanover, one of the Saber snipers, said over the taclink.

Fischer and Robalt exchanged confused looks.

"Did he say Pegasi?" Fischer asked.

"Overwatch, Actual, say again?"

*"I have eyes on what appears to be a Pegasi military officer
disembarking a shuttle on the far side of the bay. Rank on his
shoulder says he's a Colonel in their PKE."*

"We're re-tasking a drone to verify," Captain Chambers said.

The PKE, or Peacekeeper Elite, were the special forces arm of
the Pegasi military, like the Alliance's MARSOC Marines. They
deployed on any number of missions, up to and including assassi-
nation of enemies of the state, both foreign and domestic.

Robalt swiped the correct panel up, enlarging the image as the
drone moved into position high above the new arrival. The officer, dressed in traditional red and black of the PKE, stood talking
with one of the raiders, seemingly relaxed and comfortable. The
officer was in his forties, clean-shaven, and fit. Like all in the
special operations lifestyle, it was a requirement of the job.

"Can we get audio?" Fischer asked, leaning closer to the
panel. "He's Pegasi, all right. What the fuck is he doing out
here?"

Robalt nodded. "It'll be a few seconds for the drone to get
without range. There's a lot of background noise to scrub
through."

The door opened, and Eliwood stepped in. "They're
offloading."

On another screen, three six-wheeled loaders approached
Firestorm's loading ramp.

Fischer watched the loader roll up to the first container,
wrapped its giant lifting clamps around it and lifted it off the
deck. As it rolled away, the second loader took its place, picking
up the next container. In less than two minutes, the workers had

removed three containers and were setting them on the deck in front of *Firestorm's* cargo ramp.

"It's not going to take them long to unload all those crates," Robalt observed.

"We might need to expedite this," Fischer said.

"Right now, stealth is a much more valuable asset that our firepower. The longer we can remain quiet, the better for everyone involved. Means less shooting, and that means less dying. For us and them."

"I highly doubt these raiders would stand against your team," Eliwood said.

"And I don't disagree," Robalt said. "But we aren't super-soldiers. We're not invulnerable. Even a poorly aimed, horribly operated weapon can kill. And once the shooting starts, it won't stop until we've completed the mission or they're dead."

Fischer noted that he didn't say mention the possibility of the Sabers not surviving. The warrior mentality these men and women had wasn't suited to thinking in those terms. What was that old adage? In a gunfight, keep fighting because you'll never know if you lost. There was no quit in these Sabers, and right now those were the kind of people that Fischer desperately needed.

A soft tone chimed.

"We've got audio," Robalt said.

The sound quality wasn't great and came in at a tinny pitch, but considering the size of the hangar bay and the amount of background noise, it was still pretty good.

"...on schedule," the Pegasi officer was saying as he stepped off the shuttle's boarding ramp.

The raider nodded. "Of course. We've just been waiting on this latest shipment. Now that it's here, we'll be able to start Phase Three."

"Excellent. Cardinal is anxious to move forward. Have you inspected the weapons yet?"

Cardinal again, Fischer thought. He was almost as desperate to know who this Cardinal fellow was as he was to get his hands on Young again.

"No, we're just now offloading them," the raider said, pointing toward *Firestorm.* "Sanderson's overseeing the operation. Shouldn't take us too long. Then we can get that damn freighter out of here. I don't know why Gav decided to use a third party for this shipment. Doesn't make a whole lot of sense."

"Have you talked with him yet?"

The raider shook his head. "Bastard's probably still doing his hair."

"We're too close to the endgame now," the Pegasi said. "We can't afford to have our people out of position for too long. A simple weapons delivery is something we can contract out."

"We're getting ready to stage at Delta," Captain Chambers advised over the taclink. On the map next to the video feed of the Pegasi Colonel, a group of six stacked at the end of a short corridor leading to the room Young was in. *"Agent Fischer, what's your assessment? Go or no go?"*

"Once they go through that hatch, shit's going to get dicey. Hold up." Robalt raised a hand. He pointed to one of the video feeds on the panels in front of him. A woman appeared behind the Pegasi officer, ducking as she stepped through the shuttle's exterior hatch.

Fischer scooted around the Marine for a better look. Someone new had arrived—a woman with blue hair dressed in a long, black overcoat that hung almost to the floor.

"Where are Fero and Danva?" the woman asked, brushing strands of blue hair from her face and giving the engines a frustrated look.

"Let's go, Colonel," the blue-haired woman said, leading their small party toward *Firestorm.* "I want that freighter dealt with as soon as possible."

"Shit," Fischer said and headed for the hatch.

"What's wrong," Eliwood asked, staying on Fischer's heels as he jogged through the bay.

"Our blue-haired mystery woman," Fischer said. "She's here."

"Do you think she knows who…" Eliwood trailed off.

"Yeah, she knows," Fischer said. "If Gav knew, she knows."

"What are you going to do?"

Fischer shook his head. "I have no fucking idea."

They reached the ramp just as the blue-haired woman, Sanderson, and Jade did. The blue-haired woman was breathing heavily and stomping toward them, pointing.

"Let's go, you morons. We haven't got all day here!" the blue-haired woman shouted.

"Hey now, we're going as fast as we can," Sandy threw out his arms to the side. "You don't want us to mess anything up, do you?"

"What the hell is going on?" Fischer asked, trying to keep any nervousness out of his voice. "Who the hell are you?"

The blue-haired woman sneered. "Who am I? Well, you would know that if you were actually Fero. But, as I've met the *real* Fero, and you obviously don't know who I am, it's painfully clear that you aren't him."

"Look," Fischer said, "I don't know what the hell his going on, but Fero hired us to bring this shit out here. I don't know anything other than that."

The Pegasi office came up behind the woman. "What's going on here? I—" His eyes fell on Fischer and widened in obvious recognition. His hand dropped to the pistol holstered on his hip. "Oh, fu—"

His head exploded in a cloud of red mist and gore. Blood sprayed across the woman, Sanderson, and the others behind him; all standing in utter shock. The officer's body stood there for several seconds, and for a brief moment, Fischer wondered if it was going to fall. Then, finally, it slumped to the ground, collapsing on top of itself.

"Valkyrie Actual, Overwatch, hostile target down. I have engaged," Hanover advised. *"I say again, I have engaged hostile contacts."*

"Fuck," Fischer said, moving for cover.

CHAPTER 42

Corridor Four-B
Raider Outpost, Astalt System
4 August 2607

Sheridan peered around the corner, MOD27 finally in his hands where it felt most comfortable. They were about ten meters from the target room. Sergeant Rocha and Richards were behind him in the stack, with Cole and Reese holding rear security, making sure no one snuck up on them while they were prepping the breach.

The corridor was dark, lit by sporadic light strips on either side of the ceiling. Sterile white light reflected off the sheer rock face. Strips of glittering minerals curved their way through the dull gray rock, twinkling in the light from the panels. Air ducts and power conduits hung from brackets drilled straight into the rock.

Sheridan could feel the adrenaline start to flood into his system as the anticipation grew. The target hatch was positioned directly between the two corridors the team was now stacking in. In the other passage, outside of Sheridan's view, Team Two's explosives and demolition technician, Sergeant Dustin Oliver, was prepping his charges.

"... I say again, I have engaged hostile contacts."

Sheridan's stomach tightened as Hanover finished his report.

Son of a bitch, he thought. *That didn't last long.*

"Oliver, move," Chambers said over the taclink. *"Eyes up, team. We're moving."*

The explosives tech didn't answer over the comms, but a second later, he appeared around the far corner, moving quickly up the hatch to place his charges. Sheridan brought his rifle to bear, covering Oliver, gritting his teeth and holding his breath.

It took less than five seconds to place his charges, one over the top hinge, one over the bottom hinge. When they were secure, Oliver doubled back around the safety of the corner.

"Fire in the hole," Oliver advised. "Three, two..."

Sheridan jammed a finger into each ear and closed his eyes. Even from behind cover, without his helmet's sound dampeners, the blast would be deafening. The charges blew a second later, and Sheridan felt the concussion wash over him, the explosion still loud, despite his finger-plugs.

A half-second later, his hands found his rifle, and he was peering around the corner, eye squinting against the cloud of smoke and dust. He sensed rather than felt his teammates behind him and pressed through to the hatch. Nguyen and Guerrero appeared ahead of him, on the opposite side of the now blown hatch.

Sergeant Nguyen motioned to himself and pointed through the hatch to Sheridan's side of the room. Then, to Sheridan he pointed a knife-hand back his direction. Sheridan nodded understanding and Nguyen stepped into the room, searching.

Sheridan followed him, stepping through the hatch, rifle up and sweeping across the far bulkhead. A chair had been blown over from the blast, which he moved around with practiced grace, turning and continuing down the bulkhead to the back of the room. A meter in front of him, a man was pushing himself off the floor.

"Stay down!" Sheridan shouted, driving a knee into the man's back, right between his shoulder blades. He pushed him to the deck, looking forward, seeing two more picking themselves up, obviously dazed from the blast. Movement behind an overturned table caught his attention. He put all of his weight onto his knee, forcing the man down, and pointed. "Movement!"

"Don't fucking move!" Cole shouted, moving past Sheridan.

A chorus of shouting and curses filled the room. Sheridan swung his rifle around behind him and pulled a pair of electrocuffs from his back pocket. He grabbed the man's arms, pressed them together, and slapped the cuffs around his wrists.

On the other side of the room, Nguyen, Guerrero, and Kennedy were taking another one into custody as Reese and Rocha moved past them.

"Stay down, or you're dead," Sheridan shouted, standing.

Two shots rang out. Someone yelled out in pain. Across the room, Kennedy stumbled backward.

Sheridan swung his rifle around. At the back of the room, a man in a black jacket was getting to his feet, hand extending, holding a pistol. Sheridan fired at the same time three others did. The man spasmed as multiple bullets hit him. He fell against the far bulkhead, then slid to the deck, gun falling from his fingers.

"Go!" Chambers shouted, patting Sheridan on the shoulder, taking his place watching the prisoner.

Sheridan edged around Cole, who was also standing. There were two behind the table. The closest was struggling to pull the charging handle back on a rifle. Sheridan didn't give him the chance. He fired twice, putting two rounds into the side of his head. The man's skull burst, spraying the underside of the table behind him with blood. The impact shoved his body sideways, landing on a woman who was scrambling away from the collapsing corpse.

"Stop!" Sheridan shouted. "Don't fucking move!"

On the other side of the table, Nguyen tossed a chair out of the way, clearing a path to the woman. She looked over her shoulder as if trying to determine whether or not she could escape.

Sheridan stepped over the man he'd killed, closing on the woman. "Don't fucking move!"

Nguyen reached her, quickly yanked her to her feet and spun her around, pressing the electrocuffs around her wrist in a matter of seconds. That was when Sheridan noticed what she was wearing.

"Pegasi?" he said, confused.

The woman wore a black Pegasi Peacekeeper Elite uniform, complete with rows of colorful ribbons and metals. The rank insignia identified her as a General.

"Go fuck yourself," she shouted, then spat at him. She missed.

"Clear!" Nguyen said, stepping back from the woman, but keeping a hand on her arm.

"Trevion, check Ken," Captain Chambers said. He crossed the room to where Sheridan and Nguyen stood with the Pegasi General.

The two other captured raiders were being carried to their feet, cursing and trying to pull away. Panic started to wash over Sheridan as he scanned the room and over the faces of the two people they'd killed, praying they hadn't been ex-Admiral Young. He was only slightly relieved that they weren't.

"Where the hell is Young?" Sheridan asked.

"You're a little outside your jurisdiction, Captain," the Pegasi major sneered. She fought against Nguyen's grasp, and he jerked her back.

What the hell is going on? Sheridan thought.

His eyes flicked to the man he'd shot by the table and for the first time, realized he was also wearing a Pegasi uniform—he, too, a general. The dead man in the corner, wore an expensive-looking suit, now dotted with multiple bullet holes, blood staining the white shirt he wore beneath. It wasn't Young.

"Captain, you will stand down," the PKE general said.

Nguyen pulled on her arm. "Quiet."

"Where's Marcus Young?" Chambers asked the general.

The woman smiled at him. "Admiral Young's time here was over. But, as you've committed an act of war against the Pegasi Empire on her sovereign soil, perhaps his mission was a success after all."

"What does that mean?" Chambers asked. "What mission? Where's Young?"

"I don't have to answer your questions. You have no authority—"

"I'm not going to argue jurisdiction with you," Chambers said. "Where the hell is Marcus Young? And don't give me any bullshit about him not being here. We tracked his beacon directly to this room."

The woman laughed. "His beacon? You think we would just allow him to keep such a device? It was taken from him almost as soon as he arrived here."

"Bullshit," Sheridan said.

"See for yourself," she said, motioning to the floor beside the overturned table, to a six-inch case made of hard, black plastic, partially covered by an Alliance military uniform.

Cole pushed the table out of the way and picked up the case, giving Sheridan a questioning look. He visibly tensed, holding his breath as he popped the latch, then opened the case. He shook his head. "Son of a bitch."

Sheridan craned his neck to see. Inside, a tiny, silver device, no bigger than the end of his thumb, rested on foam padding, the smooth alloy skin stained with blood in several places. A look at the Alliance uniform on the floor gave Sheridan no doubts as to whom this implant had once belonged.

Sheridan stepped closer to the Pegasi general. "That doesn't mean he's not here. But if he's not here, where is he? You know where he is, and you're going to fucking tell us."

Still smiling, she said, "Your arrogance to think your position is an advantageous one is what will bring your Alliance to its knees."

Sheridan grabbed the general by her jacket and yanked her roughly toward him. "Where the fuck is he?"

"Sheridan, stand down," Chambers said.

Sheridan hesitated for a moment, eyes locked on the general's, then let her go and backed away, grinding his teeth.

Chambers turned to where Trevion was treating Kennedy. "How is he?"

"I'm good, sir," Kennedy said, blowing out a pained breath as the medic worked.

"One hit the armor, the other was a through and through to the upper arm," Trevion said. "Tissue damaged, no major arteries hit, no broken bones. Pushing some meds on now and sealing."

Chambers nodded and tapped his taclink. "Overwatch, Actual, what's your status?"

"Well," the sniper paused, the sound of gunfire echoing in the background. *"They know we're here."*

"Roger." Chambers looked around the room, jaw muscles clenching.

"Sir, we can't afford to get tied down in those passages out there," Kline said.

"You're never going to make it out of here alive," the general taunted.

Chambers nodded, ignoring the Pegasi.

Sheridan couldn't stop himself. "We can't leave. We have to find Young!"

348

Chambers turned to Sheridan, eyes hard, but sympathetic. "I'm sorry, Sheridan. But right now, room to room is out of the question. We need to get moving before we get pinned down."

"But, sir—"

"Not now," Chambers said, lifting a hand. "Overwatch, we're going to you."

"Roger," Hanover replied.

"And the prisoners?" Master Sergeant Kline asked.

Chambers looked around at the three prisoners. Only the woman was in a uniform. The other two were dressed in civilian clothes.

"You're going to die," the general said. "There's no way this ends well for any of you."

Sheridan turned and punched the general square in the face. He felt the cartilage in her nose crunch, and her eyes rolled back into her head. Her legs gave out underneath her, and she slumped down. Nguyen grunted, catching her before she hit the floor, his expression shocked.

"What the hell, Sheridan?" the Saber asked.

"You remember what happened to the others," Sheridan said. He looked to Chambers, half-expecting a reprimand for the action, but the captain didn't seem upset. In fact, he seemed to be considering Sheridan's words and actions in regard to the two remaining prisoners.

"Richards, can you?" Chambers let his question hang in the air as the medic stood up from helping Kennedy.

Richards looked from the captain to their two conscious prisoners, then back again, shaking his head. "I don't—"

Before he could finish, Chambers motioned to Kline. "Sergeant."

"Roger that, sir," Master Sergeant Kline said. He stepped forward and rammed the butt of his rifle into the side of the first man's head. His body collapsed, legs buckling underneath him, and Cole struggled to keep him upright as Kline continued to the next.

"What the—" the second man never finished his question. Kline's butt smacked against the side of his head. Oliver hefted the man's limp body onto his shoulder, gritting his teeth under the weight. Nguyen and Cole did the same.

"All right," Chambers said. "Rocha, Richards, clear us a path."

"Roger," they said in unison and left the room.

Sergeant Nguyen lifted the general and grunted as he ducked through the hatch after Kline. Cole followed with his prisoner, then Oliver with his. Sheridan brought up the rear, hesitating before stepping back out in the passageway. He looked over the room one last time, feeling like he wanted to vomit. Every fiber of his being screamed at him to go and find the bastard. He *knew* Young was here. Reluctantly, he followed the rest of the team through the hatch and back into the dim corridor.

"Contact," Rocha said. Gunshots rang out ahead of them, followed by shouting.

The unencumbered members of the team rushed to address the attack while the three carrying their prisoners hung back, advancing slowly as the lead elements pushed forward. Sheridan alternated between walking backward, and side-stepping, gritting his teeth as the exchange of gunfire continued ahead of the group. They weren't slowing, which suggested the enemy was falling back, but in this maze of corridors and rooms, a retreating enemy wasn't necessarily a good thing.

"They're cutting off Charlie," Rocha said, over the taclink. *"We're going to have to backtrack to Bravo."*

In front of Sheridan, Kline opened his link. The orange hue illuminated his face and brought up the outpost's layout. "Damn it."

"Actual, Overwatch, be advised, I have eyes on what looks

like an assault team forming near Charlie," Hanover reported. *"My guess is they're getting ready to hunt."*

"Roger that," Chambers said. "How's Bravo look? If we back-track, can we make it to *Firestorm*?"

"If you move fast, probably," Hanover said. *"But the world's going to shit pretty fast out here, Captain. A lot of ships are launching."*

"It's going to shit everywhere, Sergeant. Break. Valkyrie Actual, Legend Actual, be advised, we have engaged hostile contacts and are proceeding with exfil."

"Roger that, Valkyrie Actual," Captain Ward said. *"We are moving to assist. Do you have the package?"*

"Negative, *Legend*," Chambers said. "No joy."

CHAPTER 43

Hangar Bay
Raider Outpost, Astalt System
4 August 2607

"... No joy."

"Son of a bitch!" Fischer shouted as another barrage of rounds ricocheted off the weapons container at his back.

Four meters away, Robalt was pressed against another container, reloading his rifle. Gunshots echoed around them, accompanied by shouts and curses from the raiders throughout the compartment. In the distance, engines spun up as ships lifted off the hangar deck, heading for the void.

"I told you!" Eliwood shouted beside Fischer. "Shit always goes sideways."

On the deck between them and *Firestorm's* cargo ramp, four bodies lay dead, the Pegasi Colonel's head completely gone. Fischer didn't think he was ever going to get that image out of his brain. The fourth member of the raider's welcome party had made it ten meters before one of Hanover's bullets found him, taking him in the back and dropping him to the deck. Fischer had put two in the blue-haired woman's chest. She'd been mid-drawn, pulling a pistol from the small of her back. Her hand was still on the grip when she died. Eliwood had killed the first woman they'd seen, and Hanover had taken out Sanderson.

Now they were hunkered down among the unloaded weapons containers, exchanging sporadic fire with several raiders trying to get at them from behind the frigate on *Firestorm's* starboard side. Fischer leveled his pistol and fired off several shots, more to keep them pinned down than to actually hit anyone. Though he wouldn't have begrudged any of the rounds had they found soft targets.

Robalt saw what Fischer was doing, saw the group of raiders, and added his own fire to the mix, creating a shower of sparks spraying off the underside of two frigates parked closely together.

"What do you think?" Fischer asked, reloading his pistol.

"Fucked up like a football bat." The Saber leaned around the edge of the container behind them and fired off several bursts before retaking cover.

The second group of raiders had found refuge behind a shuttle, not wanting to cross the twenty meters of open deck between them and their prey. That was just fine with Fischer. The problem was *they* didn't have anywhere to go either.

Fischer, for his part, couldn't agree more. "We can't stay here."

A loud whoosh filled the air, and Fischer looked up just in time to see the rocket trail before the *Firestorm* shook under the impact of a violent explosion against the side of her hull. Smoke and flames curled down off the starboard side, raining twisted debris across the hangar bay. A second later, another explosion ripped through the hull, sending twisted chunks of steel and alloy through the air.

"What the fuck is that?" Eliwood shouted over the groaning of

Firestorm's landing rails as they strained to keep the heavy bulk of the ship upright.

"Rockets," Robalt called over. "They're attacking the freighter."

The high-pitched whine of engines screamed above them as a small corvette, almost like a two-seater Nemesis fighter, flew above them. The deck vibrated under them, and the thrumming drives reverberated in Fischer's chest. The corvette banked around, slicing through the smoke curling off the hull and headed for space.

Movement at the top of *Firestorm's* ramp caught Fischer's attention—Jones and Loomis running out of the bay and immediately ducking for cover as rounds sparked off the bulkheads around him. Robalt flipped around the side of his container and fired a long barrage, keeping it going until both men were clear of the ramp and ducking behind another of the containers.

"Son of a bitch!" Jones screamed, running down the ramp. "We need to get the fuck out of here!"

At least we're on the same page about that, Fischer thought.

The group near the frigates ahead were moving again, but this time, it looked like they were retreating, not advancing, running for something Fischer couldn't see.

"Where the hell are they going?" Eliwood shouted, obviously seeing the same thing.

"I don't know." Robalt keyed his taclink. "Hanover, you see anything? It seems like they're backing off."

"That's affirmative. Looks like a group just boarded a sprinter and are in the process of lifting off," the sniper reported. *"But that main group is shifting toward Bravo. I can't tell for sure, but it looks like they're moving in some heavy weapons. Might be an MG26 or something similar. On the far side of some long-term storage bins. They get those things set up we're going to be in a*

bad way. I don't have a shot. Captain, you're going to want to hurry, sir."

"Because we're not in a bad way already?" Fischer asked, Robalt, not over the taclink.

"We need to stop them from setting up that weapon," Robalt said, pointing across the bay. "We can't let them cut off the team's exit."

"We *need* to find a ride off of this fucking rock," Jones shouted.

Fischer's mind raced as he glanced around the bay, searching for options. There was a distinct lack of good ones. His gaze fell on the row of four frigates off to their right, between them and the raider group setting up their crew-served weapon. Two of them looked like they'd been recently gutted. A third looked like it was in the process of being put back together. The fourth and final frigate looked like most of the repairs and modifications had been completed, but there were still an awful lot of components strewn around the deck underneath it. It was a relatively small ship, compared to *Firestorm* at least, but it would be able to lift all of them out of here, and that's all that mattered.

If we can get it running, Fischer thought. He flinched at another barrage of twangs on the side of his container, sending sparks flying and vibrating the steel.

"Jones, can you fly one of those?" Fischer shouted.

Jones followed Fischer's gaze to the frigates, then immediately turned back. "You can't be serious."

"As a heart attack. Can you do it?"

"Yes, I can fucking fly them, but how the hell do we even know if their space-worthy? The damn thing could fall apart around us, and then we'd be fucked."

"It's either that or this." He motioned to the *Firestorm*.

Jones considered the vast bulk of the freighter and shook his head. "Son of a bitch."

Fischer looked over at Robalt. "If we can get that thing up and running, it'll give us wings and guns."

"That's a big 'if.'"

"It always is."

"This is crazy, Fish," Jones said. "You don't even know if that damn thing has power."

Fischer motioned the fuel cells lined up on the deck underneath the port side engine nacelle. "Those external fuel cells should." He turned to Robalt. "Right?"

Robalt chuckled. "It's slightly more complicated than that, but we might be able to make it work."

"We don't have much of a choice," Fischer said. He peered around the corner, checking to see where the first group of raiders had gone. A flash of movement at the shuttle caught his eye, and he saw a man raising a rifle. "Shit."

Fischer ducked back around the corner a second before the rounds slammed into the steel.

Overwatch," Robalt said, "you have eyes on?"

Hanover's voice was calm and steady. *"Affirmative."*

Fischer bounced on the balls of his feet, taking several long breaths. "Jonesy?"

Reluctantly, Jones got to his feet. "I don't know why I always let you talk me into the shit."

Fischer turned to Eliwood, who nodded at him. "Let's do this."

"I'll cover your move, then you cover mine," Robalt said, peering around his container, giving their deck behind them a quick scan. He fired off two three-round bursts and yelled, "Go!"

Fischer lunging forward at a full sprint. Ahead, Jones, and Loomis took off as well, Eliwood keeping pace slightly behind him. He weaved his way through the few remaining containers and reached the open deck. To his left was a group of three raiders who were in the middle of loading several containers into a small shuttle. One looked up as Fischer emerged from a cluster of containers and began frantically tapping on his companion's shoulder, pointing and shouting.

Fischer didn't hear the shot, but just as the second man was turning to see what his friend was warning him about, the first man's head disintegrated. The force of the impact pushed the first raider into the second, sending them both crashing to the ground.

"One down," Hanover said.

A rapid three-round burst sounded behind him, and the third man doubled over. Fischer glanced over his shoulder and saw Robalt lowering his rifle and beginning to run again.

"Go!" The Marine shouted, waving Fischer onward. "Go! Go!"

A man next to the fallen raider looked up, eyes wide in surprise, frantically trying to get his gun level. A cloud of red exploded from his chest, just below his clavicle. The impact knocked him back into the shuttle, and he fell to the deck.

"Two down," Hanover said.

The third shouted something Fischer couldn't hear and moved away from his fallen comrades, picking a rifle up off the deck, eyes locked on Fischer and his group. Without slowing, Fischer extended his pistol and fired one-handed, knowing his shots wouldn't find their target. The attack had its intended effect, however, forcing the raider to duck back into the shuttle as Fischer's rounds sparked off the deck and fuselage.

He reached the frigate, dropping to his knees and slid behind one of the maintenance carts under the port side engine nacelle, breathing heavy. Jones crouched down, looking back over the top of the cart, watching. Loomis sat with his back pressed against the cart, his breath coming in ragged gasps. He probably hadn't run like that in years, if ever.

Eliwood reached them, ducking behind one of the aft landing rails. Between breaths, she said, "This is really bad, Fish!"

Fischer pointed to the shuttle as Robalt approached. "There's still one in there."

The Saber knelt down behind a crate that wasn't anywhere big enough to conceal him. His rifle pulled into his shoulder, he leveled it toward the shuttle. "Got ya covered." He fired off several controlled bursts, twangs echoing as the rounds smacked into the shuttle.

From his new position, Fischer could see the majority of the hangar bay, and the raiders setting up to their MG26, ready to slaughter the Sabers trying to make their escape. Several were shouting and cursing, firing down the length of the access tube. Others were finishing the set up of their weapon.

We need to—

The MG26 barked, its report loud and steady. The raiders cheered as the weapon fired, and Fischer didn't need to see the target to know whatever was at the business end of that position was being wholly obliterated. They needed to do something and fast.

"Jones," Fischer said, motioning to the frigate's open personnel hatch halfway down the fuselage. "See if you can get her started."

Jones looked at Fischer, frowning, almost as if he hadn't understood what Fischer had said.

"Jonesy!" Fischer snapped his fingers.

"Shit," Jones said, shaking himself out of his trance. He eyed the frigate, then nodded. "Right."

Sparks erupted from the front side of the cart just as Jones was getting to his feet. He cursed, dropping to the deck. Flat on his chest, he looked up at Fischer, red-faced. "I fucking hate getting shot at, Fish! Hate it!"

"Yeah, well—"

Another round of incoming bullets peppered the hull of the frigate above them, cutting Fischer off. Crouching behind the cart, Fischer glanced around. This had been a great idea when he had been protected by large steel containers, but now, hiding behind practically nothing, the plan didn't seem nearly as clever.

To his left, Robalt cried out, falling to his rear, holding his left arm, his teeth bared in obvious pain.

"Robalt!" Fischer yelled. He started to get up, but another barrage kept him pinned down. "Son of a bitch!"

Eliwood rushed to the Saber's side, pulling him back behind the frigate's landing rail.

"I'm okay! I'm okay!" Robalt growled as she helped him to his feet. He grimaced, clearly in pain, and brought the rifle up, holding it awkwardly in one hand.

"Here," Eliwood said, reaching for the MOD27. "Switch."

Robalt hesitated for a moment, the relented, handing the rifle over and taking Eliwood's proffered pistol. Eliwood looped the sling over her head, then raised the weapon to look down through the sights. The gun bucked slightly in her grip as she fired, but not as much as Fischer had anticipated. She put a few bursts toward the shuttle, then another burst back at the containers they'd left moments before.

"Fish, whatever the hell you're going to do, you better do it now!" Eliwood shouted.

"Jones," Fischer said, "Go!"

Keeping low, Jones went for the hatch as Fischer ran to Eliwood and Robalt. "You good?"

"Fine," Robalt grunted.

"Come on, let's get you inside."

Fischer pulled the Saber to his feet and laced his uninjured arm around his neck. Together, they made for the ladder leading to the hatch. Jones was already climbing inside, and Loomis was right behind him. Eliwood kept pace beside them, every few steps firing off another burst from the Saber's rifle. They weren't aimed shots, just enough to make the enemy second-guess making an appearance.

He helped Robalt up first. The Saber's climb was awkward without the use of his left arm. Fischer followed closely behind, helping the man keep his balance, all the while acutely aware of how exposed they all were.

Inside the ship was dark, the passageways lit only by pale yellow emergency lights along the top corners of the bulkheads. A small airlock was just inside the hatch, about five meters across, the opposite hatch leading to a corridor that spanned the width of the ship.

"Well, there's power, anyway," Loomis said.

"Can we get her started?" Fischer asked, helping Robalt to the deck. The Saber grimaced again, then sucked in a pained breath as he adjusted his position against the bulkhead.

"This is a Matrix Model L, put out of service for faulty air circulator units, among other things," Loomis said. "Pegasi manufactured, so it's debated whether or not the systems are all functional, but if the drive is intact, we should be able to fly at least."

"Do you think you'll be able to get that railgun up there working?" Fischer asked.

"Railgun?" Jones asked. "Are you out of your—nope, you know what? Scratch that." He pointed to Loomis. "I'll head to the bridge. You good for engineering?" Loomis nodded and headed down the passage as Jones took a ladder upward. He called down as he disappeared into the shaft, his voice echoing. "And someone's probably going to need to keep those bastards occupied while we do this!"

"I can do that," Robalt said, grimacing as he spoke. He put one hand against the bulkhead and took a long, controlled breath.

"You can barely stand," Fischer said.

Robalt shook his head. "I'm okay." He turned and knelt just inside the exterior hatch, hand out for his rifle. "Trust me, if there's one thing I can do, it's shoot. Just do me a favor; reach in my back pouch there. I've got a stim kit—grab me a hit, would you."

"Yeah," Eliwood said. Bending over, she rummaged for a moment, and pulled out the small injector. "Here."

Robalt flicked the cap off with his thumb, then pulled up his shirt and depressed the injector button. There was a barely audible hiss, and Robalt's face visual relaxed.

"Oh, damn. That's better."

"You good?" Fischer asked.

The Saber nodded. "Fantastic."

"Aniyah, stay with him."

Eliwood checked the magazine in her pistol. "Where are you going?"

Fischer jerked a thumb to the ceiling. "I'm going to get a bigger gun."

CHAPTER 44

Transfer Tube - Waypoint Bravo
Raider Outpost, Astalt System
4 August 2607

"Sergeant!" Sheridan shouted. He flicked his wrist, jerking his MOD27 over and ejecting an empty magazine. "We've got more coming up behind us!"

Master Sergeant Kline moved up parallel to him and fired off a burst as Sheridan slapped in another magazine. Sheridan flinched as more rounds from the MG26 *pinged* off the bulkhead ten meters ahead of their position. Each impact sent tremors through the passage around them.

The team was hunkered down just outside the entrance to Waypoint Bravo, the transit tube that would take them back to the hangar bay—or would have if not for the MG26 laying waste to the bulkhead at the end of the passage. Sheridan and Kline were busy keeping the raiders behind them from getting any closer, while the others focused on keeping their prisoners down and figuring out a way out of the dead end they'd run into.

Kline pushed his MOD27 around behind him on his sling and

stood. Then, he worked his way to the other side of the passage and grabbing hold of one of the storage lockers there. "Give me a hand!"

Sheridan quickly shifted to his side and together they were able to tip the locker. It slammed down hard on the deck without bouncing, and slid a few centimeters to a stop. Sheridan dropped down behind it just as a raider came into the corridor thirty meters away. A three-round burst dropped the man mid-stride, falling to the deck like a rag doll.

Two more appeared from either side of the adjoining corridors, rifles firing. Sheridan dropped behind the locker and felt the impact of the rounds slamming into the back side, filling the passage with musical twangs. Kline's rifle fired twice, then twice again.

"Two down," Kline said, ducking to reload.

"We're not going to be able to stay here, Sergeant," Sheridan said.

"Yeah."

Sheridan looked over his shoulder at the rest of the team. At the far end, Rocha pulled the safety clip from one of her dazzlers and tossed it into the tube. It detonated a few seconds later, bright multi-spectrum light flashing from around the corner. As soon as the light faded, she pushed her MOD27 around the corner and fired off a string of three-round bursts, shouting curses at the enemy.

"Valkyrie Actual, Overwatch," Chambers said over the taclink. *"We are pinned down outside of Bravo and we have enemy encroaching from the rear. We don't have an exit. I say again, we do* not *have an exit."*

"Roger, Actual," Hanover said. *"It looks like the flight team is working on a solution to your problem now, sir. Two-Echo and I are moving to assist."*

"Solution?" Chambers asked. *"Agent Fischer, report."*

Sheridan had to strain to hear the conversation over the impacts from the MG26 and gunshots reverberating up from the other end of the passageway. Every few seconds, he'd look around, trying to figure out another way out of this bucket they'd found themselves in, but was just nowhere to go. He eyed their unconscious prisoners, now sprawled out on the deck as their carriers engaged the enemy and prayed the cacophony wouldn't rouse them.

"Well," Fischer intoned. He said something else but a barrage of impacts on the locker behind him drowned out the rest of the words. Sheridan ducked lower to the deck, shifted his position, lifted his MOD27 over the top of the locker, and fired.

"Son of a bitch," Sheridan said.

"Make it quick, Fischer," Chambers said.

"Mother fuckers," Kline growled, reloading. He, too, fired blindly over the locker, working burst after burst across the width of the passage.

Sheridan glanced up at the rest of the team. Chambers was kneeling next to the bulkhead, swiping through his link, studying the map of the station, obviously looking for another route. The way he was shaking his head, however, suggested he wasn't having any luck.

Kennedy crouched next to the bulkhead in front of them, adjusting his grip on his rifle. His wounded arm wasn't completely useless, but it wasn't one hundred percent either. Richards had cut away his sleeve to patch the wound. Dried blood covered his arm and shirt, and while the armor had protected him from fatal injury from the other bullet, the Saber was obviously in pain, wincing with every breath.

Kline rose up again, firing two controlled bursts. "Sir, I don't know what he's doing, but we're not going to be able to stay here. We need to push up or back."

"I understand, Sergeant," Chambers said, looking back down the passage the way they'd come.

He's wrong, Sheridan thought, looking at Kline who popped up to fire again. The only thing backtracking would get them was more raiders and more crisscrossing tunnels. If they were going to get out of here, they needed to push forward. They had no other options.

Another barrage of MG26 rounds chewed through the bulkhead ahead of them, sending chucks of debris spinning through the air. Plumes of dust puffed out from the impact craters and sparks filled the air. A series of flashes illuminated the interior, electrical cables shorting out and sending streaks of electricity arching in all directions.

"Valkyrie Actual, Agent Fischer, what is your status?"

"Working on it!"

"That son of a bitch needs to stop working on it and start fucking doing something," Kline shouted.

Sheridan didn't disagree. He found another target—a female raider firing her rifle one-handed as she reached for one of her injured companions. He dropped her with a burst to the chest.

The thought of making it all this way for nothing turned Sheridan's stomach. Young should've been here, but they'd been too slow. The worst part about the whole situation was that Sheridan couldn't really put the blame on anyone in particular. No one had really messed up. It had just been a run of shitty luck. But even knowing that, rage still burned inside him at not being able to get his hands on the that traitorous bastard.

CHAPTER 45

Hangar Bay, Raider Outpost
Astalt System
4 August 2607

The holodisplay flickered and winked out again.

"Goddammit!" Fischer pounded a fist against the console next to the gunner couch and immediately regretted it, wincing as pain shot through his hand. "Jonesy! You got to give me something here!"

"And what exactly do you think I'm doing?" Jones asked, sounding agitated.

The screens flickered again, barely adding any illumination at all to the glow of Fischer's link. It was a cramped space with room enough for the gunner couch, the weapon controls in front of him, and a series of holodisplays. The hole to the ladder he'd climbed up was cut into the hull to right of his couch. The turret had obviously been constructed after-market, attached to the frigate's outer hull by a pivot ring. The feed tray snaked around the interior of the turret, around the left side of the couch, disappearing behind Fischer into another compartment through a second hole also cut into the hull.

Fischer didn't want to think about the craftsmanship involved in securing the weapon to the ship. If even the smallest weld was out of place, it wouldn't matter whether he got the gun working or not. Once they hit the void, they'd have real problems to deal with.

Eliwood rose up through the hole in the floor of the turret. "Still nothing?"

Fischer shook his head. "Jones? How long?"

"It'd be sooner if I didn't have to stop and answer you every five seconds."

"We've got a group advancing on us from that shuttle," Robalt said before Fischer could reply. *"And they don't look happy."*

"Do what you can to keep them off our ass," Fischer said. Then to Eliwood, "He's going to need help."

Eliwood started back down the ladder, then paused, looking back up at Fischer. "If we don't get up and running…"

Fischer ground his teeth together. "I know."

"All right, I think I found something," Loomis said. *"Looks like a couple of the jumpers were misaligned. Getting them back into position now."*

"Finally, he does something useful," Jones said.

Loomis didn't respond.

Fischer could hear gunshots through the turret's thin armor plating but didn't have any way of knowing whether it was friendly fire or not. He pushed those thoughts from his mind, trying to focus on something else, anything else, but sitting alone, inside the darkened interior of the turret, there wasn't much else he could think about.

The screens flickered, twice then winked out again. Fischer was just about to slam a fist down on the console again when they flashed to life, twin displays illuminating the interior with a bright orange light. The screens were blank for a moment, then finally, a loading icon appeared at the upper left-hand corner.

"Yes! You did it, Loomis!" Fischer shouted. "I've got power! The systems booting up."

Around him, additional lights came on as the system continued to initialize. The deck and couch began to vibrate under him, and the ship began to hum as the frigate's engines began to cycle up.

The loading icon vanished, and a real-time view of the frigate's exterior appeared on the left monitor, the targeting, and fire control systems on the right. The targeting system was still loading, several different panels running multiple programs and diagnostics.

"Come on. Come on." Fischer tapped a finger on the left display, shifting the view slightly to the right. Unseen servos whined as the turret rotated, following his direction.

He centered the view on the group of raiders clustered near a row of containers, and the MG26 crew-served weapon on the deck just the right of the last container. A single gun sat on the floor behind the weapon, feet propped against the two front legs of the tripod, and both hands on the firing controls. The weapon shook violently as it fired out its stream of deadly projectiles, tossing links and casings to the deck. Several of the raiders added to the barrage with fire from their own rifles, but by now, they were looking for additional targets in the bay, as the MG26 had the definite advantage.

A targeting reticle appeared on the right screen. He manipulated it with his fingers, zooming in on the group of raiders. They were laughing.

"Bastards," Fischer growled, wrapping both hands around the fire control handles. "Not going to be laughing for long."

He clenched his teeth and pulled the triggers.

Nothing happened.

"What?"

A flashing message panel on the upper right screen informed him that he hadn't loaded any ammunition.

"Oh, you've got to be kidding me." He tapped through a series of selection menus. It was a relatively simple operating system, for which Fischer was extremely grateful. Even as straightforward as it was, he was having a hell of a time focusing on what he needed to do for all the adrenaline pumping through his veins.

"What are you waiting for?" Jones asked. *"Shoot those moth-erfuckers!"*

"Yeah! Right!" Fischer shouted, finally finding the proper menu and jamming a finger onto the 'load' button.

A series of whirs and clanks sounded behind the chair as the solid tungsten projectiles were fed into the tray. More servos hummed as the ammunition entered the hopper, then the chamber. The panel flashed green, indicating the weapon was loaded and ready to fire.

"Here we go," Fischer said.

The railgun shook in Fischer's hands as he fired. The rate of fire wasn't anything to write home about, the rhythmic *thump thump thump* rumbled. The first rounds riddled the deck just forward of the MG26 and the raiders around it. The impact sent a spray of steel, sparks, and dust into the air.

Fischer cursed under his breath and shifted the fire to the right, toward his target. Raiders scatted, though some ran straight into the line of fire, their bodies ripped apart by the large rounds, becoming so much bloody mist and gore. The MG26 disinte-grated, as did the gunner who'd only had enough time to let go of the weapon before he too was cut down. Two more dropped under the assault before the remaining attackers found cover, most still unsure of where the attack was coming from.

"Fischer to Chambers, the gun's down, but there's still raiders in the vicinity," Fischer said.

"Roger, we're moving!"

"Jones, how are we look—"

The turret shifted around him, and for a brief moment, Fischer thought they'd been hit by more rockets only to realize that ship had lifted off the deck and was now rotating toward the destroyed weapon emplacement. He twisted the controls, centering the targeting reticle back on the ruined patch of deck where the gun had been only moments before.

Raiders scattered, running in all directions, searching for cover wherever they could find it. A few even brought their rifles up to shoot at the frigate, for all the good it did them. Their small munitions simply sparked over the ship's armor plating, causing only minimal scratching, if that. Fischer adjusted the turret, lining up on and the area between two cargo containers we several raiders were trying to use to shield themselves from the tunnel. Obviously, the Sabers were on the attack again.

Fragments of steel splintered and raiders dove for safety as round after round pounded the deck and the containers, tearing through men and women without mercy. Fischer gritted his teeth as he white-knuckled the controls, feeling no guilt at all for the devastation he was raining down on them. There was nowhere to hide. For an instant, he felt like one of the Four Horsemen, bringing forth the apocalypse.

An alert chimed, and a warning panel appeared on his screen. Enemy tracking computers were attempting to lock-on to their frigate.

"Fish! Someone's painting us!" Jones shouted over the taclink.

"Shit," Fischer grunted, trying to locate the source of the signal. He swiped his fingers across the screen, shaking his head. It wasn't responding fast enough.

He grabbed the controls again and twisted right. The turret responded immediately, mirroring his movements. He only had to pan for a second before he saw one of the smaller assault boats they'd seen on their way in, banking across the bay, toward them. Just as Fischer realized its wing-mounted launchers were open, the weapons fired, sending a stream of rockets out.

"Jones! Look out!" Fischer yelled, even as the first rocket streaked by. The frigate shifted underneath Fischer, its engines roaring. He adjusted his sights, centering the reticle on the shuttle and fired. Like the raiders' rockets, Fischer missed with his first several rounds, finally connecting with the craft, his rounds punching through the fuselage and exploding out the other side. It was obviously only lightly armored, if that. A fireball erupted through far side of the craft, sending streamers of flame and smoke arching in all directions.

"Holy shit," Fischer said, his fingers loosening on the triggers, gaze fixed on the plummeting spacecraft. It crashed into another shuttle, still parked on the deck. A secondary explosion ripped through the first shuttle's aft section and sent the second skidding away. Flames burst from torn sections of the fuselage. Smoke curled up from both wrecks.

Fischer didn't see any survivors.

"Nice fucking shooting, Fish!" Jones cheered, laughing over the taclink.

Fischer nodded, but didn't answer, he went back to searching for more raiders. Sporadic groups were appearing and disappearing all over the hangar deck, popping up every now and then to fire at their stolen frigate or down the transit tunnel where Fischer the Sabers were.

"Valkyrie Actual, to all Valkyrie elements, moving to extract!" Chambers shouted over the taclink, his words accompanied by the sounds of gunfire in the background.

The frigate shifted again, turning to face the open bay doors two hundred meters away. Fischer saw more raiders scattering, and sent rounds downrange, pushing them farther and farther back. More corvettes lifted off the deck, but instead of coming to attack, they banked away, their engines flashing as they raced for the exit.

"Jones, you hear that?" Fischer asked.

"Yeah, I got it," Jones answered.

Fischer tracked another group of raiders, all running full speed for a shuttle that was already lifting off. His fingers hovered over the trigger, but he didn't fire. Instead, he rotated the turret around, back toward the transit tunnel, and saw the first of the Sabers emerging into the bay, her weapon up, sweeping the area ahead of her. Two more came out, then another, all carrying unconscious people over their shoulders. Sheridan brought up the rear.

The Team slowed as they exited the tunnel, spreading out to either side, each sweeping their own sector of fire. Each seemed to automatically know where they needed to focus their attention, and they all moved as sync with each other. Even the ones loaded down with the weight of their prisoners seemed intent and focused.

Chambers came over the taclink. "Robalt, where the hell are you?"

"Valkyrie Actual, Two-Golf, we are descending toward you now," Robalt said. *"We... uh... acquired some new wings."*

Fischer's chest ached, and he couldn't help but grind his teeth as he looked from prisoner to prisoner, not seeing Young. Chambers had said it already, but Fischer still held to some hope that the captain might have just been mistaken. He could see now that he'd been correct. The man he'd been chasing for almost three months was not among them, and that, more than anything, infuriated Fischer.

Abruptly, the frigate dipped back and to the right. Fischer braced himself.

The ship corrected itself almost immediately, the thrumming of the engines reverberated through the hull as they increased power to compensate.

"What the hell was that, Jonesy?" Fischer asked.

"This piece of shit..." Jones trailed off, his voice sounding strained.

"We're good," Loomis said. *"We're fine."*

"All right," Fischer said, not entirely convinced. "What—"

"It's fine," Loomis repeated. *"Engines are a little janky, that's all."*

"A little janky doesn't sound fine," Fischer countered.

"Oh, for shit's sake, shut up. I'm trying to concentrate here," Jones growled.

The frigate flared as Jones lowered them to the deck, the engines kicking up a cloud of dust around the craft, partially masking the Sabers approach. As it settled on its rails, Fischer rotated the turret back toward the exit. Three raiders emerged from behind a small two-person fighter, weapons up and firing. Fischer squeezed the trigger, and the railgun barked twice. The frigate rocked as he fired, and soon after, the deck underneath the raiders exploded, sending them spiraling into the air.

"All right, everyone's on board," Eliwood said. *"Let's get the hell out of here!"*

CHAPTER 46

Unnamed Frigate
Raider Outpost, Astalt System
4 August 2607

Fischer turned the turret, following the computer's targeting alerts as the frigate shot out of the hangar bay into the void. A dozen icons appeared on his screens, ships of all classes and sizes, all heading multiple directions at multiple speeds. It took the computer several minutes to identify the classes of spacecraft, most of which were frigates like they one they were in or smaller corvettes, all of them actively engaged in a vicious battle with *Legend's* squadron of Nemesis II fighters.

"Legend Command, Valkyrie Actual," Captain Chambers said. *"Be advised, our transport has been destroyed. We are now in a secondary craft and are flashing friend-or-foe. Inbound on a Model-L frigate. Do not fire. I repeat, do not fire."*

Fischer spun the turret, glancing back and forth between the targeting screen and the viewpoint feed. A flight of three Nemesis IIs shot past, heading toward the output, their guns blazing. Several hundred kilometers in front of them, one of the frigates exploded, and each Nemesis pulled away, heading off in different directions. If *Legend* didn't get the message, and their frigate caught one of the pilots' attention, they wouldn't last long. There wasn't much Fischer could do against the most advanced fighters in the fleet.

Just hope and pray, he thought, rotating the turret until he located *Legend*, still two-hundred thousand kilometers away.

Legend's response came through the taclink. *"Roger that, Valkyrie Actual. Legend Command passes Fury."*

"Valkyrie passes Leviathan."

There was a brief pause, then, *"Authentication confirmed, Valkyrie, you are clear to approach,"* the controller said. *"IFF codes assigned and transmitted through mil-net."*

Identification, friend-or-foe designations, allowed ship-board battle computers to assign priority targeting packages and reduce the danger to unintentional friendly-fire casualties. It was a system that had been incorporated in all advanced targeting systems for hundreds of years and was generally something that most spacers took for granted. It was just standard operating procedure to allow the computer to target based on its IFF returns.

Now though, flying through a field of battle where either side might turn and attack, the impact of such capabilities really hit home for Fischer. At least now all they had to worry about was getting voided by the raiders, and Fischer doubted any one of them would have the foresight to run an IFF scan on a frigate that was very obviously not an Alliance ship, which only left one alternative.

Not like they'd have much opportunity to engage us even if they did, Fischer thought.

A head appeared in the ladder tube—one of the Sabers. Corporal Reese if he remembered correctly.

"Captain wants you in the bay as soon as possible, sir," the

Saber said, his head level with Fischer's couch. "I'm supposed to take your place."

Fischer suppressed a cringe at the formality and nodded. "Right."

Corporal Reese slid down the ladder, giving Fischer room exit, then immediately climbed back up.

"Hey, Reese," Fischer said, grabbing one of the rungs as the Saber climbed into the seat above.

"Yeah?"

"They don't know we're not one of them."

The Saber frowned briefly, looking up at the holoscreens in front of him, then understanding registering on his face. "Roger that, sir."

Fischer opened his mouth to correct him, then shut it quickly, shaking his head.

He found Captain Chambers, the rest of the Valkyrie team, and their prisoners in the frigate's small cargo bay. The compartment was slightly bigger than *Doris's* bay, with barely enough room for all of them. The prisoners were laid out on their backs, still unconscious. The female, a general in a Pegasi military uniform, had dried blood on her mouth and nose.

Chambers looked up from his conversation with Kline. He took something from his jacket pocket and tossed it to Fischer. "I'm sorry. We were all hoping he was going to be here."

Fischer caught the thing, and couldn't help but grind his teeth at the sight of the implant, immediately knowing who it belonged to.

"Let's see it," Robalt called from the side of the bay.

"Here," Eliwood said, taking it from Fischer and passing it on.

Fischer didn't say what he was thinking, that the device was likely wiped clean. He turned back to their prisoners. He didn't recognize the general, but that wasn't at all uncommon. There were thousands of high-ranking officers in both the Alliance and

Pegasi militaries. Knowing the names of every single officer would've been impossible.

"We'll need to grab the link data," Fischer said. "That's the first thing. Next, we need to separate them for the trip back. No contact whatsoever." He turned to Richards. "And check their teeth. Can you give them something to keep them sedated?"

"I've got some biosynthine, but nothing that will work long-term."

"Use it," Fischer said.

Eliwood grabbed Robalt's linkclone and went to work on the general.

"I just don't understand. What the hell are the Pegasi doing out here?" Chambers said. He stood over the general, looking down at her unconscious form.

"Well, it damn sure wasn't for the sights," Eliwood said, tapping on her link.

Fischer had been trying to work out the same thing ever since the colonel had appeared in the hangar bay. The idea that the Pegasi Government was involved in state-sponsored terrorism didn't surprise him in the least. They'd been doing that for years, if only on a smaller scale than what they'd found here. Hell, their entire Peacekeeper force were basically mercenaries working under the guise of liberators and benevolent minders. The idea of collaborating with the raiders to effect more direct operations was the next logical step.

The only question in his mind then was, where did Young fit into all this? His escape proved he wasn't working alone. Not to mention the seemingly limitless connections their people had in all the right positions. The ability to delete security records, not only from Cathcart station but also from Alliance military facilities like Haroldson Memorial on New Tuscany, spoke to that.

The only thing that made sense was that Young was working for the raiders, or the raiders were working for him, but that didn't explain why the Pegasi military was present all the way out here in the middle of nowhere. Unless...

"They're working together," Fischer said as soon as the realization struck him.

Chambers frowned. "Who?"

"Young, the raiders, the Pegasi, they're all working together." Even as he said it, Fischer didn't want to believe it. Despite his dislike of Young as a person, Fischer hadn't ever envisioned the former admiral as a traitor. A bastard, sure, but turning his back on his own people? The thought of Young working with what amounted to the sworn enemy of the Alliance was something else entirely.

"That doesn't make a lot of sense," Chambers said. "The Pegasi have hated us for years, why the hell would they be working with us now? And to what end?"

Fischer's mind raced. He thought back to the Stonemeyer mission. The Ambassador there, Tobias Delaney, had been overseeing one of the largest weapons smuggling operations in Alliance history, and the general consensus was that he'd been supplying the rebels with weapons to overthrow the local government, but what if that hadn't been the case?

"What has this whole thing been about?" Fischer wondered aloud.

Eliwood looked up from her link display. "What? Young?"

Fischer nodded. "Well, yeah, but I'm talking about the big picture. Young's a part of it, but what about the whole thing? What's the end game?"

Eliwood pursed her lips, obviously considering his question.

"Chaos?" Sheridan asked.

"Chaos for whom?" Fischer asked. "I'd say there's already enough of that to go around, even without all this mess. We've been at odds with the Pegasi for years, and I don't see any sign of that getting any better any time soon."

"Almost everything we've seen so far has been about weapons," Fischer said. "From Stonemeyer to *Firestorm*, it's been about amassing weapons to supply their forces. And these aren't small operations either. These aren't backroom deals for a couple dozen raiders hijacking freighters and shuttles. These are large-scale deals meant for hundreds, if not thousands."

"But what does that have to do with Young and the Pegasi?" Chambers asked. "And I don't care how many weapons they have. From everything I've seen, these bastards aren't, in any way, equipped or prepared to go to war with the Alliance. They might get a few quick blows in before we could mobilize, but there's no way in hell they'd be able to go up against our entire military. No way."

"I don't think that's what they're planning either," Fischer said, remembering something Campbell had said about Pegasi military operations on their side of the URT. "The problem with the raiders isn't confined to our side."

"What?" Chambers asked.

"Before this whole thing with Young kicked off, the reports we were seeing showed increased raider activity, not only on our side of the URT but on their's as well. Pegasi naval units were being deployed to combat increased attacks, just like ours were."

"Wait, so you're saying the raiders were attacking their own benefactors?" Chambers asked. "What sense does that make?"

"None, if the Pegasi were their only benefactors," Fischer said, putting the pieces together in his mind even as he spoke.

"No way," Eliwood said. "I know you're not going to say what I think you're going to say. That's crazy, Fish."

"It's the only thing that makes sense."

Chambers looked from Fischer to Eliwood, then back again. "Don't tell me you're suggesting the Alliance and Pegasi are working together on this."

Fischer shook his head. "I doubt it's the actual governments.

Even for the Pegasi, that seems like a stretch. But splinter cells of high-ranking officers and government officials? I'd say that's more than likely considering what we've seen so far. Young isn't the only Alliance officer involved. That's a simple fact. Who knows how many are on his side."

"His side? What is *his* side?" Master Sergeant Kline asked, stepping up next to Chambers. "What reason could he have for *willingly* working with the same people we've been enemies with for years?"

Fischer nodded at the unconscious Pegasi general. "Did she say anything to you before you knocked her out?"

Sheridan looked like he wanted to say something but kept it to himself.

"She said he'd already left," Chambers answered. "And that his mission was over. But didn't elaborate on what that mission was. That's when we found his implant."

"And you don't think they just killed him?" Eliwood asked.

Chambers shook his head. "I didn't get that impression."

"Neither did I," Sheridan added.

"His mission was over?" Fischer asked, more for himself than anyone else. "His mission for what? Stonemeyer was a disaster. If that was his mission, it wasn't just over—it was a total failure on his part. They didn't get any of them."

"If rogue members of the Pegasi Empire and Holloman Alliance are working together, we need to get that information to Command," Chambers said. "We need to shut it down as quickly as possible."

"I agree," Fischer said. "But running back home and blasting the information out for everyone to see isn't going to help our cause. In fact, it'll probably make things worse for us."

"How could it possibly make it worse than where we're at right now?"

"Because right now, we have the advantage," Fischer said.

"Right now, we know that there are double agents within our ranks, and those agents don't know that we know."

"Yeah, well, it won't take them long to find out," Kline said. "Not after what happened here."

Fischer nodded. "Time is short, I agree. We need to get back and watch everyone—see who flinches when the news hits. If we can ID them soon enough, we might be able to shut them down before shit hits the fan."

Eliwood stood, the linkclone still working. "I don't mean to burst your bubble, Fish, but there could be people onboard *Legend* we can't trust. We already know there are people inside ASI that we can't, and Young's evidence enough to see that the Navy's compromised and has been for a while."

"I don't think we'll need to worry about anyone on *Legend*," Chambers said. "Her entire crew was hand-picked by Admiral Hunter himself. This project is his baby. He wouldn't have risked its success with unreliable people."

"Except that he didn't know anything about Cardinal when he made those assignments," Eliwood said. "None of us did."

"This is another reason why putting this information on blast is a bad idea," Fischer said. "Panic. Look at us, we're already looking at each other, wondering if we're working for the other side. Imagine that on a multiplied scale. I don't see that we have any other choice, we're going to have to sit on this."

CHAPTER 47

Command Information Control - ANS *Legend*
JumpLane 4821 - En Route to Alliance Navy Command,
Solomon System
4 August 2607

"You've got to be kidding," Captain Ward said, folding his arms across his chest. "You can't really expect us to sit on this? Possibly the biggest conspiracy in the history of the Alliance?"

"I don't see that we have a choice," Fischer said.

Legend's CO chewed on the inside of his cheek, considering everything Fischer and Captain Chambers had just relayed about what they'd learned.

Eliwood and two of the ship's computer techs were running the information she's cloned from their raider's links through *Legend's* computer, pulling out any relevant data they could. The rest of the command staff was also present, along with the Saber's leadership.

Richards and the ship's medical team had found and disabled a small explosive device in each of their captive's brainstems, and the activation module: a faux molar. Their links had been disabled after they'd been successfully cloned, and now they all sat under guard in *Legend's* brig.

"Even if we go on complete blackout, we're going to have bring Hunter in," Ward said finally. "There no way we can't."

"I agree," Fischer said. "I've already sent a message to my boss, instructing him to meet us at the Phoenix in person. This is definitely not something we can discuss over the net."

"Hunter I know we can trust. Are you sure you can trust your boss?" Ward asked.

"One hundred percent," Fischer said. "Unfortunately, I can't say the same about others in the office. We're going to have to proceed very carefully."

Ward shook his head. "This whole thing is almost unbelievable. Double agents, assassinations, government conspiracies. You see that shit in movies, not real life."

"It's real all right," Eliwood said, looking over a row of holo-screens.

"Okay, so why, though?" Ward asked. "What's it all for? Why all the raider attacks? Why push both nations toward war? Who does that benefit?"

"Cardinal," Sheridan muttered from the side of the room, his eyes flicking up from the deck as everyone turned to face him. The expression on his face suggested he hadn't intended to speak aloud. "I'm sorry, sir."

"Cardinal," Ward repeated. "Just who in the hell is this Cardinal?"

"I don't think it's a person," Fischer said.

"What is it then?"

"I think Cardinal is the thing we're after—the thing we're trying to prevent. It's a group or force behind everything that's happening. No one has been able to give us a clear answer, even Gav side-stepped the question. He even told me, 'I don't know what *it* is?' He said 'it.' Cardinal is this whole thing."

"But it still doesn't shed any light on why they're doing what they're doing," Ward said.

"They're obviously trying to push us into war with the Pegasi," Fischer said. "It's really the only thing that makes sense at this point."

"Okay, but what does war with the Pegasi do for them?" Ward asked. "The raiders are already doing a bang-up job of putting the two nations on edge, what more is war going to do besides get a lot more people killed."

Fischer had been thinking about that very prospect and while he could come up with numerous reasons why someone on the outside would want war between the two superpowers, the most obvious was if the Alliance and Pegasi were fighting each other, it would allow others to operate with impunity while both militaries were engaged with each other. But as to why members of both nations would work together to set the conflict in motion, Fischer had only been able to come up with one reason.

"Money," Fischer said.

Ward stopped short, frowning. "Money? What do you mean?"

"Tensions between us and the Pegasi have been high for years," Fischer said, pacing around the CIC. "But, with the exception of a few skirmishes here and there, things have been relatively quiet. It's been more than ten years since the last time we were legitimately shooting at each other and until recently, I didn't think we'd ever get back to that point. We've actually been the process of downsizing and cutting back military spending. Ships are being produced, weapons manufacturing has been at an all-time low, and even some technology markets have taken a hit in the last couple of years.

"I know this," Fischer continued, "because while doing work on the Stonemeyer case, we kept coming across the name Alistair. Alistair Holdings specifically. One of the large tech corporations in the galaxy, and one that's been taking big hits because of the cutbacks in military spending."

"Without a war, there's nothing to spend our money on," Eliwood said.

Fischer nodded. "So, if you don't have one…"

"You start one," Ward finished for him. "My god."

"That's insane," Chambers said. "You're suggesting that someone wants to start a war to make money?"

"Like I said, my guess, it's not just one person. Something as big as this, it would have to be a collective of people from multiple backgrounds and specialties."

"Cardinal," Eliwood said.

"Cardinal," Fischer repeated.

"But we stopped them, though, right?" Ward asked. "By figuring it out before the fighting started. The war isn't going to happen now."

"I highly doubt what we did today stopped anything," Fischer said. "This thing has too many moving parts to be stopped on a dime. Slowed it down, maybe. Gave us more time."

"So, not only are we going up against some of our own people, but also one of the most powerful interstellar corporations of our time. We don't have any idea where to start."

"I wouldn't say that," Eliwood said. She'd been working on her terminal the entire discussion, filtering through the information they'd pulled from the cloned links. She tapped in a few commands and three faces appeared floating over the screens, rotating slowly.

Fischer looked at the faces. "Of course."

"Councilman Kramer?" Ward asked, stepping toward the holograms. "I don't recognize the other two."

Eliwood tapped on her console. "Lieutenant Commander Sullivan, Naval Intelligence, currently assigned to the *Phoenix* Battle Station, and—"

"Major Glen Fredericks," Captain Chambers said. "What is this?"

"Contact information pulled from the general's link," Eliwood said. "I'd say they're obviously part of this Cardinal operation."

Chambers shook his head. "Not a chance. I've known Fredericks for years. He's as loyal as they come. He'd never do anything to harm the Alliance."

"I'm sure most of the people involved in this will turn out to be people we'd never assumed," Fischer said.

"Does it say anything else?" Chambers asked Eliwood.

"Still processing," Eliwood said. "Those names were the first thing that popped up."

"Maybe they're targets," Chambers suggested. "People they knew they needed to be weary of or they needed to take out before things got out of control. I refuse to believe Glen Fredericks has anything to do with this, whatever *this* is. Kramer doesn't surprise me at all though, he's been calling for escalated military operations for months. But he's also been calling for the eradication of the raider menace, not going after the Pegasi."

"Window dressing," Fischer said. "Once the machine is in motion, it's hard to get it to stop."

"You think the raider problems we've been dealing with were manufactured?" Captain Ward asked. "That our own people created the problem we've been assigned to eliminate?"

"At this point, Captain, I wouldn't put anything past these people," Fischer said. "But at least now we do have somewhere to start."

"What are you going to do—arrest the Councilman? On what grounds, conspiracy? His information on a Pegasi's link is hardly evidence of any wrongdoing. And I'll be damned if we're going to be arresting Fredericks or Sullivan without anything more concrete in our arsenal."

Fischer shook his head. "No, we don't want to show our hand

too early. We watch and we wait. At least until we have more to go on than what we have right now."

"Surveillance on our own people?" Ward asked. "Alliance military personnel are prohibited from conducting operations inside Alliance borders unless actively engaged in combat with enemy attackers. Domestic operations are strictly out of the question."

"And you don't think we're engaged with the enemy?" Fischer asked.

Ward opened his mouth to answer, then shut it again without answering.

"Whether we like it or not," Fischer said. "Whether with the raiders, or the Pegasi, or Cardinal, we're engaged about as much as you can be. I hate to say it, but unless we can stop it, the Alliance is on a collision course with the Pegasi Empire and war."

To be concluded in…
Essence of Valor

FROM THE PUBLISHER

Thank you for reading *Echoes of Valor,* book two in the *Valor* series.

We hope you enjoyed it as much as we enjoyed bringing it to you. We just wanted to take a moment to encourage you to review the book on Amazon and Goodreads. Every review helps further the author's reach and, ultimately, helps them continue writing fantastic books for us all to enjoy.

If you liked this book, check out the rest of our catalogue at www.aethonbooks.com. To sign up to receive a FREE collection from some of our best authors as well as updates regarding all new releases, visit www.subscribepage.com/AethonReadersGroup.

JOSH HAYES is a USAF veteran and retired police officer turned author. In addition to the Valor series, his work includes Stryker's War (Galaxy's Edge) and The Terra Nova Chronicles with Richard Fox, as well as numerous short stories.

His love of military science fiction can be traced all the way back when he picked up his first Honor Harrington novel, as well as a healthy portion of Tom Clancy and Michael Crichton.

He is the President and host of Keystroke Medium, a popular community for writers of all levels, which produces weekly content including live YouTube broadcasts, craft discussions, and author interviews. www.keystrokemedium.com

When he's not writing or podcasting, Josh spends time with his wife Jamie and his four children. You can find out more about his books at www.joshhayeswriter.com.

Join his Facebook Fan Club: www.facebook.com/groups/joshhayes/

Receive his newsletter: www.joshhayeswriter.com/free-books--more.html

SPECIAL THANKS TO:

ADAWIA E. ASAD
BARDE PRESS
CALUM BEAULIEU
BEN
BECKY BEWERSDORF
BHAM
TANNER BLOTTER
ALFRED JOSEPH BOHNE IV
CHAD BOWDEN
ERREL BRAUDE
DAMIEN BROUSSARD
CATHERINE BULLINER
JUSTIN BURGESS
MATT BURNS
BERNIE CINKOSKE
MARTIN COOK
ALISTAIR DILWORTH
JAN DRAKE
BRET DULEY
RAY DUNN
ROB EDWARDS
RICHARD EYRES
MARK FERNANDEZ
CHARLES T FINCHER
SYLVIA FOIL
GAZELLE OF CAERBANNOG
DAVID GEARY
MICHEAL GREEN
BRIAN GRIFFIN

EDDIE HALLAHAN
JOSH HAYES
PAT HAYES
BILL HENDERSON
JEFF HOFFMAN
GODFREY HUEN
JOAN QUERALTÓ IBÁÑEZ
JONATHAN JOHNSON
MARCEL DE JONG
KABRINA
PETRI KANERVA
ROBERT KARALASH
VIKTOR KASPERSSON
TESLAN KIERINHAWK
ALEXANDER KIMBALL
JIM KOSMICKI
FRANKLIN KUZENSKI
MEENAZ LODHI
DAVID MACFARLANE
JAMIE MCFARLANE
HENRY MARIN
CRAIG MARTELLE
THOMAS MARTIN
ALAN D. MCDONALD
JAMES MCGLINCHEY
MICHAEL MCMURRAY
CHRISTIAN MEYER
SEBASTIAN MÜLLER
MARK NEWMAN
JULIAN NORTH

KYLE OATHOUT
LILY OMIDI
TROY OSGOOD
GEOFF PARKER
NICHOLAS (BUZ) PENNEY
JASON PENNOCK
THOMAS PETSCHAUER
JENNIFER PRIESTER
RHEL
JODY ROBERTS
JOHN BEAR ROSS
DONNA SANDERS
FABIAN SARAVIA
TERRY SCHOTT
SCOTT
ALLEN SIMMONS
KEVIN MICHAEL STEPHENS
MICHAEL J. SULLIVAN
PAUL SUMMERHAYES
JOHN TREADWELL
CHRISTOPHER J. VALIN
PHILIP VAN ITALLIE
JAAP VAN POELGEEST
FRANCK VAQUIER
VORTEX
DAVID WALTERS JR
MIKE A. WEBER
PAMELA WICKERT
JON WOODALL
BRUCE YOUNG

CPSIA information can be obtained
at www.ICGtesting.com
Printed in the USA
FSHW020411091119
63804FS